MURDER CAN WRECK YOUR REUNION

A DESIREE SHAPIRO MYSTERY

by Selma Eichler

A SIGNET BOOK

SIGNET
Published by New American Library, a division of
Penguin Putnam Inc., 375 Hudson Street,
New York, New York 10014, U.S.A.
Penguin Books Ltd, 27 Wrights Lane,
London W8 5TZ, England
Penguin Books Australia Ltd, Ringwood,
Victoria, Australia
Penguin Books Canada Ltd, 10 Alcorn Avenue,
Toronto, Ontario, Canada M4V 3B2
Penguin Books (N.Z.) Ltd, 182–190 Wairau Road,
Auckland 10, New Zealand

Penguin Books Ltd, Registered Offices:
Harmondsworth, Middlesex, England

First published by Signet, an imprint of New American Library,
a division of Penguin Putnam Inc.

First Printing, January 1997
15 14 13 12 11 10 9 8 7 6 5 4

Printed in the United States of America

PUBLISHER'S NOTE
This is a work of fiction. Names, characters, places, and incidents either are
the product of the author's imagination or are used fictitiously, and any resemblance to actual persons, living or dead, events, or locales is entirely
coincidental.

BOOKS ARE AVAILABLE AT QUANTITY DISCOUNTS WHEN USED TO PROMOTE
PRODUCTS OR SERVICES. FOR INFORMATION PLEASE WRITE TO PREMIUM MAR-
KETING DIVISION, PENGUIN PUTNAM INC., 375 HUDSON STREET, NEW YORK, NEW
YORK 10014.

To my agent and friend Luna Carne-Ross
with much appreciation

ACKNOWLEDGMENTS

Many thanks to—

Captain Alan G. Martin, of the New York State Police, who provided some much-needed technical information

Buddy Addabo, Esq., of Addabo and Greenberg, for his valuable legal input

Danielle Perez, my always helpful and encouraging editor

Nikki and Julian Scott for their tireless legwork

My Sister in Crime, mystery author Elizabeth Daniels Squire, who has been so generous in sharing her experiences and who has given me some of the best advice I've ever received

Raven Costa for "lending" me her name

And finally, my husband, Lloyd, for his unflagging help, support, and patience

Chapter 1

"A *what*?"

"A *divorce* party," my niece repeated. "Sybil's divorce became final a few weeks ago—you remember Sybil, my friend from college, don't you?"

"I never met her, but it sounds familiar. I think I remember hearing about her."

"That's what I meant. Anyhow, she's throwing this big bash over the weekend to celebrate her divorce."

"How very nineties of her," I remarked sarcastically.

"Oh, come on, Aunt Dez," the voice on the other end of the wire coaxed. While not exactly accusing me of getting stuck in some kind of time warp or even—God forbid—of not being "with it," Ellen's patronizing tone made it fairly obvious she was thinking along those lines.

Of course, some divorces really are cause for celebration. But as for actually serving as a reason to throw a party, well, that's a bit too *now* for my taste. I told Ellen as much.

"It's a lot better than sitting around and feeling sorry for yourself," she countered.

I conceded that maybe it was. But grudgingly.

"Anyway, I mentioned the party to you before."

"Not a word," I contradicted.

"Oh, I thought I did. Four of us have been invited for the weekend," she chirped. "We'll all go out on Friday and stay over until Sunday. The real festivities aren't until Saturday night, but Sybil lives in this wonderful house in Clear Cove—you know, out on Long Island—"

"I *know* where Clear Cove is," I broke in, just to remind her that I wasn't born yesterday (although come to think of it, she had certainly made it clear she was aware of that fact).

Ellen went on unperturbed. "Yes, well, she has this charming old house with a swimming pool and tennis courts and everything—it's really gracious living, Aunt Dez. A bunch of us used to spend weekends there during summer vacation. You remember that, don't you?"

"I'm not senile!" I shot back mean-spiritedly.

I guess I should explain that I was in a lousy mood even before Ellen called. And it wasn't because I'd had a bad day at work—which I hadn't. Or because I'd just gotten my period—which I had. The reason I was behaving like such a class A witch was that I'd returned home only minutes earlier from a Bloomingdale's white sale. And let me tell you, if you're in the market for a truly unnerving experience, I can recommend a Bloomingdale's white sale. What made things even worse, though, was that after doing battle with practically every ambulatory female in Manhattan, all I had to show for my considerable efforts was one crummy fingertip towel, one broken fingernail, and two very sore feet. But, of course, I had no business taking things out on Ellen.

"You were even getting together out in Clear Cove after you graduated—you and your friends—weren't you?" I asked in a more cordial tone.

"Only once. Sybil got married at the end of her junior year in college, so then we started meeting for lunch in the city every so often instead—you know, whoever could make it. I'm really looking forward to going out there again; I used to absolutely adore that place."

"Can Mike get away for the weekend?" I asked, Mike being—the way I liked to look at it—Ellen's almost-husband or, at the very least, almost-fiancé. He was doing his residency at one of the local hospitals, and I didn't remember him ever having the luxury of an entire weekend off. (Of course, in the not-to distant future they'd have to let him take a lot more time than a weekend. Two weeks would be just right for a honeymoon in Paris or maybe for a romantic Caribbean cruise—I was flexible.)

"No, Mike's on duty," Ellen informed me. "But men—even husbands—aren't included, anyway. Not to spend the weekend, that is. They've just been invited to the party on Saturday night. I think the whole town's been invited to *that*."

"But you're going out on Friday?"

"Uh-huh. I'm leaving the store early, so I can catch the five-thirty train." ("The store" in Ellen's life was Macy's, where only recently they'd acquired the good sense to promote her from an assistant buyer to a full-fledged buyer.) "Sybil said she'd have someone pick me up at the station. I'm just *thrilled* about seeing everyone again, Aunt Dez." Then abruptly the animation left her voice and she murmured, "I wish Mike could get away and come to the party, though. I feel a little funny about going off like that while he's so hard at work."

"It's only for a couple of days, for heaven's sake. And it's not as if he'd be able to spend any time with you if you stayed in the city. So don't be silly; just go and enjoy your friends." And then I gushed, "I'm sure you'll have a wonderful time."

Of all the dumb platitudes! I wasn't sure of any such thing, and I had no business saying I was.

But in my own defense, there was no way I could have anticipated that thanks to this harmless little get-together, my only niece would wind up a murder suspect.

Chapter 2

Just look at her! Tight, almost thigh-high skirt, long, *long* legs ending in stiletto heels that are more like stilts, and there she is taking out three bad guys, one right after the other, with perfectly executed karate chops and a few on-target kicks to the groin. And if that doesn't strain your credulity—I mean, a flesh-and-blood human being would hardly be able to walk in shoes like that, much less acquit herself so heroically—the woman doesn't even work up a sweat! The only visible effects of her life-threatening encounter are this sweet little smudge on the tip of her nose, along with a slight rearrangement of her long blond hair—which is now mussed just enough to make her look sexier and more adorable than ever.

It could really make you toss your lunch.

I was so annoyed I'd have turned off the TV in a second and gotten rid of Ms. Perfect. The only problem was that the remote was on the other side of the room, and I'd just plopped down on the sofa, exhausted, after filling in for Charmaine, my every-other-Saturday cleaning woman. (Who hadn't put in an appearance for so many Saturdays that I wasn't sure anymore which Saturday she was even supposed to be here.) So I sat there immobile, forced to subject myself to Hollywood's ridiculous conception of a female private investigator.

Not that I'd expect the heroine to look like me, you understand. I could have lived with the fact that she was a good half a foot taller than my five-two. And that her reedlike frame was I-don't-know-how-many-pounds slimmer than this amply proportioned figure of mine. And also that most of the pounds she *had* accumulated appeared to have settled in her chest area. I swear, I wasn't even particularly disturbed that she'd celebrated a few less birthdays than I had (and I have no intention of telling you just how few less, either). No. I'd have been content with a PI who was at least *believable*, who didn't attempt to convince me she could lick the world in her four-inch heels. . . .

I woke with a start to the ringing of the phone. (It appeared that I *had* managed to escape Ms. Perfect, after all.) The living room clock informed me that it was just after five.

"Aunt Dez? It's me." The words were muffled by tears. Which, partnered with the blaring of the television and the fact that I was not yet fully awake, made me wonder if I'd even heard right.

"Ellen?" I said stupidly.

"Y-y-yes." Ellen only stutters under the most extreme circumstances. In fact, come to think of it, I'd only known her to do it once before.

"What's wrong?" I asked sharply.

"It's R-r-raven. She's dead."

"Oh, my God!" I responded, even though I didn't have a clue who Raven was. "What happened?"

"C-can I come over? I'm at Grand Central now."

"Sure. Of course. But are you all right? Do you want me to come and get you?"

"No, no. I'm okay. I'll just hop into a cab."

A dozen or so tissues and a substantial shot of blackberry brandy later, Ellen was finally able to string some coherent sentences together. And after establishing that Raven was one of the guests at the divorce party, she went on to relate the circumstances of the girl's demise.

"It was just awful," she said, her voice close to a whisper. "We were all at breakfast—all except Raven, that is—and it was after ten. So Sybil asked Winnie, who's Raven's sister-in-law, if she'd mind going upstairs and getting her to come down. I said I'd go up with her, because everyone was asking to see Mike's picture, and it was in my wallet in the bedroom.

"Well, I had to pass Raven's room to get to my own, so I was there when Winnie knocked on her door. When there wasn't any answer, I was kind of of curious, so I stuck around. Anyway, after a while Winnie tried the door and went inside, and I took maybe two or three steps into the room. You could see right away that it was empty. And her nightgown and I think a matching robe were lying in this crumpled heap right in front of the terrace door. I figured she must have gotten dressed in a big hurry and gone out somewhere. But then Winnie said, 'Maybe she's in the bathroom,' and she went and checked. And that's when we heard this terrible scream coming from the back of the house. We both ran out on the terrace—the terrace door was wide open—and then I saw . . . it."

Ellen's hand flew to her mouth, and she squeezed her eyes shut and shook her head slowly from side to side. I had the impression she was trying—and with very little success—to block the scene from her mind. A moment later the dark eyes opened, and they were filled with horror. "There were three or four people—the caterers, I think they were—standing over by the swimming pool, and Raven was lying there, at the bottom of it. Of course, I didn't realize it was Raven at the time. All I could see was this . . . this nude figure." She heaved a deep sigh, and a tremor shook her slight body. "The pool was . . . it was empty, Aunt Dez," she concluded.

"Good Lord," I murmured. "Does anyone know how it happened?"

"Well, the police came a little while later, and they had some ideas."

"Which were?"

"The chief of police there said it looked like she had dived into the pool—most likely the night before—from her bedroom terrace, which was right above it. She—oh God!—everything was all broken, her whole body!"

"How terrible" was all I could think of to say. I felt a little sick.

Ellen swallowed hard, then sat there silently for a moment. She licked her lips before going on. "She used to pull that stunt when we went there for weekends back in college—diving into the pool from the terrace."

"Pretty gutsy of her, wasn't it?"

"Very gutsy. That's how she was. Plus she was a real showoff." Ellen's face immediately turned a brilliant scarlet. "God, I don't know how I could have said that—about her being a showoff. Not after what happened to her, I mean. It slipped out. I must be—"

"You didn't say anything so awful. Besides, just because she's gone doesn't make it any less true."

"Yes, I know, but—"

"Did she always stay in the same room?" I put in hurriedly, denying Ellen any further opportunity to beat up on herself.

"Always."

"What makes them think the accident occurred on Friday night, anyway?"

"I heard the chief telling one of the other men that he figured it must have been at night; otherwise, she would have seen that there wasn't any water in the pool."

Of course! I nodded, feeling stupid.

"He said they'd know more about the time of death after the autopsy, though. Poor Raven," Ellen murmured. "The thing is, the rest of us had all been told about the pool being repaired. Sybil apologized Friday evening at dinner that we wouldn't be able to use it that weekend. Seems she'd hired someone weeks before to do the work, but he got sick or something or *said* he was sick or something—Sybil really didn't believe him—and he hadn't gotten around to finishing the job. She was really ticked off at the guy."

"How come Raven was the only one who wasn't aware of this? Wasn't she at dinner, too?"

"Uh-uh. She didn't get out to the house until after ten, and the meal was over by that time. And it doesn't look like anyone mentioned it to her later on—we had this little cocktail party afterwards, just the six of us." There was a pause before Ellen said softly, a catch in her voice, "If anyone *had* . . ." There was no need to complete the thought.

"What a tragedy. What a horrible, horrible tragedy!" I exclaimed, reaching over on the sofa to give her a brief emotionally supportive hug. "You were the one who called the police?"

"No. The housekeeper did. But I secured the scene," she reported. "After I went downstairs I asked one of the maids to go up and stand outside the bedroom door until the police came." She glanced at me expectantly, and I got the idea a word of praise might not be out of line.

"Good thinking," I said, so as not to disappoint her.

A wan little smile flitted across her lips. "A chip off the old block, I guess."

Now the fact is, Ellen and I couldn't possibly be lugging around the same genes. She was actually my husband Ed's niece, may he rest in peace. But I think she sometimes forgets that; I know I do. Anyway, at this point I happened to look at my watch. It was almost eight-thirty. "Listen, Ellen, when was the last time you ate?"

She shrugged. "I'm not hungry."

"I think you should have something or you'll make yourself sick. I know you were very fond of Raven, but there's—"

"But I wasn't fond of her at all—none of us were," Ellen protested. "And that's putting it mildly. We couldn't even stand to be in the same room with her."

I wondered why, under those circumstances, Sybil had invited the girl to her party, but Ellen continued talking, and the question flew out of my head.

"Even Winnie's had plenty of problems with Raven, although I guess she—Winnie, I mean—more or less had to stay on halfway decent terms with her because of Dick. That's Winnie's husband."

"He was Raven's brother?"

She nodded. "Anyway, that's why Winnie was the one Sybil asked to go upstairs and get her." And then Ellen's face crumpled, and an instant later she was in tears.

I handed her the box of tissues that was sitting on the end table next to the sofa and moved closer to her, putting my arm around her shoulders while she cried it out. After a while, the tears subsided. "I can't bear to think of her lying there like that, Aunt Dez. I just f-feel so damned guilty about f-feeling the way I did about her."

Uh-oh. The stammering was starting again. "I realize how upset you are, but your feelings toward Raven had absolutely nothing to do with her death, Ellen."

"I know that, but—"

"And now we're going to do something about supper. And don't you dare give me a hard time, because I'll never forgive you if you go and faint on me."

Ellen didn't even smile. "I don't think I'd be able—"

"I could order from Ping Chow's," I offered enticingly. I doubted that even in this agitated state, my niece would be able to resist an offer of Chinese food.

She proved me a prophet. "We-ll, maybe I could force myself to have just a little something. . . ."

Ellen stayed over that night. I more or less insisted on it. Mike was working until all hours, and I didn't want her to be by herself. She was still pretty traumatized.

On Sunday morning, though, she was a lot calmer. She was even up to preparing breakfast for us. (Ellen's culinary expertise is, for some inexplicable reason, restricted to the area of breakfast.) She whipped up a truly delicious batch of apple pancakes that we both consumed with gusto, and then we sat around and chatted over coffee for a while. At about one o'clock she headed for home.

It took over an hour after she left for me to talk myself into getting out the ironing board and pressing some of the things that had been accumulating in my laundry basket for weeks now. I kept at it until a little after four, at which time I quit and had myself a nice, leisurely bubble bath, following which I put on my makeup and slipped into a decent dress. Then I combed my glorious hennaed hair—which for once was reasonably accommodating—spritzed it with a mega-dose of hairspray on the off-chance I'd encounter a windstorm, and proceeded across the hall for dinner.

My neighbor Harriet Gould was going to be entertaining her husband's boss for the first time the following week, and she wanted to give the menu a dry run. So I had been pressed into service. "I can't trust Steve's opinion," she'd explained. "He'll eat anything that can't get up and walk off his plate."

It turned out to be quite a feast. For starters, there was a shrimp and scallop mousse in puffed pastry, which was not to be believed. This was followed by the kind of salad I love. The thing had absolutely everything in it: three kinds of lettuce, red cabbage, scallions, eggplant appetizer, artichokes, olives (black *and* green), cucumber, green pepper, radishes, cherry tomatoes, croutons, Parmesan cheese, and probably a couple of other things that I can't remember. The main dish was a sensational creation called Turkey Orloff that's made with turkey breast scaloppini, mushrooms, onions, and cheese. "A Julia Child recipe," Harriet confided. "It took forever to prepare, especially since I'm so pokey, but it's worth the trouble, don't you think?" I agreed that it certainly was. Dessert was a store-bought—but really excellent—tarte Tatin. Even now, months later, the recollection of that dinner almost brings tears to my eyes.

And what did husband Steve have to say about his wife's efforts?

"Now, don't get me wrong, Harriet, it was a nice meal." *A*

nice meal? "But, geez, this kind of stuff . . . what I'm trying to tell you is that Bob's a plain guy. He goes bowling a lot."

I left right after Harriet finished carrying on about Steve's having been born without taste buds and just as she was demanding to know what the hell bowling had to do with Julia Child's Turkey Orloff, anyway.

I was back in my own apartment before 10:00, and since there was nothing much on television, I read for a couple of hours—a new mystery that I soon found out had nothing at all to do with the blurb on the back cover. Still, it was pretty suspenseful. Right around midnight, though, I had to put it down. I was just too tired to focus any longer. But on the other hand, I was too stuffed to go to sleep.

And that's when I thought about Raven again.

What a senseless way to die! If only she had gotten to Sybil's a little earlier, she'd have learned that the pool was empty, and she'd be alive today—right now.

And then I began to wonder why Ellen—and apparently the rest of the group—had disliked her so much. I hadn't wanted to pry yesterday—it had seemed inappropriate at the time. And anyway, Ellen would fill me in when she was feeling up to it. My niece and I didn't keep secrets from each other.

Or so I thought.

Chapter 3

But Ellen didn't tell me why she felt the way she had about Raven. Not for quite a while.

When I broached the subject a few days later she quickly sidestepped the topic with, "It isn't important anymore. So let's not talk about it now, okay?"

And even being as nosy as I am there was nothing much I could do about a response like that. Short of putting lighted matches under my dear niece's fingernails, that is.

A little over a week passed. And then late one afternoon—it was on a Tuesday, I remember—just as I was about to leave my office, I got the phone call.

"Aunt D-d-dez?"

Oh, my God! She's stuttering again!

"What's wrong, Ellen?"

"The p-p-police just came to see me at the store."

"Police?"

"The Clear Cove police—the chief, anyway. He wanted to ask me some more questions about Raven."

"What *about* Raven?"

"I think that *he* thinks I k-k-killed her."

The idea of Ellen as a murderess was so absolutely preposterous I almost laughed out loud. As it was, I couldn't refrain from a fleeting smile. "You're just imagining that, I'm sure," I told her. (After all, Ellen *had* been known to jump to conclusions once in a while.) Then I tossed in a pertinent reminder. "Raven's death was an accident, for God's sake."

"I th-thought it was. But they—this Chief Brady—was talking m-murder."

I could barely take in what I was hearing. "He really thinks she was *murdered*?"

"Well, he said they were investigating the p-possibility."

"Did he say why?"

"He said that there were a couple of things that seemed a little su-suspicious."

"He didn't say what they were?"

"No."

"Well, what did he want with you?"

"Someone told him that Raven and I had had an argument recently."

"Oh." Then after I digested that: "Look, Ellen, I think maybe you'd better clue me in on just what happened between you and Raven."

"Yes, I will; I want to. I'm leaving work now. Do you think you could m-meet me at my apartment? I should be there in about a half hour."

"I'll see you then."

Now, Ellen has never been the calmest person I know. (A very large understatement, if you really want the truth.) The fact is, I often refer to her as a nervous Nellie. And that night, seated in her living room, she more than did justice to the nickname.

The stuttering, of course, persisted. Add to that the white, pinched look on her face, along with a freshly acquired habit of gnawing on her lower lip at frequent intervals. What's more, she had positioned herself on the edge of her chair, as if ready to vacate the premises at a moment's notice. She was really so close to the edge that a couple of times I worried that any minute she'd wind up on the floor.

"I'm so s-scared," she murmured.

"I know. But you don't have to be. We'll straighten this thing out, I promise."

"Do you really think so?" she asked, her eyes filled with such childlike trust that my heart constricted.

"Of course I do. But first off, tell me just what this police chief had to say to you."

"He said there was some reason to believe a c-crime might have been committed, and he made me repeat how I'd gone upstairs with Winnie when she went to w-wake Raven that morning. And then he wanted to know what I had ag-gainst her."

"And you told him?"

"Well, I had to."

"And what did he say?"

"He nodded a lot, and then he thanked me and told me he might wa-want to talk to me again." The large eyes opened even wider. "You don't think that's b-because he's already g-got me p-p-pegged as the k-k-killer, do you?"

Ellen's stammering appeared to be getting more and more pronounced. So after assuring her that the chief's visit was just routine (although I admit I was a little concerned myself and anxious that she might pick up on it), I reverted to what had done the trick the last time. "How about I pour you some brandy? Or a glass of wine."

"There's some amaretto in the c-c-cabinet. I think I c-could probably use some of that. But you must be hungry. Why don't we order something to eat, now, t-too," she suggested between gnaws on her lower lip.

I shook my head. "In a little while," I told her. "Let's both have the amaretto first."

Ellen nodded. "I'm n-not very hungry, anyway."

"Go ahead, have some," I instructed a couple of minutes later, handing her a wineglass more than half filled with the almond-flavored liqueur. She dutifully sipped, and I did the same. "All right. Tell me about this disagreement or whatever it was between you and Raven," I said after a time.

"Well, it has to do with what happened my freshman year at college. The b-b-breakdown, I'm t-talking about."

"Oh," I responded softly, those terrible events of more than a decade ago returning in a flash. . . .

There had been a lot of anxiety involved in Ellen's decision to attend a school away from home. She had been eager for some independence, but on the other hand, she'd never been on her own before, and it frightened her. Holden, a small liberal arts college in central New York State, presented the perfect solution. It was too far for a commute but still close enough so that she could come home every weekend if she wanted to.

Right from the beginning, Ellen was happy there. Her first day of school she made friends with a girl who was staying in the same off-campus boardinghouse—Georgiann, her name was—and the two of them became fast friends. I mean, they really bonded.

Georgiann acquired a boyfriend only a few weeks into the

term. And before long, Ellen began dating, too. Everything was peachy. Georgiann and this boyfriend of hers, Cary—or was it Gary?—soon became serious. The two of them were even, so Ellen told me afterwards, talking about a June wedding, with Ellen slated to be maid of honor.

And then, inexplicably, Cary broke it off. No explanation. No apology. Nothing. "I don't think this is working" was all he said to the poor girl. That was it. Just "I don't think this is working."

Well, Georgiann was very young—much younger than most of the other freshman girls—and very naive. She'd been a virgin until this Cary came along. In fact, she'd never even had a boyfriend before. And she took the breakup hard. She couldn't eat. She couldn't sleep. She couldn't study. About the only thing she *could* do was cry and blame herself, insisting that it must have been her fault, that she must have done *something* to precipitate that dirty little punk's departure.

Ellen was very understanding, very kind. That's the way Ellen is. She listened. And comforted. And bolstered. She did everything possible to try to help her friend. But, of course, Ellen had her own life, too, and she couldn't be on call twenty-four hours a day.

Don't get me wrong, though. She didn't by any stretch turn her back on Georgiann; she spent hours on end with her. It's just that she wasn't able to devote *all* of her free time to the girl.

Then one night a week before Christmas vacation, it happened.

Georgiann knocked on Ellen's door that evening about 6 o'clock. "I'm kind of depressed," she said, or words to that effect. "Do you mind if I come in for a while?"

Ellen explained that she had a dinner date and had to leave in five minutes but that she didn't expect to be out very late. She told Georgiann she'd check to see if there was a light under her door when she got back. "If you're still up, we'll talk then," she promised.

I don't have to tell you, do I, that Ellen never saw her friend again. When she returned to the boarding house just before ten, Georgiann was being carried out on a stretcher, a white sheet covering her face.

Ellen was more than willing to shoulder the blame for Georgiann's suicide. "I should have canceled my date that night. I should have been there for her. I should have realized how desperate she was to talk. I should have . . . I should have . . . I should have . . ."

She left for Christmas vacation early—two days after Georgiann's suicide—and she never returned. She had what I guess you'd call a breakdown of sorts. It wasn't anything that required institutionalizing, but still, it prevented her from functioning normally. She didn't seem to want to do anything or see anyone. Mostly she just sat around the house, a good deal of the time with tears streaming down her face. And none of us—her family or her friends—was really able to get through to her. We told her over and over again that no matter how much she might have wanted to, it would have been impossible to monitor Georgiann around the clock. We tried to convince her that the suicide would have occurred regardless of whether she'd stayed in that evening or not. That if Georgiann hadn't done away with herself this night, it would have been the next one or the one after that.

But Ellen tuned us all out.

Fortunately though, at my sister-in-law Margot's insistence, she began seeing a psychiatrist before very long, visiting his office four days a week for over six months. And with his help and the passage of time, she was finally able to shed, at least for the most part, the awful guilt with which she'd saddled herself.

The following September Ellen transferred to Walden, another small eastern college—this one in Pennsylvania. She met Sybil and Raven and the others there. And in the spring she joined their sorority.

"You do remember about the b-breakdown, don't you?" Ellen was asking now.

"Of course, I do. But I wouldn't exactly call it a break—"

"Well, that's what R-Raven h-had on me," she said, taking a few more sips of the amaretto.

"I don't understand."

For a moment she chewed on her lip again. Then she gazed at me intently and drew in her breath. "Okay," she said, the word coming out as a sigh, "I'll fill you in.

"When I moved into the K-kappa Gam house," she began,

"Raven kind of adopted me. You know, took me under her wing. She knew what had happened with Georgiann—there was this transfer from Holden who told everyone on campus— and she really went out of her way to make me feel comfortable and everything. We got pretty t-tight, the two of us. It wasn't exactly the way it was with Georgiann, of course, but I liked her a lot, and we began hanging out together—going to dinner, the movies, things like that. But then she had this argument with one of the other girls—Lee. It started with some remark Lee made to her, something about her hair. It was pretty innocuous, it really was, but it made R-Raven furious; she was extremely sensitive. Anyway, they had this big, d-dumb fight, and I tried to smooth things over. Raven thought I was taking Lee's part, which I wasn't. But that's the way she saw it, and it put a kind of s-strain on our friendship. But then after a while things got back to normal again. Sort of, anyway. Although it was never the same between us after that. Not really."

"This Lee. Was she at the divorce party, too?"

Ellen shook her head. "Uh-uh. I don't think anyone stayed in contact with her after graduation."

"Okay, go on. I assume there's more."

"There is," Ellen confirmed after breaking briefly for a return visit to the amaretto. "At the end of our junior year, Sybil got into terrible trouble. Someone had set her up, you see. Anyhow, she blamed Raven, but I couldn't accept that Raven was even capable of such a thing—maybe because I didn't want to. And so I decided Sybil must have made a mistake, that it was somebody else. "And then later on, when we were seniors, something happened to Carol Sue Kessler, one of the other girls in the sorority. She *was* at the party, by the way. Well, it was something really horrible, Aunt Dez. *Really* horrible. I was just s-sick about it; we all were. And the thing is that Carol Sue was almost positive Raven was responsible for spreading the rumor that started everything in motion. She had no real proof and Raven, naturally, denied it. But C-carol Sue didn't believe her."

"What did you think about Carol Sue's accusation?"

"I didn't *think* Raven was involved, but I couldn't be sure. It's different now, of course. Now I'm almost sure that she *was*. Anyway, I did say that I didn't believe Raven would do something like that. But I suppose I wasn't that wholehearted about it, and Raven told me I should have stuck up for her more, should have really defended her. But how could I, unless I truly felt she had nothing to do with that story? And I just didn't know. Carol Sue was dating this guy Raven was interested in, and Raven was pretty t-ticked off about it. And not even because she cared that much about him. But because she had this need to always be on top, to be first with everyone. She was almost obsessive about that, and . . . well . . . it made me wonder. Plus in the back of my mind, I suppose, there was the Sybil thing, too. And so I couldn't bring myself to support her the way she would have liked. You can understand that, can't you?" she asked earnestly.

"Of course. And she held this against you?"

Ellen nodded. Then we both took time out for some more of our libation before she went on. "She n-never forgave me. I felt just awful, too. She'd been so great to me at the beginning, and up until then we were still pretty friendly. You have no idea how much I wanted to believe her when she denied she was responsible. But I'd gotten to know her pretty well by that time, and like I said, I couldn't seem to shake off these doubts that I had." Here, Ellen managed a small smile. "I realize you have no idea what I'm talking about, so all this must be practically impossible to follow. Maybe I should just tell you what it was about—the thing with Carol Sue. Do you want me to?"

"Some other time," I said, an answer that was practically against my religion. But I didn't want her to get sidetracked. "I get the gist of what went on," I added. "What I really want to know right now is what happened between Raven and *you*. Something else did happen, I gather."

"Yes, something did. But much, *much* later. And it's a really funny thing, too. It took months before I could even get a hello out of her after the business with Carol Sue. And I guess I couldn't blame her; I'd probably have been the same way if the situation had been reversed. But anyway, she eventually warmed up a little and started acting fairly pleasant to me. Not that we were ever friends again, but I never thought she considered me her enemy, either. Once we graduated, of course, we didn't make any effort to keep in touch. In fact, I hadn't seen or spoken to her in years. But then this past February—well, I suppose she found herself in a position to get back at me for what she considered my betrayal."

"She waited until *then*?" I asked incredulously.

"That's right. Can you imagine?"

"Just what did she do?"

"She was at this wedding—some distant relative, I think it was—and who should be seated at the same table but Mike's cousin Candy and her husband. Mike and I had been out to dinner with Candy and Len a couple of times when they came into the city—they're from Westchester. I really like them a lot. I—"

"About Raven, Ellen," I reminded her.

"Sorry. Well, Raven mentioned in conversation that she'd gone to Walden, and Candy remembered that I had, too, and she asked Raven if she knew me. Candy must have said that I was going with her cousin, I guess. Anyhow, Raven said she knew me very well and that I was such a sweet girl and that she hoped I'd finally recovered from my breakdown, which was just such a terrible shame. Something like that, at any rate."

"She didn't!" I all but shouted.

"Oh, yes, she did."

"Candy told you this?"

"No, she said something to her mother about it, and then her mother said something to Mike's mother, and then Mike's father said something to *him* about it. What Mr. Lynton told Mike, though, was that I'd been in a mental hospital. But to be fair," she added an instant later, "I don't know if that came from Raven or if the story had been embellished somewhere along the line. Anyway, according to Mike, Mr. Lynton said he was concerned about me. I'm sure what he really said was that he was concerned about my stability."

"Was Mike aware of what had happened at Holden?"

"Uh-uh. I'd never spoken to him about it. Not because I was trying to hide anything, but because it had just never come up. But I finally told him everything, and that was the end of it. As far as Mike was concerned, that is."

"What do you mean? Didn't he explain things to his parents?" I asked, suddenly realizing that Ellen had, thankfully, been sans stutter for the last few minutes. No doubt due to the amount of tippling she'd been managing to intersperse with her narrative.

"Sure, but I've seen his mother twice since then," she answered glumly. "And both times I caught her looking at me strangely. I swear I did. She's probably worried that her son's gotten himself mixed up with a loony." She shrugged, then conceded, "But maybe I'm just being paranoid."

"And you never breathed a word to me about any of this!" I said accusingly.

"I was going to, but I was just so damned angry, and I was afraid I'd work myself up even more by rehashing everything. So I made up my mind that I'd just have to try and forget it."

"Oh," I responded, pouting a little because Ellen hadn't seen fit to confide in me. I quickly put myself down for it. After all, how infantile can you get? "Did you have a chance to confront Raven at the party?" I wanted to know.

"Oh, I had it out with her before then. I called her as soon as I found out what she'd done."

"And?"

"And she claimed it wasn't the way I was making it sound. She said that I'd always been her favorite sorority sister, even after we drifted—you know, that kind of bull. And she swore she was honestly interested in how I was and that she'd assumed Candy knew about the breakdown. More bull. She also told me she never claimed I'd been in an institution and that it was another case of someone wrongly accusing her. And then she had the nerve to tell me *she* was the one who should be upset. She said that's what she got for caring about people. How do you like that?" Ellen demanded, eyes flashing.

"The bitch," I growled. "The horrible little bitch."

"She's dead, Aunt Dez, remember?" Ellen remonstrated gently.

"The horrible *dead* little bitch," I amended.

"Ohh, Aunt Dez." So saying, she drained her glass of its few remaining drops of amaretto. And I, to be companionable, followed her lead. Then we decided to have some dinner.

Chinese takeout, of course.

Chapter 4

At 9:30 the following morning I called Jackie, my secretary, to let her know I wouldn't be in that day. (God forbid I didn't apprise her of this fact; I can assure you that hell would have been a virtual paradise compared to what life would have been like around the office.) That taken care of, I had a second cup of my truly horrendous coffee, made a couple of phone calls, picked up my Chevy at the garage around the corner, and headed for Long Island.

Driving out there, I kept thinking how silly—how preposterous, really—it was that Ellen should be suspected of any crime more serious than jaywalking. (And I had my doubts about the jaywalking, too.) I mean, the very idea that this police chief could think she might be involved in Raven's death! He might as well have accused *me* of being the killer, for God's sake! Well, I'd find out just what was going on very soon now.

Traffic in that direction was light, so I got to Clear Cove in slightly under an hour. I remember deciding that this town was about as close to immaculate as a town can get. What's more, it let you know right away—but very discreetly of course—that there was plenty of old money here.

I passed one impressive home after another—many of them more like estates—looking for someone who could provide me with directions to the police station. The litter-free streets, however, were completely devoid of human life. Probably everyone was out back playing in their swimming pools, I supposed. After all, it was an ideal day for it. According to the weather report I'd just heard on the radio, the temperature had already hit eighty, which report could be verified by every stitch of clothing I had on. I'd removed the jacket of my pale green linen suit about a half hour ago and I was now wishing I could do likewise to the yellow cotton blouse that was plastered up against my back. But alas, modesty and New York State law prevented. (I swear, the first thing I'm going to do when I win the lottery is buy myself a car with an air conditioner that works more than ten percent of the time. A Porsche would be nice, I think.)

Anyway, before long I came to a small but elegant shopping center, which while far from bustling, actually had a few real people traipsing up and down its sidewalks and entering and leaving its handful of smart boutiques. Now, under normal circumstances, I would have found it hard to resist a little browsing—particularly in the shop that was at this moment directly parallel to my Chevy—but just then I was much too anxious to have a word with the idiot who'd so mercilessly grilled my poor Ellen. So I pulled alongside the curb and leaned over to the passenger's side of the car, totally ignoring the eighteen-karat gold distractions—which I couldn't afford, anyway—that were winking shamelessly at me from the jewelry store window. I called out to the first passerby. "Excuse me!"

"Yes?" She was a tall, elderly woman, slim and smartly dressed in a beige sleeveless sheath, her thick, precisely arranged snow white hair shimmering in the morning sun. Walking toward the car, she closed the distance between us in two long strides.

"I was wondering if you could tell me how to get to the police station."

"Certainly." She was eyeing me curiously now. "You turn left at the traffic light and then go two blocks down. It will be on your left in the middle of the block. You can't miss it."

Glancing over my shoulder just before I rounded the corner, I saw that she was still standing where I left her, staring after me.

The Clear Cove police station was—like everything else I'd seen in this town so far—spanking clean. Of course, there weren't too many people around to mess it up. In the main area were just two uniformed policemen, plus a man in street-clothes at the water fountain, and a middle-aged woman in a bright print dress sitting at a computer. She was the closest person to the entrance.

"I'd like to see Chief Brady," I told her. "Is he in?"

"You bet, honey," she responded. And then calling out to the man at the fountain: "Say, Al!" The man looked in our direction. "This lady here wants to see you!"

"Hi there," he said genially, ambling over to me. "How're you doin'? Follow me. My office is right there." I obediently trudged behind him for a few yards before he preceded me into a nice-sized, glassed-in space that I can't even begin to tell you how much I coveted. It was furnished with a simple black Formica desk, a brown vinyl sofa, and three brown vinyl chairs, one of them behind the desk. The desk itself was bare, except for a telephone, a computer, a lamp, a couple of Bic pens, and a single manila folder. No wonder this guy had been hounding Ellen! Raven's accident had probably been the only case they'd had here in years to offer even a speck of hope that it could turn out to be an actual crime.

"What did you want to see me about?" Brady asked with a pleasant smile. Settling into his chair, he gestured for me to take the seat alongside the desk.

He was a big man of fifty or more with sparse gray hair and a round, jowly face that sat on a short, thick neck. His deep-set blue eyes, which were tinged with red, looked directly into mine. They were intelligent eyes, I thought.

"I'm here about Ellen Kravitz," I informed him, bending my head now as I fished around in my suitcase-sized handbag for my private investigator's license.

There was a pause before I heard, "Oh, sure. The woman I spoke to yesterday. What about Ms. Kravitz?"

"She's my niece," I answered without lifting my eyes from the bag, "and she was very upset after you told her that her friend's death might have been due to foul play." *Aha! Here it is! Damn! It's my damn key case!*

"I'm real sorry to hear your niece was upset by my visit, but I don't think I'd call Ms. Eber a friend of hers. Not from what she herself told me."

And damn Ellen, too! She was always much too up front about everything for her own good. "There might have been a little falling out of sorts between the two girls recently," I admitted, still intent on my search, but now devoting a portion of my brain to an attempt at damage control. "It was nothing serious, though. And Ellen's a very gentle person. Very." *I found it! No, it's my damn pocket diary!* "That's why she was so distressed at even the *thought* that anyone might have actually been responsible for Ms. Elber's death."

"The name's Eber, ma'am. And murder's only one possibility. Uh, but just out of curiosity, is it okay to ask what it is you're huntin' for?"

"Do you mind if I put a few things out here for a sec?" I said, finally looking the man in the face. Before he could answer, I began emptying the contents of my handbag on his desk. "I just want to show you my license."

"What kind of license are we talkin' about?"

"I'm a private investigator."

"Wonderful," he responded with a kind of groan. "Exactly what I've been prayin' for."

"I've got it!" I announced triumphantly then, removing the small black leather card-holder from its hiding place in the fold of my wallet and handing it to him.

Flipping it open, Brady took a cursory glance at the license inside. "Desiree Shapiro, huh?" he murmured, returning it to me. I thought he was trying to suppress a smile.

At least Desiree Shapiro's a memorable name, I refrained from remarking. *A lot more memorable than, say, Al Brady, for example*. "That's right," is what I said instead. Why antagonize someone you're trying to pump for information?

"Just what is it I can do for you, Ms. Shapiro?"

"I'd like to know what makes you think that Miss Eber's death wasn't accidental," I answered, shoveling everything back into my handbag. My mirror didn't make it, clattering to the floor and shattering into more than a dozen pieces.

I started to get up, but Brady put a restraining hand on my arm. "Leave it. The cleaning people'll take care of it. And anyway, I'd appreciate it if you'd just sit still for a coupla minutes. Frankly, you're drivin' me crazy."

Obligingly, I leaned back in my chair. "Sorry. You were about to say—?" I prompted.

He sighed resignedly. "Okay, I can't see where it would hurt any to answer a few of your questions. But this supplyin' you with information is a one-time-only proposition. Don't get yourself any ideas about a collaboration here. And if you find it absolutely necessary to start lookin' into things on your own, make sure you don't do anything to hamper this department's investigation in any way. Understood?"

"Oh, completely."

"First off, I never said Raven Eber's death wasn't an accident. But there are a coupla things I find puzzlin'. And when I've got myself a puzzle, I do my best to get the answers."

"What is it you find puzzling?"

"Well, for starters, Ms. Eber was never invited to that party."

"You're kidding! Do you mean she crashed?"

"Not exactly. Ms. Miller says she never sent her an invitation. Yet the deceased—"

"Oh. I wasn't aware the invitations had been *sent*. I thought the girls were contacted by phone. There *were* only a few of them."

"You're talkin' about for Friday. But there were, well, must have been a hundred or more people invited to the Saturday night shindig she was supposed to have. And as long as she was doin' up invitations for those . . . Anyway, as I was sayin', the dead woman told her brother she'd gotten an invitation. She even showed it to him."

"That's funny, isn't it?" I mumbled, mostly to myself.

"I'd say so."

"Well, what do you take it to mean?"

"It seems to me that somebody wanted the woman there. And since everybody hated her, it—"

"Not Ellen. Ellen didn't hate her. She—"

"And since everybody hated her," Brady repeated loudly over my protest, "it could very well be that someone had plans for her. Unpleasant plans. And maybe when whoever it was found out about the pool, they saw their chance. And so they very kindly gave her a helping hand off that balcony."

"But she didn't really do my niece any permanent harm," I insisted, determined to remove Ellen from suspicion. "The things Raven said about her didn't bother Mike—Ellen's boyfriend—at all."

"Maybe not, but I understand they made an impression on the boyfriend's mother. And who knows what kind of harm that could eventually cause the romance."

Oh, Ellen, Ellen, I silently moaned. *You had to tell him about Mike's mother, too?*

"So you see, ma'am, your niece, along with every one of the other women at that little get-together—and I've talked to 'em all, by the way—had a reason for not exactly wishin' this Ms. Eber well."

I opened my mouth to present a more eloquent defense of Ellen, but there was no time to get the words out.

"And then there was the note," Brady said.

I sat up straighter. "What note?"

"The charred remains of what appears was a note of some kind were found in an ashtray on one of the tables in the bedroom. There was a spent match in the ashtray, too."

"I don't follow you. What could possibly be the significance of that?"

"Well, I'm thinkin' we might have had a suicide note there."

Suicide? This was something that hadn't even entered my mind. Besides, it didn't make any sense. "But Raven wasn't even aware there was no water in the pool."

"For all *we* know, she wasn't," he corrected.

"And anyway, if she did write a suicide note, why would she burn it?"

Brady shrugged. "Maybe she decided it should say somethin' else and she rewrote it."

"But if that's the case, where's the second note?"

"You're askin' me exactly the same questions I keep askin' myself."

"It didn't have to be a suicide note at all, you know. It could have been any one of a dozen other things. Like, for instance, a love letter she changed her mind about sending or a memo to herself or just a plain grocery list or—"

Brady put up his hand, a polite way of asking me to shut up. "You're a hundred percent right. I just like to explore every possibility, that's all."

I wasn't quite ready to comply. "It could even—" *Hold it!* I suddenly warned myself. *Maybe you shouldn't be so quick to dismiss the notion that Raven took her own life.* When you got right down to it, from my point of view suicide was certainly preferable to murder. I did a hasty about-face. "But then again, the girl just might have written a suicide note and later decided against leaving one, after all."

"I haven't ruled that out, either." God, this guy was agreeable! Also, I had begun to realize, a lot shrewder than you'd be led to believe by that down-home manner of his—which seemed more appropriate to the boonies somewhere than to this affluent suburban community. "Of course," he added in that same congenial tone, "I can come up with plenty of ways to do away with yourself that are a lot less messy than divin' headfirst into concrete."

Well, he had something there. Still, I wasn't about to let him scratch the suicide thing. "But the girls had a cocktail party that night. Maybe she was just drunk enough not to think about that."

"Not accordin' to the autopsy report, she wasn't. Ms. Eber might have been a little inebriated—she had a slightly elevated blood alcohol level—but she was far from mind-numbin' drunk."

"But you do think suicide's at least a possibility," I persisted.

"The way I see it, everything's a possibility right now."

"Do you have any idea when it happened?"

"Some time late Friday night. Or I should say, early Saturday mornin', since she didn't go upstairs until almost one."

"Nobody heard anything?"

"Not a peep."

"You're not ruling out that it was an accident, though, are you?" I wanted to establish that. I mean, accident was still my first choice. Also the most logical one.

"Of course not." And then the chief leaned forward and looked at me with those sharp bloodshot blue eyes of his. "Look, Ms. Shapiro, accident was my initial impression and, chances are, accident is just what it'll turn out to be. But the fact that Ms. Miller denies sending the dead woman that invitation bothers me some. So does the burnt note. So I'm not ready to close the file on this case yet. Not until I do a little more nosin' around, at any rate."

When I left the Clear Cove police station a few minutes later, I felt much better about things. It really didn't look like Ellen had anything to be concerned about. Brady had questioned all of the girls who were there that night, and he'd learned that all of them had disliked Raven Eber—the others, as I was sure he could tell, with far more intensity than Ellen was even capable of. Which meant they had much stronger motives, right? And besides, I'd received every indication that in the end the police would most likely conclude that it was an accident, anyway.

I called Ellen as soon as I got home and told her these things.

"You don't think I'm actually a suspect then?"

"No, I don't. I don't think Chief Brady really believes there was even a crime committed here. He just wants to satisfy himself that he didn't overlook anything."

"Honest?"

"Honest."

"He doesn't think that I—"

"I'm sure he doesn't."

"You're not just saying that?"

"No, I'm not."

"I've been meaning to tell you something, Aunt Dez. Something weird. When Raven walked in that night, I didn't believe I was seeing right—I just couldn't understand Sybil's inviting her. And then later in the evening, I found out that Sybil didn't. So I figured that for God-knows-what reason, Raven must have showed up on her own. But a few days afterward, I heard that somebody sent her an invitation. None of us can imagine who, though—or why."

She sounded more perplexed than worried. Still, knowing my niece, if allowed to dwell on this piece of intelligence, she'd find some way to perceive it as casting further doubt on her innocence. "It was probably meant as a joke of some kind," I said lightly. And then I quickly segued into a few more reassurances. And by the time I hung up, I think I'd managed to put her mind at ease. Or as much at ease as her nervous system would allow.

As for me, I was very comfortable with everything I'd said to Ellen. I mean, there was no murder here. And no suicide, either. Didn't the dead girl dive into the pool from the terrace all the time in her college days? And wasn't she absent when the others learned there was no water in the pool that weekend?

Yes.

And yes.

Nobody was responsible for Raven's tragic death but Raven herself.

As for that invitation business, I decided there had to be a simple explanation for it. So I didn't intend to let it bother me. I was going to just put it of my mind.

Along with the blackened remains of some insignificant piece of paper in an ashtray.

Chapter 5

On Thursday morning at 8:30 I stopped off to see one of two new clients that, thank goodness, I had recently acquired. (Not to worry; I'd informed Jackie the night before that I probably wouldn't be in until after 10:00.)

The only previous meeting I'd had with Mrs. Wetzel was both sad and funny and when I thought about it later, a little strange, too.

A sweet old lady with sparse white hair, a thin, frail body, and false teeth that clacked when she talked, Jane Wetzel had walked into my office a few days earlier, eyes red and a kind of dazed expression on her face. She came equipped with a large wad of tissues clenched in her small fist, which she availed herself of quite frequently as she tearfully recounted her story.

The minute she began talking in that wispy little voice of hers, I wanted to cry for the poor thing. (But then, it seems I want to cry for all my clients.) Her husband of almost fifty years had gone out one afternoon last week, she told me, ostensibly to play cards at the senior citizens' center. She hadn't seen him leave, but a few minutes after he walked out the door, she realized he'd taken their dachshund with him. Well, she should have known right away that something was fishy. You see, dogs aren't allowed at the center. At any rate, when the two of them didn't come home for dinner, she called one of her husband's card-playing buddies. He said Wilbur never showed up that day!

Naturally, Mrs. Wetzel related, at first she had feared there'd been an accident or that Wilbur, the husband, and Hoboken, the dachshund, had met with foul play.

"Hoboken?" I interjected here.

"That's where we bought him, dear," she replied. "Hoboken, New Jersey." Her manner clearly indicated that I wasn't terribly bright not to have figured that out for myself.

In spite of the serious nature of her problem, I couldn't keep the grin off my face. I quickly bent my head so she wouldn't see it. "Oh," I said. And after I'd gotten hold of myself, "Go on, please."

She was just about to call the police, she continued, when *something*—she has no idea what—told her to look in the closet. And that's when she made this startling discovery: two of Wilbur's suitcases were gone, along with most of his clothes—including the silk pajamas she'd given him last year for his birthday!

"I don't understand it," she murmured, sniffling pathetically and using three or four tissues from her ample supply to blow her nose. "Everyone said we were a perfect couple." And then unaware of the obvious contradiction: "Except that he has a *thing* for waitresses."

I asked Mrs. Wetzel if she had a picture of her husband. "Certainly, dear," she replied, removing a small stack of photos from her handbag. "This is Wilbur," she said, handing me the one on top.

I was a little startled. The picture was hardly what I expected. The man appeared to be a lot younger than his wife; in fact, he looked far too young to have been married for close to fifty years. I was trying to come up with a delicate way to question my client about this when she provided the explanation. "I hope that photograph is all right," she said. "It's fifteen years old, but Wilbur hasn't changed at all since it was taken. Well, maybe he's lost a bit of weight and some of his hair. And he does have this little goatee now."

Swell. "Are those others any more recent?" I asked, indicating the remaining pictures she was holding.

"Oh, these aren't of Wilbur." She thrust the other six or seven photos into my hand. "That's Hoboken. He comes from championship stock," she informed me proudly.

After dutifully examining the snapshots (her Hoboken was really quite a handsome little fellow), I made her promise to see if she could hunt up a more recent picture of the husband. Then I said, "Do you have any idea at all where Mr. Wetzel could have gone? Are there any close relatives?"

A hasty swipe at her eyes with a tissue. "Come to think of it, it's possible, I suppose, that he went to stay with his sister. But it's more likely he's with one of his waitresses. Although why he left home in the first place, I just don't know. He had no reason. No reason at all." She looked at me with this pitiful, heart-wrenching expression.

I assured her that I was certain he didn't. "Where does his sister live?" I asked.

"In one of those states out in the Midwest," she replied vaguely.

"You don't have her address?"

"Well, not with me, dear. Henrietta and I don't get along; it's been forty years since I was in touch with her myself. The address is somewhere in the house, though; I'm pretty sure of that. Wilbur writes to her every once in a while." She was shrugging into her little cotton sweater now, which she had hung on the back of the chair. Then abruptly, she got to her feet. "I'll call you in a day or so, as soon as I can find that picture for you," she told me.

"But there are a couple of other things I wanted to cover with you," I protested.

"Next time, dear. I have to go now. Choir practice. I'm already late as it is." Smiling wistfully, Mrs. Wetzel leaned over to pat my hand. "It takes my mind off things, don't you know."

And before I even had a chance to stand up, she was out of the office, a large pile of crumpled tissues on the corner of my desk marking her visit.

Now, after receiving a phone call last night in which she had informed me that she'd come across a later photo of Wilbur, I was seated in her living room.

The apartment was in one of those old buildings on the Upper West Side that you know immediately must have been super luxurious years ago. The well-kept lobby still had a kind of elegance. Not a speck of lint or dirt showed on the worn burgundy-and-blue-patterned carpeting. The brass wall sconces had a rich, cared-for sheen. And the huge crystal chandelier was positively sparkling. A doorman had pointed the way to the wood-paneled elevators.

The Wetzel living room, I noted, was almost like an extension of the building itself, it, too, attesting to former glories. The once-beautiful Oriental rug, now almost threadbare in spots, appeared to have been freshly vacuumed. And it was apparent that the vintage furniture—which you could tell was of really good quality—was being treated with respect, the tables so highly polished you could see your face in them. I had settled myself on a faded rose damask sofa that was flanked on either side by a coordinating rose, ivory, and blue armchair. Unfortunately, in a misguided attempt to preserve any remaining vestige of their good looks, all three pieces had been slip-covered in that horrendous plastic stuff (a sizable portion of which—no matter how often I shifted positions—now clung stubbornly to my bottom). And to gild the lily, the upholstery was further shielded from human contamination by strategically placed hand-crocheted doilies.

Mrs. Wetzel had just supplied me with a picture that was totally useless—the man's face was a blur. "I found this in my bottom drawer. It's only about two years old," she said. "I didn't even know I had it."

"Are you sure you haven't got anything that would give me a better idea of what your husband looks like?" I asked.

"Well, there might be something in the photograph album. As a matter of fact, I'm almost sure there is. And the album *is* around someplace, only I just can't remember where. I'll hunt around for it, dear, but I'm afraid it could take a little while before I lay hands on it. I'll let you know the minute I do, though."

"That's fine, Mrs. Wetzel. Now, you were going to see if you could locate your sister-in-law's address for me, weren't you?" I reminded her.

"Oh, I have that for you." She got up and left the room, returning moments later with a fragment of paper that had been torn from one of those lined yellow pads. The name printed on it in large block letters was Henrietta Clark. There was an address and phone number in Ames, Iowa.

"Thanks. I'll see what I can find out from her," I said, slipping the paper into my handbag. "Uh . . . there's something else we should talk about, too, if you don't mind," I put to her reluctantly.

"Of course not, dear."

"You mentioned that you think your husband may have . . . um . . . gone off with a waitress."

Tears immediately welled up in Mrs. Wetzel's eyes. "That's right," she confirmed, helping herself to a couple of tissues from the omnipresent wad in her fist. "He was always carrying on with one or the other of 'em—every time we went out. And the good Lord knows what went on when I wasn't around. I suppose he couldn't help it, though," she confided with a kind of sob. "It's almost like a sickness with Wilbur." And then she composed herself sufficiently to announce, "He's a sex maniac, you know."

A seventy-, maybe even eighty-year-old sex maniac? I was skeptical. Also, in spite of myself, amused. Although it *was* possible, I guess, it was even more possible that Mrs. Wetzel was greatly exaggerating her mate's sexual appetite.

"They knew how to play him, too—those women," she said, a bitterness creeping into her voice now. "Played him like a fiddle's what they did. Fussed over him and made big eyes at him and giggled at all those silly jokes of his. Probably found out there was a little money there. Not a fortune, of course," she added hastily, "but enough to appeal to a gold-digging sort, I imagine."

"Do you have the names of any of the women you suspect that Wilbur might have been interested in?"

"Oh, I don't know any of their names. That's *his* department. *He* knows *all* their names. I wouldn't be surprised if he could give you their measurements, too. But I can describe them and tell you where they work. Would that be all right?"

"That would be a big help."

The old woman smiled, obviously pleased at that. "I'll start making a list later. There are a lot of them. Maybe ten."

"I'd like a list of your husband's friends, too. Anyone you can think of. It's possible he confided his plans to someone."

"All right." She stood up. "You'll stay for coffee won't you, dear? It won't take but a minute or two."

"Well, I—"

"Wilbur got me one of those automatic coffeemaker things for my birthday a couple of years ago," she said as she began to walk away. "I ask you," she put to me, turning now and retracing her steps, "is that the kind of present you give your wife for her birthday?" I was spared the trouble of wracking my brain for a tactful response. "It certainly is not," my client asserted. "Believe me, he'd never give something like that to one of his chippies." And with this, she headed for the kitchen again.

"Listen," I called out, "I'm terribly—"

"It won't be long," she informed me cheerfully. "But you just sit here and relax until I have everything on the table."

"Honestly, Mrs. Wetzel, I'd love to have coffee with you. I really would. But—"

At the door now, she stopped and looked at me gratefully over her shoulder. "Oh, I'm *so* glad. It's awfully lonely here now."

So I stayed for coffee.

Well, what would you have done?

Chapter 6

It was after 11:00 by the time I got to work that morning.

Now, sizewise my office is nothing to brag about (although I occasionally try to fool myself by telling myself it's sort of cozy). The thing is, though, it's a really good deal. I rent the space from a law firm by the name of Gilbert and Sullivan (I thought it was a joke, too, the first time I heard it), and the principals—Elliot Gilbert and Pat Sullivan—are a couple of really nice guys who try to throw me some business whenever they can. Not only that, but as part of our agreement I get to share an exceptional secretary whose services I'd otherwise never be able to afford. Jackie, I'm talking about. I mean, the woman is efficient, hardworking, helpful, loyal, pleasant, kind, and a very good friend, besides—with only one or two of these qualities suspended when I manage to upset her. And if on those occasions, she can also be one of the most intimidating people you'd ever want to meet, well, at least she brings some structure to my life.

Anyway, I spent about a half hour typing up some notes. And following that, I paid a few overdue bills, as well as the balances remaining on my credit cards—things I was finally able to take care of thanks to a conservative projection of my earnings from those two new cases of mine. Then at around one, inspired by that jewelry store I'd shown such fortitude in resisting yesterday, I decided to go out and treat myself to a pair of earrings, earrings being a major weakness of mine.

I stopped in at one of the many women's boutiques in the neighborhood and promptly fell in love with this long, dangly silver pair, set with (fake) emeralds that I knew would go perfectly with *something* in my closet. And if not right now, definitely sometime in the future. What's more, they didn't cost even a fraction of what I'd have had to spend at that swanky place in Clear Cove. But then, they weren't eighteen-karat gold, either. Or fourteen. Or even ten. But no matter. They were stunning on me.

I was on my way to Little Angie's—where they make the absolutely thinnest, crispiest pizza crust in New York City—when I passed (make that almost passed) this little cosmetic shop that had opened in the neighborhood less than two weeks earlier. Naturally, I had to stop and check out the window. And of course, after that I had to give myself an excuse to go in. Deciding that I suddenly and desperately required a new coral lipstick worked just fine for me.

Fifteen minutes later, I walked out of the store in shock. I'd obviously parked every ounce of sales resistance I possessed at the entrance to the place—along with any common sense I might have been born with. So now here I was with this little shocking pink vinyl-covered paper tote in which nestled my new coral lipstick, along with regular skin cream and night cream and eye cream and body cream and presun cream. Enough damn creams, in fact, that if they only worked, could have retarded wrinkles and sagging practically into the next century!

I could scarcely believe I'd just charged almost two hundred dollars that I hadn't earned yet on my only-paid-up-this-morning Visa card for some dubious preparations that I had doubts I even wanted. The problem wasn't with my skin; it was with my brain!

On second thought, though, I *had* acquired two new clients, hadn't I? And one of them happened to be a large corporation that was paying me a very nice fee to investigate a matter requiring some fairly long-term sleuthing. So the way I made up my mind to look at it, I could afford a little self-indulgence; I was practically a mogul these days.

After twenty minutes and three pizza slices, I was back in the office, trying to reach Henrietta Clark, Wilbur Wetzel's sister. I let the phone ring nine times, but there was no answer. Also, no answering machine. I'd have to try again later.

As soon as I postponed Henrietta, I took out the file on that corporate case I mentioned. Just to clue you in, it appeared that one of the trusted executives at this manufacturing firm—Williams and McGuire—had been embezzling company funds. I'd narrowed the suspects down to three possibilities pretty quickly. But that was the easy part; from what I'd been able to determine, they were the only ones in a position to have managed the theft. Now, however, I was faced with the multimillion dollar question: Which of the three had actually had his sticky little fingers in the till?

I was about to start doing some background checks—in fact, I'd just finished dialing one of the men's former employers—when there was a tentative knock on the door. "Come in," I called putting the receiver back in its cradle.

Elliot Gilbert poked his head in, a sheepish expression on his round, pleasant face. "Mind if I sit down for a moment Dez?" he asked. "I have something to tell you."

"Sit," I responded, gesturing to the chair next to my desk, which was also the only chair in the office not occupied by me. I was smiling, even though Elliot's manner was a dead giveaway that this visit was nothing to smile about.

He sat down stiffly, a pink flush creeping slowly up his neck. "Umm, Bob Gilchrest just called me," he began, referring to Williams and McGuire's executive vice-president. "Uh, I'm afraid the company CEO made up his mind he wanted this high-powered firm of investigators called in. I think he may have used them for something once before. Bob tried his best to convince him to give you a chance, but there just wasn't anything he could do."

"Oh," was all I could manage.

"You'll be nicely compensated for the time you've already spent on the case, of course. But I don't suppose you've had a chance to really get going on it yet."

"No, I haven't."

"I'm sorry, Dez. I realize this would have been a nice piece of business for you."

"It's okay, Elliot. These things happen," I assured him through dry lips.

"Well, don't worry. We'll get you something else that's just as lucrative . . . uh, just as soon as something comes in."

When he closed the door behind him, I kicked the shocking pink vinyl-coated paper tote sitting under my desk.

After dinner that evening I tried Mrs. Clark for the fourth time, but there was still no one in.

And then I did some agonizing over losing out on the Williams and McGuire case.

Why did you have to go and write all those checks today? I kept asking myself. But I soon got around to rationalizing. After all, it wasn't as though I'd completely depleted my checking account; there was still a little something left over. And once the company compensated me for the hours I'd already put in on the investigation, between what I'd be getting and what remained in the account, there'd be no problem at all in covering incidentals like food and shelter, along with such absolute essentials as five different kinds of skin cream. I grimaced.

If only I hadn't picked this afternoon to go on that damned cosmetic binge! But, of course, I hardly ever did anything like that. And every woman *should* give herself a little treat every so often—you know, to make herself feel special. I even dredged up that old line about my being worth it. Plus I had the Wetzel investigation to tide me over until things picked up again, didn't I?

Later, right before going to bed, I slathered on four of the new creams. I mean, I put that stuff on with a heavy hand. (And I'd have piled on the fifth cream, too, if I'd been able to come up with any reason at all for applying a presun in the dead of night.)

It was my way of pretending that I wasn't the least bit sorry I'd been so extravagant.

I even managed to convince myself—for a few moments anyway—that all that junk would actually work.

I guess I'd practically hypnotized myself into a state of blind optimism about Raven's death. I hadn't given it more than a minute or two's worth of thought all day Thursday.

But when I opened my eyes at 7:30 Friday morning, the first thing that popped into my mind was that business about the invitation.

I suppose there was really no way to keep something like that from making an appearance once in a while. I mean, although I knew it was only a matter of time before the tragedy would officially be termed an accident—ergo, Ellen had nothing to worry about—I have this thing about loose ends. And any way you looked at it, the invitation was a loose end.

Somehow, though, I was able to shoo that worrisome little item out of my head before it became too firmly entrenched there. If Raven had dived into Sybil Miller's empty swimming pool by mistake, I reasoned—and I had no doubt that was exactly what she did—what difference did it make how she happened to get to Sybil's anyway?

I was at work by about 9:15 and Jackie waved a pink telephone slip at me the instant I came through the door. "From your client Mrs. Wetzel. You just missed her call."

Rats! I'd meant to try her sister-in-law one more time last night, but then I'd gotten all hung up on my finances, and I completely forgot about it. I took the paper from Jackie's outstretched hand and read the message as I walked down the corridor to my cubbyhole. Jackie wrote: "Mrs. Wetzel says to tell you, 'He's come home, thank God.' She thanks you and says to send a bill for what she owes to date."

Well, how do you like that!

I was really pleased—in spite of the fact that just yesterday I'd lost my only other case. Something else would turn up; it had to. But for now, I was relieved to learn that Wilbur had returned and that his wife wouldn't be lonely anymore. (Sometimes I think I might be a nicer person than I think I am.)

I couldn't just send a bill, not without telling Mrs. Wetzel how happy I was to hear the news. I dialed her number as soon as I was in my office.

It was a different Jane Wetzel who answered the phone. There was a kind of youthfulness in her voice, a lilt that hadn't been there before. It came through even in her hello.

"It's Desiree Shapiro, Mrs. Wetzel. I just want you to know how delighted I was to get your message." I hesitated a moment. "Everything's okay now, isn't it?"

"Oh, everything's perfect. He was pretty tired-looking and a little the worse for wear when he walked in. But I fixed him a good meal—probably the first decent one he's had since he's been gone—and he seems fine now. He just went into the other room to relax and watch a little television—that Regis and Kathie Lee program. He *loves* Kathie Lee."

Although I was dying to find out, I refrained from asking what had prompted the randy Wilbur to take a powder. I didn't want to embarrass her. "Well, I'm very glad things turned out the way they did," I said. "You stay well. And be sure you give Mr. Wetzel my regards, okay?"

The response was slow in coming. "Mr. Wetzel? You think I've been talking about *Wilbur*?"

"Uh, yes. Haven't you?"

"Why, no, dear. It's *Hoboken*. I thought I told your girl that. He showed up in front of the building at seven o'clock this morning—Lord knows how many hundreds of miles he had to travel to come home to me. Naturally, the doorman recognized him immediately—they're good friends—and brought him right up. Oh Mrs. Shapiro, it's so good to have him home again."

"Uh, but Wilbur . . . that is, don't you want me to see if I can locate your husband?"

"I only wanted to find *him* so I could get Hoboken back. I'm sure I explained that to you, dear. But now that my sweet boy is sitting right here in his own living room, what would I want with Wilbur?"

So there I was, without a single case. Or even the prospect of one. Some mogul I turned out to be!

But as it happened, it was probably fortunate that my workload had suddenly become so light. (How's that word *light* for a euphemism—or *workload*, for that matter?)

You see, before very long I wouldn't be able to focus on anything requiring more than the most minimal thought or effort. Because another job would be coming along, and it would be the most important job of my career:

Trying to keep Ellen out of jail.

Chapter 7

I had a crappy weekend.

I spent a couple of hours Saturday afternoon doing some emergency food shopping, the most pressing emergency being that my container of Häagen Dazs Macadamia Brittle had been reduced to all of about three spoonfuls. In the evening I watched a movie I'd rented: *Groundhog Day*. It was supposed to be pretty good, although you can't prove it by me—I fell asleep right in the middle of the thing. And I hadn't even been tired! But I don't know if you can take that as a critique of the movie or just my desire to escape from the world for a couple of hours.

On Sunday I took an old college friend to dinner. Jill was in from Ohio visiting her mother in Queens, and since she was flying home the next day, it was my last chance to see her for at least another six months. So even though I was feeling a little low, I forced myself to pull myself together, think optimistic thoughts, and paste a smile on my face in order to avoid depressing the hell out of the poor woman.

As soon as Jill and I sat down in the restaurant that night, I knew it was okay—almost mandatory, actually—to cool the perkiness. She immediately apprised me of the fact that her husband had recently skipped to parts unknown after twenty-two years of marriage, cleaning out their joint bank accounts while he was at it. And that was just for openers. Add to this that her younger son was on drugs, her older son had joined a cult, and that only last week she'd discovered her sixteen-year-old daughter was pregnant—and you have a pretty good idea of just how welcome some Little Mary Sunshine would have been at her table. And the meal itself did nothing to improve the atmosphere. My rare roast beef was well done, while Jill's chicken was almost raw. (And with her luck, there was every chance this would lead to salmonella poisoning.)

Still, all of this doesn't mean I was glad to get to the office on Monday. I mean, if there was anything that could match my evening with Jill, it was just sitting around wondering when I'd have something to write in my appointment book again.

It rained pretty heavily all morning and well into the afternoon, so I couldn't even kill a few hours window-shopping at lunchtime. I consumed a turkey and brie at my desk with a slice of pecan pie as a chaser and tried to convince myself things would be picking up any day now.

It was about ten after two when Jackie buzzed me. "There's a Dick Eber to see you, Dez."

Dick Eber? "Who—?" And then: "Wait." *That was the name of Raven's brother, wasn't it*? "Oh," I said, following this with a "well." After which I was a little more articulate. "Have him come in, will you, Jackie?"

"You weren't expecting him, I gather."

"Nope," I acknowledged.

Dick Eber was in his thirties somewhere. Probably his late thirties. He was on the short side and just a little chunky, with fair skin, blue eyes, and a kind of clean, open face. His straight sandy hair, which was just beginning to recede, had been a victim of the downpour and was now plastered tight against his head. He was wearing a crumpled white knit short-sleeved shirt, open at the throat, and slightly baggy khaki pants, both of which were seriously water-logged. In his hand was a dripping—and judging from his appearance, not very serviceable—umbrella that he seemed to be totally unaware of at that moment.

Now, maybe Eber had expected to see a clone of that leggy blond in the television movie I told you about, I don't know. But it was apparent that he *hadn't* expected to see me. And he wasn't able to conceal his surprise, either. Not with his eyes bulging and his mouth open like that.

"Please sit down, Mr. Eber," I invited, ignoring the expression on his face. (It was pretty much the same one my clients usually wear at our first meeting.) "I'm Desiree Shapiro." I extended my hand, which he shook almost automatically.

"There's an umbrella stand right behind the door," I pointed out.

He glanced down, disconcerted. "Oh, I'm so sorry. I completely forgot about this for a minute," he apologized, reddening. Then he dutifully placed the umbrella in the stand and took a seat. He was still looking at me as if he couldn't quite believe I was who I purported to be, but I guess he decided to give me the benefit of the doubt. "I, uh, know I should have called for an appointment first," he said, "but I really had no intention of coming to see you. This was a spur of the moment thing. I'm here—in Manhattan, I mean—cleaning out my sister's . . . cleaning out my sister's apartment. My sister is Raven Eber—*was* Raven Eber, that is to say. I know your niece told you what . . . what happened."

"Yes. And I'm sorry—very sorry—for your loss."

"Thank you," he responded in this hushed tone. It didn't require any great intelligence to see that the poor man was stricken. "I'm here because . . . well, because of a conversation I had with Ellen the other day." He cleared his throat before continuing. "She was calling to speak to Winnie—that's my wife—but Winnie wasn't home at the time, so Ellen and I had a pretty long talk. She mentioned that you were certain the police would eventually conclude that Raven's death was an accident."

"That's right," I assured him, assuming he'd be pleased. Or at least relieved.

"That would be a mistake," Eber said flatly. "My sister didn't have any accident. And she didn't commit suicide, either. She was murdered."

I was taken aback. "What makes you think that?"

"I don't *think* it. I'd bet my life on it. Raven was pushed off that balcony by one of those sorority sisters of hers. There isn't a doubt in my mind about it."

"But how can you be so positive? Ellen tells me Raven was a"—*showoff* was what Ellen had called her—"daredevil," I substituted hastily. "Ellen said that back in their college days your sister dived into the pool from that same balcony many times. And it appears that no one told her about the repairs, so—"

"Listen, Mrs. Shapiro, you didn't know Raven." And with this, his features softened, and there was the trace of a smile on his face. "She was such a little ham," he said in this far-away voice. Momentarily caught up in his reminiscences, he absentmindedly swiped with the back of his hand at a tear that had just left the corner of his eye and was poised to roll down his cheek. "Such a little ham," he said again. Then abruptly the mood changed. "Raven would never have done a thing like that just for kicks," he went on determinedly. "In fact, she told me on a number of occasions that diving off the balcony like that made her a little nervous."

"Then why—"

"Because she loved playing to an audience; she wanted to entertain people."

"Look, she'd just been to a cocktail party," I ventured, "and maybe the drinking made her—"

Eber interrupted. "I don't care how much she had to drink." His voice rose. "Don't you understand? Raven didn't even *like* the water that much."

"All right. But why are you so certain she didn't commit suicide? There may have been something troubling her, something she never told you about."

"There wasn't anything. We were extremely close. If there'd been anything—anything at all—I'd have known about it, believe me." It's possible that I looked a little skeptical because then he added, "She always shared her thoughts and feelings with me, ever since she was a child."

"Even if she normally confided in you, maybe—"

"There are no maybes," he said shortly. "And besides, for her to have committed suicide that way makes no sense at all. Didn't you just tell me yourself that she didn't know about the pool being empty?"

"I said it didn't *seem* that she knew about it," I corrected.

"Okay. But it still doesn't make sense. Everything had been going exceptionally well for Raven lately. She'd gotten a pretty substantial raise only about a month earlier. And right after that this man she'd been interested in for the longest time finally asked her out. He had to go to the West Coast for a few weeks on business, so they made a date to have dinner when he got back. That would have been the Friday after . . . the Friday after she was murdered." Eber closed his eyes for an instant and then swallowed a couple of times before murmuring, "Raven was so excited she was acting like a little kid about it." Now he swallowed a few more times, after which he sat up in his chair, shoulders back and spine ramrod-straight. When he spoke again there was a new urgency in his voice. "But even if you don't put much stock in any of this, there's something you *have* to consider. I suppose you're aware, aren't you, that Raven was never even invited to that party? Not by Sybil. Or anyway, that's what Sybil claims." The emphasis on this last word was slight but unmistakable.

"Yes, I heard that," I acknowledged.

"Whoever invited her, though, did it for only one reason: to murder her." He paused to ensure that this sank in before continuing to make his case. "Look, none of the women who were there that weekend had any great love for my sister. And that includes your niece. Just ask her," Eber challenged. I opened my mouth to respond—how, I wasn't quite sure—but fortunately, he went right on. "And with one of them, apparently, it went a lot deeper than that."

"How did your wife feel about Raven?" I had to ask.

He hesitated before making the admission. "I suppose Winnie wasn't very fond of Raven, either. No, I want to be completely truthful with you. I *know* Winnie wasn't very fond of her. Just like I know she'd never have harmed her. She was aware of what Raven meant to me."

"Tell me this. I assume your sister knew how the others felt about her. So why on earth would she even go to that party?"

Eber shrugged. "Because she was invited. Also, I think she might have looked at it as an opportunity to bury the hatchet— with one or two of them, at least."

"She must have been surprised to receive the invitation."

"She was. Very."

"Didn't it occur to her that it might have been sent as a sort of spiteful little joke, to maybe—oh, I don't know—make her uncomfortable in some way or other?"

"Of course. It occurred to me, too. Although it didn't dawn on me the invitation could be a phony—I was just concerned about the reason Sybil was inviting her. Anyhow, I tried to persuade her not to put herself in a position like that. You can see how much good that did," Eber said miserably.

"Do you think Raven suspected the invitation was bogus?"

"Maybe. She didn't say. But she was certainly suspicious of why she was being invited; that much I can tell you."

"But she went anyway."

"You didn't know Raven," Eber reminded me for the second time. "A thing like that would have made my sister all the

more anxious to show up. Right away—on her lunch hour—
she went out and bought herself a new nightgown to take away
with her. She didn't get much use out of it, did she?" he muttered, his voice close to breaking with the bitter irony of the
words. "The fact is," he told me a moment later, "Raven took
pride in being able to handle herself. She had this . . . well, I
guess you could say this almost compulsive need to rise to a
challenge. Listen, the poor kid survived a lot worse in her life;
take my word for it. And her experience—that's how it affected her."

I was about to ask him to elaborate, but at that instant, I
thought of something else. "You saw the invitation, I understand."

"That's right. I had to drive into the city to take care of
some business on the Wednesday before that weekend, and
Raven and I met for dinner. It had just come in the mail that
day. To her office."

"What did it look like?"

"Nothing like the printed ones Sybil sent out to the other
women, if that's what you're asking. Chief Brady showed me
a sample of those. No. This one was different. It was the kind
you get at card stores. You know, where they leave these
spaces for you to write in the date and time and all that. I remember asking Raven if she had to respond. And she showed
me that there wasn't even an RSVP on the thing." *No. There
wouldn't be.* "That should have made me realize it was a
phony," Eber said disgustedly.

"I got the impression before that you still think it might
have come from Sybil, though."

"It could have. It's possible she sent Raven something like
that just so that if anyone saw it—the way I did—it wouldn't
look like it came from her."

"You make a good point there."

"God!" Eber exclaimed then, grabbing his head with both
hands. "Why didn't I try harder to talk her out of going? Why
didn't I—?"

"From what you've told me about Raven, no matter what
you said, she would have checked out that party."

"That's probably true," he conceded after a moment.

"Tell me, did you mention the invitation to your wife at
all?"

"No. When I came home that night, Winnie was already

asleep. And she was late for work the next morning, so we didn't really talk. And then I more or less forgot about it. Winnie was completely floored when Raven turned up that weekend."

"Mr. Eber, you said something—"

"Dick."

"And I'm Desiree. Or Dez. It's your choice," I informed him with a smile. "You said something a couple of minutes ago about what Raven had to survive."

"That's right. And I'd like to tell you about it if you can spare me a few more minutes. I think it will help you to understand her a little. . . ."

Chapter 8

Dick Eber was looking at me intently now. "My mother died when Raven was only four," he said, "and I had just turned thirteen. So my aunt—my mother's sister—who was single, came to live with us and help raise us. At the beginning, Raven and I weren't too crazy about Aunt Gerri. For one thing, she was pretty strict. And for another, she wasn't a warm person. By that, I really mean that she wasn't at all demonstrative. At least, not with us. Things were different, though, when it came to my father. Before long—within a month, I'd say—they began sharing the same bed." I noticed that at the words "my father," Eber's —that is, Dick's—lips had curled into an almost imperceptible sneer. "Still, for a while—" He stopped abruptly. "Do you think I could get a drink of water?" His voice had that sound you make when your mouth is bone dry.

"Of course. There's a fountain right outside. I'll get you a cup. Unless you'd rather have some coffee? I'm sorry. I should have asked you before."

"Don't give it a thought; I'm not much of a coffee drinker," he assured me. "Water'll do just fine. But I'll go out to the fountain myself, if you don't mind. I'd like to stretch my legs."

When he returned, Dick sat down with obvious reluctance, and there were two sharp lines between his eyes now. I sensed that he was ambivalent about proceeding, but he let out a long sigh, shifted around in his seat a little, and then forged ahead. "Where was I?"

"Your aunt," I prompted.

His face was blank.

"Sharing the bed with your father."

The lines deepened. "Oh, yes. Well anyway, in spite of the

fact she and my father were sleeping together—which made me pretty uncomfortable at first—things weren't actually too bad initially. Naturally, Raven and I missed our mother, but Aunt Gerri did the best she could. I think the problem was that she just wasn't comfortable with kids, which is what gave me the impression—and I think Raven, as young as she was, had the same take—that she felt she'd been saddled with us. But still, she took very good care of us. Prepared our meals and saw to it I studied and that we wore clean clothes and went to the dentist—all of that stuff. And then three of four months after Aunt Gerri moved in, my father got fired."

"What did he do? For a living, I mean."

"He was a bartender. But he was never at one job for very long. He had a quick temper, and he was always getting into arguments with the customers or with one of the other bartenders or a waiter or the boss—*somebody*. Well, I guess the buzz about him started making the rounds, because this last time he was finding it tough to get any place to hire him. My aunt had been a legal secretary before she became a substitute mother, so she said she'd go back to work until he landed something. Just so they'd be able to pay the bills, she said. She got something right away, too, and so while she went out to work, my father stayed home and looked after Raven. Supposedly." There was an almost frightening animosity in the way he spit out this last word.

A knot was forming in the pit of my stomach now, and there was this hot, prickly feeling at the back of my neck. "That didn't work out too well?" I asked stupidly, dreading what I was sure I would hear yet knowing that I had to hear it.

"You might put it like that," Dick agreed with a short, bitter laugh. "Being a complete dunderhead, though, I had to wait for the sky to come crashing down on me before I tumbled to what was going on. I was in school most of the day, of course, so all these years I've been telling myself that was a big part of it. But I should have realized what was happening, anyway. When I look back now, I can't understand how I missed it. Raven's behavior alone should have given me some idea. She'd suddenly become a lot more quiet, almost withdrawn at times, and she had always been such a lively, happy little kid before. But I just figured that was because of our mother's death. We'd both taken the loss pretty hard, and I wasn't exactly a barrel of laughs myself in those days. At any rate, I eventually found out the truth: Dear old Dad was, it seems, molesting her."

My "oh, no" was barely audible. Dick had said exactly what I'd been steeling myself for, yet for some reason, when it was put into words like that, it was still a shock. "I'm terribly sorry." Since it was no longer possible to say that to Raven herself, it seemed perfectly natural at that moment to convey my feelings to the one person in the world who had really cared for her.

Her brother acknowledged this sentiment with a nod. Then moistening his lips with his tongue, he muttered, "I should have known. The signs were there. I should have—"

"Don't blame yourself, for God's sake! You were still a kid, too."

"But I was a lot older than Raven was. And I'd promised my mother I would always look after her. I had the clues. I had the—" He broke off, sighing deeply. And then in a choked voice: "It's been almost twenty-five years, and I still can't forgive myself for letting it happen."

I couldn't allow him to go on flagellating himself this way. "That's crazy. How could you possibly know the change in Raven was due to anything other than your mother's death?"

"Because of my father. Because of what he was like. You have to understand about him. The man had this ego thing. He was Mr. Machismo. And here he was, out of work and what was worse, dependent on a woman for his bread and butter. I had to be an idiot not to realize he'd need to prove to himself he was still a big man."

"My God, stop it! You weren't a trained psychiatrist. You were only thirteen years old!"

He completely ignored me. "And how does he prove it?" he went on in a tone literally pulsating with hatred. "By molesting his own four-year-old daughter!" And with that, Dick Eber slammed his fist against the side of my desk with such force that I came damn close to shooting out of my chair. He seemed startled himself. "I'm sorry," he murmured, massaging his hand. "I don't know what got into me."

"Are you all right?" I asked, concerned.

"I'm fine. Embarrassed, but fine." His discomfort was reflected in his complexion, the pale skin on fire now."

"Are you sure?"

"It's just a little sore, that's all."

"I hope nothing's broken."

"Believe me, it'll be fine."

"Oh, I wasn't referring to your hand," I joked, trying to take the edge off things. "It's the desk I'm worried about."

"I usually have more control than that. I'm sorry," Dick repeated.

"Listen, I'd like to lay that son of a bitch out myself, so please stop apologizing." I glanced down at the injured hand; the knuckles were red and bruised. "I think I'd better get some ice for that."

"No, please. It sounded worse than it feels," he assured me with a shamefaced grin. And then very soberly: "I'd like to finish telling you about Raven."

"Well, all right, if you're positive . . ." His nod gave me permission to pose the question I'd been about to put to him before the assault on my furniture. "How did you finally find out what your father had been up to? Did Raven say something?"

"No. I don't think she would ever have done that. But one day I came home from school early—an upset stomach. He was just leaving her room. He was fully dressed by that time, but there was this look on his face. I can't even describe it, but I just *knew*. Raven was standing next to the bed in her panties, pulling this little shirt over her head. When she saw me, she just froze. I walked in and threw back the quilt, and all the proof I needed was right there—on the sheet."

"What did you do?"

"I went and got my baseball bat. I think that if he'd hung around, I would have killed him right then and there. But he didn't; he'd already left the house. So I went back to see how Raven was. I found her cringing in the far corner of the bedroom, sobbing. When I finally managed to calm her down a little, I found out that she thought everything was her fault— God knows what kind of crap he'd been feeding her—and she was mortified that I'd discovered what was going on. She was worried it would make me hate her. Can you imagine?" he said disgustedly.

"The poor little thing," I responded, shaking my head.

"My father was quite a guy, wasn't he?" Dick growled.

"How was he with Raven before the sexual abuse? Had he been treating her all right until then?"

"Are you kidding? He used to abuse her verbally before he graduated to that. He'd tell her she was stupid and that she'd never learn anything and that other kids her age could do everything so much better and quicker than she could. What a sweetheart, huh? She's still just a baby, and he's handing her that kind of garbage, undermining her confidence and, as it turned out, scarring her for life. The truth was that she was a pretty smart little kid. But he just had no conception of how much you could expect from a four-year-old, how much they were capable of. Or if he did know, he didn't care."

"What did your Aunt Gerri have to say about the way he spoke to Raven?"

"Oh, he was pretty careful not to let her hear any of it. In fact, he played the role of Decent and Loving Father when she was around."

"Was he the same way with you? Verbally abusive, that is."

"Sort of. A while back, anyway. But never to the same degree. Plus my mother used to muzzle him whenever she caught him putting me down. She was some feisty lady, my mother," Dick informed me with pride. "Especially when it came to her kids. And she was also three inches taller than he was and solidly built—did I mention my father was skinny and sort of runty-looking? Well at any rate, he wasn't about to take her on. And then when I got to be around ten, he seemed to ease up on me. Maybe he decided I didn't make quite as good a victim anymore."

"And he had your sister to concentrate on by that time."

"Not right away. He started working on Raven when she was three or so. The trouble was, by then my mother was in a pretty bad way, so she didn't have that much control over him anymore."

"Cancer?"

"No, she had a weak heart. And having to put up with a husband like that—well, the cards were pretty much stacked against her surviving, I suppose. Ever since I can remember, my father was always giving her some kind of grief.

"You know, before I found out he was molesting Raven, I wouldn't let myself so much as *think* that he bore any responsibility for my mother's death. I wouldn't even admit to myself how much I hated the man. I was *that* terrified of alienating him. You see, he was all we really had, the two of us. Or so I thought, anyway. Can you understand?"

"Of course."

"But the day I saw him coming out of my sister's room like that, everything changed."

"Did you tell your Aunt Gerri what happened?"

"Yes, but I hadn't planned on it."

"What do you mean?"

"Well, after I got through trying to convince Raven that she didn't do anything wrong, I shoved everything of hers that would fit into this little suitcase. And then I went and packed my own stuff. Don't ask me where I intended going or what I intended to do when I got there. Anyway, I had close to a hundred dollars hidden in the closet—money I'd saved from a paper route and doing odd jobs in the neighborhood. And I found another fifty by scrounging around in my aunt's dresser drawers. I figured I'd leave her a note saying that we had to go away and that I'd pay her back as soon as I could. In fact, I'd already begun writing it when she came home from work."

"So then you had to tell her."

"Yes. I tried stonewalling it for a while, because I didn't think she'd even believe me. And besides, I was ashamed—he *was* my father. But eventually she wormed it out of me. She said to unpack my suitcase, that she'd handle everything. I didn't know what to do; I was really torn. On the one hand, I was worried about how Raven and I would make it on our own. But on the other hand, I knew I couldn't let her stay in that house—not with him there. I never did have to come to any decision, though. Because while we were still hashing things out, my father showed up, the picture of innocence, acting like there was absolutely nothing wrong. Aunt Gerri convinced me not to start anything, to just go to my room. 'Leave it to me,' she said. 'Everything will be all right.'

"They had quite a battle, the two of them. You've never heard so much shouting and cursing! And mostly on my aunt's part, surprisingly enough. She had always seemed to be so devoid of emotion, and now suddenly she was like a tiger. I could hear a lot of what was said—shouted, I mean; the acoustics were great in that place. She called him every name in the book—a lowlife, an animal, a pig, and some things I wouldn't even consider repeating to you. Words I didn't even know she knew." Dick laughed then. For the first time, he was actually enjoying his narrative.

"Did your father admit to what he'd done?"

"*Him?* He denied everything. But my aunt wasn't having

any. She screamed that she wanted him out of there. And then he screamed back that he had no intention of leaving, that it was *his* house. Of course, my grandparents—my mother's parents—were the ones who put up the downpayment and the place was mortgaged up to here, besides"—Dick stretched his arm above his head to illustrate—"but that didn't stop him from going ballistic. Aunt Gerri cut him dead. She told him she'd call the police and have him locked up if he didn't pack his things and get out. And right away, too—tonight, she told him. He yelled that it was his word against the lies of a couple of snot-nosed kids. Something like that. And she said that no, it wasn't. She said she'd swear she saw him do that to Raven."

"Good for her! And he left?"

"You bet he did. Oh, not without a lot more screaming. And he did try putting his fist through the wall a couple of times in protest." With this, Dick automatically looked down at his own newly damaged appendage.

I followed his glance. "I wish you'd let me get some ice for that," I offered again.

"It feels better now, honestly." And then he added in a tight little voice, "I guess this sort of thing runs in the family."

"I hope that wall was all your father hit," I put in quickly. "It sounds to me like punching out a woman would have been right up his alley."

Dick actually guffawed at this notion. "You never saw my aunt. She was built a lot like my mother—only even more so. Let me put it this way. If there'd ever been a head-on collision between my Aunt Gerri and one of those giant tractor-trailer rigs, the smart money would have been on Aunt Gerri. My father wouldn't have dared lay a hand on her! Like most bullies, he was basically a coward. An ex-boss of his once told me that the people my father used to get into those arguments with at work were all smaller than he was. Or older. Or frailer."

"That must have been a pretty terrifying night for you," I observed then.

"It was. It's funny, though. As soon as things became really heated, I went into Raven's room to check on how all that yelling and screaming was affecting her. And when I saw that she was back in that corner again, shaking all over, I forgot how scared *I* was. I sat down in the corner with her, comforting her, and the two of us went on sitting there and hanging on to each other until the smoke cleared."

"Your father left that same night?"

"Early the next morning. Before I got up for school. And we never saw or heard from him again."

"Do you know if he's still alive?"

"I don't give a damn if he is or not. In fact, I prefer not."

"I can't blame you. And your Aunt Gerri?"

"She passed away ten years later—fifteen years ago. And you know something? I still miss her. From the day my father took off, things were different with her—easier. I don't mean that she suddenly started to smother us with hugs and kisses or anything like that—it wasn't in her nature. But she was less strict. She even smiled more. I don't know why, but I think his leaving made her more comfortable about raising us."

"The three of you lived together until she died?"

"That's right."

And then Dick, plainly exhausted from what had been a very emotional outpouring, asked if I'd excuse him while he made another trek to the water fountain. I'm not even sure he wanted the water. I think he desperately required another break.

When he returned, however, he seemed revitalized. "That's about it," he said. "After my aunt died, we sold the house. The mortgage was paid up by then—she'd seen to that—so we made a fairly nice profit. I used part of the money to buy a small condo for us—for Raven and me—and what was left over I put into a fund for Raven's college.

"But the reason I've told you all this—and I had no idea I'd be so long-winded about it—was because I wanted you to know about my sister. Know what made her tick."

"Oh, I—"

"Please understand. I'm not denying that she occasionally hurt people—although I can't accept that she was responsible for all of the things her sorority sisters accused her of. But anyhow, in other cases, like the incident with Ellen, I'm positive it was more the result of a misunderstanding than anything else."

Well, I couldn't buy that. But I wasn't about to make Dick face up to his sister's true nature, either. His illusions about her were sustaining him. And he'd earned the right to keep them.

"Listen," he was saying, "right after Ellen chewed her out, Raven called me. She swore that it never occurred to her that the concerns she'd expressed at that wedding—and they *were* genuine concerns—could cause Ellen any trouble. She felt really awful. I happen to know that she'd always been extremely fond of your niece. And while there's no question she misspoke—particularly since she was talking to someone related to Ellen's boyfriend—I can tell you one thing for sure: There wasn't any malice there. She hadn't seen Ellen in years, and she was sincerely interested in finding out how things had been going for her."

I didn't have the heart to protest.

"I don't want you to think I'm whitewashing her, though," Dick hastily assured me. "There were times when Raven's motives were much less altruistic. You see, she had no self-esteem. None. That was part of our dear father's legacy to her. You have to take into account that for a long time he reminded her on an almost daily basis of how inferior she was to other girls her age. And it stuck. She always had to convince herself that she was as good as anyone else—*better*. It was the only way she could survive."

Well, naturally I was appalled—no, *mortified*—by the abuse, both verbal and physical, that Raven had had to endure. But citing it as the source of her abominable behavior more than two decades later was just too simplistic an explanation for me. I mean, this may sound callous, but you can blame the past for just about anyone's misdeeds. Maybe Attila the Hun didn't have such an ipsy-pipsy childhood, either. But did that give him the right to go trampling through country after country butchering and doing God-knows-what-else to all those people? And where was Dick Eber's license to practice psychiatry, anyway? *Oh, come on*, I wanted to say to him.

And then he added something excruciatingly sad.

"Do you know what she once told me? She was maybe ten at the time, and one day, out of the blue, she asked me if I remembered when our father did what she used to call 'that thing' to her. I said I did, and then she said that in a way it had made her happy. It made her feel like maybe he thought she was worth something, after all."

That poor, poor kid! I can't even describe the intensity of the ache I felt for little Raven and—at that moment, anyway—for the young woman she'd become.

"Look," Dick went on, "what I'm trying to say is that because of the self-image my father had inflicted on her, Raven sometimes did harmful things to other people. But it wasn't to deliberately bring them down; it was to pull herself up."

"You were a good brother," I told him then.

"I tried to be," he responded with a wan smile.

"I don't suppose Raven ever got professional help."

"Unfortunately, no. My aunt wasn't very sophisticated about things like that. And after a while, Raven did seem to be doing okay. *I* thought she was coming along just fine," he said with a terse, self-derisive laugh. "I imagine if she hadn't appeared to be dealing with everything so well, sooner or later Aunt Gerri would have seen to it she got the help she needed."

Suddenly, Dick partially rose from his seat to inch his chair closer to mine. Then he leaned forward, his face not much more than a foot away when he spoke again. "It wasn't easy for me to reveal all these terrible things about my own family; I'm normally a very private person. But I thought you ought to know that there was a very good reason Raven was . . . the way she was."

"Why is that so important?" I inquired gently.

"Because I want you—I want *someone*—to care what happened to her that weekend in Clear Cove and to do something about it."

"But the police—"

"Didn't you tell Ellen that the police are very likely to rule out homicide?"

I thought fast, "Yes." I answered, "but Ellen was very upset by your sister's death, and I figured an accident would be easier for her to accept than a murder. That's primarily why I said what I did. But Chief Brady's not ready to close the investigation yet; I know that for a fact. And if it *was* murder, I'm sure the police will find evidence to that effect."

"I would feel a lot more confident if you'd look into things."

"I think—"

"I don't know how long the police will take to wrap this up. Or even *if* they'll wrap it up—correctly, I'm talking about. And in the meantime, I haven't had a decent night's sleep since— Listen, I want to know how my sister died; I *have* to know how she died." And then he put in with a little semi-chuckle, "You've got to say yes. You're the only private investigator I know."

Well, I'd been praying for a new client and *voilà*! I'd gotten one—and in record time, too. The only problem was, I had to say no to him. "I don't think it would be ethical for me to take the case," I explained. "Not with Ellen involved—however innocently. Protecting her interests would always be my overriding concern, and while right now I can't imagine how that would affect the investigation, somewhere along the line I might find myself facing a conflict of some kind."

Dick looked so crestfallen that I said, "I could recommend another investigator to you, if you like. But if you want my opinion—and you'll get it even if you don't—" I tittered, "I suggest you wait another week or two before calling anyone in. After all, the Clear Cove police *are* continuing to check things out, and Brady appears to be a very competent and intelligent man."

"He struck me that way, too. But . . . well . . . I don't know. Do you really think he's considering the possibility it could be murder—seriously considering it, I mean?"

"I really do."

It was the truth. Which didn't make what I'd told Ellen any less true. I mean even though Brady had pretty much led me to believe that Raven's death would eventually be labeled an accident, for the time being, at least, he hadn't come to any definite conclusion. So that meant he was seriously considering murder, too, right?

Funny, isn't it, how you can take the same basic facts and— by slanting them just a little—use them to justify whatever point you're anxious to make at the moment.

"Well, I guess I could give it a little more time, anyway," Dick conceded. "But I still wish you'd change your mind."

"I just can't," I said regretfully.

But of course, you know, don't you, that I eventually wound up doing for nothing what my stupid principles refused to let me get paid for.

Chapter 9

It was on Wednesday that the you-know-what hit the fan again.

I'd just gotten home from work, having forced myself to stay until 5:00 just in case something turned up—which it didn't. To keep occupied, I'd spent almost the entire day reading magazines and making personal calls. Late in the afternoon, I even resorted to giving myself a manicure, mangling three cuticles in the process.

But at any rate, as soon as I set foot in the kitchen that evening, I remembered that I was out of milk. Well, since I would probably die without a cup or two of coffee after my meal and since I can't stand drinking it black and since I was still fully dressed, I decided to haul my reluctant body downstairs and pick up a carton.

The phone rang right after I locked the apartment door behind me and dumped the keys in my handbag. I quickly reached back into that portable junk shop I lug around with me. It was only a second ago that I'd deposited the keys in here, so wouldn't you think they'd be right on top? Well, they weren't; they never are. Almost frantically—I hate missing phone calls—I dug deep down into the bag, but the ringing stopped long before I made contact with my key case again.

I went back into the apartment anyway, so I could retrieve any message that had been left on the answering machine. What I heard when I pressed Playback was a very disappointed Ellen.

"Ohhh, I was hoping you'd be there. I don't know what to do now. I thought maybe be you'd come over and have dinner with me—that is, if you didn't have any plans. Mike just left; he was feeling terrible. He broke out in a sweat, and then he started getting the dry heaves, so I sent him home. He must be coming down with the flu or something. You should have *seen* the poor thing—he turned positively green. But the thing is, I'd already called Mandarin Joy and ordered all this food because he insisted he wasn't that sick—that was right before the dry heaves—and the delivery guy should be here any minute now." A pause. "Well, I suppose I could freeze some of it, but Chinese food is never really the same after it's frozen. At least, I don't think it—"

My answering machine had run out of patience.

I returned the call immediately. "I'm on my way," I said.

Ellen greeted me at the door in one of those long skinny shifts that make her look her most Hepburnish—as in Audrey, that is. (Have I mentioned that the resemblance is really quite startling? Well, maybe not startling exactly, but it's definitely *there*.) This little number was black with white piping and so narrow I had doubts it would even have made it around my index finger.

"Oh, I'm so-o-o glad you could come," she squealed, acting like I was rescuing her from some kind of dire fate. "I'd have *hated* to see all that wonderful food go to waste." She demonstrated her appreciation of my presence with an almost bone-crushing hug. I've never been able to figure out where she gets all that strength. If there's even a single muscle in that tall (from down here, five six is tall), super thin frame of hers, it's very cleverly concealed. "The order arrived about ten minutes ago," she informed me, mercifully releasing me and thereby providing me with an opportunity to exhale. "I put everything in a low oven to keep warm. Wait'll you see what we've got," she enthused.

There were really no big surprises, which was fine with me. The meal turned out to be practically a duplicate of the one Ellen and I had shared the last time I'd been up there, except that Mike had opted for the scallion pancakes over the dim sum. I supposed he was entitled, although I had a little difficulty accounting for his preference. Nevertheless, I assisted Ellen in demolishing the pancakes, along with a heaping tinful of spareribs. And then we turned ourselves loose on the lemon chicken and the shrimp in black bean sauce. Later, there was even Häagen Dazs for dessert. And while it wasn't Macadamia Brittle—after all, she hadn't been expecting me—well, okay; I've learned how to make do.

We were clearing the table when the downstairs buzzer sounded.

"I can't imagine who that could be," Ellen said. Her hand rested on the intercom phone for a second. "Probably somebody just wants into the building. You don't know what's been going on around here lately."

But it turned out to be much worse than a ploy by some neighborhood slime.

"It's Chief Brady, ma'am," the voice informed her. "I wonder if I could talk to you for a few minutes."

"Oh, my God," she whispered, her face suddenly the color of chalk.

I ran for the amaretto.

Ellen had fortified herself with a number of healthy gulps of the liqueur before Brady made his appearance, and she was able to conduct herself with relative calm. I was sorry I hadn't done a bit of imbibing myself. This unscheduled visit had set off a little alarm in my head.

"I hope I'm not intrudin'," he began when we were seated in the living room. "I stopped off at Macy's, Ms. Kravitz, and they said you were home sick. Do you think you might be able to answer one or two questions for me? Won't take very long, I promise. But naturally, if you're not up to it, we could do it another time."

Ellen responded with downcast eyes—a dead giveaway to her embarrassment. "No, no. I'm really fine. I was playing hooky," she confessed with a forced smile.

Brady gave her instant absolution. "We all need us a little break sometimes, don't we?" he told her in his most ingratiating down-home manner. "Listen, there's this one point that's come up. Probably doesn't mean a thing, but I happened to be in the city today"—*Oh sure; he "happened" to be here*—"and so I thought I'd check it out with you. It's somethin' Ms. Miller's maid just this mornin' contacted me about."

"What's that?" a frightened Ellen inquired. And then her upbringing took over. Before he had a chance to respond, she was playing hostess. I swear it was like a reflex with her. "Oh! I'm sorry. I haven't even asked you. Would you care for a drink, Chief Brady? Or some coffee? I have some Häagen-Dazs in the freezer if you'd like—Belgian Chocolate and Pralines 'n Cream."

I wanted to shake her! *This is not a social visit!* I silently shouted.

She totally ignored ne. "But maybe you'd rather have some fruit." I'll tell you, sometimes Ellen's good manners can be positively maddening.

"No thanks, Ms. Kravitz. I 'preciate the offer, but I just had myself a meal that'll last me through to tomorrow night. What I wanted to talk to you about, though, was this altercation the maid says you and Ms. Eber had at that cocktail party."

"Oh." Whatever tiny bit of color had crept back into Ellen's cheeks during the last few minutes vanished completely. I reached for the near-empty glass of amaretto she'd deposited on the end table, quickly refilled it, and shoved it into her hand. She took a good-sized swallow followed by another good-sized swallow. Then she said in a small voice, "I didn't think anyone was around then."

"Well, it appears that this maid—Hannah her name is—she was under the impression everyone had gone upstairs already, and she was comin' in to straighten up the library. That's where you had that little party, wasn't it—the library?" And when Ellen responded with a nod: "But then she heard you and Ms. Eber shoutin' at each other, so she thought she'd better hold up awhile on that straightenin'. Just as she was about to turn around and go back to the kitchen, though, she heard you threaten Ms. Eber. Anyhow, that's what she was tellin' me."

I had been really quiet up to now, not wanting to antagonize Brady since down the line his goodwill might be important to me. But there *are* limits. "Oh, for heaven's sake!" I blurted out. "The woman's crazy! Ellen wouldn't threaten anybody!"

Brady glared at me, but when he spoke it was in his usual polite, low-keyed style. "Why don't you let your niece do her own talkin', ma'am. She's the one with the firsthand knowledge." And to Ellen: "*Is* Hannah lyin', Ms. Kravitz?"

Ellen shook her head. "No," she whispered.

Flustered, I put in quickly, "Well, uh, just because you say a few words in the heat of the moment, well, that doesn't mean—"

Brady cut off the protest with a soft-spoken, "Please, Ms. Shapiro." But I got the feeling from the way his lips were twitching that at that moment it would have given him much pleasure to reach over and crush my windpipe. "Listen," he said to Ellen, "I know that ninety-nine times out of a hundred threats of this nature don't count for a darn thing. I'm just gatherin' my facts, that's all. Hannah claims she heard you say, 'I could murder you' or 'I'm gonna kill you.' Somethin' of that sort—she wasn't too sure of the exact words. Is that substantially correct?"

"Yes," was the whispered response this time. "Only I don't think I ever said "I'm *going to* kill you.' It was probably 'I *could* kill you.' But I really don't remember exactly."

"Well, naturally you don't!" I put in. "Because it didn't *mean* anything—whatever it was." Then I challenged Brady. "How many times have you said that same kind of thing yourself? And where's this Hannah been all this while, anyway? If she thought for one moment that Ellen had been serious, she'd have reported that conversation to you a long time ago."

"A course, that's one way of takin' it. But the thing of it is, until yesterday Hannah had no idea we were even lookin' into the possibility this might be a homicide. And then this friend of hers whose daughter's keepin' company with someone on the force told her murder *was* considered an option, so she decided to come forward and tell us what she knew." He fixed his eyes on Ellen. "There was somethin' else, too, wasn't there?" he asked quietly.

Ellen didn't respond. She sat there silently, chomping on her lower lip. She was going at it so furiously that I considered it likely she'd be drawing blood any second.

"Wasn't there?" Brady repeated.

She stopped chomping. "Umm . . . I'm . . . I don't know what you mean."

"I mean that Hannah saw you throw that drink in Ms. Eber's face."

"Ellen!" It just slipped out. I could go along with almost anyone in the world doing something like that if sufficiently provoked. But not the Pope. Or Mother Theresa. Or my sweet, gentle Ellen.

She looked at me with this pitiful expression. "You don't understand. I—she—it was what she said to m-me." She was starting to blubber now, and her eyes were filling up rapidly. I figured they could overflow at any moment, so I jumped up to fetch a box of tissues from the bathroom. When I returned, Ellen was dabbing at her face with a crumpled tissue and Brady was handing her the glass of amaretto, which she'd once again placed on the end table. She acknowledged his thoughtfulness by eking out a faint smile through her tears.

"Just take your time," he told her kindly.

"Thank you," she sniffled. "I'll be all right in a second."

"No problem."

It took about two minutes for Ellen to polish off the remainder of the amaretto, blow her nose half a dozen times, mop up the wetness on her cheeks, and regain some modicum of composure. All this accomplished, she stared down at the rug. "I've never done . . . I would never have thought I'd ever be capable of a thing like that," she told the floor covering, shamefaced.

"She must have really pushed you to your limit," I got out, in spite of the fact that this revelation about the tossed drink had left me practically numb.

"Ms. Shapiro—*please*," Brady cautioned, his tone finally reflecting his exasperation. And to Ellen: "Just what did Ms. Eber say to upset you to that degree?"

Ellen lifted her head. "The thing is," she answered, looking directly at him now, "for practically the entire evening, I'd been able to avoid her. After what she told Candy—Mike's cousin—I didn't want to have anything to do with her, you know?"

"I can see why you'd feel that way," the policeman responded, taking the cue.

"But right after the party broke up, when I was about to leave the room, she stopped me. She said she wanted to talk. I figured I should at least listen to the woman"—*wasn't that just like Ellen?*—"but she gave me the same story she had originally. I mean, about my misunderstanding the reason she'd said anything to Candy. She kept insisting it was only because she'd been so anxious to find out how I was."

Ellen glanced over at me. I got the impression she was in need of a little bolstering, and I nodded encouragingly. Then she returned her focus to the chief.

"I told her that I didn't believe a word she was saying," she continued, "and that it was pointless to talk about it anymore. And she said that she should have expected as much from me. She said that the truth was, I'd always been emotionally unstable and that that was why I'd hooked up with someone like Georgiann in the first place. Georgiann was that close friend of mine who committed suicide years ago," she hastily explained to Brady. "Anyway, Raven told me that people like us—like Georgiann and me—sought each other out. And she made a few other nasty remarks that I don't remember. And then she said—and she was sneering when she said it—'What a sick pair the two of you must have made.'

"That's when I lost it. There was an almost full glass of champagne on the sideboard next to me, and before I was consciously aware of what I was going to do, I picked it up and let her have it in the face." The tears were surfacing again, but Ellen managed to get out one last sentence. "I didn't mind so much that she ridiculed me, but when she talked about Georgiann like that . . ." And now the dam broke.

She sobbed for a good two or three minutes before she was able to collect herself. Then she said in a voice thick with emotion, "When I think that that was the last time I ever saw Raven and that there was so much animosity between us, I just feel so awful about it. We'd been such good friends when we were younger. I wish we hadn't had those words. I wish I hadn't thrown the drink at her. I wish I'd never ever gone out there that weekend!"

It was anybody's guess whether this would lead to another crying jag, and an uncomfortable-looking Brady wasn't anxious for the results to come in. "You . . . uh . . . you take it easy now, huh, Ms. Kravitz?" he mumbled awkwardly, quickly rising. "And I thank you for bein' so forthcoming."

I walked him to the door. "It was nice to see you again, Ms. Shapiro," he told me with a straight face.

Well, if he wasn't above that kind of thing, neither was I. "You, too," I said. And my face was every bit as straight.

Chapter 10

Brady needn't have worried. When I returned to Ellen, she was harmlessly slipping off her sandals. "I suppose I should have been more understanding of Raven," she murmured, leaning back on the sofa and tucking her feet up under her body. "I'm sure that her father's molesting her when she was a child had a lot to do with why she pulled some of the things she did. I should have taken that into consideration; we all should have."

So Ellen knew about the incest! And apparently the others did, too. Well, that shouldn't have surprised me. Not with Raven's sister-in-law a member of their little group.

"I did tell you about Raven's father, didn't I?" Ellen was asking.

I didn't say that, no, she hadn't. Or that I'd learned about the abuse during a visit from Dick Eber. I'd been careful not to even mention that visit, because I knew Ellen would ask why Eber had come to see me. And that, of course, would have led to my having to disclose that he was so adamant Raven had been murdered he had wanted to hire me to prove it. I mean, the last thing Ellen needed was to have her worst fear reinforced like that. So I just ignored the question. "Look," I reasoned, "what Raven's father did to her was absolutely horrendous. But that doesn't mean people had to make allowances for her behavior forever. You weren't responsible for her being molested. And you certainly couldn't be expected to take it into consideration when she sabotaged you the way she did. And the same goes for everyone else whose life she messed up."

"I suppose you're right, but I still wish I'd been a little more understanding."

I let it drop, and a moment later Ellen said, "Can I ask you something, Aunt Dez?"

"Sure."

"Are you still so positive Raven's death was an accident?"

Actually, even though Eber had been pretty persuasive, I did have some problems with his reasoning. Still, I was no longer able to totally discount the possibility that his sister had been assisted in her precipitous exit from this world. What I mean is, *positive* was just too strong a word. But even if you threatened to pull out my fingernails, I wouldn't have owned up to it just then. "Yes, I am," I stated with all the conviction a well-intended lie can generate. "But I'll tell you what. If you're concerned about things, I'll prove it to you. And to that gung ho police chief, too."

"You're going to investigate Raven's death?"

"That's right."

"Oh, I'm . . . I'm just *so* glad," Ellen informed me. The way she was tilting in my direction, I knew I was an instant away from one of those lethal hugs of hers. I shot out of my seat. "Suppose I make us some coffee."

I want you to know that while I'd been disturbed by Brady's dropping in like that—and certainly by what that little interrogation of his had revealed—I wasn't actually worried about Ellen's being a serious candidate in any search for a killer. Not at that point. The reason I'd decided to sniff around a little was just to put her mind at ease. And maybe my own, too, while I was at it. My intention was to somehow establish that Raven Eber's death was either (a) an accident or—and much less likely—(b) a suicide. And in the far-fetched eventuality (as I was still determined to regard it then) it *should* turn out to be (c) a murder, I was going to see to it that the blame didn't get attached to my innocent and defenseless niece.

And besides, what else did I have to do?

I called Sybil Miller on Thursday morning, and she agreed to let me come by at two o'clock that afternoon.

Sybil's house was built like one of those antebellum mansions you see in movies about the Old South. Large and white (although barely—it really needed a paint job), it had massive columns supporting a wide front porch (porticos, I think they're called) and stood imposingly on a slightly elevated knoll. From here, it was able to overlook its not-very-impressive domain: a sizable expanse of lawn that screamed out for a mower and a scraggly border of wilting, late-blooming flowers that I wasn't able to put a name to.

A uniformed maid—*Hannah?* I wondered—opened the door and showed me into a small parlor just to the right of the entrance. "Mrs. Miller will be with you shortly," whoever-she-was informed me brusquely.

Sybil Miller came into the room not more than three or four minutes later. Tall and slim, with an olive complexion, deep brown eyes, and thick, almost black hair held neatly back with a red elastic, she might easily have been a native American. The little makeup she wore was expertly applied—a pale coral lipstick, just enough blush to highlight her enviable cheekbones, and, I suspect, a touch of mascara to accentuate these incredibly long, curly lashes. She was dressed in very clean white jeans, not-so-clean white sneakers, and a red T-shirt. Walking over to my chair, she shook my hand. Her voice was pleasantly husky. "I'm Sybil Miller," she told me, smiling, "and you, of course, are Ellen's Aunt Desiree. I've been hearing about you for years, Mrs. Shapiro."

"Desiree," I corrected, concluding that while she wasn't exactly pretty—her mouth was kind of funny and she didn't have quite enough chin—Sybil was really a very attractive girl. (Yes, I know. But unless you're over thirty—obviously over thirty, that is—you're still a girl to me.) More important than her looks, though, was the nice, friendly way she had about her.

After offering me some lunch—which I politely declined, since I'd stopped off at a coffee shop for a bite on the drive down here—she said, "You wanted to talk to me about that weekend."

"Yes, I won't take up much of your time. I should be out of your hair in five or ten minutes." (An underestimate, if there ever was one.) Then I added in my most sincere and ingratiating manner, "I just have a couple of questions." (An out-and-out lie.)

"Don't worry about it. Go ahead."

"Well, for starters, I understand that Raven hadn't been invited to the festivities. At least, not by you."

"That's right. I almost fell flat on my face when she walked in Friday night."

"You never thought of asking her to leave?" I'd been wondering about that.

"Of course I did. And naturally, I could have kicked myself later for not tossing her right out on her ear. But at first I was so dumbfounded that I couldn't seem to do anything. That sounds ridiculous, I know. Maybe I was in shock. Or maybe it was just that I can be such a marshmallow sometimes. Then, too, she was Winnie's sister-in-law, and I didn't want to cause any family hassle for Winnie." She broke off here to clarify things, in case they needed clarifying. "Winnie's one of my other sorority sisters, and she was here that weekend." Her expression led me to regard this as a question.

"Yes, I know," I answered.

"I even had it in my head for a while that Winnie might have told her to come. Which was really dumb. I never made any secret of how I felt about Raven; none of us did. Besides, it's the last thing Winnie herself would have wanted—having her beloved sister-in-law around for two days."

"Raven's presence must have really put a damper on things," I remarked.

"You can't imagine. I forced myself to talk to her, because nobody else would. I couldn't even saddle Winnie with the job. The poor thing had a bad case of laryngitis and wasn't able to get two words out Friday night." Sybil sighed. "The end result was that since it was my house, I felt obligated to at least address a few innocuous phrases to the woman. Much as I hated to do it." A grin. "I told you I was a marshmallow. Not completely, though. I had made up my mind to send her on her way on Saturday, right after breakfast. And it would have been none too soon, too. Carol Sue Kessler had already let me know that she'd be cutting out the next morning, that she couldn't stand to be anywhere near Raven—a sentiment I could definitely relate to. I told her not to worry, that Raven wouldn't be staying."

"I'm surprised it would have been necessary for you to resort to that. I would have thought that after being shunned by everyone the way she was, she would have been chomping at the bit to get out of here."

"Not Raven! Sometimes I think she thrived on situations like that. Maybe she regarded them as a challenge. Who knows? But think about it. Who else would have had the nerve to show her face at that party under the circumstances?"

Which led to the big question. "Do you have any idea who might have sent her an invitation?"

"Not *who* sent it. But I do have this theory. What I believe took place is that one of my sorority sisters mailed her the invitation as a little joke, never actually expecting her to put in an appearance. I could have predicted that that's exactly what Raven would do, of course. It was like waving a red flag in front of a bull. But at any rate, whoever it was apparently didn't read her as well as I did and was probably mortified at seeing her that night. Most likely this mysterious invitation-sender—and I'm damned if I can figure out which of my friends it could be—didn't say anything at first, because she was afraid the rest of us would be angry with her. And later, when Raven ended up dead, she was just too shook up to mention what she'd done. There's even a possibility she felt a little guilty. After all, if it weren't for that invitation, Raven never would have had the accident. I have a—" Sybil interrupted herself then, obviously misinterpreting whatever it was she saw on my face. "And yes," she interjected here, "I realize that the same thing could apply to me. If I'd let Raven know the pool was empty, she wouldn't have had the accident, either. But I never even thought about her not being there when I told the others about the repairs. And anyway, who could have imagined she'd do a thing like that at one in the morning when she was supposed to be going up to bed?"

"There was no way you could possibly have anticipated it," I assured her. "But you were saying something about the person who sent the invitation. . . ."

"Just that I think she would have fessed up eventually if it weren't for the police coming up with the bright idea that Raven might have been murdered. She must realize that if it does end up being a homicide, whoever was responsible for getting Raven here would be the A-number one suspect."

"But you yourself are certain that Raven's death was accidental?"

"Absolutely."

"And you have no inkling at all to who might have sent her that invitation?"

"None, honestly. When I heard about it, I wracked my brain trying to decide on someone, but frankly, I'm at a loss. It doesn't seem to be the kind of thing that would even occur to any of them."

"I understand that all of you hated Raven for one reason or another."

"That's true. For one *good* reason or another. But if you've got it in your head that one of us killed her, you're wrong. Not that we didn't all daydream about it at various times in our lives—and frequently, too. But that doesn't mean any of us acted on it. Look, I'm not sorry she's dead; I'm sure nobody really is—except her brother, of course. But none of my friends is capable of committing murder." Then almost as an afterthought: "And by the way, neither am I."

I looked at her quizzically, opened my mouth, and promptly shut it again.

She responded as I hoped she would. "What is it you wanted to say?"

"Well, I was just wondering what that girl could possibly have done to you that would make you feel the way you do about her even after she's gone?"

Something that was somewhere between a laugh and a snort—but much closer to a snort—escaped from Sybil's lips. "Let me tell you about little Raven. . . ." she said.

Chapter 11

They'd both been excellent students—she and Raven—Sybil told me. In fact, at the end of their junior year of college a local bank was to present an award to Walden's most outstanding woman business administration student. And Sybil was first in line to receive it, with Raven a close second.

"From what I've heard about Raven's competitive nature, I wouldn't assume that being second would have sat too well with her," I remarked.

Sybil's "hardly" was accompanied by a sound that, this time, was pure snort.

"She did something to stack the cards in her favor?"

"You bet she did. She got me thrown out of school!"

I was nonplused. "How in heaven's name did she manage that?"

"I'll tell you how. We were both scheduled to take this history exam—it was on April 12, I remember. Now, that morning Raven had asked to borrow my tan windbreaker so she could run over to the bookstore. Her room was on the third floor—mine was on the first—and she didn't feel like trudging all the way upstairs to get something, she said. I planned on wearing that jacket to classes later—I'd been practically living in it for days, since it was the lightest one I owned and the weather had been pretty warm that week. So I told her she could have it if she brought it back by lunchtime. Raven said no problem, that she'd return it in a few minutes, which she did.

"Anyway, as soon as I walked into history class that afternoon, the professor demanded to see my jacket. He'd been waiting at the door for me. I took it off and handed it to him. I was really wondering why he would be interested in it; I even thought that maybe he wanted to get one like it for his daughter. *That's* how naive I was. And then he reached into the pocket and pulled out these notes—these *crib* notes! I was dumbfounded. I'd never seen them before in my life. *Somebody* had planted them there."

"You think it was Raven?"

"I'm positive it was, although she's always denied it. Naturally."

"She told the professor to check your jacket?"

"He'd received an anonymous phone call to that effect, I found out later."

"Were you out of your room at all that morning, either before or after Raven borrowed the jacket?"

"Yes, a few times."

"And the door was unlocked?"

"Listen, Desiree, I understand what you're getting at. But no one else had any reason to set me up like that. In fact, I couldn't imagine Raven doing it, either. Until I remembered about the bank award. And suddenly, it all made sense."

"What happened after that?"

"There was this hearing, and of course, I kept insisting I didn't know anything about the notes, that someone had gotten ahold of my jacket and slipped them in the pocket."

"You didn't say that it was Raven?"

"No, I had no proof. All I said was that I knew who did it. But there was this one creep on the faculty who fancied himself a Sherlock Holmes or something. He made this big announcement that he'd checked the typewriter in my room and that the notes had been typed on my machine."

"Seems she thought of everything, didn't she?" I muttered under my breath. "But wait a minute. Just because you have some notes in your pocket doesn't mean you're going to pull them out and use them to cheat on an exam."

"It was against the rules at Walden to bring anything like that into class when you were taking an exam."

"Oh." And a moment later: "So Raven wound up with the award, I assume."

"Uh-huh. While I wound up getting suspended. And I was so upset by the whole thing, by their not believing me—despite the fact I was an A student and wouldn't have needed any damn crib notes to pass their stupid test—that I decided I never wanted to set foot in the place again."

"Did you end up at another school?"

"No. That summer I met Jack Miller. I married him a month later, and I just pushed college out of my mind." Sybil made a sour face. "To this day, I have no idea why I married that pompous idiot. Most likely it was out of spite."

"I don't follow that. Who were you spiting?"

"I'm not really sure. I think it was Walden—the people there who had suspended me, I'm talking about. It was like saying, 'Who needs your damn school? Look at this brilliant marriage I made.'" This was punctuated by a reprise of the snort sound. "Like they would have given a damn even if they knew about the marriage, which I'm sure none of them did. And if by some chance a couple of them happened to hear about it, well, they could hardly have regarded it as brilliant, anyway."

I felt I should come up with a response of some sort, but then Sybil added, "Or maybe I married him because I just didn't want to deal with trying to get into another school."

"So you never went back to college?"

"No," she answered bitterly. "I became the perfect helpmate instead."

"You continued to live here after you were married?"

"Oh, you bet we did. Jack said it was only temporary. Until we could afford a nice place of our own, he said. But even after his business took off, he didn't want to budge. Why should he, when he could sponge off my mother? Anyway, she died last year. And a few weeks after that I threw him the hell out"—she was smiling almost mischievously now—"for reasons too numerous and disgusting to mention."

"You know," I remarked a couple of minutes later, "I certainly can't blame you for how you feel about Raven. But that *was* eight or nine years ago, wasn't it? A long time to hold a grudge." (I surprised myself with that gem. Prototypical Scorpio that I am, I could hold one for a century or so with no strain at all.)

"You don't understand. What Raven did is affecting me right now. Today. I realize I have no business blaming her for my jumping into marriage like that. It was my own stupidity, of course. Although the fact is, it would never have happened if I hadn't been suspended from school. Putting that aside, though, there's one thing I *can* lay directly on her doorstep: I'd always planned to be a lawyer someday. But thanks to my friend Raven, I had to scratch that little idea."

"That's ter—" I stopped abruptly. "But it's not too late; you could go back to college—maybe even this year," I suggested eagerly. "And after you grad—"

"Uh-uh. With that cheating thing on my record, I'd never be accepted to law school. I resigned myself to that a long time ago." There was a brief silence before Sybil spoke again. "Ever since my split from Jack, I've been trying to figure out what to do with the rest of my life," she said plaintively.

"You didn't work while you were married?"

"Sure I did. In my husband's public relations firm. And I hated every second of it. I loathe that whole PR business." And then she attempted to lighten the mood. "But look, Dear Abby," she joked, "don't get any gray hairs on my account. I'll come up with something one of these days. In the meantime, what else did you want to know?"

"I'd like to see the bedroom that Raven was using that weekend, if I could."

She was instantly on her feet. "Let's go."

The room we had just entered was large and bright. Although far from ornate, it was very comfortable, with substantial-looking cherry furniture, a couple of cushy, chintz-covered chairs, even a small sofa.

Automatically, I turned around and examined the door. "No locks," I observed.

"Why? Did you expect any?" I hadn't been aware I'd said it aloud. "Don't tell me you have one on *your* bedroom door," Sybil added, looking amused.

"Three," I responded, grinning. But I was embarrassed. "Never hurts to check," I felt compelled to add. "Do you know anything about some burnt paper that was in an ashtray here?" I asked then.

"Chief Brady had the same question for me. I have no idea what it could have been. But anyway, whatever it was, the police found it in that ashtray over there." She was indicating a round table about two yards in from the door, a small armchair beside it. The table held a white china reading lamp, some issues of *People* magazine, a *Cosmopolitan*, and a recent *Ladies' Home Journal*. There was also a large square dish that might have been a piece of Lalique crystal, which the process of elimination—along with the tiny gold matchbox right next to it—led me to presume did occasional service as an ashtray.

"Brady checked with Hannah, my maid—she's the one who cleans up in here—and she swears there was no paper in that ashtray, burnt or otherwise, before Raven took over the room. I believe her, too. She's very thorough."

I nodded. "Is it all right if I go out there?" I asked, gesturing toward the terrace.

"Of course."

It was a narrow terrace, just wide enough to accommodate its tiny green plastic table and matching folding chair. Taking the few steps required to get to the edge, I noted that the wooden railing surrounding it reached to a little above my waist. I calculated that if someone climbed over that railing there'd probably be just enough space on the ledge to afford the leverage needed to execute a dive of some kind. I peered down at the pool almost directly below. It was empty. "I see you still haven't gotten those repairs done," I commented to Sybil, who had joined me at the railing.

"No. I decided to wait. As you've probably noticed, there are a couple of other things around here that also need doing. To tell the truth, I've really been letting the place go to pot for quite a while now. The other day I finally began trying to find someone to replace the gardener, who quit last month. I also have to call in a roofer. And then I've got to get someone to give the house the paint job it should have had five years ago. Those things take priority. Besides, I pretty much lost interest in using the pool this summer after what happened to Raven. And it's the one thing I never did neglect, too." She smiled then. "See? That's something else she ruined for me." The smile didn't fool me for a minute. I knew the comment had been made only partially in jest. If there'd been any jest in it at all, that is.

"Tell me, was it unusual for Raven to do her diving at night?" I said at this point. It was a question I'd meant to put to Ellen many times and then on Monday to Dick Eber. But somehow I kept on forgetting to ask it.

"Not at all. She often did."

I looked down at the pool area again. "When those lights are on, do they illuminate the pool itself?"

"Sure. But that Friday the lights out back were turned off as soon as everyone went upstairs. There was a full moon that night, though, so she still would have been able to make out the outlines of the pool. That is what you wanted to know, isn't it?"

"Yes," I said, "exactly. But just one more thing. Are you aware that Raven didn't care for the water?"

Sybil looked at me skeptically. "Didn't care for the water?"

"It's something her brother told me. According to him, she only did her diving bit to entertain her friends. He claims that she wouldn't have made that dive unless she'd had an audience."

"What he really meant was that she was a damn exhibitionist. I don't know whether she liked the water or not, Desiree. All I know is that she never once came here without going off this balcony. But it could be she was just practicing on Friday night for the next day when she figured she *would* have some people to play to."

A couple of minutes later we were on our way downstairs. But when we reached the landing, I stopped. "By the way, did you visit Raven's room for any reason after the party?"

"Of course not." *As if she'd admit it if she did!*

"Do you know if one of the others might have gone to see her?"

"Raven was not murdered!" Sybil said emphatically.

"I wasn't implying that she was. Maybe somebody just wanted to have things out with her."

"Listen, wild horses couldn't have dragged any of them into that room. Or me, either."

I was about to head downstairs again when Sybil put a restraining hand on my shoulder. "You probably think I'm a real bitch for the way I've been bad-mouthing a dead woman," she said.

"Oh, no, not at all. Not after that business at Walden."

She went on as if I hadn't responded. "And Ellen probably told you about Raven's degenerate father."

"I heard about him," I hedged.

"Dick was always telling Winnie she had to make allowances for that. But Winnie never bought it, and neither did I. Which makes me seem even more heartless, I know." There wasn't time to contradict her, to say that I agreed with her; she didn't even pause for breath. "But nobody will ever be able to convince me that's why Raven did all those unconscionable things. Now, I'm not saying that the incest didn't have any effect," she amended hastily. "It was perverted, and it was horrible, and there's no question it was very traumatic for her. But you can't put the blame for all her actions on something she went through twenty-five years ago. Not when it comes to some of the stuff she pulled. And besides, other little girls have been molested, and they didn't turn out like that, did they?"

She answered her own question. "Uh-uh. I'm convinced that there was a kink in Raven's nature. If I had to use one word to describe her, do you know what that word would be?"

I cocked my head and looked at her inquiringly.

"Raven Eber was evil, Desiree." And then very slowly, giving the words the dramatic impact they warranted: "Just . . . plain . . . evil."

Chapter 12

I had an early ophthalmologist's appointment on Friday, so I didn't get to work until 10:30. Almost immediately, I dialed the number Sybil had given me for Winnie Eber's office.

It was more than likely Sybil had alerted her friends about our meeting yesterday, because Winnie said, "Oh, yes," when I gave her my name. She informed me that she was having her hair done in Manhattan on Saturday, and she suggested we get together for coffee afterward.

I spent most of what was left of the morning bemoaning the dormant state of my business and then went on to tackle the formidable task of deciding what, if anything, in my wardrobe would be appropriate attire for my anticipated residence in the poorhouse. (Assuming I was able to secure accommodations, that is, and that there even was such a thing anymore.) I hadn't arrived at any definite conclusions when Elliot Gilbert rapped gently on my open door. "Got a minute?"

I flashed him my most courageous smile. "These days? Quite a few of them." *That's right*, I scolded myself, *make this sweet, compassionate guy feel even more responsible for your indigent condition than he already does.*

Turning a very pretty shade of pink, he came in and plunked his short, stocky torso on the empty chair. "I promised you another case, and well, I have something for you. Unfortunately, it's nothing very big, but, uh, I'd be grateful if you could take it on."

If I could take it on! Leave it to Elliot to make it sound like *I'd* be doing *him* a favor. You really had to love the man!

"Of course. I'll be happy to help out," I responded magnanimously. "What's it all about?"

And so he proceeded to fill me in on this old family friend who wanted to unload (my word, not Elliot's) his spouse of more than forty years.

"Herm—Herman Moody, his name is—is certain his wife Muriel's having an affair. I'd like you to look into it and see what you can find out. Okay?"

"Sure. What can you tell me?"

"Suppose we wait on that. Herm forgot to bring along any photographs of Muriel when he came in to see me yesterday. He's going to drop a few off on Monday, and I'll come by then and give you the particulars."

Jackie and I took a very extended lunch hour that day. After stopping off for burgers, we made the rounds of the neighborhood dress shops. Jackie was looking for something to wear to a Labor Day dinner dance she was attending with her beau Derwin, a taciturn and tightfisted gentleman whose most striking attribute was the thickest—and most obvious—silver toupee any male person of advanced years could ask for. Anyway, she flipped out over a dark navy silk at the last place we tried. The cut was very flattering, whittling her hips to practically nothing and making her tall, large-boned figure appear almost stately. Not only that, but the color seemed to bring out the blond in her blondish brown hair. Plus, it was the sort of dress that was appropriate for just about any occasion any season of the year. But it was out of her price range. Way out. She left the store almost in tears.

"I could borrow my sister's navy silk shoes," she mused as we were walking the two short blocks back to the office. "They're a little tight, but it would just be for a few hours. And you'd lend me that little silver bag of yours, wouldn't you? I'd be careful with it."

"Of course."

"I would be saving a lot of money that way, so maybe I *could* swing it."

"I'd give that some thought, Jackie. Three hundred and seventy-five dollars is still a lot for a dress," I reminded her, like the busybody I always try not to be.

"Yes. You're right. It's just that it looked so . . . But you're right. Definitely. I plead temporary insanity. I'm sure I'll find something else. Something I can afford. I'll just have to shop around some more"

Fortunately, by the time I was once again closeted in my cubbyhole there wasn't much left of the afternoon. Before I knew it, it was 3:30, and I had an early date that night. It wasn't a *date* date, of course. Which was just as well, I suppose. I hadn't been on one of those in so long that I probably wouldn't have known how to act, anyway. (I mean, are *we* holding doors and pulling out chairs for *them* these days?) At any rate, since I was getting together with my friend and next-door neighbor Barbara Gleason in just a little over two hours and since I'm one of the pokiest people ever to wield a mascara wand (to say nothing of serving as a magnet for minor, although time-consuming personal disasters), I probably shouldn't even have bothered coming back here after lunch.

Grabbing my bag, I practically flew out of my office, slowing down at Jackie's desk to wish her a good weekend on my way out. She was on the phone.

"Chez Lisa? I'd like you to put aside a dress for me. It's a navy . . ."

I grinned. I was surprised she'd held out until now.

To tell you the truth, I hadn't exactly been looking forward to Friday night. In fact, you might say I'd been dreading it.

Barbara was treating me to an evening of "theatuh," via an off-Broadway show that had opened only a week before and was hanging on by a thread. I can't remember the name of it anymore, but it had garnered some of the most atrocious reviews you've ever read. And compared to the word of mouth on the thing, they'd been laudatory. "It was a really painful experience," according to another friend of mine, Pat Martucci, who sneaked out less than halfway into the first act.

One of Barbara's fellow grade-school teachers had, however, raved about the play. And Barbara, of course—and if you ever met her you'd understand the "of course"—has decided that the average theatergoer just couldn't appreciate the nuances of such literate dialogue, "which my colleague had assured me is so much more thought-provoking than anything that's been around in years." And so she had immediately purchased two tickets, one of them for me.

Now, the reason for Barbara's largesse was that a few months earlier I'd taken her to see *Cirque du Soleil* in Ellen's place, my niece having come down with food poisoning a few hours before the performance. And while Barbara didn't exactly love the show—she claimed it was highly overrated—she was hell-bent on reciprocating. Whether I wanted her to or not.

Anyhow, I put on my makeup, gritting my teeth. (And if

you think it's easy to apply lipstick that way, you've never tried it.) Surprisingly, considering how rushed I felt, there were no mishaps that night. No spilled foundation. No broken eyeliner. Not even any smudged mascara that wound up under my eyes and made me look like a raccoon. Which was fortunate. We were going to dinner before the show, and Barbara had threatened my life if I should dare be late. "I don't want to choke on my food," she'd informed me, "and I certainly don't want to miss any part of the play."

The only real problem arose as soon as I finished doing battle with the most stubborn head of hair in Manhattan: It started to rain. At first, it was just a drizzle. But—and Barbara's admonition notwithstanding—I still thought I'd better switch to my wig, which is an exact replica of my own hair but which handles inclement weather with a great deal more grace. Naturally, that meant combing and coaxing and cursing and spritzing all over again. But at least the wig didn't put up that good a fight.

Then, while I was getting into my clothes, the drizzle became a deluge. So now I had to stop and ponder which pair of shoes I'd least mind ruining at the same time that the rest of my brain was thinking about how lovely it would be if on a night like this I could just sit in my own dry, air-conditioned living room and curl up with a good murder mystery—preferably one I was able to solve.

Somehow, though, by a quarter of six—the designated time—I managed to get myself all together. (Fear, I've discovered, can be an incredibly powerful motivator.) I was reaching for the doorknob, umbrella in hand, at the precise moment Barbara rang my bell.

"Oh, I'm glad you're ready," she said when I opened the door. And then positively aghast: "But where are your rubbers?"

Is she nuts? "I can't wear those things in this heat; it must be ninety degrees out there," I told her, glancing down at the black vinyl ankle boots that encased her 9½ AAAs, which would, I was willing to bet, swell to 9½ Cs before the evening was over.

"Well," she sniffed, her long, thin face mirroring her disapproval as she eyed my sacrificial tan leather pumps again, "if you're determined to get soaking wet, it's certainly not up to me to argue."

There didn't seem to be any response to that.

*   *   *

The restaurant, a nice little continental cum seafood place, was in Greenwich Village, three blocks from the theater. Now, since Barbara had sprung for the tickets, I felt it would be really tacky of me not to pick up the tab for dinner. (Things may have been tight financially, but that's what credit cards were for, weren't they?) As the host, to start with I ordered a carafe of white wine, which Barbara prefers to red. And for a brief time, we just sat and chatted over our drinks.

Barbara told me earnestly that she was hoping I would enjoy the play. Which—because I already hated it in advance—made me feel guilty as hell. Then she said that she sometimes got the feeling I considered her pretentious. I almost spilled the Chablis all over myself at that one.

"Don't be silly," I responded. "I don't know what would give you an idea like that." But I could feel the telltale flush on my face contradicting the protest.

"It's all right, Desiree," she told me, smiling, "I know my tastes aren't what you would call mainstream. I've always had this penchant for psychological dramas, plays that take you beneath the surface of things." Another smile. "You can blame it on my upbringing. My parents took us—my sisters and me—to see Ibsen and O'Neill and Tennessee Williams when we were practically still in diapers. And what was particularly wonderful about it was that afterward we'd all sit around and discuss what the play was saying." And then wistfully: "That was a marvelous time of life for me."

"I imagine it must have been a terrific experience for a kid. I didn't even set foot inside a theater—aside from a movie theater, I mean—until I moved to New York. And I was in my twenties by then."

For a brief time Barbara didn't respond. And then when she spoke again, her voice seemed to be coming from far away. "My parents made everything so special when they were alive. But they were both dead by the time I was seventeen."

"I'm sorry," I mumbled uncomfortably.

"It's okay." She even managed a laugh. "That *was* a few years ago, you know."

Barbara asked some questions about my own pre-Manhattan years then, following which she said a couple of other things about her family and growing up here. And I suddenly realized I had begun to feel very warm, almost protective, toward her. Because of this revealing exchange, I suppose.

After that, however, we got down to the business of ordering. And the closeness that had sprung up between us only minutes earlier took a powder.

What it all boils down to is that Barbara and I should never attempt a meal together. Although she's sworn at least a dozen times not to monitor my selections, I've come to the conclusion that she just isn't capable of that kind of restraint. And while in the past there'd been many times I was able to ignore her gratuitous dietary advice, lately it seemed that *I* wasn't capable of that kind of restraint.

For an appetizer, I ordered the escargot. Barbara—who was having a sensible fresh fruit cocktail, along with an equally sensible main course of grilled monkfish—made no comment. But her eyebrows lifted almost to her hairline, and I hate when she does that! Then the waiter, a little cherub of a man—plump, rosy-cheeked, and cheerful—asked for my entrée. Now, there was a very nice filet of sole on the menu, and I'd decided on that. But when I opened my mouth to say so, somehow "sole" came out "scampi." I couldn't believe it myself. As much as I love scampi, I'd had no intention of ordering it that night. And I still have no idea whether the switch was the result of a last-minute change of mind or whether it was plain perverseness—prompted by Barbara's eyebrows—that was responsible. One look at her expression, though, and I could see she'd been pushed over the edge. My scampi has done that to her more than once.

"You're going to OD on garlic, for God's sake!" she hissed right in front of the waiter.

"You're not planning on kissing me good night, are you?" I teased, with what I thought was good-natured humor. The waiter thought so, too; he was chuckling when he walked away.

Barbara, however, was stone-faced. "Did you ever hear of the word cholesterol?" she asked evenly, sounding precisely as if she were addressing her class of third-graders. "Just stop and consider the amount of cholesterol there is in that meal you intend consuming. First, the escargot with all that butter sauce, every single drop of which I have no doubt you'll be sopping up—and with buttered rolls, I'm sure!" Her tone was getting shriller now. "And then you follow that up with another dish drenched in butter! For God's sake, Desiree, think about your arteries!"

I tried to keep from exploding, reminding myself that she

meant well. At the same instant, I hastily enumerated all the
qualities I admired in her. There was one in particular: Barbara
Gleason was the quietest person ever to live next door to me,
bar none—a major attribute when you're forced to exist within
the cardboard-thin walls of a typical city apartment. So I said
to her gently, in my most reasonable voice, "You told me you
wouldn't do this anymore, Barbara."

She was defensive. "I know I did. But you have to understand that when I see you acting so—"

"Please, Barbara," I broke in. As much as I'd hoped to
avoid it, I had been forced into one of my "butt out" speeches,
which I always do my best to couch in friendly language. As
usual, I began by recalling for her that I was a grown-up. I
then let her know that I was abreast of the medical warnings re
cholesterol and that even if by some miracle I had overlooked
the findings of the experts, she herself had been hammering
the message home to me for years. I could, therefore, I pointed
out, hardly be unaware of the dangers to which I was exposing
myself. I concluded on a conciliatory note, with a sentence
that opened, "I know you mean well, but . . ." to assure her I
was, nonetheless, grateful for her concern.

She listened stoically. And when I was through, she just
hunched her shoulders and said resignedly, "It's your life."
But I could tell she was hurt.

Well, as I said, she really did mean well, so I couldn't leave
things like that. "I appreciate your caring, Barbara. I really do.
But look, my cholesterol was checked just last month when I
was at the doctor's, and he was pretty pleased. He said it was
ten points lower than the last time I was there. So stop worry-
ing, huh?"

She sighed. "All right. And I'm relieved about the cholesterol. But there *is* one more thing." And before I could even
work up a dirty look for her, she was off and running again.

"Now, don't get mad, Desiree, but I do wish you'd start trying to take off a little of that excess weight you carry around.
And believe me, I wouldn't even *mention* this, but it's a real
shame because you have—"

"—such a pretty face," I finished for her. Is there a woman
alive more than ten pounds overweight who's been spared that
tedious routine? "If you're so anxious to talk weight, Barbara,
why don't we discuss yours?" I put to her, seething. I gave her

skin-and-bones frame one of those obvious once-overs that are guaranteed to make even Heather Locklear feel insecure.

Barbara felt insecure. "What's that supposed to mean?"

I hadn't intended to retaliate with this allusion to *her* lack of physical perfection, but the harping had really gotten to me tonight. However, I'd begun to feel ashamed of my response about two seconds after I made it. My reprieve came in the form of our jovial waiter, who was now arriving—beaming at me—with our appetizers. As soon as he left, though, I was back in the hot seat. "Just what did you mean?" Barbara demanded again.

The wonderful garlicky aroma of the escargot dissipated any remaining vestige of my anger. By now I was far more interested in attacking the snails than Barbara. "Nothing, honestly. I don't even know why I said that."

"I guess it wouldn't hurt if I put on a few pounds," she conceded, much to my surprise. "But it's not easy. Especially for someone who prefers simple food and who doesn't have much of an appetite to start with." She was looking at me with genuine understanding now. "I suppose you have the same problem, don't you? Only in reverse." Then in an uncharacteristic display of affection, she reached over and patted my hand—the one that at that moment was engaged in a duel with a very slippery escargot. "I promise I'll mind my own business from now on, all right?"

I knew she'd never live up to a promise like that. She couldn't. But I put a lot of feeling into my "all right," anyway. I mean, I have made it clear, haven't I, that Barbara means well?

We spent the rest of the meal as newfound—although transitory, I suspected—soul mates. Later we sloshed over to the theater, and in a few minutes we were dripping all over two of the only eight occupied seats. (The other six were almost definitely filled by relatives of the cast's.)

All I can say about the production itself was that it lived down to its reputation. I mean, it was a real stinker. Barbara's verdict was that she found it difficult to accept how "the comparatively minor tensions of that dysfunctional family could have accelerated to the point of producing such an unlikely and precipitous denouement."

I suppose what she was trying to communicate was that she thought it was a stinker, too.

Chapter 13

Saturday was bright and clear and replete with that delightful "green" smell you sometimes get after a summer storm. (Even in Manhattan there's some greenery—not much, but some.) For a too-brief interlude, there was actually something in the air to compete with the gas fumes.

The rain had cooled things off a lot, too, and for the first time in weeks the temperature was hovering around seventy. All in all, it was one of those outstanding, great-to-be-alive days. Perfect for taking a brisk walk or a nice, leisurely stroll or, if you're like me—without one energetic bone in your entire body—for hopping into a cab.

I was meeting Winnie Eber at 2:30 at a coffee bar just twelve blocks south of my apartment. But because you can never predict how many of your neighbors will outmaneuver you for a taxi, I allowed myself fifteen minutes door-to-door time. It turned out to be almost ten minutes too long. As soon as I stepped off the curb my transportation screeched to a stop in front of me, nearly side-swiping me in the process. And to further speed things along, there was absolutely no traffic that afternoon. Half the city, it seemed, was bent on flexing their leg muscles. The other half had, in spite of yesterday's downpour, vacated as usual to spend the weekend in places like the Hamptons and Amagansett and Fire Island.

When I walked into Lonnie's Coffee Bar, Winnie was nowhere in sight. I was able to determine this even without having met the girl, since there was only one occupied table, seated at which were a handsome and very dignified elderly couple. They both looked up and gave me a nice, friendly smile when I walked in. I chose a little booth a few yards away, toward the rear, and sat facing the door so I could see Winnie when she walked in. The description she'd furnished me with was, "I have blond hair, and I'm medium height and on the chunky side." Not very definitive; still, I imagined I'd be able to pick her out of the rest of the clamoring horde demanding entrance here.

I figured I might as well have some coffee while I was waiting, so I went up to the counter and ordered a mug of the house blend, resisting the temptation to get a pastry to keep it company.

I'd sat back down and had taken maybe one or two sips when that couple up front—you know, those very dignified folks—got into a slight argument.

"You're a liar!" the woman screamed. "And I've reached my limit! I won't stand for it a minute longer! Not one single minute! Do you hear me?"

The whole city undoubtedly hears you, I responded. But not out loud, of course.

The man, although red-faced, was soft-spoken and reasonable-sounding. (Which I considered a fairly reliable clue that he was going to be lying through his dentures.) I had to strain a little to hear him, but being an inveterate eavesdropper, I somehow managed. "Shhh, there are people here, dear," he damn near whispered, glancing over his shoulder at me. I quickly lowered my eyes to gaze with apparent fascination into my coffee mug. Then he was back to a vain attempt at pacifying his wife. "It's not what you think, honestly. Let's go home, where we can discuss it quietl—"

"We'll discuss it this instant! And don't shush me!"

"I can't imagine what gives you the idea there's something going on," he told her, his voice even lower now. (He was making this a real hardship for me.) "Believe me, Nettie, there's nothing between us. I just happened to bump into her again this week, that's all. At Zabar's—on Tuesday, I think it was."

"Spare me, will you? Listen, mister, you've been carrying on with that tramp for years. I've known about it all along, so don't think you've been putting anything over on me. But *this*—this is too much. Now you actually have the gall to say we should have her over *for dinner*?"

"But, Betty—" (I could have sworn he'd said Nettie before.)

"Don't 'but, Betty' me! And don't bother denying it! I want you to promise me it will stop! And immediately!"

"I swear, Betty, I'll never see her again." And then a moment later, almost fearfully: "All right?"

"Ha! I thought you hadn't been seeing her in the first place! 'Believe me, Betty, I just *happened* to bump into her at Zabar's,' " she mimicked. "Believe *you*, you lying, senile old satyr? No more!" And with this she rose, at the same time scooping up the large and undoubtedly jam-packed Louis Vuitton handbag that had been sitting on the floor, next to her chair. And then while her miserable, cheating SOB-of-a-husband was still in the process of getting to his feet, she let him have the handbag—right in his midsection. This accomplished, she marched out of Lonnie's establishment, chin held high.

The stunned gentleman—and I use the term in its most liberal context—cast another embarrassed (or was it guilty?) look in my direction before hurrying out himself.

With the exit of Betty and the satyr, I was the only one in the place. But after a few minutes a young couple came in, and in another few minutes a woman pushing a baby carriage sat down.

But still no Winnie.

I checked my watch. I had been here twenty-five minutes so far. But I'd arrived close to ten minutes early, so she wasn't all that late—only fifteen minutes. I'd finished my coffee in what for me was record time, though, so I got myself another cup just for something to do. And then I sipped and waited. And sipped and waited some more.

When I checked my watch again, another fifteen minutes had gone by.

Now it was decision-making time. I looked down at my empty mug. Should I get still another cup of coffee that I didn't really want and hang around a little longer? Should I get that third cup of coffee and—the hell with it—maybe a brownie? Or should I just call it a day?

Exploring these alternatives required all of my concentration (although I'll level with you, right from the start I was leaning hard toward the coffee and brownie), and I momentarily forgot about keeping an eye on the door. And that's when I heard this soft, hesitant "Ms. Shapiro?"

I jumped. Practically touching my right elbow was a girl I had every reason to believe was Winnie Eber. "Winnie?"

"Yes. And I am *so* sorry." She seemed to be terribly anxious, but I had an idea this might be a normal state for her. The round, almost plain face exhibited all sorts of signs of wear and tear. Permanent signs. There were deep furrows in her forehead, frown marks etched between her eyes, even fairly pronounced lines bracketing her nose and small, tight-set mouth. And how old could she be, anyway? A lot younger than she looked, I'd have bet. Probably, she wasn't even thirty yet. "Tino—my hairdresser—is always on time," she explained. "But wouldn't you know it, the one day I have an appointment with someone afterward, he's running late. How long have you been here?"

I didn't want to add to her discomfort. "Not that long. I was late myself," I graciously lied. "And anyway, those things happen, so don't worry about it. Sit down, and I'll get you some coffee."

"Oh, no, I can get it."

"Sit!" I commanded in the exact tone that had always produced such immediate obedience in Brewmeister, my beloved and long-since departed German shepherd.

"No, *you* sit," Winnie insisted obstinately. (Maybe I should have included the hand signal.) "Which kind would you like— you'll join me, won't you?"

Now, the coffee was really good in this place, but I was up to here with it at this point. However, when you're pumping someone for information, it makes the process seem a lot more amicable if you're doing it over a beverage of some kind. "Of course," I replied. "And I'll have the house blend—regular, please."

"How about a pastry or something, too?"

"No, thanks. I think I'll pass on that," I answered stoically.

I watched her waddle toward the counter in her tight pink pants and pink-and-white striped blouse, her oversized cheeks swinging slowly from side to side. Winnie Eber was way past the "chunky" designation she'd assigned herself, I decided. Following her progress, I was vividly reminded of why I don't even own a pair of slacks. I vowed to keep this picture of Winnie forever emblazoned in my memory, in the unlikely event I should ever be tempted to relax my dress code.

In about three minutes she was back, carrying a tray that held two steaming mugs of coffee. "I did try calling you here three or four times once I knew I'd be held up," she informed me, sliding into the booth, "but the line was always busy." She tossed her head in the direction of the counter, and I looked over. The boy behind it—he couldn't have been too far removed from puberty—was talking on the telephone, as he had been ever since I first set eyes on him. More than likely it was just one long, interminable conversation, too. I mean, he hadn't hung up either time he served me—just put whoever it was on hold long enough to rid himself of the unwarranted interruption. "Kids," Winnie remarked irritably.

I figured I'd give her a chance to unwind for a few minutes before bombarding her with "just a couple of questions." So I said, "Why don't you have some of your coffee first, and then we'll talk."

"Oh no, that's okay. I've kept you long enough already."

"Drink!"

This time she provided an appropriate response. "Okay, if you don't mind." Accompanying this was the first smile she'd favored me with since she came in here.

While she sipped, I found myself fixated on her freshly coifed hair. I decided that this Tino person deserved to be hauled in front of a firing squad for even allowing her to walk out of his salon with a hairdo like that. The short, curly style couldn't have been less flattering to that round face of hers, causing it, from certain angles, to bear an uncanny resemblance to a full moon. Besides, although the curls had had a certain amount of spring when Winnie first arrived, they were already beginning to wilt. And as if those things weren't bad enough, her obviously just-bleached hair was this horrendous shade that bordered on lemon yellow. Reflexively, I patted my own glorious hennaed locks. Now *this* was a color!

Winnie broke the brief silence. "How is Ellen?" she asked.

"She's okay, thanks. Aside from being upset about what happened to your sister-in-law, of course."

"Yes, we're all upset about that."

If there was a tactful way to say what I had in mind now, I wasn't able to figure it out. But I did the best I could. "I understand you and Raven weren't really close."

"That's putting it tactfully," she responded with a short, harsh laugh. *Sometimes I just don't give myself enough credit.* "I detested Raven. Ask Ellen what she was like."

"She's already told me."

"Still, it's horrible that she died like that. Particularly horrible for Dick—that's my husband—who was completely devoted to her." *Well, from the sound of that, it appeared that Dick Eber hadn't apprised his wife of his visit to me.* "My heart breaks for him; he's absolutely devastated." The large brown eyes were filled with sympathy. They were pretty eyes, too, I thought, soft and warm. "I've been trying to get him to take two or three weeks off from work," she added. "He needs a vacation; we could both use one. But he says he wants to wait until this thing with Raven is resolved. He's sure somebody murdered her, you see." And then she paused. "But so are you, I suppose. Otherwise, you wouldn't be going around and asking us all questions, would you?"

"You've got it wrong. I don't think Raven was murdered," I corrected. "In fact, if I had to make a bet right this minute, I'd put my money on accident. But the police aren't totally convinced—it appears there are some loose ends—and as long as they're continuing to investigate, I thought I'd look into things, too."

The large eyes seemed to narrow a bit. "Why?" Winnie demanded. "Did somebody hire you?"

I answered the question truthfully. "No, but Chief Brady has been around to see Ellen a couple of times. And if the police should eventually discover that Raven *was* murdered, I don't want her to wind up being the patsy."

"Ellen? Why would anyone suspect Ellen?"

"Well, for one thing, someone informed Brady that she'd had a, well,"—I searched for a word to minimize what had occurred—"a falling-out with your sister-in-law at the cocktail party that Friday night."

"It wasn't me," Winnie put in quickly.

"I wasn't implying that it was. Brady—"

"I didn't even know about any falling-out," she persisted. "You say it happened during the cocktail party?"

"After the rest of you went upstairs. In fact, what I started to tell you is that Sybil's maid passed the information on to the police."

"Oh."

I took a few sips of coffee now, mostly to get my questions in order, and then I said, "By the way, how did you happen to get together with Raven's brother? Did she introduce the two of you?"

"Not really. That is, originally I guess she did—he used to come down to school to visit her. But nothing developed between Dick and me until much later. Maybe because there was such a big age difference—big at the time, I mean. And besides, he had a girlfriend when we first met. Naturally, Raven saw to it that *that* didn't last—although, of course, Dick's always insisted she had nothing to do with the breakup."

"But you're certain that she did?"

"Listen, she even bragged to a few of the girls about how she managed it. My husband, however, could have caught that sister of his pushing someone off a cliff, and he'd have made himself believe he didn't see what he saw. Or if he did accept the evidence of his own eyes, he'd have blamed it on poor Raven's having had such a abominable childhood." Winnie made a face. But whether it signified anger or frustration or just plain resignation, I wasn't sure. "That's the way it was with him."

"So when did you actually begin seeing each other—you and your husband?"

"I ran into him at the ballet about five years after I graduated from Walden. We were both with dates, but we stopped to talk for a couple of minutes. And then he called me later that week, and well, that started it. I knew it was just a matter of time, though, before Raven would try to do me in, the way she had all of my predecessors. And believe me, she gave it her best shot. Raven didn't want her brother to have a serious relationship with anyone—but especially not with me." Now came a tentative, surprisingly sad smile. "But it seems her best just wasn't quite good enough."

"And what was 'her best'?"

"I guess I'll have to backtrack a little to explain. You see, when we were sorority sisters, Raven and I had actually been friends—good friends. For a while, that is—until she pulled one of her doozies. But anyway, in those days I used to confide in her, and that's how she got the ammunition to use against me later, with Dick."

"What doozie did she pull on you at Walden?" I asked, curious as to whether whatever it was could possibly measure up to the diabolical little plot the dead girl had hatched to take care of Sybil.

"Well, at the beginning of my junior year I was dating this guy—Keith Fein—and then suddenly, out of the blue, Raven became interested in him, too. In retrospect, I recognize that he wasn't even all that much. But that was Raven all over; she always wanted what somebody else had. At any rate, Keith's fraternity was having this big formal dance, and I went out and bought a really gorgeous gown. It was ivory silk, and it looked smashing on me. At least *I* thought it did." She tittered self-consciously. "Anyhow, that night I was all dressed and just fixing my hair when Raven walked in. She was carrying a glass of tomato juice."

Oh, no! I could envision the disaster even before Winnie related it.

"She came over to me and fingered the skirt—to see what fabric it was, she said afterward—and a split-second later my brand-new ivory dress was bright red!"

"Are you sure it was—"

"Yes, it was deliberate!" Winnie snapped, anticipating my next word. "And I was just furious. Also heartbroken. It was the only formal I had. That spiteful bitch, of course, pretended to be mortified. She apologized a million times and even offered to lend me something of hers—knowing very well that it would be four sizes too small for me."

"So you didn't go to the dance?"

Winnie grinned. "As it happens, I did. Beth Shore—another sorority sister—was right out in the hall at the time. She heard all the commotion and came running in. She said this friend of hers on campus who was more of less my size had a really nice gown and that she'd call and ask her if she'd lend it to me. Well, her friend said sure, that I was welcome to borrow it. And damned if that dress wasn't a perfect fit!" The grin widened. "And so poor Raven wasted a good glass of tomato juice for nothing."

"And that, I assume, ended the friendship."

"You bet it did. From then on, I barely spoke to her. And after we graduated, I was blissfully out of touch with her—right up until Dick came into my life."

"I'm surprised he'd take up with someone who was on such bad terms with his sister. In view of their being so close, I'm talking about."

"He didn't even remember that Raven and I hadn't gotten along. After all, this was years later. Or it's possible she never mentioned it to him in the first place."

"She didn't discourage his seeing you?"

"Not that energetically. Not in the beginning. I really lucked out there. You see, when Dick and I started dating, Raven was pretty preoccupied. She was tangled up with this married man, and from what I could gather, she was so busy concocting schemes for inducing him to leave his wife that she couldn't really concentrate on me. I wasn't spared completely, of course. She did resort to one or two of her little tricks, but it was nothing major, and I escaped relatively unscathed. That is, until she realized Dick intended to marry me."

"Uh-oh," I said.

All at once, every line in the girl's face became more prominent. "'Uh-oh' is right. Almost as soon as we announced our wedding plans, Raven felt it was her duty to inform Dick that I'd had an abortion years earlier."

"I take it this is what you meant a few minutes ago about her getting ammunition against you in college."

"Yes," Winnie replied softly, looking miserable. "Back when Raven and I were close, I'd foolishly poured out my heart to her one night."

"How old were you when you had the abortion?" I asked gently.

"Only sixteen. And do you want to hear something dumb? I wasn't even that upset about getting pregnant. I thought I was madly in love and that since I was going to be marrying the little creep anyway—I'm referring to the baby's father—what difference did it make if we marched up the aisle a little sooner than we'd intended? But eventually reality caught up with me, and at long last it sank in that there wasn't going to be any happy ending here. And, well . . ." Her voice trailed off, and she sighed plaintively.

"You have to appreciate that I come from a pretty religious family," she explained, "and some of it must have rubbed off on me, because it's only recently that I've been able to forgive myself for the abortion. That's why I couldn't work up the courage to tell Dick about it. But at any rate, when Raven saw how serious things were between her brother and me, she dredged up my unhappy little secret and shared it with him."

"How did he take it?"

"Not well. Not well at all. He said it was mostly because I hadn't told him myself. But I've never been really convinced that was true—although I'm sure *he* thought it was. You see, in his own way, Dick's a pretty straight and narrow kind of guy—old-fashioned, actually. That's one of the things I love about him. But anyway, Raven was very clever about the whole thing. According to Dick, it disturbed her no end that she had to betray my confidence. He swore that it was only after much soul-searching that she'd decided he had a right to know and that, of course, her first loyalty was to him. She even had the nerve to tell him how much it bothered her that I'd had to go through something like that so young—her sneaky little way of reminding him how much more she herself had gone through when she was even younger. Incidentally, she did that reminding bit a lot and—" Winnie stopped. "You do know that Raven was sexually molested as a child?"

I nodded. I wasn't exactly anxious to revisit that topic, either. So I put in quickly, "Apparently, all that hard work didn't get her any farther than the tomato juice had."

"Fortunately," she responded, her expression dead serious. "But it was touch and go for a while there. Dick really lit into me for not being honest with him—and justly so, I admit—and after letting me have it, he stormed out of my apartment, leaving me a total basket case. I didn't hear from him for over a week, but finally he called and said we should talk. So he came over and that's what we did: talked. We talked all that day and all that night. And then at around dawn we just sort of agreed to put the whole thing behind us."

I mulled things over for a few seconds. *Maybe Winnie wasn't being altogether fair here. I mean, it was possible Raven really had felt that Dick was entitled to know about the abortion.* "Look, don't be angry that I'm bringing this up," I brought up, "but I've been wondering: Is it conceivable that in this instance, at least, Raven really did have her brother's interests at heart?"

"Not on your life! With Raven, it was just one thing after another. She did anything and everything humanly possible to cause trouble between Dick and me."

"And your husband never made an attempt to get her to cool it?"

"Whenever she came out and said something obvious, he did. But that rarely happened. Raven wasn't only a bitch, she was an insidious bitch." Now Winnie colored, asserting almost defiantly, "And the fact that she's dead doesn't change that."

"I agree with you completely," I assured her. "Tell me, though, after you and Dick got married, did Raven let up at all?"

"Are you kidding?" Her voice was strident now. "If anything, she was even more determined to see us split up. Getting me out of Dick's life was my sister-in-law's pet project, right up until she died." Suddenly, Winnie's manner changed, and her tone became confidential. "Listen, if I told you about all of that woman's machinations, we'd be here at least until Christmas. But let me give you just one example of how that devious mind of hers worked . . .

"This happened only two or three months after the wedding. What inspired it, I'm sure, was that there had recently been a couple of crack-related hit-and-runs in Stonehaven. That's where we live, Dick and I, and where Raven lived at the time—she didn't move to Manhattan until almost a year later. Oh. In case you've never heard of it, Stonehaven's on Long Island," she amplified, "about a half hour's drive from Sybil's place. Anyway, both victims were under ten years old, and it really got everyone in town up in arms about drugs. Now, Raven was nothing if not opportunistic. So what did she do? She started spreading her lies, telling at least a dozen people in that oh-so-convincing way she had that I was an addict and how very concerned she was whenever I got behind the wheel of my car. There was no talking to me, she claimed, although God knows, she'd tried. And she had no idea *how* she could possibly break the news to her brother that his wife had this terrible problem. She had her doubts he would even believe her, she said.

"And then she just sat back and waited.

"It didn't take long. One day Bill Weaver, a man we knew only slightly, walked into the store—Dick's a partner in a hardware store—and said something to Dick about how I was an addict and that Dick had better confiscate my car keys immediately and then get me into a treatment program. Naturally, Dick tried convincing him that he was mistaken about me, but it didn't do any good. It finally got to the point where my husband—who's normally a pussycat—was ready to flatten this Weaver. His clerk actually had to stop him from hurdling the counter to get at the guy.

"Well, Dick never mentioned a word to me about the incident—I guess he realized exactly what I'd think. But a week later I ran into our neighbor Jake Whital when I was coming home from work. As soon as he saw me, he said something like, 'I never figured that husband of yours for a temper like that, heh-heh'—Jake had been at the store when it happened, you see. And then he said, 'Good for him, too. I'd have felt the same way if someone had talked about *my* wife like that.' The man's a bachelor," Winnie advised me with a fleeting grin. "Anyhow, Jake just assumed Dick had told me all about it, and I let him continue assuming. Before long I'd gotten him to fill me in on every last detail.

"And that," she informed me, "is how I found out why so many people were averting their eyes or whispering or pulling their kids closer to them every time I passed them on the street.

"Oh, my," I muttered lamely.

"Needless to say," Winnie went on, "I realized immediately where that miserable, vicious rumor had originated. Where else but with my miserable, vicious sister-in-law?"

"The whole thing is so . . . so Machiavellian, so *sick*!" I exclaimed. And then I added hesitantly, "Uh, I suppose you know for a fact that Raven was responsible."

"For an *absolute* fact. It was confirmed to me by a number of the people she'd spoken to. But anyhow, I made the mistake of accusing her when I brought up the subject with Dick. I should have anticipated his reaction—he was furious. He said that I always blamed Raven for everything. 'If they had an earthquake in Japan tomorrow,' I remember him telling me, 'you'd find a way to put that on Raven, too.'"

"Did you ever confront *her* about it?"

"Yes, but I knew it wouldn't do any good, and it didn't. She swore that she had nothing to with the story and that anyone who claimed she did was a liar. And then she told me she'd heard that same rumor herself and had been just appalled by it. *Appalled* my backside!"

"I don't understand something, though. What did she hope to accomplish with a lie like that?"

"I didn't always understand Raven's motivations, either; you'd have to think the same way she did—God, forbid—to know what she had in mind. But what I figure she was after is that I'd accuse her to Dick. Which—not having too much smarts—is exactly what I did. And that, of course, produced the friction she was hoping for. Although not to the degree she'd hoped for, thank goodness. Then, too, there was the extremely satisfying fringe benefit of having me viewed as a pariah in my hometown."

"But wasn't she afraid that your husband would try to get to the bottom of things?"

Winnie responded with a smile filled with irony. "Raven knew Dick very well. She realized he wouldn't pursue it, that he was too afraid of learning the truth."

Now, although I am not above covering my ears and gluing my eyes shut when conditions merit it, this was altogether different. I mean, Dick Eber should have run that story down for his wife's sake—sister or no sister. I suppose my expression reflected my feelings, too, because Winnie felt obliged to come to his defense. "Dick's a wonderful man, believe me. Raven was his one blind spot." And then with a poignant smile, she held out her palms and hunched her shoulders, which I translated to mean, "Well, you have to take the bad with the good." Or something like that. A second later, though, the smile disappeared. "Do you know that there are some people in Stonehaven who are still convinced I'm a junkie?"

"But that was years ago. I don't—"

"Look, I own this agency that supplies temporary office help. When the drug story first started making the rounds, business took a nosedive. I didn't even know why at the time. It was quite a while, too, before things gradually started to pick up again. But to this day I'm not doing as well as I once did. And I probably never will again."

"You must have been thrilled when Raven moved to Manhattan," I commented then.

"Oh, I was, believe me. But you know, the move didn't improve things to the extent that I thought it would. Raven was a true genius at coming up with new ways to try to undermine me with Dick, and I found out soon enough that her base of operations wasn't that significant."

"Did you have to see very much of her?"

"A lot more than I wanted to, I assure you. Listen, Ms. Shapiro—"

"Desiree."

"Desiree," she acknowledged perfunctorily. "The thing is, I'm crazy about my husband. He's the kindest, most loving man I've even known. And he and Raven had this incredibly strong bond—he was really more like a father to her than a brother. So I realized that if I tried to get him to break his ties with her or made it difficult for him to keep up the relationship, all I'd accomplish would be to alienate him—the last thing in the world I wanted to do. That's why I'd invite her to dinner on holidays, and once in a while—a great while, I might add—I even let Dick talk me into joining them when he took her to the theater or the ballet or something.

"What made me really crazy, though, was when *she'd* get tickets for the three of us. 'See?' Dick would say. 'She's trying, even though she knows how you feel about her'—after which he'd throw in something to pacify me like 'Not that you don't have your reasons, of course.' And then he'd usually go into his 'I'm aware that Raven isn't perfect, but who is?' routine, pointing out that because of his father, she had a lot better excuse than most of the rest of us for not always 'taking the high road,' as he liked to put it."

"You were a damn good sport to have gone along with things," I observed.

"What choice did I have? I wanted to make Dick happy. I just did my best to try and hide my feelings when I was with her. But I'd clench my teeth so hard the entire time that it's a miracle I didn't wind up with lockjaw."

Winnie folded her hands on the table at this point in what I assumed to be a gesture of finality. "So," she concluded, "while I'm sorry about *the way* Raven died, particularly because of Dick, I don't regret for an instant that she's dead." Then she lifted one cheek off the seat, leaving no doubt that flight was imminent.

I spoke hurriedly. "I won't detain you much longer, but I wanted to talk to you about the weekend of her death. Uh, I only have one or two questions."

"In that case, I'll be right back." She began inching her way out of the booth. "I'm getting myself another cup of coffee," she announced. And now she said what I was praying I wouldn't hear. "You'll keep me company, won't you?"

Chapter 14

I made a quick trip to the ladies' room, then rejoined Winnie in the booth. I tried to look pleased at seeing that fourth mug of coffee sitting there, staring me in the face.

"What was it you wanted to ask me?" Winnie inquired almost at once.

"I was just wondering if, by any chance, you stopped in to Raven's room that Friday after the party. I'm only asking because her manner could have provided a clue as to her frame of mind that night."

"You're not serious! My one goal in life was to be able to stay out of her way."

"Uh, I don't suppose you know if anyone else paid her a visit."

"I seriously doubt it. A leper would have been more popular with our group than Raven was."

Well, it was a long shot. "Tell me about Saturday morning. About your going to her room to get her, I mean."

"There's very little to tell. When Raven wasn't down for breakfast by ten-fifteen or so, Sybil asked me to see what was keeping her. Ellen needed something upstairs, so she came with me. I'm sure Ellen's already filled you in on this, though, hasn't she?"

"Yes," I acknowledged, "but she may have overlooked something."

Winnie's expression made it clear that she considered this replay a complete waste of time. But she humored me. "Well, I knocked on the door, and when there was no answer, I went in. Then I heard a terrible—Oh, I almost forgot. I peeked into the bathroom, just in case Raven might be in there combing her hair or something. And right at that moment I heard this ear-piercing scream. The catering crew had discovered her body in the swimming pool."

"You knew your sister-in-law as well as anybody did," I put to her then. "What do you think happened that night?"

The response came without hesitation—as if she had already answered that same question for herself. "I think she went upstairs and got ready for bed. And then it occurred to her that she'd be doing that dive of hers off the balcony at some time over the weekend—if *she* had anything to say about it, that is—and I think she became a little concerned. Raven always had to be perfect at everything, you see, and it had been years since her last unforgettable performance at Sybil's." There was no mistaking the derision in Winnie's voice now. "Well, she decided a rehearsal was in order. So she slipped off her sweet little peach peignoir and her matching little peach ballerina nightgown and then went—" She broke off abruptly. "Don't look at me like that, Desiree. I told you. I wasn't in her room that night. I know what she had on because her things were lying over by the terrace door when I went to wake her on Saturday."

Of course! Ellen had mentioned that. Only I'd forgotten all about it for a moment there, so I guess I *had* been looking at the girl kind of strangely. But naturally I assured her that I hadn't been and urged her to go on.

"That's all there is. Evidently, no one had mentioned anything to Raven about the pool being empty, and the dive killed her." She didn't say this with either sadness or glee. It was just a plain, matter-of-fact wrap up.

"It's sort of funny," I remarked then. "I wouldn't have figured your sister-in-law as the peach nightgown type. Black lace would have been more in keeping with my mental picture of her."

Winnie laughed. "You've never seen an actual photograph, I gather."

"No, I haven't. What did she look like?"

"Well, she had this tiny upturned nose and these big blue china doll eyes and long, straight blond hair that—"

"You mean Raven was *blond*? With a name like 'Raven'?"

Winnie laughed again. "I know. The name didn't exactly match up with her looks. Or with the sweet, wholesome image she projected."

"Sweet, wholesome image?" I parroted. Another distortion of my mental picture!

"Oh, yes. We're talking about a real girl-next-door type here. Raven was innocence personified, and she worked hard at making sure it came across, too. She went easy on the makeup—I don't think she even owned any eye shadow or mascara. And she'd always wear these nice, simple clothes—not *overly* simple, though, but not overly stylish, either, if you understand what I mean. And most of the time she'd have her hair in a perky little ponytail, tying it back with a ribbon that coordinated with her outfit. Or when it was loose, she'd put on one of those headbands—I'm talking about the type they used to wear in the sixties or whenever. I guess she thought they made her look like Alice in Wonderland."

Winnie screwed up her face. "Some Alice," she scoffed. "I once saw this television movie—Elizabeth Taylor was in it. The title of the thing stuck with me for obvious reasons; it was called *Malice in Wonderland*. Now, *that* was more like our Raven! But anyhow, she stayed in character right to the end. She even had a peach ribbon in her hair when they found her in the pool. Did you know that?"

I didn't know it. And I supposed it didn't make any difference at this point what color her ribbon was. Or even that she was wearing a ribbon at all. But I was suddenly very interested in the dead girl's appearance. And I'm not even sure why. It's possible I hoped it would give me some further insight into her character. (Which was silly of me and which, of course, it turned out not to.) It's even more possible, though, that I was just curious. "You wouldn't happen to have a snapshot of Raven with you?"

"You've got to be kidding!"

"Well, was she tall or short?"

"Tall—almost as tall as Dick. And she was thin—she could have used a good ten or fifteen pounds, if you ask me." (I had to stifle a smile at that one.) "Listen, if you like, I could get some photos together and send them over to your office. You'll have to return them when you're through with them, though. Dick would kill me if he knew they were even out of the house."

I told Winnie that I'd appreciate it and promised to get the pictures back to her. Then I said, "I guess you're aware by now that Sybil never invited Raven to that party, that someone else sent her an invitation."

"Yes, to lure her there and kill her—according to one theory, at any rate. But don't look at me. For a while, I didn't even know if I'd be going myself. I had a bad cold all that week."

"You must have some thoughts, though, as to who was responsible for that invitation."

"I'm at a loss there. Let me tell you something. Every one of those four sorority sisters of mine is a very bright lady in her own right. But as far as I'm concerned, the bunch of them together couldn't have cooked up that kind of a plot."

I wanted to be sure she understood. "We're not necessarily talking murder here, you know. What if someone just wanted to get her to that party in order to confront her or embarrass her in some way? Or maybe the invitation was intended as a joke, and Raven wasn't even expected to show."

"I'd have to give you the same answer. It has nothing to do with motive. I was talking about the creativity involved in something like that."

All right, I'd try another tack. "Forget about the invitation," I instructed. "If by the slightest chance it was determined that someone killed your sister-in-law, who would you suspect?"

"Me," she replied promptly with a chuckle. "Seriously, I can't conceive of any of them murdering someone—even Raven." She gave it a little more thought. "No. There isn't one of them I can see as capable of it," she asserted firmly.

"How about suicide?—which is something else the police are exploring. Can you think of any reason at all for Raven to want to kill herself?"

"Frankly, I have no idea why she'd do a thing like that. She had a terrific career—she was a stockbroker, and a pretty successful one, too. And Dick said that there was a new man in her life." She grimaced. "That lucky fellow has no idea of the grief he's been spared! Oh, that sounds awful, doesn't it?" Her already wrinkled forehead pleated up like an accordion now. "I can't help how I felt—how I feel—about her, though, can I?"

"No, of course you can't."

"Anyway, what it amounts to is that if Raven did commit suicide, I haven't a clue as to what might have triggered it."

Now, I was a little surprised to hear Winnie say that. I

mean, I had expected her to immediately pooh-pooh the notion. And I told her so.

"Look, I'm not saying I think she killed herself," she clarified. "In fact, I'd be really shocked if that's what happened. But with Raven, well, you could never be certain of anything, that's all." She seemed to be turning something over in her mind then. "On the other hand, though," she added a moment later, "there's a very good reason for *discounting* suicide."

"What's that?"

"Me."

"*You*?"

Winnie grinned mischievously. "There's no way my sister-in-law would have permitted herself to make me that happy."

Chapter 15

After I left Winnie, I stopped off at the cleaner's.

Now, Stylish French Cleaners and Professional Tailors had changed owners three times since I'd moved to the neighborhood about twelve years ago. The most recent change had occurred only a couple of months earlier when Charley, the then proprietor, sold his business at age forty-nine in order to move to South Carolina and play golf every day all year long. I figure I was a major depositor in that retirement fund of Charley's—a largesse I had also extended to his predecessors and was now well on my way to bestowing on his successor.

The thing is, I'm almost a fanatic about personal cleanliness. It has to do with my weight, I suppose. I mean, while I might prefer to be described as "amply proportioned" or "full-figured" or—and this I don't hear nearly often enough—"voluptuous," I learned a long time ago that there'll always be some insensitive peabrain who refers to me as fat. However, I refuse to give that peabrain an excuse for referring to me as fat and *sloppy*. That's why any time there's even a microscopic spot on anything of mine, I rush it straight over to the cleaner's.

It was well after 4:00 when I got to Stylish. Myron, Charley's replacement, was behind the counter. He favored me with his usual broad, slightly bucktoothed smile. Obviously, the man knew who his most reliable contributor was when he saw her. "How are you today, Miz Shapiro?" he asked when I handed him the cleaning ticket.

"Just fine. And you?"

"Not bad. Not bad at all," he responded cheerfully. "Be right back."

He returned almost immediately with my gray suit, and I paid him, after which I held out my hand, foolishly assuming

I'd be redeeming my property. Myron, however, was not prepared to relinquish it. He just stood there, the plastic-covered garment over his arm, shifting awkwardly from one leg to the other. Finally, he said, "I was wondering, Miz Shapiro, if maybe . . . well, if maybe . . ." He cleared this throat. "I know this isn't much notice, but I said to myself, 'Myron,' I said, 'she might not have anything to do, and so maybe she'll be glad of the company.'"

Oh, shit! I wasn't altogether sure what he was getting at (no doubt because I didn't want to be), but still, I wasn't any too comfortable with my suspicions.

"For dinner," he clarified. "I thought maybe we could have dinner tonight." Then, still holding the suit for hostage, he looked at me inquiringly.

Damn! He is! He's asking me out!

Now, I probably have some kind of nutty nurturing complex, because I'm uncommonly attracted to men who are small and pathetically skinny and needy-looking. But despite the fact that this description fit Myron to a T, the man did absolutely nothing for me. Less than nothing, even.

To begin with, he had this completely bland personality. And besides that, he sweated a lot. (I know, I know. Considering the nature of his working environment, this wasn't fair. But I couldn't help it, could I, if I found it a turnoff?) And I'm not even mentioning his watery little eyes. Or the prominent Adam's apple that I wasn't able to take my eyes off whenever he opened his mouth. "Gee, Myron, that would have been nice," I said. "But I have other plans tonight."

"Yeah, well, I knew it was kinda last minute. We could make it tomorrow, if you want."

"Oh, I'm sorry, but I'm expecting company tomorrow night."

Having gotten himself up for this, he was not about to let go. "You wanta make it during the week?"

Oh, why hadn't I just told him right away that I was engaged or something?

Because you're an idiot, that's why, I had to admit.

And of course, it was too late to trot out that excuse now. "I never go out during the week; I always have to bring work home with me," I tried instead. "But thanks for asking," I added in what I intended as a gently dismissive tone. And then

I leaned over the counter, my hand extended again, to remind him that I'd come in here for my suit.

Myron was a pit bull now. "I don't like to plan so far in advance," he proclaimed, while involuntarily (I think) stepping backward and holding the suit a little closer to his sunken chest. "But seein' that you're such a busy lady, we can make it for the following weekend. How's Friday?"

"Well, I—"

"Saturday's good with me, too. We can even get together Sunday, if that's better for you."

I threw in the towel. "All right," I acquiesced. I just couldn't think of what else to do. "Let's make it Friday."

"Swell." And then, at last, Myron forked over the suit.

When I got home, I found a message on the machine from Ellen. She wanted to know if I had had a chance to look into Raven's death yet.

I returned the call as soon as my hard-won suit was back in the closet.

"I realize there hasn't been much time for you to do anything, but I just wanted to know if you had any news at all for me," she said, sounding apologetic.

I told her I had spoken to Sybil and Winnie so far.

"And? Did you find out anything?"

"Nothing to lead me to believe me there was a crime committed here. So relax, will you?"

"I'm relaxed. I was just curious," she responded. But her tone didn't convince me. "I'll see you tomorrow," she said then.

And that's how the conversation ended.

I hadn't lied to Myron about Sunday; I *was* having company—Ellen and Mike. So after a quick supper, I prepared and baked the eggplant parmigiana—tomorrow's entrée. (I always prefer Italian food reheated—and the more reheats the better, too.) And while the eggplant was in the oven, I made the baked clam appetizer and got started on the little meatball hors d'oeuvres.

It was almost 1 A.M. by the time I was through cooking and close to two when I finally finished cleaning up after myself. (I somehow manage to use half the pots and pans I own even when I'm not doing much more than boiling water, so you can imagine the mess I had to contend with that night.) At 2:15

I crawled into bed. The second I closed my eyes, Myron and his overbite materialized in my head. It was not a welcome picture. The last thing I remember before dropping off to sleep was saying hopefully, almost prayerfully, to myself, *Think positive. There's always a chance you'll get hit by a truck before Friday.*

On Sunday morning I made the cold lemon soufflé—which had been requested by Mike via Ellen and which is my most special dessert. And then I devoted myself to the salad: washing, drying, slicing, and/or chopping half the things in my refrigerator.

Right after that I housecleaned, this being necessitated by the fact that my every-other-week cleaning woman was still among the missing. One of these days I was going to have to fire that Charmaine and start looking around for someone else. But how can you fire someone if she doesn't show up and never returns your calls? Anyhow, I didn't do any of the heavy stuff. No windows got washed, no mattresses got turned—nothing like that. I just concentrated on putting the place in the kind of shape that would preclude Mike's deciding that his almost-fiancée had sloppy genes running around in her family. It didn't even matter about Ellen and me being only related by marriage—you just can never tell how someone will see things. At any rate, when I'd finished with my chores, I sat down on the sofa and closed my eyes for only a minute or two. . . .

The insistent ring of the telephone pulled me out of the best dream I'd had in weeks. Startled, I jumped up and grabbed the receiver, glancing at my watch at the same time. It was past 6:00. Damn! I still had quite a bit left to do, and Ellen and Mike were due at 8:00.

As soon as I said hello the voice on the other end launched into a pitch for some charity I'd never heard of. I agreed to send five dollars, anyway. After all, whoever it was had, however inadvertently, certainly done me a good turn.

I put up the folding table and set it with a speed I didn't have any idea I was capable of. Following this, I jumped into the shower and then hurriedly slapped on my makeup. It only required a little extra time to wipe off the mascara globs under my eyes, mop up the foundation on the bathroom floor, and pick up the broken bottle pieces. After that, I took care of all the last-minute food preparation, and then got into my clothes.

I was just coming out of the bedroom when Ellen and Mike arrived.

They really are a handsome couple, I decided, as I always did whenever I saw them together.

"I'm so pleased you could finally make it," I told Mike. "It's been a while now."

"Yes, it has. And you can't imagine how much I've been looking forward to another one of your dinners." He quickly amended that. "And to seeing you, too, of course."

"Mike even got a haircut in your honor," Ellen informed me. And giggling: "But then again, it might have been in honor of the lemon soufflé."

I couldn't comment on the haircut at that moment. Mike extends up so high that I have difficulty seeing much above the top button on his shirt. But a little later when we were sitting down nibbling hors d'oeuvres and sipping the merlot he and Ellen had contributed to the meal, I remarked on how nice his hair looked.

"Thanks," he mumbled. He was actually embarrassed, which I thought was really adorable. "Ellen told me you were checking into her sorority sister's death," he said a few seconds afterward.

"That's right. But only to convince this worrywart niece of mine that there was nothing sinister about it."

"I'm glad you're doing that. And I know what you mean by 'worrywart,'" he said, squeezing Ellen's shoulder affectionately. "I keep telling her it had to be an accident. But she's practically certain that any day now the police will come breaking down her door to drag her off to the slammer."

Ellen glowered at him. "That's not it at all. It's just that with a thing like that, well, you can never be too sure *who's* going to fall under suspicion." And then before either Mike or I could call up any of our oft-repeated reassurances, she changed the subject.

We started to chat about all sorts of other things now: movies, our respective careers, even—and I can't, for the life of me, recall how we stumbled into this one—our favorite colors.

At the dinner table a short time later, we covered books, cars, and restaurants, segueing into Italian versus Chinese food. I explained to Mike that while I was passionately fond of both cuisines, I rarely prepared any Chinese dishes for Ellen, since Mandarin Joy did such an estimable and frequent job of it. It wasn't until his second—or was it his third?—helping of the lemon soufflé that I told them about my upcoming date with Myron.

Mike's response came first. He suggested—in a very tentative way and with a surreptitious peek at Ellen—that I give the guy a chance. "You really can't tell about people until you get to know them a little. With Ellen and me, it was actually loathe at first sight," he joked, "but then we kind of grew on one another."

As I'm certain he expected, Ellen countered at once. "Don't listen to him, Aunt Dez." And then she pointed out to Mike, "She's obviously dreading this, so why should she put herself through it? In fact, she owes it to *Myron* to break that date."

Mike grinned. "All right, I'll bite. How would canceling out be to Myron's advantage?"

"Because that way she wouldn't be leading him on. Can't you see that?" And turning to me: "Don't listen to him," she reiterated. "It's okay for men to talk to *us* about getting to know someone. But just try telling one of *them* to give some *woman* a chance! Ha! You want my advice?" She was apparently confident that I did. "You call Myron and tell him the truth."

"Which is—?" I asked.

"Which is that your old boyfriend has come back into your life again."

"The truth," I echoed. "Of course." And then the three of us began to laugh.

When the laughter subsided, Mike came close to putting me in shock. "I was wondering if I could have another cup of coffee."

I tell you, I really had some concerns about this guy's taste buds! I mean, Ellen is used to my abominable brew, but very few others have been known to even make it all the way through cup No. 1.

"I wouldn't mind a little more coffee, either," Ellen piped up.

"I'll bring in the cups," Mike offered the instant I rose.

I was thinking about what lovely manners he had as he followed me out of the room. But as soon as he'd placed the cups on the kitchen counter, he said very softly, "Uh, I wanted to talk to you."

Well, at least I wouldn't have to waste any sleep over his taste buds. "Is there something wrong?" I asked anxiously.

"No, it's nothing like that. I just wanted to know if you meant what you've been telling Ellen—that you're sure Raven's death was an accident."

"Yes, I did. I can't be positive, of course"—I lowered my voice with this admission—"but it certainly looks that way to me."

"I'm very relieved to hear it. That drink in the face thing— I've been worried that it might wind up causing Ellen some trouble, that's all."

Honestly! I mean, why point out to your husband-to-be that you've ever had any less-than-perfect moments? "She told you about that?" I asked rhetorically. I felt like gagging her.

"Yes, and I wouldn't want the police to zero in on it. It's really so uncharacteristic of Ellen. She normally has such a gentle, forgiving nature." He smiled sheepishly. "As I'm sure you didn't need me to tell you."

"Everything will be fine; you'll see," I said firmly.

But I couldn't have been more wrong. And ironically, it was that normally gentle, forgiving nature of Ellen's that was eventually to land her in so much trouble.

Chapter 16

I reached Carol Sue Kessler at home on Monday morning. I explained that I was Ellen's aunt and that I had some questions I wanted to ask her about Raven's death. "It won't take long," I assured her.

"I don't understand this," Carol Sue responded petulantly. She had a whiny, nasal voice that I found very grating—in spite of the fact that I'd been predisposed to feel sympathetic toward the girl. "Why is there still an investigation? Raven jumped into the pool and accidentally killed herself, and that should be the end of it."

"Oh, I agree with you—one hundred percent. But there are a couple of matters the police have to clear up first, and I'd like to speed things along, if I can."

"I've already spoken to that chief of police—Brady—three times, and I've told him everything I know. I don't see what more I can tell *you*."

"Why don't you let me come by, and I'll explain? We can do it any time it's conv—"

"I'd really rather not."

"I honestly *do* think I can help put this thing to rest. It shouldn't take more than five or ten minutes. That's a promise." (I did have my fingers crossed when I said it.)

"No, I can't see you." She was adamant now. "Look, I don't want to be mean or anything, especially since you're Ellen's aunt. But the whole subject of Raven Eber is painful to me, and I just want to put it—*her*—out of my mind."

"But that's what I'm trying to do. Wind things up, so you can *all* put this out of your minds."

"I'm sorry. I really am. And please give my best to Ellen."

And with that, she was gone.

For a minute, I sat there holding the dead receiver. I think I must have been glaring at it, too, because I heard this very soft throat-clearing sound. And when I looked up, Elliot Gilbert was standing just outside my office, grinning. "I've never seen anyone who looked like they wanted to murder a telephone before," he said.

I laughed. "I'm just feeling a little frustrated at the moment. C'mon in."

"Herm Moody dropped off some photos a couple of minutes ago." He had a large manila envelope in his hand, I saw then. And as soon as he sat down next to my desk, he emptied its contents on the desktop. There were two eight-by-ten photographs and five snapshots.

"This was taken five months ago," he said, handing me the first eight-by-ten, a color portrait of an attractive older woman with soft gray-green eyes, lovely silver hair, and a smooth, virtually unlined face. The subject, in spite of the fact that she was no longer young, could even have been characterized as glamorous. "I'm afraid you can't go too much by this picture, though," Elliot cautioned. "Muriel hasn't really looked like this in years. The photographer seems to have been a pretty gifted retoucher."

The other eight-by-ten, which Elliot told me dated back two years, had been similarly enhanced. "I think the snapshots'll give you a truer likeness," he said, passing along a photo of the woman with a distinguished-looking, if portly gentleman whose silver hair was a perfect match to her own. "This one was taken last September. That's Herm, my—I mean, *our*—client with Muriel." The pair had been shot standing on the top step of a brownstone, both of them elegantly decked out in formal attire.

"This is their home?" I asked.

"That's right. On the Upper West Side."

I noted that the Moodys had positioned themselves so far apart from each other that it looked as if they'd have preferred not being on the same planet, let alone the same stoop. If body language was any criterion, I thought, the trouble between the two dated back to September, at least.

"They were leaving for Debbie's wedding reception here," Elliot told me. "She's their only daughter." I had to hold the picture practically against my face to see the woman's features, and even then I could just barely make them out. And it wasn't because I need glasses, either—there's absolutely nothing wrong with my eyesight, thank you. It was only that whoever took that snapshot obviously hadn't considered it necessary to be anywhere in the couple's immediate vicinity.

The four remaining pictures were shot from much closer up. And now I was able to ascertain—almost regretfully—that Muriel Moody wasn't nearly as attractive or youthful-looking as those first two photos had led me to believe. I was also positive I'd have no problem identifying her when I saw her. I informed Elliot of this.

"Good," he responded. And then: "Look, I've never been overly fond of Muriel. She's too much of a social climber for my tastes. Also, I've always suspected that she was a rather manipulative woman. And she has absolutely no sense of humor, either. None. When you say something funny to her— and I'm not talking about anything off-color, you understand—she always gives you one of these insipid smiles that lets you know how hard she's trying to be tolerant.

"Basically, though, I think Muriel has a good heart. And besides, she and Herman have been married for a lot of years— although from what he tells me now, things have been sort of rocky between them the last year or so. Still, Herm said they seemed to be getting along a little better recently. Until this cheating—this *alleged* cheating business, that is."

Flushing a little, Elliot broke off then and grinned in embarrassment. "What I've been trying to say in this long-winded soliloquy of mine is that I really hate to see this. I want you to know that I tried very hard to convince Herm the two of them should consult a marriage counselor or that he should at least try talking things out with her, but he stubbornly refuses to consider either alternative. He's sure she's having an affair, and he's a very proud man—too proud sometimes. Anyway, he seems to have absolutely made up his mind to a divorce." Elliot was silent for a moment. "I did my best; I really did," he murmured sadly.

"I have no doubt of that, Elliot. Tell me, though, what evidence does he have that Muriel's been seeing someone?"

"Well, once a week she supposedly meets a friend of hers for lunch. Adrian Wyatt, the woman's name is. This Mrs. Wyatt lives in New Jersey, incidentally, and Muriel claims she comes into Manhattan every Tuesday for her doctor's and dentist's visits or to take in a show or do some shopping or whatever. At any rate, one afternoon—in April or May, it was—Mrs. Wyatt phoned to talk to Muriel. But Muriel had already left the house by then, ostensibly to have lunch with this woman. Now, as it happens, Herm was at home when the call came in. Seems he'd been feeling ill that morning and had only remained at work for a couple of hours. In fact, when the housekeeper took the message, he was right there in the kitchen with her."

"The friend wasn't calling to cancel lunch, I take it."

"No. From the housekeeper's end of the conversation, Herm was pretty certain of that."

"Did he say anything to Muriel when she got in? About the call, I mean."

"Not a word. Just asked her how Mrs. Wyatt was and where they'd eaten and if they'd enjoyed the meal."

"And naturally, she didn't let on that she hadn't seen the woman that day."

"Correct."

"You know, Elliot, what you've been telling me really doesn't amount to very much. Let's say Muriel knew in advance that Mrs. Wyatt wouldn't be coming into the city that week. And let's say she wanted to do something that she wasn't anxious for her husband to find out about—I don't know, maybe treat herself to a massage or go to a play or even meet some other female friend, one that he didn't especially care for. I can see where she wouldn't say anything about her original plans falling through, can't you?"

"Of course. But there's more. The following Tuesday after Muriel went out, Herm dialed this Mrs. Wyatt's house. Not to speak to her—he planned on hanging up if she answered the phone—but just to see if she was at home. And unfortunately, she was."

"Oh." I can't tell you why, but I was really sorry to hear this. Possibly it was because of all the years the couple had invested in one another.

"And he did the same thing again a week or two after that."

"Mrs. Wyatt was home then, too?"

"I'm afraid so."

"Oh." Now I felt even more dejected. "Let me ask you something," I put to him a few seconds later. "This Tuesday lunch thing—has it been going on for a long time?"

"Not that long. Maybe a year. Which Herm claims should have made him suspicious right from the beginning. The two women have been friends since they were both at Vassar, and they used to talk on the phone once or twice a month. But as for actually getting together, well, that would only happen about once a year—if *that* often."

"I see." Well, there didn't seem much doubt that our client's wife had gotten herself involved with *something*. But whether that something was another man still remained to be seen.

"There's one more thing," Elliot was saying. "Lately, Muriel's also taken to going out in the evening on a fairly frequent basis—to play Bingo, she says."

"How frequent are we talking about?"

"Sometimes every week, sometimes once every two weeks. It varies."

"Any particular night?"

"No. But she's smart enough to make it when one of the neighborhood churches actually has a Bingo game scheduled."

"Did the husband say whether or not she ever had any interest in Bingo before?"

"He says he never heard her even mention the word before."

"And this started—when?"

"I can't say exactly. A couple of months back, maybe." He reached over now and scooped up the pictures spread out in front of me. Then he returned them to the envelope, which he handed to me. "So there you are; that's all of it," he said. "Oh, I'll write down the Moody's address for you." Tearing a slip of paper from the small yellow pad on my desk, he jotted something down. "Oh, and Muriel leaves the house at about eleven-thirty on Tuesday mornings," he added, getting to his feet. "And when she goes out to play Bingo—*allegedly* to play Bingo, I imagine I should say—that's usually right after supper. Around seven, seven-thirty."

"I can keep these for a while, I assume?" I inquired, waving the envelope at him.

"Sure, for as long as you need them. Herm'll probably burn them when I give them back to him, anyway."

As soon as Elliot walked out of my office, I tried to contact Ellen at the store. She wasn't available, so I left a message for her. I heard from her right after lunch.

"I was in the *longest* meeting," she explained. "Anyhow, what's up?"

I told her about Carol Sue.

"I'll call her." And then, in a very conciliatory tone, she added, "Don't judge Carol Sue too harshly, Aunt Dez. She's very bitter about Raven, and I can't blame her. The thing is, what Raven pulled on her? It really took its toll. It had an impact on her whole life, actually."

"I'm not criticizing her, but I think you could say the same about what was done to the other girls."

"I know. But, well, it was different. Sybil and Winnie could handle it better. I always felt Carol Sue was more fragile than the others. And besides, with Carol Sue the consequences—to my way of thinking, anyhow—were the most traumatic. But I suppose that's beside the point right now. Listen, I'll talk to her. I think I'll be able to persuade her to see you."

It wasn't until after 5:00 when I was getting ready to leave the office that Ellen phoned again. "I was finally able to get in touch with Carol Sue—we kept missing each other all afternoon," she reported. "Anyway, she's agreed to meet with you."

"How did you manage that?"

"I told her it was the only way we could all reach some closure on this."

"I told her the exact same thing. More or less, anyway."

Ellen giggled. "Yes, but you can't get her a discount on a new sofa."

"You're kidding! *That's* what did it?"

"No, of course not. I *am* kidding. It was all those years of friendship that did it. 'Old sorority sisters never die,' " she paraphrased. " 'They just—' "

Suddenly, she was struck by the meaning of her words. "But they do die, don't they?" she said in a hushed voice. "And sometimes pretty horribly, too."

Chapter 17

It was definitely my week for pictures.

The photographs of Raven Eber arrived at my office on Tuesday morning at 9:30, five minutes after I did. They were accompanied by a short, typewritten note from Winnie:

Dear Desiree—

Well, here they are. Now you can see what I mean about Alice in Wonderland.

Please call me at the office as soon as you're ready to return the photos, and we can make arrangements.

Best to Ellen,

Winnie

P.S. I didn't say anything to Dick about these being "on loan," so guard them with your life.

There was a total of six pictures, carefully protected by cardboard and obviously covering a span of years. The first one I laid hands on was a snapshot taken from fairly close up of a smiling Raven, arm in arm with her equally cheerful brother. They were dressed in similar khaki shorts and white shirts, which served to emphasize the already very strong family resemblance. I mean, the pair had almost identical smiles. And they were about the same height, too. Also, both were blond, with slim, almost angular builds. I turned the photo over. Somebody had jotted down on the back: "Raven and

Dick, Fourth of July, '88." Well, Dick Eber had certainly been a lot thinner and blonder in those days. But what made the biggest impression on me was how on-target Winnie had been about the dead girl's appearance. (I'm not talking about the Alice in Wonderland thing—Raven's hair was pulled back in a ponytail in this shot, so it didn't even apply.) I'm referring to Winnie's remarks about her sweet wholesome image. I'll tell you, it was really tough to reconcile this fresh faced ingenue with the conniving bitch who had devoted her short life to causing those around her so much grief.

The second shot was of a ponytailed Raven on a city side-walk, surrounded by furniture. In this one, she was dressed in blue jeans and appeared to be staggering under the weight of the good-sized toaster oven she was carrying. Still, she was smiling gamely. There was someone in the background, too. Bent over a large carton was a wide, pants-clad figure, its der-riere pointed heavenward. That derriere was very familiar. Grinning, I flipped the picture over. It was inscribed "Raven moves to Manhattan." I decided that this might have been the only time Winnie was actually happy to help out her sister-in-law.

Next, I picked up a Polaroid of a very young Raven in a simple, full-skirted blue gown, a corsage of what appeared to be gardenias pinned to her shoulder. She was positively beam-ing at the gangly young man in the tux standing next to her. In this picture, by the way, she did have on one of those head-bands, and yes, she did look sort of Alice in Wonderlandish. Or my conception of Alice, anyway. There was no notation on the back of that photo, but it obviously dated back to Raven's high-school days.

The other snapshots showed a smiling Raven at a barbecue with a group of friends and a smiling Raven on skis. The one likeness of an *un*smiling Raven was a five-by-seven portrait in a cap and gown. I imagine the photographer had suggested the uncharacteristically pensive expression as more in keeping with the milestone of a college graduation. At any rate, in this larger study, you could really appreciate the girl's wide blue eyes and lovely shoulder-length hair. After some scrutiny, though, I decided that Raven Eber hadn't been what you would call beautiful. In fact, while she was certainly pretty, she wasn't even my idea of *unusually* pretty. I speculated that if I had to pick just one word that would best describe her appearance, I'd have to borrow Winnie's *wholesome*. But then again, maybe *fresh-faced* would be better. (I regard that as one word.) Eventually though, I opted for *clean*. I know that sounds strange, but the girl looked as if someone had taken a scrub brush and gone over her face until it shone.

Anyway, once I'd arrived at this carefully deliberated—and totally extraneous—conclusion, I gathered up all the photographs, replaced them in the cardboard, and slipped them into a fresh manila envelope. Then I made a quick call to Winnie to put her mind at ease. She sounded relieved when I told her that I'd finished with the pictures, and we agreed that I'd Fed Ex them to her office.

A short while later, I went downstairs and picked up my Chevy, which I'd deposited at the garage around the corner from the office that morning. And at ten after eleven, I was stationed behind the wheel on a nice tree-lined block on the Upper West Side.

The Moody brownstone was on a one-way street. Which meant that at least I hadn't had to toss a coin to decide which way to face the car so I'd be in the right position to follow the (allegedly) errant Muriel. To get the best view of the house, I'd double-parked directly across the street, in front of a shiny new black Mercedes that was just my speed. (Although, unhappily, someone else's automobile.) Fortunately, it was a fairly cool day, so I was pretty comfortable sitting there with the windows rolled down, marking time. Anyway, I was keeping one eye on the brownstone and sneaking occasional covetous peeks at the Mercedes with the other, while listening to this incredible tape of Judy Garland, my all-time favorite singer—when suddenly this gray head poked itself in the passenger-side window of the car. I swear, I almost landed in the coronary care unit!

The head belonged to an irate, matronly type woman. "What are you doing here?" she demanded.

"Uh, waiting for a friend," I answered as soon as I'd regained the power of speech.

"*What* friend?"

"Ellen Kravitz."

The woman—who obviously had no immediate plans to remove her topmost portion from the interior of my Chevy—

jerked her thumb behind her. "There's no Ellen Kravitz in this house."

"Oh, she doesn't live around here. She's visiting someone on the block."

Now she sucked in her cheeks. "Really," she said sweetly. "And just who might that be?" I had the feeling I was involved in a little cat-and-mouse game here—and guess which part had been assigned to me. "I'm familiar with everyone on this street," she let me know.

"Uh, well . . . uh, I can't remember the name."

"Is that so?"

"I think it might begin with an 'R,' " I attempted lamely.

"Look, let's cut the crap, all right?" Gray Hair responded sharply. "I've been watching you from the window. You've been parked in front of my house since before eleven o'clock." *Eleven-ten*, I corrected silently. "And if you don't get out of here immediately, I'm going to go straight inside and call the police." Her eyes bored into me. "Understood?"

I had to admire the woman. I mean, she was sixty if she was a day, and for all she knew I could have been Jackie the Ripper. Yet neither of these facts seem to give her pause. I got the distinct impression there wasn't much, if anything, that would frighten this lady.

But my appreciation of them notwithstanding, those brass balls she was displaying presented a real problem. Especially since I had no doubt as to how far a protest would get me. Well, what could I do? I nodded perfunctorily, then turned away, resigned to making my departure. In the same motion, I glanced across the street.

At that precise moment a taxi—which I was a hundred percent certain was transporting Muriel Moody—pulled away from the curb. Before I could even switch on my ignition, the cab sped away and a minute later disappeared from sight.

I was really frustrated. Also angry. (Although I'm not even sure at who—make that *whom*.) Anyhow, the way I looked at it, I owed it to myself to make a stop at Little Angie's. It was therapy.

So before heading back to the office, I paid a visit to that worthy eatery and was soon seeking to counteract my negative emotions with tomato sauce, mozzarella, and anchovies served on top of the thinnest, crispiest pizza crust in the five bor-oughs.

By the time I'd finished my third slice, though, I had to admit there'd been no improvement in my psyche; I was still extremely distressed about the aborted stakeout. But at least I'd enjoyed trying for a remedy.

I was at my desk by 1:15, dialing Carol Sue Kessler.

Even the girl's hello was jarring. She really had *such* an un-pleasant voice. She agreed—although none too graciously—to let me drive out to see her the following afternoon. But just when I assumed everything was set, she made a last-ditch ef-fort to dissuade me. "By the way, you do know I live upstate, don't you?"

I told her I knew.

"I'm close to three hours from the city."

I told her I knew that, too.

"Well, wouldn't it make it easier all around to do this on the phone, then?"

"I don't mind driving up there at all. I really don't," I as-sured her. "I'll see you tomorrow." And then before she had a chance to utter even one more syllable, I very gently placed the phone back in its cradle.

Chapter 18

Right after I got to the office on Wednesday, Elliot dropped in to ask just what I was afraid he was there to ask. "You have a chance to look into the Muriel thing yesterday?" And when I nodded: "So? How'd it go?"

"Uh, not too well." I could feel my face getting warm.

"What happened?"

My recounting of Tuesday morning's fiasco, brief as the events themselves might have been, was extended by a whole lot of hemming and hawing. Elliot, however, actually seemed to enjoy it, chuckling when I was finished. "Foiled by a little old lady, huh?"

"She wasn't *that* old," I objected. "And she was a lot bigger than I am. Uh, heightwise, anyhow."

Realizing now that I was genuinely upset (have I mentioned that the man is a real sweetheart?), he was instantly solicitous. "Don't worry. There's always next Tuesday. And the one after that. And I've told Herman to give us a call the next time Muriel has one of those Bingo nights of hers."

"I should never have parked there for so long, not in broad daylight," I grumbled. "No wonder the woman was suspicious. I should have driven around the block a couple of times."

"And what if Muriel had left the house a few minutes early that day? Look, you had to keep a constant watch on the place. How were you to know that Miss Marple herself lived right across the street?"

I had to smile at that one. It definitely helps to have people around who'll tell you that you didn't screw up when you know damn well that you did.

*　　*　　*

I was standing on the porch of the small white clapboard house at five after three, right on time for my between-3:00-and-3:30 appointment.

"You're Ms. Shapiro?" the girl framed in the doorway inquired.

"Desiree."

"All right. Desiree." She smiled, exposing tiny, not-very-even teeth. "I'm Carol Sue." She didn't have to say that; I'd have recognized that voice of hers anywhere.

Short—probably an inch or two shorter than I am—Carol Sue Kessler was thin to the point of scrawniness. She was dressed in cut-off jeans and a too-tight faded yellow T-shirt, which items of clothing plainly revealed that she had absolutely no hips and even less of a chest. I gave the rest of her a quick once-over, too. Her chin-length reddish brown hair was straight and plainly styled, her eyes on the narrow side, and her nose slightly too long for her tiny face. Plus her one concession to the cosmetics industry was a pale orangey lipstick that, unfortunately, only seemed to emphasize her sallow complexion.

Now, I realize I'm not painting too pretty a picture here. And the fact is, Carol Sue in total wasn't nearly as unappealing as that cursory description of her individual parts might have led you to believe. At second glance, I noted that her lips were full and well shaped. And I saw that her hair had a nice healthy shine to it. What's more, her eyes were really a lovely shade of green. But most of all, there was a kind of vulnerable quality to her appearance that was actually quite endearing. Or maybe it was just that nurturing thing of mine again.

Motioning me inside, Carol Sue preceded me down a short passageway. "How was the drive up?" she asked over her shoulder.

"Fine. It took a lot less time than I thought it would."

"I was concerned you might run into traffic, although you usually don't this time of day. Barring an accident on the thruway, of course."

The girl was certainly a lot more amicable than our phone conversations had led me to expect. And even the whiny, nasal voice was somehow less annoying now that I was experiencing it in person.

We entered a postage-sized living room crowded with unmatched, but serviceable furniture. At Carol Sue's suggestion,

I settled myself on the oversized gold sofa. She promptly took a seat opposite me, curling up in a Queen Anne wing chair upholstered in a blinding electric blue-and-crimson paisley. "I figured you might be thirsty from your trip, so I prepared some lemonade for us," she told me. A pitcher, two glasses, and a plate of assorted Pepperidge Farm cookies stood on the narrow rectangular cocktail table between us.

"Oh, that was really thoughtful of you. And I'd love some," I said untruthfully, having consumed a large Coke not more than fifteen minutes earlier in a diner just outside town.

Carol Sue poured, looking pleased, and we sat there for a while sipping and munching and making small talk, which I kicked off with, "I understand you're a teacher." It was something Sybil had mentioned when she gave me her friend's phone number.

"That's right. Junior high."

"I gather you're off for the summer."

"Not entirely. I'm still doing some tutoring. I'd go crazy just sitting on my duff until September. Besides, it helps pay the mortgage."

"It must be great having a whole house to yourself. I've got a one-bedroom apartment, and I'd sell my soul for a little more space."

"Oh, I don't live here alone. I live with my mother and sister. They're in Delaware for the week, visiting my aunt."

We went back to the subject of her vocation now, with Carol Sue telling me how much she enjoyed teaching in a small town and comparing the schools there to those in urban areas. "I don't think I could handle the New York City school system," she confided. She started to elaborate, then stopped abruptly. "But this kind of thing isn't what you've driven all this way to hear, is it?"

I smiled. "I guess not," I admitted, hastily adding, "although I've really been enjoying our conversation. But I suppose we *should* start getting into the business of Raven's death. After all, I promised I wouldn't take up much of your time."

"I still don't know what I can tell you, but . . ." She left it at that.

"I was wondering if you had any idea who sent Raven that invitation to the party. I assume you do know that it wasn't Sybil."

"Yes, of course. But I really can't imagine who could have been responsible. Or what purpose it was supposed to serve."

"The purpose just might have been murder. I'm not saying that's the case, but it *is* possible, at least, that somebody wanted to get Raven to Sybil's that weekend in order to dispose of her."

If Carol Sue was disturbed by this thought, there was no indication of it in her tone. "I don't believe it," she said matter-of-factly. "Raven had an accident, plain and simple. I can't imagine why anyone would have a problem accepting that."

"But you do admit, don't you, that it was a little strange— her getting this phony invitation?"

She shrugged. "Maybe someone sent it as a joke."

"Uh, I understand you were pretty upset when she showed up," I threw out then.

"Everyone was."

"You even threatened to leave, from what I heard."

"I wouldn't call it a threat," the girl contradicted, her normally peevish tone even more so now. "I just didn't want to be in Raven's company. I hated being anywhere near the woman, if you want the truth."

And now I took a deep breath. I was getting to the part that I knew with absolute certainty Carol Sue would not take terribly kindly to. I tried paving the way for it. "Listen, I want you to know that I'm not just being a busybody questioning you like this. I'm interested in gathering whatever facts I can for only one reason: so that maybe we can put an end to the speculation about what killed Raven." I took another deep breath. "And the thing is, I've learned that sometimes the smallest piece of information or the most remote incident—remote in time, that is—can shed some light on an investigation." At this point I put in quickly, "I should make it clear that my own feeling is that Raven's death was an accident. Which is just what I'm hoping to prove. I—"

"Why?"

A little taken aback by the question, I repeated it automatically. "Why?"

"Why is it so important to prove anything—anything at all?"

"Well, primarily because Sybil's maid told the police that Ellen and Raven had had an altercation at Friday's cocktail party, and now Chief Brady is poking around to find out if

Ellen might have had something to do with what happened that night."

"Ohh," Carol Sue mused. "So that's who it was."

"What do you mean?"

"Brady asked me if I knew about Raven getting into an argument with one of the other women, but I didn't have any idea he was referring to Ellen."

"Uh, look, what I started to say before, Carol Sue, is that it might be helpful if you'd fill me in on just what it was that transpired between you and Raven when you were at Walden together."

"That's something I won't talk about. I put it behind me years ago, and I'm not going to let it mess up my life for the second time."

"I can appreciate how you feel, honestly I can. But there's always a chance it could be relevant."

"How?" she challenged.

"I can't know that until I hear what happened."

"You're talking as though Raven *was* murdered," Carol Sue pointed out.

"You don't understand. I'm trying to *eliminate* the possibility of murder."

"Well, I'm sorry," the girl said firmly, shaking her head. "But nothing could induce me to dredge all of that up again."

"Every one of the others had problems with Raven, too, remember, and they—"

"Look, they're entitled to do what they want to do. But so am I. I didn't tell the police what went on back then, and I'm not about to tell you. Just take my word for it that whatever it was had no bearing on Raven's death."

I could recognize a stone wall when I ran into one. Eventually, at any rate. So I gave up. Besides, although I would have liked to hear Carol Sue herself explain the reason for her animosity toward the dead girl, there was always Ellen.

Apparently Carol Sue's thoughts had been paralleling my own. "Don't look so disappointed," she told me. "You can always find out from Ellen, you know." But she didn't sound any too pleased about the prospect.

"Yes, well, I certainly don't want to cause you any more pain," I responded softly. "Look, I have just one more question—if you wouldn't mind, that is."

"Go ahead," she agreed resignedly.

"Did you, by any chance, visit Raven's room after the cocktail party?"

"Of course not. I—" She stopped short. "Why do you ask? Did someone say that I did?"

"No, nothing like that. As I told you before, I'm collecting whatever facts I can, that's all. Just one more question," I said one more time. "You wouldn't know if any of your sorority sisters paid her a visit that night, would you?"

"Not that I'm aware of. But I tend to doubt it." And after a little further thought: "No, I don't see that." And then still more definitely: "Uh-uh. I really can't see that at all."

On the drive home, I was just burning with curiosity. So as soon as I walked in the door, I went straight to the phone. There was a message from Ellen asking me to call when I got in. Which is exactly what I had intended doing, anyway.

She didn't waste any time after my, "Hi, Ellen."

"What happened with Carol Sue? Did she agree to see you?"

"She did. And I just got back from there."

"You're kidding! Already? Were you able to learn anything?"

"Nothing. And she refused to tell me anything at all about that fight she'd had with Raven in college.'

"I wouldn't call it a fight exactly."

"Whatever you want to call it then. At any rate, I'd like for you to fill me in on it."

To my surprise, Ellen hesitated before replying. "Well . . . umm . . . all right," she got out at last. "If you really think it could be important."

"There's always that possibility. But what's the problem? You offered to enlighten me weeks ago," I reminded her.

"Yes, but that was before."

"Before what?" I asked crossly.

"Before *she* refused to. Look, don't be angry, but Carol Sue evidently doesn't want anyone to know about it, so I can't help feeling a little guilty. It's as though I'll be betraying her."

"Don't be silly." I was exasperated now. "It's going over the incident *herself* that bothers your friend. Evidently, talking about it is still painful for her. But she even suggested that I ask you to tell me what went on." (I omitted a mention of the girl's tone of voice at the time.)

"Really?"

"Really."

Ellen wasn't through yet, however. "But, umm, Aunt Dez?"

"What?" I took pride in the fact that I managed to say it without screaming.

"Do you think something that happened such a long time ago could actually help you find out how Raven died?"

"Most likely not. But you never know. And I don't want to overlook anything." Well, that was the truth. Or a big part of it, at least. So I didn't feel obligated to add that I was also just plain nosy.

Ellen didn't voice any further doubts. And it was finally arranged that we'd meet for a late supper the following night when she was through with work, at which time she'd supply me with the information—albeit still a bit reluctantly.

I hung up thoroughly annoyed with her for being so damned honorable. And even more annoyed with myself for faulting her on it.

Chapter 19

The hot pastrami wasn't so hot. And you can feel free to take that both ways. First off, it was somewhere between cool and chilly. And besides that, the few parts of the meat that weren't fatty were stringy. The French fries were even worse: cold, oily, and just a couple of minutes away from raw. The Second Avenue Deli this wasn't. But then the Second Avenue Deli was nowhere near Macy's.

Ellen and I were, however, starved.

We determinedly got through the sandwiches and even made a pass or two at the fries. But I drew the line at the apple strudel. I mean, if I'd dropped that thing on my foot, I would have been maimed for life. Ellen, on the other hand, gave it a valiant try before putting down her fork, delicately wiping her lips and regretfully shaking her head. When I asked her how she'd managed to choke down even that much of the Dessert from the Cement Factory, her response didn't surprise me in the least. "I thought about all the starving children in Somalia," she admitted, blushing.

My sister-in-law Margot certainly knows how to plant those seeds of guilt in her kids, doesn't she?

At any rate, when Ellen had finally pushed away the strudel, all we had to deal with was the bitter vetch that Irving's Kosher Delicatessen lists on the menu as "coffee"—and which made even my brew seem palatable. It appeared to be a good time to get around to the reason we were there to start with. (I just don't think conversations on topics like murder—or even accidents or suicides—can add to your enjoyment of a meal. Although, in the case of *this* meal, I guess it didn't really make any difference.)

"Tell me about Carol Sue," I instructed after a grimace directed at my coffee cup.

Ellen still didn't seem too comfortable when she said okay. She even found a way to briefly postpone her narrative. "Oh, I hear you're going to be seeing Jeannie on Monday," she put in, referring to Jean Brooks, the sixth Kappa Gam who was at Sybil's for that fateful celebration.

"Yes. That was the earliest she could make it. She's going away for a long weekend in the morning." And then it occurred to me. "But how did you know?"

"Well, it's not because I'm clairvoyant," Ellen asserted with a giggle. "Jeannie called me at work today to tell me."

"Uh, Ellen? About Carol Sue," I prodded.

"I'm sorry. I got sidetracked." But now she engaged in still another delaying tactic. Removing her napkin from her lap, she placed it on the table, smoothed it out, folded it with deliberate care, and then finally set it alongside her cup and saucer. I watched her perform this task with equal parts of astonishment and annoyance. But I didn't utter a word (this momentous accomplishment managed by biting down hard on my lower lip). And at last she began. . . .

"Well, Carol Sue had this boyfriend—Graham his name was, but everyone called him Gray—and they'd been going out regularly for about two months, when they had a fight and broke off. They only split up for a week, but during that time Gray took Raven home from a fraternity party, and I think she kind of liked him. I know she expected to hear from him again. But he and Carol Sue made up a day or two later, so . . ." Her shrug completed the sentence.

"What was the fight about, do you know?"

"I'm not really sure, but I think it had something to do with Gray's drinking too much that night—the night they had the fight, that is."

"Okay. You were saying . . . ?"

"Well, pretty soon after they got back together, this story started going around. I didn't hear about it at the time, but lots of people did—including a few of the girls in the sorority. The gist of it was that Carol Sue's little sister—who was only two or three years old then—was really her own daughter."

Leave it to Raven immediately jumped into my head. "That's cute," I said disgustedly. "I'm supposing it wasn't true."

"No, it wasn't."

"But her boyfriend believed it?"

Ellen's scornful, "He was such a jerk!" gave me my answer. "And it seems he was *doubly* upset," she went on, "because he and Carol Sue had been seeing each other all that while and she still wouldn't sleep with him. But at any rate, Carol Sue herself wasn't even aware of that sick, malicious rumor. Not until the night . . . the night of the attack."

"This Gray *attacked* her?" I gasped.

"No, not him. What happened was that they had been out to a movie that evening, and well, Carol Sue sensed there was something wrong from the minute Gray picked her up. He was acting really, really weird, she said. Anyhow, on the way home, she confronted him. She told him that if whatever was bothering him had anything to do with her, he owed it to the relationship to level with her. So he pulled the car over—they were on this quiet street then, about a mile from campus—and he repeated the damn story.

"She couldn't have been more shocked. And she was furious that knowing her as he did—or should have, anyway—he would put any credence in something like that."

Ellen chewed on her lip now, looking very much as though she wanted to cry. But after a moment, she forged ahead. "And then Carol Sue made this terrible mistake," she said softly.

"Mistake?"

"She got out of the car."

Oh, no! All sorts of possibilities began flashing through my mind, none of them pleasant. "What happened?" I asked nervously.

"Well, Gray drove along next to her for a couple of blocks, trying to persuade her to get back in the car, but she said she'd rather walk. And finally he got so ticked off at her for being stubborn that he just took off and left her there—the creep. Later on, whenever he talked about that night, he said he was sure she'd be safe enough. And it *had* always been a low crime area, I'll give him that much."

"But she wasn't. Safe enough, I mean."

"No. Three men jumped her a few minutes later, and they dragged her into this vacant lot and took turns r-r-raping her."

"Oh, God." I could barely get the words out.

Just then the waitress, carafe in hand, came over to ask if we wanted refills on our coffee. Well, as putrid as the stuff was, it was the only excuse we'd have for sitting there any longer.

And since neither of us had gagged all that much in getting the first cup down, we both bit the bullet.

After the woman walked away, we sat there quietly for a time, each of us struggling with our feelings about the rape of Carol Sue Kessler—and what had led up to it. Then Ellen, her expressive face mirroring her anguish, murmured, "When she came back to the house that night, they say she was really hysterical. I didn't see her myself; I was sound asleep by then. But I did see her in the morning, and while she'd calmed down some, physically, she was in pretty terrible shape. Her face and arms were bruised—one of those animals kept punching her—and her lip was all puffy and her eye was swollen shut."

"Did anyone report the attack to the police?"

"No, Carol Sue wouldn't hear of it. She wouldn't let anyone take her to the hospital, either. She stayed home from classes that week, and then the following Monday, she resumed her normal schedule—I still don't see how she managed it. But for a long time afterward, she was—I don't know—like a zombie almost."

"And she was fairly certain the rumor originated with Raven." Since Ellen had apprised me of that weeks ago, it wasn't really a question. What's more, from everything I'd learned since then, I was sure Carol Sue's judgment had been on the money. This little hatchet job had the fingerprints of the deceased all over it.

"She was almost positive it did," Ellen responded emphatically. "And she had actual *proof* that, at the very least, Raven was *spreading* that garbage."

"What kind of proof?"

"Well, aside from the fact that Carol Sue had been hearing that Raven was interested in Gray, she—Raven, that is—had had a lot of problems at the house by then. There was that terrible thing with Sybil and, before that, a nasty incident with Winnie, where Raven spilled tomato juice all over—"

"Yes, Winnie mentioned it to me."

"And also that silly thing with Lee that I told you about—you know, where Raven thought I took sides. Oh, and she'd also gotten into a big argument with Rickie, Carol Sue's roommate. I forget just what it was about, but I don't think it was anything major. I—"

"Wait. Are you saying that because these others had trouble

with Raven, Carol Sue took it as proof she was the culprit here, too?"

"Oh, no. That's only why Carol Sue—and almost everyone else—had no doubts about whether this fraternity brother of Gray's was being truthful when he told his girlfriend who told Moira—one of our sorority sisters—that Raven had been the one who told *him* the story. If you follow me."

I followed her. (I usually do, and sometimes it scares me.) She didn't wait for confirmation, though.

"And then this other fellow we knew saw Raven and Gray talking together in a coffee shop," she continued. "John didn't hear what was said, but he claimed they were both whispering and that Gray seemed really shook up." Ellen paused for effect before offering up the final piece of evidence: "And *this* was only one day before the attack."

"Did anyone ever get around to asking Gray if it *was* the little sister thing he and Raven were whispering about?"

"Well, naturally." a somewhat offended Ellen responded with a sniff. "In fact, two or three of the girls did. But he never really gave them a straight answer. Eventually, Carol Sue put the screws to him, too, but he was even evasive with *her*. He swore he couldn't remember what they'd been discussing—if you can believe *that*."

"Tell me, did Carol Sue and Gray ever start dating again?"

"No. She refused to have anything to do with him. I have a feeling he was secretly relieved, too. I think he preferred not having her around as a reminder of what he'd done."

That niece of mine never ceases to amaze me! At times it's hard to believe she's right on the heels of thirty; I mean, she can be as naive as any going-on-twelve-year-old. But then at other times she'll come out with something so wise, so perceptive that I find myself questioning which of us is really the more grown up here.

"You've probably got something there," I told her. "But how about Raven? Did Gray start seeing *her*?"

Ellen shook her head. "It's funny. Raven was very pretty, maybe even beautiful. But still, she wasn't all that successful in the romance area. I'm not saying she didn't date—naturally, she *dated*. But well, for some reason she wasn't quite as much of a femme fatale as you might imagine. Maybe a lot of guys were scared off because she *was* so pretty."

"Could be. It could also be that they sensed there was something not quite right about her. But there's even a third possibility."

"What's that?"

"Maybe some of them actually had enough character to judge the opposite sex on more than looks."

Ellen feigned shock. "*College* boys?" We both laughed. It was our first light moment since the conversation began.

A minute or two later, however, I brought the subject back to Carol Sue. I wanted to know if she'd ever been married.

Ellen's expression was instantly somber again. "No. The thing is," she said sadly, "before Gray, Carol Sue was very shy, and she wasn't very popular with men. And after being . . . raped like that, well, she just wasn't interested. A few of us tried talking her into blind dates from time to time—much later, of course—but she wouldn't even consider it."

I'd purposely brought an unopened packet of tissues with me, and from the way Ellen's mouth was trembling now, I thought I'd better start poking around in my handbag for it.

But she faked me out. "You know, Aunt Dez," she concluded, still dry-eyed and in a surprisingly steady voice, "once she started going with Gray, Carol Sue really seemed to be coming into her own. She became more self-confident. Happier. Even more gregarious. Raven put an end to all of that."

"Hold it," I said then, a lot more stridently than I'd intended to. "The way I see it, Gray has to be held accountable for that night, too. Even if he was convinced Carol Sue was her sister's mother"—that does sound bizarre, doesn't it—"and even if he was mad as hell at her for jumping out of the car, he had no business leaving her to make it back to campus on her own." It wasn't that I was defending Raven, you understand. I was just reminding Ellen that the blame wasn't the dead girl's alone.

"Yes, you're right. But if it hadn't been for Raven's lie, the whole thing wouldn't have happened in the first place, would it?"

I couldn't argue with that.

Later, lying in bed, I thought about the impact of Raven's evil (and I don't use that word lightly) machinations on her sorority sisters.

Look what she'd done to Winnie. She'd placed her sister-in-law's marriage in jeopardy on an almost constant basis and—

for a while, anyway—had even caused her to become an outcast in her own hometown.

And what about Sybil? In getting that lovely girl expelled from school, Raven had also crushed all her hopes of having a career. I should put in, though, that I was beginning to have some reservations there—about the career part, I mean. Maybe Sybil could no longer get into law school—and I was assuming she was right about this—but that didn't mean she hadn't been free to pursue any one of dozens of other possibilities. It seemed to me that Sybil was taking the easy way out, assigning the deceased responsibility for everything from an unfulfilled ambition and an unhappy marriage to a loss of interest in a swimming pool.

I returned my attention to Carol Sue now. I had to agree with Ellen. Raven's handiwork had apparently produced the most tragic results here, scarring her target for life. I wondered idly what Carol Sue had been like before the attack. Maybe she'd taken more pains with her appearance in those days. Maybe she'd even been less of a whiner. Immediately, I felt guilty for letting that whine creep into my head. After all she'd been through, Carol Sue was entitled to do a little whining. Or even a lot of it, if she wanted to.

Ellen, I decided, had been pretty lucky. The reaction of Mike's family to her so-called breakdown, notwithstanding.

I began to speculate then about the remaining member of that weekend group. What had the malevolent Raven done to Jean Brooks—and what had provoked it? (I took it for granted the girl hadn't escaped her acquaintanceship with the scourge of Kappa Gam unscathed.) Was a man involved? I wondered. Or had Raven been envious of Jean's scholastic ability? Or—? I decided I'd find out soon enough. Resolutely, I squeezed my eyes shut tighter and rolled over on my stomach. It was time I got some sleep.

I was halfway there when, suddenly, I remembered what had been crowded out of my thoughts for most of the evening. And I shuddered.

Tomorrow was Friday.

And Myron.

Chapter 20

It still isn't too late, I repeatedly goaded myself. So practically all of Friday I kept lifting up the receiver and then putting it down.

The minute I was settled in my cubbyhole that day I'd begun thinking that there were probably any number of ways I could get out of my dreaded date tactfully—and for good. The last part being positively crucial. I mean, I was definitely not interested in a mere postponement.

This criterion immediately eliminated a burst appendix. Also, a car crash, a scorpion bite, and beriberi. Unless there was absolutely no chance of recovery, I'd still be in trouble.

Okay. So what could get me off the hook once and for all? A brand-new husband would qualify. Or how about a sudden impulse to enter a convent? (After all, I *am* Catholic—not a practicing Catholic, I admit, but still, I'm the right religion.) And of course, there was always the option of getting someone else—like Jackie—to deliver the bad news about a death in my family. My own, I'm talking about.

Then around midafternoon, I made a ninety-degree turn. *What are you, anyway—a woman or a bowl of Jell-O?* I'd just tell Myron something had come up, and I couldn't see him tonight. Period. That's all. Nothing more. And I wouldn't let him corner me into rescheduling, either.

But each time I was on the brink of dialing, I chickened out. The same as I had earlier. *Oh, hell*, I decided finally, *you let yourself get talked into this thing, so just go through with it. Like a person.*

Now, interspersed with this internal wrestling of mine, I want you to know that I did manage to get some work done. In the morning I typed up my notes on last night's meeting with Ellen, and then later in the day I carefully read over my entire

file on Raven Eber. And concluded there was absolutely nothing—nothing I could see, at any rate—to suggest there'd been
any foul play here.

Oh, sure. Maybe none of those girls was too broken up that
the deceased was six feet under, but I couldn't find a thing to
suggest that any of them had put her there. Besides, they'd all
been completely candid about their animosity toward the victim, even detailing the reasons for it (except for Carol Sue, that
is—whose reluctance to go into specifics was, I felt, completely understandable). The point I'm trying to make is, if any
of them had murdered Raven, would the guilty party have leveled with me like that?

Of course she would, stupid, I shot back. Everyone in the
group seemed to be aware of Raven's relationship with the
others. So it would have been fruitless to try to conceal anything. (And this was particularly true considering that my own
niece was familiar with virtually all of Raven's charming little
plots against her sorority sisters.) The killer—if there *was* a
killer, which I was still almost positive there wasn't—could
even be thinking that the more forthright she was, the less suspect she'd be.

Well, I still had one more girl to talk to. But I didn't antici-
pate that my trip to Jean Brooks's Pennsylvania home on
Monday would turn up any giant revelations, either.

I went back to the promise I'd made to Ellen about proving
Raven's death was an accident. Well, it didn't look as if there
was any way I'd actually be able to *prove* it. But I told myself
that was okay. Any day now, I fully expected the police to
concede that they weren't dealing with a crime here, after all.

When the taxi dropped me off at the restaurant Myron had
suggested, my jaw dropped. No wonder I'd never heard of
Darcy's. It wasn't a restaurant at all; it was a damn coffee
shop!

I was only about ten minutes late, which in my book is practically like being on time. I mean, while I all but kill myself to
be right on the dot for business appointments, I have to admit
that I normally don't feel quite the same degree of pressure
when it comes to anything of a social nature.

At any rate, I walked into the place to find Myron already
seated at one of the little square Formica-topped tables, mop-

ping his face. He broke into a wide grin as soon as he laid eyes
on me.

"I'm glad you got here okay, Miz Shapiro," he told me,
shoving his handkerchief into the pocket of his mustard-
colored slacks and rising politely.

I managed an insipid little return smile before sitting down
to join him. "You sound surprised. And, please, call me Desiree." Much as I might be regretting it, we were, after all, on
a—and the very word was making me cringe now—date.

"It's just that you were so late." I started to dispute this, but
then he went on. "I was afraid you might have changed your
mind."

"Don't be silly," I mumbled. But talk about feeling guilty!

"So-o. How have you been?"

"Fine. Just fine. And you?"

"*Mezzo-mezzo*. That's Italian." (He pronounced it Eyetal-
ian.) "It means *just fair*."

"Yes, I know. Have you been sick?"

"Good and sick, since you're asking. Couldn't even go to
work. I came down with the flu or something on Monday, and
for a coupla days I didn't stop vomiting. Every time I managed
to get something into my stomach, back up it came. And as if
that wasn't enough, I had *some* case of diarrhea. All I'll say
about it is that I was considering moving my bed into the bathroom, heh-heh."

I managed a few sympathetic clucks.

"But enough about that," Myron said.

Amen!

"For a while there, though, I was concerned I might have to
cancel. And I didn't want to do that to you. I know how you
girls are. I figured . . . that is, it occurred to me you might even
have gone out and bought a new dress or something." He was
giving me the once-over. "But I think I've seen that one before, haven't I? You ever bring it into the shop?"

"You cleaned it for me about a month ago."

"Yeah, I thought so. Looks very nice on you." In spite of the
flattering words, he seemed disappointed that I hadn't made an
addition to my wardrobe in honor of the occasion. "Anyway,"
he concluded, "thank God I started to feel better by Wednesday—and so here I am."

"Well, I'm happy to see you." The truth would not have
been nearly as kind.

Now, all the time he'd been talking, Myron's outsized Adam's apple had—in spite of the serious efforts I'd expended to avert my gaze—been drawing my attention like a magnet. So I was very much relieved when the waiter approached and handed me a blessedly large and cumbersome menu.

Burying my head in the thing, I vowed to make the best of the evening. I certainly wasn't going to be deterred from this by a protruding Adam's apple—I have to acknowledge that I'm not exactly Heather Locklear myself. I also didn't intend to let my nose get out of joint because of what I considered a piss-poor choice of location for our little get-together. And by the way, just to set the record straight on that, I want you to know I've had many a decent meal in a coffee shop—only not on a dinner date. (The thing is, too, there wasn't even a place-mat on the table, for heaven's sake! And I'd have settled for one of those flimsy paper jobs, honestly.) Finally—and this was the *real* concession—I was even going to try my damnedest to make believe Myron had never uttered a single syllable regarding vomit or diarrhea.

It didn't take long, though, for my tolerance to be put to the test from another area entirely. As soon as I laid down the menu, I was greeted by the sight of my companion now drip-ping with moisture. And this, despite the fact that the air con-ditioner was turned up so high a fur coat would not have been inappropriate. But after all, I quickly reminded myself, the poor guy couldn't help it if he sweated, could he?

"What's your poison, Desiree?" he asked with a little chuckle, indicating my menu.

"Oh, I'll try the shrimp cocktail to start with, I think. And for an entree, the open steak sandwich with French fries. And I was wondering if maybe you care to split a side dish of the French fried onion rings."

"Those things give me indigestion; they're always so damn greasy." Then getting out his handkerchief again, he wiped off his face. "But listen," he added magnanimously, "you go ahead and order them, if you want to."

"What are you having?"

"A chicken salad sandwich. I'm not a very big eater my-self."

Ouch! There was just enough emphasis on the *myself* to make me wince. Myron obviously had me pegged as a glutton. Probably a gold digger, too—unless, of course, he was planning on our going Dutch. (As I may have mentioned at some time or other, it had been so long since I'd been out with anyone of the male gender that I really didn't know what the protocol was on these things anymore.) That didn't seem too likely, though—the going Dutch, I'm talking about. After all, *he* had invited *me* (and invited me and invited me). What's more, the way I saw it, the prices in this place were so reasonable—*cheap* might have been more descriptive—that Myron had no doubt chosen it to ensure that even if I wound up eating everything but the fixtures, he could still manage the tariff.

"Uh, I hope you don't want a drink, Desiree," he said then.

Funny. At that very moment I was thinking that was *just* what I wanted. I mean, there was always the chance a glass of wine might numb me a little. "Well, as matter of fact—"

"They don't serve liquor here."

No, of course they don't, I realized. "That's okay. I wasn't really in the mood for anything, anyway."

It was right after we ordered that a suddenly emboldened Myron blurted out, "Don't mind my asking, but how come you and your husband got divorced?"

"We didn't. I'm a widow," I clarified for him.

"I was talking to someone—I can't tell you the name—and she was positive your husband left you."

"I don't care *how* positive she was. I'm a widow," I reiterated.

"Me, I'm divorced; it was a year last week." This, accompanied by a slight quiver of the lips. "Happens to the best of us, I guess. Especially these days."

I was spared the necessity to respond, because just then my shrimp cocktail was set before me. There were only four shrimp—although nice large ones, I was pleased to note—but I made the mistake of offering a shrimp to Myron. He helped himself to two.

"It was very hard," he murmured.

"What was very hard?" I asked absently. I was concentrating on the shrimp—they were quite tasty.

"Getting divorced like that."

"Yes, I imagine it was," I concurred, sopping up some of the sauce—which had just the right amount of bite to it—with a cracker.

"You were lucky," he remarked an instant later, "if you're a widow." The *if* was my clue he wasn't convinced.

Well, so what? "I wouldn't exactly call that lucky," I said caustically.

"I didn't mean because you lost your husband. I meant that at least he didn't throw you away."

Uh-oh. I noticed then that Myron's eyes were moist. "Oh, I'm sure that—" I have absolutely no idea what would have come out of my mouth next, but fortunately, I didn't have to proceed.

"Who gets the steak sandwich?" a voice behind me interrupted.

I had just begun to enjoy the steak—it was actually very good—when Myron decided to tuck his napkin up under his chin (and for a chicken salad sandwich, too). For a couple of minutes there, I could barely swallow. And then while I was still in the process of recuperating from that one, he attacked my diminished appetite from another direction, by proceeding to unburden himself about his failed marriage.

Sniffling and wiping his eyes at frequent intervals, he poured out the whole unhappy story, which necessitated my frantically wracking my brain again and again for words of solace. Myron's depression, however, did not prevent him from eating every last crumb on his plate, as well as sharing my fries—uninvited—and consuming a sizable portion of the onion rings for which, only a short while earlier, he had voiced such disdain.

Nevertheless, I really did feel for the man when I heard how dearly he had loved Honey—his ex—and how devastated he had been when she suddenly took off with their doorman, who was half her age.

I tried to be encouraging. "Maybe it won't work out," I suggested. "It's possible that she'll be back."

His head dropped almost to his chest, and he began sniffling in earnest now. "No, she won't," he told me, the words barely intelligible. A few moments later he looked up at me, his face a study in anguish. I couldn't tell whether all that wetness on his cheeks was the result of grief or perspiration. But he swiped at whatever it was with his forearm, following which he tore his napkin from his shirt collar and blew his nose into it three or four times. Then he provided an update.

"They got married last month," he said, "and Honey's expecting a baby in October. She never wanted one when *we* were together." At this point, Myron put both arms flat on the table, buried his head in them, and sobbed. And at a fairly decent volume, too.

Mortified, I surveyed the room. There were five other occupied tables, and I caught the people at every one of them turning quickly away. They looked almost as self-conscious as I felt.

Anyhow, after that emotional outpouring, Myron was not up to ordering dessert—naturally. But he still appropriated a liberal chunk of my pecan pie, glomming up almost all of the whipped cream in the process.

As soon as *we'd* demolished *my* pie, I went into this little spiel about what a busy day I'd had and, in fact, what a terribly hectic week it had been, making it clear that I couldn't remember when I'd been so completely exhausted.

Taking the hint, Myron called for the check.

"I'll chip in with you," I said when it arrived. I thought I should at least make the offer, although I was a little concerned it might offend him.

It didn't. "Oh, that's not really necessary," he protested weakly. So weakly that I felt compelled to make the offer again.

"It's okay," I told him. "How much do I owe you?"

"All right, if you insist . . ." he acquiesced, hastily extracting a ballpoint from the pocket of his Hawaiian shirt. Then he leaned over to the empty table next to us and grabbed a clean paper napkin.

"Well, you *did* have a bigger dinner," he reminded me before putting the pen to the napkin. And then: "Now, let's see. You started with . . ."

Chapter 21

The sound seemed to be coming from very far away. I tried to ignore it, smothering my face in the pillow. But it was becoming more and more demanding, unbearably shrill now. Reluctantly, I dragged myself awake and slowly opened one eye at a time. Then reaching out for the telephone that sat on my night table, I squinted at the clock alongside it. I saw that it was 8:30—A.M., that is. Not early enough to make me worry that this was a dire emergency of some kind, but way too early for a Saturday morning communication. As far as I was concerned, anyhow.

I mumbled a passable facsimile of hello into the receiver and was rewarded for this effort with a "Hi, Desiree" in a disgustingly cheerful male voice.

Oh, no! I recognized that voice instantly. It was the property of Diamond Jim himself. "Myron?" I asked the question automatically.

"Yeah. I was just about to hang up. I hope I didn't wake you—I waited until a decent hour." A little chuckle. "Or I should say what I thought was a decent hour."

"That's okay. I guess it was time to get up anyway." It was about as gracious as I was able to manage.

"I called to tell you what a wonderful time I had last night."

I didn't know how to respond. On the one hand, I didn't want to be unkind. But on the other, I didn't want to offer the man any encouragement. No. At all costs, I had to avoid encouragement. "I enjoyed myself, too," I said after a brief interval—but with zero enthusiasm.

Apparently, Myron opted to take the words at face value. "I'm really glad to hear that." I could just picture the toothy smile now, and it was not the sort of thing one should be exposed to before her morning coffee. "Listen," he went on, "as

long as we both had such a good time, why don't we do it
again?"

My stomach flipped over. "Uh, well, I'm—"

"I thought maybe we could go out Sunday. You know, make
a whole day of it."

"I'm really sorry, Myron, but I already have plans for Sunday."

"I could work something out for tonight, I guess, if that's better for you. I'm supposed to be going to my sister's, but—"

"Tonight's no good, either. I have theater tickets."

"What about next weekend? How's Saturday night?"

God, it's rough being a man trap! "I'm going to be away the
entire weekend. A friend of mine invited me to her summer
house in the Poconos."

"You're a busy lady, aren't you?" Myron commented casu-
ally. He didn't appear in the least discouraged. "I'll tell you
what. You just name the day you're free, and whenever it is,
that's when we'll get together." He seemed to hesitate before
pulling out his ace in the hole: "And the next time, dinner'll be
on me."

"Oh, that's not—"

"Listen, don't give it a thought. It'll be my pleasure."

There was no escaping it. I had to make myself permanently
unavailable. I quickly scanned my malfunctioning brain for a
plausible out and settled for: "I guess I should have mentioned
this before, but I've kind of been seeing someone." (I know, I
know. But it was the best I could come up with on such short
8:30 A.M. notice.) I realized the second I spoke, though, just how
lame this sounded, so I immediately embellished a bit, hoping
that this would somehow give the lie the ring of truth. "Umm,
we sort of broke up for a while, Andrew and I"—I've always
had a fondness for the name Andrew—"but then he called on
Thursday night, and we decided to see if we could work things
out. I suppose I should have canceled our date then—yours and
mine, I mean—but it was so last-minute that I felt awkward
about it. Anyway, I hope you understand."

"Sure I understand," Myron retorted, his tone close to strident. "What I understand is, you're handing me some cock-and-
bull story."

"Oh no, I—"

"Look, Desiree, give me a little credit, will you? I'm not stupid, you know."

"I didn't—"

"If you don't want to go out with me anymore, just say so, and I won't bother you again. I'm a big boy now; I can take it, believe me. All I'm asking you for is a little honesty."

At that, my mouth went completely dry. He was right, of course. He was entitled to honesty—or as much of it as I dared provide without making mincemeat of the man's ego. "I'm really sorry, Myron," I said gently, "and I don't blame you for being angry. I *should* have leveled with you. I guess I was just making things easier on myself." I drew upon whatever meager amount of spine I possess and forged ahead. "Uh, the fact is, I think you're a terrific person; I really do. But, well—" I broke off, groping for the words that would inflict the minimal amount of damage. "What I want to say," I tried again, "is that it has nothing to do with you—you're extremely nice. But, umm, the thing is . . . uh . . . I don't think we're really compatible."

Whew! I wouldn't have been surprised if at that moment I felt a lot worse than Myron did. But at least it was over and done with.

Or so I thought.

"How can you say that?" Myron demanded. "You hardly know me." And a second or two later: "Listen, why don't we give it one more shot? You owe me *that* much, anyway."

A short while afterward I was sitting at the kitchen table, holding my coffee cup with wet, trembling hands. I could have given my erstwhile admirer plenty of competition in the perspiration department just then. I mean, the man had really made me squirm. It had taken three turndowns—each a little firmer than the last—before he finally slammed down the phone. For once, however, that despicable sound—which normally makes my teeth ache—was like music to my ears. And while right now I was feeling a little sad, a little shook, and more than a little damp, I was also very much relieved.

And then the worst part of the entire Myron business suddenly hit me: I'd have to find myself another dry cleaner!

I was wondering if I should give that place on Second Avenue another try—they hadn't done such a great job on my yellow dress the only time I'd ever been in there—when the phone rang.

"Hello there, stranger," trilled my good friend Pat Martucci, formerly Altmann, formerly Green, formerly Anderson.

"Hello yourself," I responded somewhat testily. "Where have you been lately, anyway?"

"Been?"

"I left about three messages on your machine in the last few weeks."

"Oh, Dez, I'm *so* sorry I didn't get back to you. I intended to, honestly. Every night I said to myself, 'I'm going to give Dez a call tomorrow.' But—I don't know—the next day something would come up, and I'd tell myself I'd call you the day after *that*. In my own defense, though, I *have* been really swamped at the office. And then after work, of course, there's Burton. You know how it gets when you're involved with someone."

Sure I did. How it gets for Pat, anyway. All of her loves—and they have been many and frequent—have ranked as nothing less than *the* love of her life. And when she's caught up in her affair du jour, she tends to put the world on hold. As for my own involvements, they were so far back I could barely remember the name of the involvee, much less anything relevant about my behavior.

"You forgive me, don't you?" Pat was saying in this wheedling, little-girl tone she sometimes affects.

I refused to let it get me as crazy as it usually did. "There's nothing to forgive. I just wish you'd make contact a little more often so I'd know you're okay."

"I'm not just *okay*, I'm wonderful!" she declared excitedly. "Burton and I are—well, sensational together. In fact, I'm sure that he's going to be making a real commitment to me any day now."

"Pat!" I squealed. "Are you telling me you two are getting married?"

Most of the excitement dissipated then. "I wasn't talking about marriage," she replied evenly. "I meant that I'm expecting Burton to ask me to move in with him. Which is really what I prefer—and that's the truth. After all, none of my ventures into matrimony was exactly a glorious success. The important thing is Burton's willingness to commit to the relationship." And an instant later, somewhat uncertainly: "Don't you think?"

Damn! Leave it to me to deflate her like that. For the second time that morning, I tried my hand at damage control. "What's important is that you're happy," I answered. And then I put in for good measure: "And you're a hundred percent right. It's the willingness to commit that counts."

"Absolutely. And anyway," she confessed, "I look like shit in white."

We both laughed, following which Pat informed me that Burton had just flown out to California that morning for his aunt's funeral. "He'll be gone until tomorrow evening," she said. "And I thought if you didn't have any plans, maybe we could take in a movie later."

"It happens there's just been a cancellation on my social calendar."

"Good. I'm in luck then. Well, I won't keep you any longer. There'll be plenty of time to do our catching up tonight." Which meant I could expect to be getting an earful on the many virtues of Burton Wizniak.

But I really didn't mind. I was glad things were going well for Pat now. And it's not that I'm so selfless, either. Sure I'd have liked to be in a serious relationship of my own, but that had nothing to do with her. Besides, I'm okay with taking out my own garbage forever, if I have to. What I mean is, I don't *require* anyone. Not so Pat. She's one of those women who couldn't exist without a man in her life—not for very long, anyhow. So I was actually relieved that she'd found someone to care for again.

We met in front of the theater at 7:30. There was a crowd milling around the box office, but I spotted Pat at once. A large woman both vertically and horizontally, she's pretty impossible to overlook. I've always maintained that with her blond hair and very ample bosom, it would just take a braid—and a decent singing voice, of course—and she'd be the perfect prototype for Brunhilde or one of those other Amazonic Wagnerian heroines. At any rate, I spent the next couple of hours fidgeting through a Steven Seagal movie, being that Pat loves Steven Seagal and there wasn't anything I particularly wanted to see. And then afterward we went to this new pasta restaurant on Third Avenue, where, as I'd anticipated, a good part of the dinner conversation centered around the sublime Burton, his matchless character, and indisputable sex appeal.

We were just finishing our coffee when Pat's hand suddenly flew to her cheek. "Oh, am I an idiot!" she exclaimed.

"You won't get any argument from me," I joked. "But what, precisely, makes you say that?"

"I've got something to tell you. I meant to tell you about it this morning, and then it slipped my mind. And now I almost forgot again."

"What did you almost forget?"

"You remember Brian—Burton's cousin from Chicago— don't you?" she asked, referring to this horrendous blind date she had arranged for me a few months earlier, which in the end had turned out to be not so horrendous after all. "Yes, of course you do," she answered for me.

"You're right," I told her dryly, "I certainly do remember Brian. Only his name is Bruce."

"You're kidding." Pat's not very big on names. "But anyway," she continued, unfazed, "I thought you might like to know that the reason you haven't heard from him is that he still hasn't gotten here." (Bruce was scheduled to be transferred to his company's New York office not long after our date.)

"Oh?"

"That's right. Something about his first having to finish up this project he's been working on. Burton mentioned it the other night. He says Bruce—that *is* his name, isn't it?—is winding things up, though. He could be making the move any day now."

"Well, thanks for telling me, Pat. But it's not exactly like I've been waiting for his call." (Which was not precisely true.) "To be frank, I'm not even sure I'd want to go out with him." (Which was, in fact, quite true.) I was, as you can gather, very ambiguous in my feelings toward the man.

"Why not, for Christ's sake?"

"Because he's rude and nasty and—"

"And sexy. Don't forget sexy." Sexy is definitely a top priority with my friend Pat.

"I wouldn't say he was sexy." Even physically, Bruce wasn't my type. But still, there *was* something about him. I had no inclination to concede this, however.

"Well, *I'd* certainly call him sexy," Pat countered. "And he's also very bright."

That much I'd give her. "You've got me there," I admitted. When Bruce and I had finally buried the hatchet that evening, the conversation turned out to be quite stimulating. Even fun.

"If you don't go out with him again, you're out of your mind."

"I'll think about it—if and when the time comes."

"It'll come," Pat predicted. "You wait and see."

Suddenly I got this funny little flutter in one of the more private parts of my anatomy. And I couldn't figure out why. I mean, like I said, Bruce Simon wasn't my type at all.

Chapter 22

On Sunday I forced myself to clean the apartment—I'm talking *really* clean it. And right on the heels of that I had to rely on still more coercion, this time to get myself to take on the job that held duel honors (along with scrubbing out the toilet bowl) for my most despised chore of all. As a result, I was soon digging into the ironing basket to tackle the two months' worth of hideously crinkled clothes that lay in wait for me.

After I was through with all that scouring and dusting and pressing, I was more worn out than my lavender print dress—which, I discovered, was practically threadbare now. So when Harriet Gould called with an invitation to come in for dinner, necessity mandated that I decline. Thanks to this sudden burst of fastidiousness, I could barely make it into my own kitchen, much less all the way across the hall. In fact, after I'd finished with supper, I sat at the table for an extra fifteen minutes before I felt I'd regained sufficient strength for a trek back to the living room—where I could sit some more.

As soon as I plopped down on the sofa, I switched on the TV remote. After catching what was left of *Sixty Minutes*, I settled in for what was, for me, anyway, another irritating but addictive episode of *Murder She Wrote*. Half annoyed and half envious, I watched my old friend Jessica Fletcher just about *divine* the solution to the publishing executive's brutal murder—and then talk the killer into confessing the whole dirty deed. As she always did. Oh, if only I could, even once in my life, find such a cooperative murderer. Well, this time, at least, I wouldn't have to worry about that. After all, it was highly unlikely that Jean Brooks would have anything more revealing to disclose than her sorority sisters did. And in the absence of even one iota of evidence to the contrary, I could finally rule Raven Eber's untimely death an accident—to my own satisfaction, at any rate. Which was precisely what I'd been hoping to do all along.

Then why was I suddenly feeling so uneasy just thinking about it?

I didn't sleep much that night. Thoroughly exhausted, I had gone to bed before 12:00 (a practically unheard-of occurrence) and then proceeded to toss myself around for hours. It really surprised me. Given the condition I was in, I should have conked out as soon as my head made contact with the pillow. *No doubt all that physical exertion just didn't agree with you* was how I eventually rationalized this exasperating wakefulness.

Before dropping off sometime before 3:00 I remembered to threaten Charmaine in absentia. *If you don't put in an appearance soon,* I told her, *I'll have to find myself another cleaning woman.* She probably didn't take me seriously, though.

It was weird. At some point during those many sleepless hours, I'd gotten this strong premonition that my meeting with Jean Brooks would be different from the others, that—like it or not—this time I *would* learn something. So it was with a kind of fear-tinged excitement that I set out for Millville, the small Pennsylvania city where Jean made her home.

The weather was beautiful that morning—not too warm and with a lovely, cooling breeze. I kept the car windows open wide, confident that not even one small strand of my glorious hennaed hair would be disturbed. After all, when you spritz on half a can of extra-extra-hold, you *should* feel secure.

Jean and I had arranged that I'd be at her house at about 12:30, and it wasn't even ten of twelve when I arrived in Millville Center. I drove around looking for somewhere suitable to kill a half hour or so. You see, as much as I knock myself out not to be late for a business appointment, personal experience has convinced me that turning up early is at least a hundred times worse. (I can't tell you how uptight I get when the doorbell summons me while I still have only one foot in my panty hose. Or more aggravating yet, before I've even had time to draw on my eyebrows.)

The three- or four-block area comprising the city's hub consisted mainly of inexpensive retail shops and moderately priced restaurants, along with a movie theater and a couple of office buildings. None of the structures here appeared to be less than thirty or forty years old, but everything looked well kept and in decent repair. There was, I thought, a sort of blue-collar feel to the place—not flashy, but solid and respectable.

At any rate, halfway down the second block, I spotted a McDonald's. Being predisposed to such judgments that day, I considered it an omen that there was a parking space almost directly in front of the place. I really felt I had no choice; I *had to* stop off for a Big Mac and a large order of fries. The fact that I was hungry hardly entered into things.

Thirty-six Morton Drive was one of a tract of eight or ten modest two-family town houses on a quiet, tree-lined street.

The door opened even before I rang the buzzer. "I was watching from the window," Jean Brooks explained.

She was the tallest of the girls I'd met with—at least five nine—and solidly built. Her most outstanding feature was her hair, which was light brown and wavy and extended almost to her waist. There was something about her expression—it struck me as thoughtful; contemplative, really—which, when coupled with the thick wire-rimmed glasses she wore, led me to peg her as the intellectual member of the group. Even her very brief navy shorts and navy-and-white tube top didn't detract from that impression, nor, I decided glancing down, did the lavender rubber beach thongs. It actually took a minute or two before I realized that wrapped around Jean's substantial, well-toned legs, and almost hidden from view, was this tiny person who was peeking timidly up at me with oversized dark eyes.

"I've heard so much about you. It's really a pleasure to meet you," Jean said after I'd introduced myself. "Please. Come on in." She held the door open wider.

Once inside the vestibule, I knelt down to address the tiny person. "And who might you be?" I asked in my perkiest, most nonthreatening manner. Said tiny person—I couldn't even determine if it was a boy or girl—immediately vanished behind its mother's legs.

"This is my daughter Cornelia," Jean told me. "We call her Corny."

"Oh, that's a *darling* name," I gushed, addressing myself to Jean's left leg, which was now encircled by small, tanned arms. "And how old are you, Corny?"

Not a word. Not a sound.

"I think I may have frightened her," I mumbled apologetically. "She's very shy isn't she?"

Jean laughed. "Not once she gets used to you, she isn't. It takes Corny a while to warm up, that's all."

"How old is she?" I asked. She could have been anywhere from one to ten, for all I know about kids.

"She'll be four next month, won't you, Corny?" Jean responded, glancing over her shoulder at the back of her legs. "But look, let's not stand here. Let's go into the living room and sit down."

Dragging her extra appendage with her, she led the way into what was, without exception, the messiest room I've ever seen.

Listen. I know that children have to express themselves and all that, but this was ridiculous. Toys, books, crayons, and drawings were strewn everywhere. There was even a large rubber swimming pool, empty at present, near the entrance to the room. Colorful scribblings decorated one of the walls. While Scotch-taped to two of the others—almost on top of each other—were lined notebooks pages covered with additional artwork. The fourth wall was brick, with a fireplace at its center. And in the hearth, lying on its side right next to a snoutless and one-eyed Miss Piggy, was an extremely large dollhouse, miniature furnishings scattered all around it.

"Sit down," Jean said, waving me toward a worn and soiled blue corduroy sofa.

I stepped over the remnants of the chocolate lollipop that was stuck to the area rug I was standing on and quickly obliged. Jean's anguished, "No, wait!" came too late to prevent me from depositing my posterior atop a half-eaten Yankee Doodle.

"I'm so sorry," she murmured as she was brushing me off. "I'd better get a damp rag." She firmly detached her child, who immediately reattached herself.

"No, don't bother. It needs a good cleaning anyway," I assured her of my cream-colored linen dress, which, in truth, was actually having its first outing since being rehabilitated two weeks ago by my now former dry cleaner, Myron.

"I'm very sorry," she said again, tossing a stuffed animal off one of the two shoddy navy armchairs facing the sofa. Eyeing the dirty, mangled elephant she'd just displaced, she sighed.

"Ever since Corny was able to crawl, I've been trying to get her to put her things in that toy chest"—she indicated a large wooden box in a corner of the room—"but, as you can see . . ." Making a face, she shook her head. "Listen, can I get you something? Some iced coffee maybe? Or if you're hungry, there's some tuna salad in the fridge."

"Thank you, but I just ate," I told her, sitting back down on the sofa—but only after scrutinizing the target area twice.

"You're sure?" As soon as I nodded, she once again separated her daughter from the rest of her. Then she took the seat vacated by the pathetic-looking elephant and hoisted the child onto her lap. I saw now that Corny was dressed in a yellow halter outfit and that there was a matching yellow ribbon tying back her shoulder-length blond hair. It made me think of Raven, and for a brief moment, I was terribly and inexplicably sad.

"What is it you wanted to know?" Jean asked, as she absent-mindedly patted the bare back of her progeny, who was now burrowing her face into her mother's shoulder.

"Whatever you can tell me."

"About Raven?"

"About Raven, about the weekend, about anything."

"Where do you want me to start?"

"How about starting with the invitation. I'm sure you know about the invitation Raven received."

"Yes, of course. But I can't tell you who sent it. It really bugs me, too—not knowing."

Now, even though this was the kind of response I'd been accepting with equanimity all along, at that instant it just got to me. Maybe it was because this silly premonition of mine had primed me to expect something more. Or maybe I was suddenly up to here with that same old story. I mean, all of these girls had sat in front of me—the way Jean was doing just then—impressing me with their candor. And one of them, for whatever reason, had been lying through her teeth. Could be Jean Brooks was that one.

"Look," I snapped, "so far everyone's denied knowing a thing about that invitation. But one of you *did* send it. And it's what brought Raven to the party." Then I threw in—mostly, I suspect, to be perverse—"And very likely got her killed!"

"Well, I can't help you," a now far-from-friendly Jean informed me tartly. "All I can say is that it wasn't me. And what do you mean, anyway, by 'very likely got her killed'? I understood you regarded her death as an accident, just like the rest of us."

I did some spur-of-the-moment plotting. "That *was* true— until very recently. But something's come to my attention, and I'm not at all sure about that anymore."

"You mean you think it was *murder*?"

"I think it could very well be."

She seemed almost dazed by the thought. "Oh, I never believed . . ." Her voice trailed off. A minute later, however, she was sufficiently recovered to glower at me. "Listen, I don't know why one of my friends would have sent her that thing, but I can tell you this much: It wasn't so they could push her off any balcony. Not that the little shit didn't deserve it. Cover your ears, Corny."

Corny, her face still embedded in her mother's shoulder, immediately obeyed this tardy instruction—for all of a second or two. But the action seemed to mobilize her. As soon as she removed her palms from her ears, she sneaked a quick look at me and apparently came to the decision that I wasn't so threatening, after all. At least, not threatening enough to require her to remain in hiding forever. Sliding off her mother's lap, she ran to retrieve the coloring book and crayons lying on the floor (where else?) about three yards from the sofa. Following which she deposited herself at Jean's feet, her back very deliberately facing me.

"Let me ask you this," I said to Jean, attempting to repair our little rift by employing the most ingratiating voice I could muster. "Do you happen to know if any of your sorority sisters visited Raven in her room after the party?"

"I'd be willing to swear none of them did. Nobody wanted to have anything to do with her. And to spare you the trouble of asking, I myself went straight to bed once the festivities were over."

Oh, what the hell! "Well, uh, that's not what I was told. There's someone who claims to have seen you entering the dead girl's bedroom late Friday night. Would you mind telling me why you went there?"

"That's bullshit!" an incensed Jean retorted. "And whoever said it's a lying shit! A son of a bitch, lying shit!" *Did I say she was the intellectual one in the group?* "Cover your ears, Corny," she ordered hastily.

Dropping her crayons, Corny once again went through the

pretense of attempting to block the offending words from her hearing.

I managed to keep the grin inside me. But it took real effort.

"Who was it?" Jean demanded.

"I'm afraid I can't tell you that."

"What do you *mean* you can't tell me!" Her face had turned almost purple, and I was concerned that at any moment the girl might have apoplexy.

"I'm sorry; I gave my word. But please don't upset yourself. To be honest, I didn't really place that much stock in the thing." It was time for a little further improvising. "Actually, the person who came to me with the story did say that it was pretty dark in the hallway and that she couldn't be absolutely positive it was you."

"Well, all right," Jean mumbled petulantly after some brief consideration. "But that wasn't the way you put it to me before." She still didn't look any too happy, but at least her color was normal again. "I really think I'm entitled to know who it was anyhow, though," she groused.

There was no way I could oblige her, of course, so I said, "I'm sure it was a case of mistaken identity." And then I quickly headed for safer ground. "Listen, I wonder if you'd mind telling me what sort of trouble you had with Raven when you were at Walden together."

"I'm afraid I can't do that."

"I'm just trying to get a complete picture of what she was really like." Jean was looking at me without expression. Well, I could blame my own stupid lies for that! I wasn't about to give up, however. "Uh, the others were all very forthcoming," I cajoled.

She shook her head determinedly.

"But—"

"I can't do that," Jean said at last, "because I never *had* any trouble with Raven back in college."

And with that, her lips curved in a mischievous smile.

Chapter 23

She sat back in her chair, looking much too smug for my taste. "Well, you certainly had me going," I conceded. I was even gracious enough to summon up a little chuckle to accompany the admission. "But how about after you graduated? Did Raven cause any problems for you then?"

"I'd use a stronger word than 'problems,' but the answer is yes," Jean responded, suddenly turning serious. "Only it was a long, long time after graduation."

"She was okay with you all through school, though?" I persisted, still somewhat surprised by this information.

"To tell you the truth, I never had that much to do with her when we were in college. I didn't join Kappa Gam until I was a sophomore, and I didn't begin living at the sorority house until the middle of my junior year."

"You roomed off campus until then?"

"I commuted. My hometown wasn't much more than a half hour's drive from Walden, so I couldn't see any reason for boarding at the house. But Sybil finally convinced me I was missing something—this rah-rah campus life and all that. Ironic, isn't it? A couple of months after she talked me into moving in, she moved out."

"That was when she left school?"

Jean nodded. "Thanks to that phony cheating business. You heard about it, I suppose."

"Yes. Sybil told me."

"What a crock," she muttered.

"You and Sybil were very close, I take it."

"We still are. Ever since we were in the same freshman psych class. She introduced me to the others: Ellen and Winnie and Carol Sue and, of course"—now venom entered her tone and she spat out the word—"Raven."

"But you didn't spend much time with Raven. Is that right?"

"That's right. Or with Carol Sue, either, for that matter. Not that I had anything against Carol Sue—or even Raven, in the beginning. We just didn't pal around together."

"Tell me what happened between you and Raven *after* you got out of school."

"I had the goddamn luck to run into her again a couple of years ago—at a cocktail party in Manhattan. Corny and I were in the city visiting a cousin of mine, and she—my cousin Mickey—dragged me along to this awful *thing* she'd been invited to. You know the kind of thing I'm talking about: where about a hundred people are crammed into a teeny weeny apartment trying their damnedest to look like they're having a good time and make clever conversation over an absolutely incredible din. Mickey and I were just getting ready to cut out when I turned around, and there, waltzing in the door, was Raven Eber. God! If only she'd walked in five minutes later. Or if we'd gotten the fuck out of there—cover your ears, Corny—five minutes earlier."

I glanced down. Now, that was a well-trained child.

"At any rate," Jean went on, "she spotted me before we had a chance to leave, and she came right over and greeted me like I was her long-lost buddy. She even hugged me, for Christ's sake!"

"That must have been awkward for you."

"It was. But not as much as I'd have thought. Raven had always made my skin crawl—at least, once that thing happened with Sybil. But it was so long ago that I guess a lot of the hostility had worn off by then."

"So you were friendly to her at the party?"

"It hadn't *all* worn off," Jean protested. "No, I wouldn't say I was friendly, but I didn't cut her dead, either. Raven acted like she was positively *thrilled* to see me again, though—she knew how to turn it on, believe me. She suggested we go out for coffee, so we could catch up on each other—you could barely hear yourself think in that place. Well, I wasn't exactly dying to spend any time with her, so I told her I had to get back to Mickey's because I'd left Corny there with a sitter. Which, incidentally, was true enough. But then Mickey popped up and said I didn't have to rush back, that she'd go home and take care of the sitter. She was under the impression I really wanted to visit with Raven, you see."

"It doesn't sound as though that left you much choice."

"Yeah, I guess," Jean concurred with a flick of her shoulder. "Anyway, we went to this luncheonette in the neighborhood there, and Raven started right off by saying that she knew I resented her because of what happened with Sybil but that it had all been a horrible mistake. She swore up and down she didn't plant those crib notes in Sybil's jacket, that someone else must have done it after she returned the jacket to the room. She told me that no matter what she said, though, she could never get Sybil to believe that."

"She was criticizing Sybil, then?"

"Oh, no," Jean scoffed. "Raven was too smart to risk alienating me by doing anything of the sort. She made it sound as if they'd both been victims. And then she fed me this crap about how some of the other girls wouldn't even speak to her after the Sybil thing and how she was still grateful to me for being so civil to her."

"Was that true? Were you civil to her?"

"Not the way I remembered it, I wasn't. In fact, I thought I pretty much ignored her. Maybe I grunted a hello or something when I saw her; that was about the extent of it. But since I'd never had a lot to say to her in the first place, I figured it could be that she wasn't even aware I'd cooled off."

"How about Carol Sue?"

Tilting her head to one side, Jean frowned. "I don't follow you."

No wonder. She would have needed a road map! "I can't exactly blame you; I can barely follow myself sometimes," I admitted sheepishly. "What I meant was, how did you react to Raven after Carol Sue was attacked?"

She thought for a moment. "About the same, I suppose. I didn't get too caught up in that mess. At the beginning of my senior year I met Danny Brooks, who eventually became my husband. And right away we started spending practically every spare minute together, so I wasn't very tuned in to what was going on in the house."

"But you were *aware* of what happened to Carol Sue?"

"Naturally. It was just that I was so self-involved in those days that . . ." Breaking off, she smiled ruefully.

"How long were you and Raven in the luncheonette?" I asked then, eager to get back to the more recent past.

"I don't know. Probably an hour or thereabouts."

"And you decided, you and Raven, to keep in touch after that?"

"Oh, no. When we said good night, I figured that was that. It wasn't like I was looking to get friendly with her or anything—that was the last thing I wanted. Although I have to admit that she did manage to make me feel kind of sorry for her. Even after all these years, she couldn't seem to forget how she'd been treated at Walden. 'Like a leper' is what she said."

"You didn't think she'd brought it on herself?"

"Yes, of course, I did," Jean replied hastily. And then a deep flush spread rapidly from her neck all the way to her forehead as she made a confession. "Look, I still thought Raven had set Sybil up. But there'd never been any real proof, you know, so there was no way of being sure. Not *absolutely* sure, anyhow. There was always the chance Sybil could have been mistaken about Raven's being the one. Or, at any rate, that's what flashed through my mind—if only for a minute."

I began phrasing another question in my head, but I was preempted. "And as for the Carol Sue thing, even way back then I wondered how everyone had come to the conclusion it was Raven who was responsible for that story. Right at the start it occurred to me that maybe she was being blamed because she was such a likely candidate. As a result of the incident with Sybil, I'm talking about."

"Did—"

But Jean still wasn't through explaining away the conflicting feelings she'd experienced during this meeting with her old sorority sister. Feelings she no doubt regarded as disloyal to her friends. "Listen, I don't know if I'm making myself clear," she put in anxiously. "It wasn't that I really believed what Raven told me—in fact, far from it. But I had to admit to myself that there was at least a *chance* they'd been bum raps. Both of them."

I mumbled something about how that was possible and then for the second time, I prodded her into leaving the Walden era behind us. "I gather you saw Raven again after bumping into her in New York."

"Yes, to my everlasting grief. One afternoon a few months later, I was working at home—I solicit customers for this new long-distance phone service, and I've been doing pretty well at it, too. But anyhow, I'd just called it quits for the day when I got this call from Raven. She said she was going to be in the area that weekend and could she take me to lunch. Well, like I said before, I didn't want to have any sort of relationship with the woman, but somehow or other—and I still can't figure out how she did it—she wheedled me into agreeing to see her. Christ! I even wound up preparing a meal for that bitch!"

I checked out the child on the floor again. This time the little hands had sprung into action even before the anticipated admonition. But Jean provided it anyway, following which she continued her narrative.

"I couldn't leave my daughter alone, of course," she explained, "and I didn't feel like springing for a sitter. Not for Raven, I didn't. And so . . ." She contorted her mouth into something that was intended to resemble a smile. "I've never met anyone who could manipulate people the way Raven could. I wish I had her talent."

"No you don't."

"You're right—I guess." Now she managed a genuine grin. And a moment later: "Where was I? Oh, yes. I made lunch for us. And, boy, did she get mileage out of that lunch! What I mean is, she kept telling me over and over again how much she loved my eggplant quiche. She even pretended to like the Caesar salad, which if you want the truth, was soggy as hell.

"I have to tell you, *nobody* had ever complimented my cooking like that—not with a straight face. In fact, Danny used to say he'd never have married me if I'd made a meal for him beforehand. Anyway—and I'm embarrassed to admit this—I lapped it up. I can't understand how I could have been such a jackass! What is it they say: 'Flattery will get you everywhere'? Well, I guess if you're non compos mentis, it will. At any rate, pretty soon Raven got on the Walden kick again and started talking about how awful those last couple of years had been for her. And she said she'd never forget me for not joining in with the rest of the pack to crucify her. She got me to the point where I didn't know what I believed anymore.

"And then all of a sudden, and I'm not sure how she worked her way around to it, but she was telling me about this new silver mining stock that had just recently gone public. Raven was a broker—in case no one mentioned it to you." She paused to look at me inquiringly.

"Yes, I heard that."

"She said she had it on the best authority that this stock was going to go through the roof, and she said that there was still time to get in on the ground floor. She went on and on about what a wonderful opportunity it was."

I shook my head sadly. "And you bit."

"And I bit," Jean confirmed disgustedly. "Danny had left me some money—he died two and a half years ago from a brain embolism. It wasn't a fortune, by any means, but it did give us a little security, Corny and me. Before long, though, Raven had me thinking that if I kept the money in the bank, I'd be doing my daughter a disservice. She told me I owed it to Corny's future to see to it that the money worked harder for us. The bitch had me all but convinced that by not going into the stock market, I was committing child abuse, for Christ's sake! And this mining stock was practically a sure thing, she said. Plus she'd be monitoring it very closely, so in case by some remote chance anything did go wrong, she'd get me right out."

Jean sighed then—a long, drawn-out sigh. "The punch line is that before the afternoon was over, I'd agreed to let her invest fifteen thousand dollars for me. I guess I should be glad I didn't turn the whole thirty thousand over to her. I'm surprised now I showed that much sense."

She leaned forward in her chair at this point, elbow on her knee, chin cupped in her hand. "You know what makes me *particularly* stupid, though?"

I waited for her to tell me.

"When we were at Walden, I used to say to myself that if I were Raven, I wouldn't stay in that sorority house a second longer. Would you—if you knew everyone in the place despised you? I remember thinking that there had to be something . . . well . . . not quite *normal* about the girl to put herself through something like that."

I nodded, my mind returning to what Dick Eber had told me about his sister's compulsive need to prove herself. "But—and you yourself said it before—that was a long time ago," I reminded her.

"You don't understand," Jean shot back angrily, the anger, I realized, directed not at me but at herself. "It even popped into my head when we went out for coffee that night and she talked about how miserably unhappy she'd been at college. I just kind of brushed the thought away then, but it must have been stored in my subconscious somewhere anyway. So, tell me, why would I go ahead and invest my money with someone like that?" And she tapped her finger to her forehead by way of answering the question she'd posed.

I was anxious to learn more of the story and, at the same time, put an end to all of this second guessing of Jean's, which, I was afraid, might at any moment reduce her to tears. So attempting to move her along, I said what was painfully obvious: "I presume the stock didn't do well."

"*Do* well? It kept dropping and dropping and dropping. Eventually the company went bankrupt."

"I'm so sorry," I murmured.

"You haven't heard the best part yet," she informed me, speaking almost with relish now as she began working up steam. "Right after I made the investment, I mentioned it to this friend of mine who sort of follows the market, which I never did—I suppose that's what made me such a terrific patsy. And a few weeks later, Clarice—my friend—called to let me know that the stock was taking a beating, and she thought that maybe I should get out before things got any worse. She suggested I check with my broker—in a hurry's what she said.

"Well naturally, I got in touch with Raven immediately, but she assured me I didn't have to worry, that all of the experts predicted the company would turn around. And then she said that, anyway, it didn't make sense to sell at that point, that I'd be taking too much of a loss."

"And you went along with her advice."

"Yes, but I started monitoring the stock myself after that. And I saw that it just kept on going down. But every time I phoned Raven about it, she insisted the company would bounce back again—when she'd *deign* to take my call, that is. She kept promising I'd still end up making money on that junk, that I should just wait and see. And then she'd give me that same old bullshit about how decent I'd been to her at Walden and that she'd never recommend anything to me that she didn't have the utmost faith in. She even went into this song and dance about how she just *loved* Corny and that she wouldn't do anything to jeopardize her interests. And I have to admit the two of them *had* hit it off that day. You know Little Miss Can't-Look-You-In-The-Face here? She ended up calling that bitcho supremo *Aunt* Raven and sitting on her lap. Other people it takes my kid forever to warm up to, but not Raven." And then, bestowing a wry look on her offspring, she observed, "Seems like she inherited her character judgment from her mother, doesn't it?"

"Is it . . . what I mean is, is there any possibility that Raven might have just miscalculated?" I ventured then, steeling myself for the response.

It came out in the form of a harsh laugh, following which Jean spoke with what little patience she could muster. "No, there is not. Raven had a pretty good idea of just where that stock was heading when she talked me into it. And how do I know? Because, for your information, she'd gotten her brother to invest in the same stock. Only she made sure *he* unloaded it—right before she convinced me to buy."

I gasped. "You're positive?"

"Winnie'll tell you."

"But why? Why would she do something like that?"

"Because all that bullshit about how nice I was to her in college? That's exactly what it was—bullshit. She felt I *had* slighted her in those days, and now it was payback time."

"She *told* you that?"

"Don't be silly. It's the truth, and Raven was allergic to the truth. But that's why she did it. I don't have the slightest doubt about it."

"Did you ever bring all of this up to her?"

"You bet your life! I went to her office and made a big stink, so everyone in the place could hear what a rotten, lowlife, swindling bitch she was. She denied she did anything wrong—just like I expected her to. She told me"—and Jean's tone became almost saccharine here, apparently to mimic the dead girl's—"'it was a *terribly, terribly* unfortunate occurrence.'

"*Unfortunate*, my potootie! Naturally, her story was that there was no way she could have predicted anything like that when she sold me that junk. And of course, she said she felt just awful about how things had turned out." Now Jean's voice rose sharply, and her eyes were blazing. "But *this* will positively slay you: For the benefit of her coworkers—who were sitting around, taking the whole thing in—the fucking bitch even claimed she'd advised me to get out weeks and weeks earlier!"

I became aware then that at some point or other, Jean had dispensed with her instructions to Corny. And either the child had become completely preoccupied with her coloring or now that the epithets were spewing forth at such a fast and furious rate, she'd wearied of continuing the charade on her own. And so while her mother cursed on, raging about how the dead girl's malice had damaged her daughter's future, Corny sat there serenely, devoting herself to her art.

When Jean had finished venting, I figured she'd told me all she could—or would—about Raven Eber, and I decided to head home.

A few minutes later, we were standing at her front door, and I thanked her for taking the time to talk to me. And then I said good-bye to her legs—behind which that peculiar little progeny of hers was in hiding once again.

There was no response, but I added with a smile, mostly for Jean's benefit, "Well, it was a pleasure meeting you, anyway, Corny."

And now, from back of the legs came this sweet, bell-like voice. "Uh-uh," it said. "That's fuckin' bullshit."

Chapter 24

Of course, I know that kids shouldn't be exposed to language like that. It isn't healthy for their underdeveloped little psyches or something. But when those words came out of that tiny, rosebud mouth—well, you had to hear it for yourself. Anyhow, I couldn't help it. For a full three or four minutes after I drove away from the house, I was still cracking up.

Then all at once, it occurred to me: The job I'd handed myself had been completed at last! And now that I'd come to the end of the line, I could finally accept that circumstances had killed Raven Eber—not one of her fellow Kappa Gams.

And if I had the slightest qualms about the verdict I'd reached, I quickly dispelled them. After all, say one of those girls *had* dreamed up that invitation business with murder on her mind—and I couldn't even be sure that had been her objective—it still didn't mean she ever got to carry out her plan. No. From where I was sitting, it looked as if Raven had been good-natured enough to save her the trouble.

I breathed a sigh of relief. It was an accident, and that put Ellen in the clear! And hey, from here on in, I could even devote my full attention to my other cases. (Okay. My other *case*.)

It was some time later, just before I turned onto the Pennsylvania Turnpike, that I remembered my premonition.

Well, it wasn't as though I'd ever really believed it, was it?

Tuesday was Muriel Moody day.

By 11:10 that morning, I was in position. This time I'd parked on the same side of the street as the now-familiar brownstone, but about fifteen feet away. I sat scrunched low in the seat, my hands on the steering wheel, my key in the ignition, and my eyes glued to the Moodys' front door—although I admit to peeling them away every so often for a nervous, split-second glance across the street. (You can color me yellow, but what if that tart-tongued, gray-haired snoop should spot me and decide to play vigilante again?)

Fortunately, Muriel made her appearance before her dreaded neighbor did. Stepping out on the stoop at 11:20, she promptly hailed a passing taxi. And immediately I was in hot pursuit.

Hell-bent on keeping the cab in sight, I plowed through one amber light after another (and even a red light once), cutting off any motorists with the gall to cross my path and coming *that close* to side-swiping a couple of pedestrians. And then on East Fifty-eighth Street, the taxi came to a sudden stop in front of a small and obviously pricey French restaurant.

Muriel had arrived at her destination.

I watched her open the intricately carved wooden doors of La Maison Bleue and disappear inside. And then for the next ten minutes or so, I drove aimlessly around, trying to locate a parking lot with the room to accommodate another car. I finally found one four blocks from the restaurant and bolting from my Chevy, practically threw the keys at the attendant. Then I hurried back to the place as fast as my seldom taxed lower limbs could carry me there. (I would have much preferred letting a cab do the carrying—but there was none in sight.)

A menu was displayed in the window, and I made a pretense of reading it, while actually shifting my eyes to search inside for Muriel and her whatever. I spotted her almost at once; she was seated at a table quite close to the window, sipping a cocktail. But her whatever was nowhere to be seen.

Obviously, he was late, I concluded. Well, apparently, she wouldn't be leaving for a while, so I couldn't see any reason at all not to pop into the croissant shoppe down the block for a cup of coffee, along with one of their incredibly flaky and buttery go-withs. And that's just what I did. When I returned to the restaurant fifteen minutes later, Muriel was still sitting where I'd left her—alone. Only this time she was attacking something that looked like mussels.

Now, that puzzled me. If she was expecting someone, would she have begun eating before he got there? It didn't seem very likely.

And then a thought struck me.

Suppose this whole thing had been a ruse. Maybe she'd never made plans with *anybody*, and she'd set up the whole Tuesday lunch business just for her husband's benefit—say, in order to arouse his jealously.

But then again, maybe not.

Could be her gentleman friend had left a message that he couldn't make it today, and Muriel decided she might as well have some lunch anyway. Of course, it was also possible he'd come in while I was down the street thoughtlessly indulging myself with that delicious little confection, and that there'd been a quarrel or something and he'd stormed right out again.

But it was possible, too, that it was none of the above.

I'd better see if I could find out.

"I wonder if you could help me," I said sweetly to the maitre d', who was standing at the lectern just inside the door. He was a tall, slender man with a thick black mustache and very little visible hair anywhere else.

"I 'ope so, madame," he responded gallantly in heavily accented English.

"I thought I saw a friend of mine come in here a few minutes ago, but by the time I parked my car . . ." I pretended to peer around the dimly lit room. "I was *very* anxious to say hello to him—it's been years—and now I don't see him anymore." I sounded so dejected, I practically had myself in tears.

"Your friend; what ees 'is name?"

Stupidly, I hadn't expected that. "It's . . . uh . . . Charles," I fumbled. "Uh . . . umm . . . Charles Manson." *My God! Did I actually say that?*

But if the maitre d' recognized the name, he hid it well. "I don't find eet," he murmured, slowly shaking his head as he scanned the reservations ledger. "What does ee look like?"

"Oh!" I said animatedly, ignoring the question. "That's his cousin over there—the woman in the green dress." I was indicating Muriel Moody. "He probably had a lunch date with her."

"Ahhh. *Zat* gentleman. Ee leave 'ere five meenutes after ee arrive. A telephone call." I was frustrated enough to spit. My no-doubt stricken expression evoked an appropriately sympathetic. "I am so sorree." But an instant later the man brightened. "We 'ave a small table available toward zee back. Per'aps madame would like to take some lunch weez us while she ees 'ere? Our *specialité* today ees *sauté de veau aux champignons*." Pressing his thumb and forefinger together, he raised them to his lips and kissed them lightly, this familiar gesture leaving no doubt as to his estimation of the offering.

To my credit, I only hesitated a second or two before regretfully declining. "I'm afraid I'm due back at work now. But I'll definitely be in again soon. And thank you; you've been very kind."

I stopped off at Elliot Gilbert's office en route to my own and presented him with a brief, rather dour recitation of this latest letdown. He was his usual upbeat self. "Don't worry, Dez. There's always next time. You'll nail the bugger yet."

A short while afterward, just as I'd begun typing up my notes on the meeting with Jean Brooks, I heard from Ellen.

I knew I should have called *her*. Yesterday, in fact. As soon as I got back from Millville. But the truth is, I just hadn't been in that great a rush to convey my big news—that Raven's death was definitely an accident, I mean.

The problem was that while I myself was willing to accept a lack of evidence as sufficient evidence of this (I do hope I'm making myself clear), I could appreciate how even Ellen—who was so anxious to put the matter to rest—might like to hear something a little more conclusive. And I'd been trying to come up with a way of presenting things to her in a more positive light.

"How'd it go with Jeannie yesterday?" she wanted to know.

"Pretty much the same as with the others. Uh, Ellen? I suppose you're aware of what Raven did to *her*?"

Now, this was a question that had occurred to me last night. You see, I happened to recall our discussion regarding the pain inflicted by Raven on the various sorority sisters—and I suddenly realized that Ellen had never so much as mentioned Jean's devastating financial loss. And it puzzled me.

"The mining stock? Of course I'm aware of it. Jeannie's not very into privacy." And after a couple of seconds: "Listen, Aunt Dez, I'm not sure this is even worth mentioning, but Raven swore to Dick who told Winnie that it wasn't like that—malicious, I mean. She swore to him she had every reason to believe the stock would do well."

"What else would you expect her to say? And explain this to

me: Why did she see to it Dick got out *before* she convinced
Jean to invest?"

"Because Dick had already made a nice profit by then, and
this other stock had just become available—a new high-tech
company that was supposed to have an even greater earnings
potential than the mining company. So Raven had him take all
of the money and put it into that."

"All right. Then answer this for me. Why didn't Raven recommend the same stock to her supposed friend?"

"Well, you see, it was more speculative, so she didn't feel it
was the right kind of investment for Jeannie."

I was incredulous at what sounded to me like a defense of
the dead girl's actions. And then Ellen added almost as an afterthought, "Or anyway, so Raven told Dick when he questioned her about it afterwards." But the tardy disclaimer did
very little to dispel my initial impression.

"And there was also some small lie of Raven's about telling
Jean to dump the stuff weeks earlier," I reminded her, "—what
about *that*?"

"Raven said she just wanted the people in her office to think
she had a better handle on things than she actually did."

"You sound as though you believe all of those trumped-up
excuses."

"Knowing Raven? Of course not." But there was something
in the tone of her denial . . .

"Admit it. You *do* think she might have been on the level
with Jean."

"Not really," Ellen responded carefully, "it's just that the
stock market is a crapshoot to start with, so it is conceivable—
although, with Raven, very unlikely—that for once in her life
she wasn't being her normal conniving self."

"If that's true, your friend's been wasting a lot of very
choice epithets on her."

Ellen giggled then. "Jeannie was cursing Raven?"

"And cursing her. And cursing her."

"Now you know why we used to call her 'Dung Tongue' at
Walden."

"Yes, I sure do," I mumbled abstractedly, while coming to
the decision that now was the time.

"By the way," I said, trying to pump some excitement into
my voice, "you can finally relax."

"What do you mean?"

"I mean that there wasn't any murder committed at that reunion of yours." I said it with all the certainty I was trying to feel.

"That's wonderful!" But then almost immediately: "You honestly—are you positive?"

"Would I say it if I weren't?"

"No, of course not; I'm sorry. But how do you *know*?" Ellen persisted.

"Believe me, I investigated thoroughly. And if there had been anything there to suggest something other than accidental death, I'd have found it."

"I'm sorry," she said again. "I know you would. And thanks, Aunt Dez, for all your efforts. That's really great news." But she didn't sound exactly elated.

"Then what's bothering you?"

"Nothing."

"Oh, Ellen. It's me, remember?"

"It's just that I hope the police have come to that same conclusion."

"Don't worry," I assured her—and myself, too, while I was at it—"if they haven't, they will."

On my way home that evening, I stopped at the video store. I was checking the section with recent releases when I heard a tentative "Desiree?"

Looking up, I saw Lionel Burke, a sweet, fussy little man who until recently had worked in the same office building I did.

"Lovely about Mrs. Wetzel, wasn't it?" he said after we'd put the opening pleasantries behind us.

I still can't quite believe it, but I actually drew a blank. Maybe because so much had happened since Jane Wetzel.

"Elderly Lady?" Missing dachshund named Hoboken?" he prompted, responding to the silence.

Of course! "I knew who you meant," I told him, embarrassed that for a moment there, I hadn't. And, now I remembered something else. "And it was you who recommended me to her, too. She's your neighbor, isn't she?"

"Yes. And we were all so happy for her—all her friends in the building—when she got that darling little doggie of hers back."

"I was happy about it, too. And imagine his traveling maybe

hundreds of miles to come home again! I've always been amazed at how they—"

"Did Mrs. Wetzel tell you *that*?"

"Isn't it true?"

"Well, ahh, no. Mr. Wetzel took a place right there in the neighborhood, only about two and a half blocks away."

My mouth dropped open. As soon as it was in working order again, I asked, "Did she *know* that?"

"I'd have to say yes and no. When the doorman brought the little fellow upstairs that morning, he told her that just the night before, one of the other tenants had seen Wilbur—her husband—entering one of the local drinking establishments. So she was aware he was in the city, anyway," Lionel admitted, looking uncomfortable.

I was shaking my head in wonder when he added generously, "But I imagine Mrs. Wetzel likes to think it *could have been* true, that Hoboken would have managed it if he had to. And I don't say he wouldn't, either. That's a very clever doggie she has there."

Later that evening, sitting in the living room with my second cup of coffee, I thought with disappointment about Hoboken's now not-so-remarkable feat. I have to confess that I much preferred Mrs. Wetzel's version of the dachshund's homecoming to reality.

Chapter 25

Wednesday was about as boring a day as I've ever spent in the office. I seriously considered cutting out in the afternoon and taking in a movie, and if there'd been anything around that I wanted to see, I suppose I would have. As it was, I occupied myself with making a few personal calls, sharpening pencils, and even straightening up (to a minor extent) a couple of my desk drawers, which as their primary function do service as handy garbage disposals. I drew the line at the file cabinets, though.

I should definitely have stopped off at D'Agostino's en route to my apartment that night, but boredom wears me out, so I was willing to go with leftovers for supper. At five after seven, however, I was standing in the middle of the kitchen thinking *leftovers*? and trying to figure out what on earth I'd had in mind.

Since there were no other options, I'd just about settled on one of my refrigerator omelets—so named (by Ellen) because they contain practically every edible scrap in my refrigerator—when just then, the phone rang.

"Hi," said this very male voice. "Have you missed me?"

There was no question in my mind as to the owner of that voice. It was the man Pat Martucci had fixed me up with a while back—you know, the one from Chicago. But I played the game. "Who is this?" I asked with some difficulty, my mouth having just gone bone dry on me.

The caller clucked a few times, then murmured with mock sorrow, "And after you swore up and down how much our evening together would always mean to you."

I didn't know when he'd condescend to identifying himself, so I folded. "Is this Bruce?" On saying the name, my heart plummeted down around my ankles somewhere.

"You didn't forget, after all!"

"No. But it's not that I wouldn't have liked to," I bantered. "How have you been?"

"We'll go into that later. Listen, how does a steak sound to you?—a thick, juicy steak. And with it, a baked potato with sour cream and chives and maybe a nice, big salad. And then for dessert, a slice of the best cheesecake you've ever had. With strawberries, naturally."

"Sounds good enough to eat," I responded lightly, wondering if he was actually asking me out for that evening. No. After all, it was past 7:00 already, and I hardly knew the man. He wouldn't have the nerve.

"Fine. I'll pick you up at eight."

"Eight when?"

"Tonight, of course," he answered, his tone leaving not the slightest doubt that he had to restrain himself from tacking "you idiot" onto that.

Well, evidently, he did have the nerve. And not only to want to make it tonight, but to cop an attitude about the whole thing, too!

It didn't matter. There was no way I was going to accommodate him. In fact, chances were, I wouldn't be seeing Bruce Simon again—ever! My last experience with him had been just that: an experience. And not an altogether pleasant one, either. "I'm sor—"

"Desiree, Desiree," he interrupted. "Don't tell me you're one of those women who requires a month's notice. I had you pegged as more down-to-earth than that." And then his voice became serious. "Look, it took a lot longer to make the move to New York than I'd anticipated—I had to finish up some business back in Chicago first. But I was looking forward to seeing you again; I thought about you a lot these past weeks."

Months, I reminded him mentally before saying aloud, "There you go, shooting from the hip again. What I started to tell you was that I couldn't possibly be ready by eight. We'll have to make it nine."

Oh, shit! What was the matter with me, anyway? On the one date we'd had together, this guy had been out-and-out obnoxious. Still, toward the end of the evening things had improved considerably. I discovered he was also bright. And witty. And—as my friend Pat pointed out not too long ago—kind of sexy.

Yes, I admitted it. He was sexy.

The buzzer rang just before quarter of nine, at the precise moment I was pulling on my panty hose. Startled, I put my foot through the damn things! I should have expected him to show up early like this, I thought. There was something truly perverse about the man. I quickly slipped on a robe so I could go to the door.

He stood there looking pretty much as I remembered—about five six or -seven, with dark hair (what there was of it) and hazel eyes. All of which I had no problem with. But then there was the rest of it . . . He was solidly built—to the extent you might even consider him on the muscular side. And he had this overconfident macho air about him. Plus the smile that played around the corners of his mouth was more sardonic than anything else. I mean, this was a fellow who definitely did not need nurturing. And, as you know, I need a man who needs nurturing. It was as simple as that.

So why was this stupid heart of mine in a free fall again?

"Hi, c'mon in," I barely managed to squeak out.

Bruce followed me into the living room. "I hope you still intend going out to dinner," he remarked, plunking himself down on the sofa. No "Hello," no "How are you?" These were the very first words he said to me.

I was taken aback for a moment. "Why do you ask?"

"When a woman greets me in an outfit like that, I have to consider the possibility she may have something else in mind."

Now, he was obviously teasing. My robe was a heavy cotton, loose, faded, and about as seductive as a laundry bag. Nonetheless, I automatically looked down to see if I'd buttoned all the buttons before retorting stupidly, "You wish." (Sometime during the middle of the night, I'd think of the sparkling comeback I should have made. I could practically guarantee it.)

He chuckled. "Maybe."

"Well, if you'd gotten here when you were supposed to, I would have been dressed," I grumbled, annoyed with us both that I was feeling defensive. And then I at least had the wit to add, "But it's obvious you just couldn't wait to see me again."

"Touché," he responded, his eyes twinkling.

I wasn't ready until 9:15. But I know that if Bruce hadn't been so damn early, I'd have had no problem being on time.

With all of that rushing, though, I got a run in a second pair of panty hose. Then only a few minutes later, I dropped an earring and had to go crawling around the bedroom on all fours, searching for it. (And in case you're interested, it didn't surface for more than a week.)

But anyway, by quarter of ten we were at the restaurant. Not surprisingly, Bruce did a lot of bellyaching at first about continental dining hours, but it was apparent this was only for effect. And it actually turned out to be a wonderful evening.

There was something almost exhilarating about being in Bruce's company. He was well versed in a whole variety of things. And that's what we talked about, *things*—books, politics, music, movies—agreeing, of course, on virtually nothing. My few attempts to get him to tell me a little about himself, however, were neatly sidestepped. And so by the end of that night I didn't know any more about him than I knew before we set out. Which amounted to his being a divorced man who worked in public relations and who also had the sharpest tongue this side of Chicago.

But I wasn't terribly disturbed that we hadn't communicated on a more personal level. Not at that juncture. It *was* only the second time we'd been out together. And besides, I had thoroughly enjoyed sparring with him.

It was about ten after one when I got home. Bruce saw me to the door of my apartment and leaning over, kissed me on the forehead. "If you want me to do better than that, you'll have to earn it," he said.

I didn't have time to dissect that. Because as soon as I walked into the living room, I noticed the red light flashing on the answering machine, and I pressed Playback for the messages. There was only one—from Ellen.

"I've got to talk to you—I just heard from Jeannie. Call me when you come in. No matter how late it is."

Well, I was pretty positive I knew what this was about, and it wasn't something I'd have expected would prompt any kind of urgency. But Ellen was nearly frantic. Or anyhow, that's how she sounded to me. I immediately returned her call.

She picked up before the first ring had finished ringing, and then she didn't even wait for my hello. "Aunt Dez?" I conjured up this picture of her pouncing on the telephone.

"What's the matter, Ellen?"

"Nothing, really. I just wanted to ask you about something Jeannie told me when she called before."

"What's that?"

For a moment, there was silence at the other end of the line, and then when Ellen did speak, it was in an unnaturally high voice. "She said you claimed someone had spotted her coming out of Raven's room that night at Sybil's. She thought maybe it came from me, that *I* was the one who was supposed to have seen her. I said of course not." And then more softly, almost fearfully: "But is—is it true?"

"It never happened."

"You m-mean you didn't s-say it or that you weren't telling the truth when you said it? Which?"

"I mean I lied," I answered bluntly. And I wasn't ashamed to admit it, either. "Look, how do you think I'm able to get information out of people?" I put to her. "Sometimes you have to set a little trap. After all, if Raven *had* been murdered, it's conceivable someone might have gotten a look at the killer sneaking in or out of her bedroom."

"Oh." But then the answer led to another question. "You didn't try anything like that before, though. How come?"

"Because it wasn't a game I could play more than once. Not with the way the five of you report to each other."

"That reminds me!" Ellen suddenly exclaimed. "Jeannie said she's getting in touch with everyone—all the women—to see if she can find out who made up that story. She's really been worried sick about it, especially since you convinced her you think one of us is a murderer. Maybe I should call her back now and tell her it's okay; the whole thing was just your way of trying to get at the truth. Would that be all right?" And before I could answer: "It shouldn't matter, should it?—not if you're really so positive it was an accident." She made it sound suspiciously like a challenge.

"Listen, you can phone her this minute if you want to, but if I were you, I'd wait until morning. It's past one o'clock, and the girl does have a small child, you know."

"Oh, my goodness. I wasn't even aware of the time."

I had the impression the conversation was pretty much over now. Or maybe I was just hoping it was. My eyelids were at half mast at this point, and I'd have given anything to have my head make contact with my pillow. But then Ellen said—and her tone was much too contentious for the Ellen I knew—"If you'd already decided there hadn't been any murder, why even bother with a trap like that?"

Courage, Desiree, I moaned inwardly. "Because I hadn't *decided* anything yet," I responded. "That didn't happen until *after* I talked to Jean. In the meantime, I wanted to do everything possible to ensure that whatever conclusion I did come to would be the right one."

"Then—"

"Look, we can talk some more in the morning if you want to. So why don't you let us both get a little sleep tonight."

But it wasn't that easy. "Then, what you're telling me is that no one saw Jeannie coming out of Raven's room, that you just m-made it up, right?"

"Yes, Ellen." I said the words evenly, which should not be attributed to my saintly disposition or anything. I undoubtedly would have shouted them if I'd had the strength. "That's what I've been telling you for hours. Or for what seems like hours, anyway."

"I guess you have," Ellen admitted sheepishly. "Aunt Dez?"

"What?"

"I'm sorry. I know I've been absolutely impossible tonight. It's just that Jeannie's a good friend, and I would hate to think she was in any kind of trouble."

"Well, she's not. And I tried to assure her of that later on. I told her I was certain there'd been a mistake. Anyhow, do you feel better now?"

"Much."

And with that, we said our good nights.

But for a brief time after we hung up, I sat there immobile, ruminating on my niece's uncharacteristic behavior. She hadn't even asked what I'd been doing until this late hour—which, Lord knows, wasn't at all like her. It was obvious that I'd just been speaking to a very troubled Ellen.

And the question I asked myself then was *why?*

Chapter 26

I wasn't able to come up with the answer that night. Or the next day, either. And it didn't help that I never really woke up on Thursday—not all the way up, anyhow. But it would be sour grapes to blame it on that.

At any rate, I still dragged myself into the office, where I accomplished absolutely nothing. (But then, I had nothing to accomplish.) I fought the temptation to put my head down on the desk and take a nap like I did when I was in kindergarten and instead devoted a good part of the morning to thinking about Ellen and Bruce.

Ellen first.

Not only had she been incredibly agitated last night—*hyper* might be a better word for it—but she'd been on the attack, too, tearing into practically everything I told her. Ellen! Who's probably the least confrontational person you'd ever want to meet.

But of course, I'd been pretty spent after that date with Bruce, so maybe my perceptions were influenced by my own exhaustion. It's very possible she hadn't been nearly as stressed out as I'd imagined. She always takes her friends' troubles to heart; that's how she is. It might have been no more than that. Come to think of it, could be she hadn't even been all that contentious. Now that I was looking back on it, that is.

And don't forget, I pointed out to myself, she'd barely stuttered, the stammering usually a dead giveaway—since this Raven thing, at least—to her being overwrought.

But then again, perhaps she'd made a little trip to the liquor cabinet before our talk. Or for that matter, to the medicine chest, where, it just occurred to me, she kept some just-in-case Xanax.

Oh come on now, I chastised, *don't look for trouble. It's most likely only a case of Ellen being Ellen.*

But I didn't really believe it.

I segued to Bruce.

If you want me to do better, you'll have to earn it. What was *with* him, anyway? Was that just a meaningless little quip? Or was it actually some kind of strategy? You know, withholding his "favors" in order to make himself more desirable. Well, if it *was* a strategy, it was a dud. I'd be perfectly content to keep the relationship platonic forever. I mean, the man wasn't *that* sexy.

I didn't make it past 4:00 that afternoon—well, 4:05, to be exact. That's when I finally had the sense to head for home. Before I could get through the front door, however, I first had to assure Jackie and then *re*assure her—the normal procedure when I decide to leave work early—that no, my health was not impaired. And no, my personal life was not in particularly dire straits, either.

"I'm just tired," I told her for the third time.

"You're sure that's all it is?" It was the third time for that, too.

I was too pooped to deal with it again. So I just smiled and waved my hand and walked away.

"Well! You might at least answer a civil question!" she yelled to my escaping back.

Shutting the apartment door behind me, I almost simultaneously kicked off my shoes. Then I made straight for the bedroom. As I stretched out on the bed, I remember thinking idly that I should really hang up my dress. . . .

When I woke up in my turquoise cotton A-line (which had suddenly become accordion-pleated), I discovered it was almost 8:00—the next morning!

I didn't exactly break my neck getting to the office that day—I mean, what for? So I could knock off early?

I made it in around 11:00 and as it happened left even earlier than I'd planned. At a few minutes before 3:00, in fact.

Because that's when I heard about Ellen.

The phone rang just after I'd finished straightening up another desk drawer—and with not very noticeable results.

"Desiree?" the man said. "It's Ellen."

Is this some kind of stupid joke? I was about to ask, when I realized that the man was Mike.

"What *about* Ellen?" I swear that for a few seconds there, my heart stopped pumping.

"Now, don't get excited. She's okay. But they took her to Clear Cove this morning."

"*Who* took her?"

"The chief—Brady."

"You mean Ellen's been *arrested*?"

"No, they wanted to get a statement from her, that's all."

I was almost afraid to ask. "Why *now*, all of a sudden? Do you know?"

"Well, uh, they're still investigating Raven's death, it seems. And, uh, they just found out something. Something new."

"Which is?"

"I think Ellen would rather tell you about that herself," Mike murmured apologetically.

"You mean they found out something that implicates *Ellen*?"

"I guess maybe the police think so." And then: "But don't worry, Dez. She didn't have anything to do with it."

How do you like that! *He's* assuring *me* that Ellen isn't a killer! "Of course she didn't!" I snapped. "Where is she now?"

"At her apartment—we're both here now. And she'd like you to come over. As soon as you can."

"Tell her I'm on my way."

Chapter 27

Mike opened the door, looking extremely concerned. Nonetheless, he welcomed me with a smile. "It's good you're here," he said.

I found Ellen sitting lengthwise on the sofa, legs drawn up, chin resting on her knees. I noted that her eyes, while dry, were puffy. And there were half a dozen used Kleenex in her lap.

Jumping up, she rushed over to greet me, leaving Mike to pick up the tissues she'd unknowingly strewn behind her. "Oh, Aunt Dez!" she cried, enveloping me in one of her bone-crushing hugs.

"Would you like some coffee or something?" she asked when she (mercifully) released me.

I'm not kidding. The building could be burning—and herself with it—and Ellen would still feel it incumbent upon her to be the perfect little hostess.

"No thanks, nothing," I responded, awkwardly patting her shoulder before taking a seat on one of two recently acquired gray tweed club chairs. As soon as Ellen had settled herself on the sofa again, I leaned forward. "Now tell me, what happened?"

"I think I could be in trouble," she said in a remarkably calm voice.

"Go on."

She moistened her lips before responding. "Well, Chief Brady came to see me early this morning—before eight, I think it was. I was just getting dressed—Mike and I both had the day off, and we'd made all kinds of plans. We were going to do some shopping—it's his mother's birthday, and he wanted to give her a silk scarf. And then we thought maybe we'd walk over to the Museum of Modern Art and after that, maybe take in a movie and—"

"Chief Brady," I interrupted to put her back on track.

"Yes, well, he said he would appreciate it if I came to the station with him to make a statement. I asked him why, and he told me he just wanted to be certain he had all his facts straight. I said couldn't we do it here, but he said no, that he'd have to have it—the statement—typed up and everything. I asked him if I was under arrest, but he said that it wasn't anything like that. Anyhow, I had to call Mike and cancel. He drove out there so he could take me home, though." She looked around then and beamed at her almost-fiancé, who was now sitting beside her, his hand resting protectively on the small of her back.

"You should have contacted a lawyer immediately," I scolded. "You realize that, don't you?"

"I told her the same thing," Mike interjected. "I thought we should call my uncle, who's a lawyer. But Ellen wouldn't hear of it."

"Well, it wasn't as though I was being charged or anything," argued this going-on thirty ten-year-old. *Honestly. You'd think someone who watches all those cop shows would have made a beeline for the phone, wouldn't you?*

"I wish you'd called *me*, at least," I said to her.

"I couldn't. Chief Brady was in the living room waiting for me, and I was rushing like crazy to finish dressing."

I was about to point out that the call would only have taken a couple of minutes when she went on. "And besides, I kept telling myself there was nothing to worry about. From what you said the other day, I figured they were finally closing the case and that this statement was probably only something they needed for the files."

I squirmed in my chair. Guilt is not a comfortable thing.

Then Ellen added, her voice a whisper now, "I wouldn't even let myself think it might be what I was afraid of."

"But it was?"

She nodded glumly.

"Isn't it time you filled me in on what this is all about?" I put to her, attempting—not altogether successfully, I'm sure—to conceal my impatience.

"I'm going to. That's why I wanted you to come over. It's just that it isn't easy. I know you'll be furious with me."

"You have my promise that I won't be. Now, please . . ."

"All right. Someone—I don't know who, Brady wouldn't say—claims to have seen me leaving Raven's bedroom Friday night."

All at once, I felt queasy. *Very* queasy. "Is it . . . it isn't true, is it?"

"No, naturally it's not true." I felt so much better.

But only seconds later, I was back to queasy again. Because Ellen expanded on her response.

"I *did* go to her room after the cocktail party; I knocked on the door and called out that it was me and that I just wanted to talk to her for a little while. But when she didn't answer, I figured it must be because she was so angry with me. How was I to know something awful had happened to her?"

She swallowed hard, so I said quickly, "That was it? You went away then?"

"Yes, that was it," Ellen replied meekly. "I suppose I should have told you about this before, but you never asked." It was true. I'd questioned all the others about visiting the dead girl that night—but not Ellen. "And anyway," she added, "it wasn't as though I actually went *inside* or anything."

"I realize that. But I still don't see why you never mentioned it."

"I guess I didn't say anything in the beginning because I'd have had to tell you *why* I went to talk to her."

"Which was because?"

"Which was because I wanted to apologize for tossing that drink in her face. I felt terribly ashamed. No matter what, I shouldn't have done anything like that. In fact, that's the real reason I went upstairs with Winnie on Saturday morning—it was a good chance to get Raven alone. I figured I'd stay behind after Winnie went back down and just tell her I was sorry."

"But I've known about the drink business for quite a while now," I reminded her.

"Yes, but by the time you found out, there really didn't seem any point in going into this, too. Don't forget," she said, jostling my memory once again (which was hardly necessary—I was way ahead of her), "you kept saying I was not to worry, that you were sure it was an accident and that you'd p-p-prove it."

"Yes, I know," I responded unhappily, "but—"

"I almost be-believed you, too," Ellen broke in, the slightest hint of reproach in her tone. "But I guess that was because I w-wanted to."

And an instant later, she was in tears.

Mike drew her to him, and she buried her face in his chest, her thin body heaving with silent sobs. Gently, self-consciously, he rubbed her back. "It's okay, it's okay," he murmured, looking stricken. "Everything'll be okay, El, you'll see."

Now, I have to say that for some reason, the tears took me by surprise. And knowing my niece, they shouldn't have. But still, until only a minute ago, she *had* been handling this really well. Much better than I'd have anticipated she would. I rose to get the box of tissues that lay on the cocktail table in front of the sofa and pressed it into her hand.

She looked up, mumbled something that might have been "thanks," and then after utilizing a single tissue, shoved the box aside and went back to irrigating Mike's chest again.

He interrupted her just long enough to ask if she'd like a glass of water. She shook her head.

"Maybe something a little stronger?" I suggested.

"She took a Xanax about an hour ago," he informed me quietly.

Well, that explained how well she'd been coping. Up to now, anyway.

When the crying ended at last and she'd wiped the wetness and mascara from her cheeks and blown her nose a dozen times, Ellen looked at me intently. "Aunt Dez," she said, "do you think I'll ever outgrow being such a weenie?" And then, astonishingly, she giggled.

Nevertheless, I knew she hadn't asked the question lightly. "You are *not* a weenie. Anyone under suspicion"—I caught myself before adding 'of murder'—"would be bound to come apart a little. Anyone with any sense, that is."

She smiled her thanks.

"Tell me, Ellen, how long after the party was it that you went to see Raven?" I asked her then.

"I'd estimate it was maybe three-quarters of an hour. I was wrestling with myself for quite a while before I decided to do it."

"You weren't concerned she might already be asleep by that time?"

"I wouldn't let myself be," Ellen admitted somewhat sheep-ishly. "I told myself she was probably still getting ready for bed. Once I'd made up my mind, well, I knew I had to get it over with."

"And you have no idea who might have seen you outside her door?"

"No. There didn't seem to be anyone else around. We were the last ones to go upstairs, Raven and I, except for Hannah and this other woman Lillian, who were cleaning up. Maybe they were still down there; I can't be certain. But there wasn't a soul in that second-floor hallway. Or so it seemed." And then she remarked with this strained little smile, "I actually would have sworn to that. Shows you how observant I am, huh?"

Almost immediately, however, Ellen's expression was seri-ous again. "You know, Aunt Dez, when Jeannie told me what you said about someone accusing her of coming out of Raven's room, I got the idea that maybe she'd been mistaken for me. I remember it *was* kind of dark in that hall, and even though we don't look the least bit alike, Jeannie and I—espe-cially with all that hair she has—well, I was practically out of my mind anyway, thinking that's what might have happened. It's the reason I was so anxious to find out if you were telling the truth. I'd never have let anybody else get in trouble be-cause of me. You believe that, don't you?"

"You didn't even have to say it," I assured her.

The three of us spent some time after that discussing the probable impact on the police of this potentially damaging new information, with both Mike and me maintaining—con-trary to all logic, really—that nothing much would come of it. And then we ordered some dinner from Mandarin Joy (where else?).

Ellen was certainly able to do justice to the meal. But I can't honestly say if it was the result of our being that convincing or of Ellen's being inordinately hungry.

I left the apartment about 10:00. Mike, with that thoughtful nature of his—those two really are *so* perfect for each other—insisted on coming downstairs with me and putting me in a cab. And almost from the moment I deposited my buns in that taxi, I began to shake. I had—now that it was no longer neces-sary to pretend—finally given myself permission to succumb to my fear: the fear that Ellen might actually be charged with murder.

After I came home, I was too upset to even consider trying to sleep. I got undressed, took off my makeup, and then sat down at the kitchen table with a cup of coffee—which happened to taste even more horrific than usual. (And it was entirely on its own tonight, too. There wasn't an appropriate morsel in my entire refrigerator to take the edge off it.)

But at any rate, as I was sitting there drinking and shaking, I became aware that at some time during the evening I'd completely abandoned any pretense of regarding Raven's death as accidental. And what's more, I was forced to accept that I'd had no business making an assessment like that to begin with.

Under ordinary circumstances, of course, I'd have immediately latched on to the notion of foul play here. You see, I'm not a big believer in coincidence. And the fact that a girl everyone despised was sent an invitation by a person unknown to attend a party at which she definitely was not welcome and at which she then met her demise would have been enough to put my suspicions in overdrive. But the thing is, under ordinary circumstances, Ellen wouldn't have been involved.

I suppose that initially I'd resisted the very idea that anyone in her nice little circle of former college chums could possibly have had a hand in anything as sordid as murder. It was just hitting too close to home. (And forget about my being a PI and therefore able to take things like that in stride. I mean, PI or not, family is family.) But anyway, then along comes Sybil's rat fink of a maid to report that champagne-tossing bit and point the finger at Ellen herself. Well naturally, Ellen's being a murder suspect was absolutely unthinkable. And something I was totally unprepared to deal with. So being the ostrich that on more than a few occasions I have demonstrated myself to be, I now chose to ignore the obvious and try to prove that what I was afraid had really happened that weekend hadn't happened at all.

God! How typical of me! In fact, I just had to go back as far as—was it only three days ago?—for yet another example of my reluctance to accept reality. But of course, opting for the fantasy version of little Hoboken's journey home was harmless enough. Whereas right now, this unfortunate tendency of mine could even cost Ellen her freedom.

I mean, the police had hardly been conducting their investigation under the same Ellen-oriented constraints that I had. What's more, Chief Brady was no lightweight in the brains department. So I could be damn sure he hadn't been exactly straight with me when he claimed that Raven's death was in all probability an accident and that he was just doing a little "nosin' around."

Uh-uh. If the man was anywhere near as smart as I judged him to be, he didn't believe in coincidences any more than I did. Which meant he'd been searching for a killer all along. And in view of what I'd learned tonight, it was a pretty safe bet he now had his sights trained on Ellen. Maybe he had almost from the first. And who could blame him? She appeared to have been the only one to do anything even the least bit suspicious that weekend.

And let's face it. Brady didn't know her the way I did.

Chapter 28

In spite of having had only about three hours of sleep, I woke up early on Saturday morning, totally refreshed. My head now out of the sand, I was armed with a new sense of purpose. I felt, in fact, as if my brain had been vacuumed.

Believe me, I would see to it that Ellen didn't suffer from my lack of judgment. There was still time to wrench her from the clutches of Chief Brady and the Clear Cove Police Department. All I had to do was present them with the *real* killer of Raven Eber.

I just wished I had some idea of how I was going to accomplish this.

After a few minutes' thought, I decided I might as well begin with a visit to Brady. So after wolfing down some breakfast, I dressed as quickly as I was capable of. Then I called the Clear Cove station just to make sure he was in.

"Is Chief Brady there?" I asked the woman who answered the phone.

"Who's calling him?" she inquired pleasantly.

"Mrs. Plotnick," I said.

"Hold on a minute, please, honey," she instructed.

I promptly hung up.

Brady was, as I'd seen before, polite enough to attempt to mask his feelings. Still, I could tell that he was not overjoyed when I showed up on his doorstep.

As soon as I was seated in his office and we'd established that I was fine and that he was fine, he tilted his chair back, locking his fingers behind his head. "And just what can I do for you t'day, Ms. Shapiro?" he asked. In spite of the smile on his lips, he was looking at me (I thought) impatiently.

"It's about my niece Ellen."

"Well now, I thought it just might be."

"Ellen was never in the dead girl's room that night, you know."

"That's exactly what she said to me herself, ma'am." The implication being, of course, that I was wasting his time.

I chose to ignore it. "Whoever saw her mistakenly thought she was leaving the *room*, but she was actually just walking away from the *door*."

"So Ms. Kravitz told us yesterday."

"I'd appreciate knowing who gave you that information, so I could ask her—it was a her, wasn't it?—about something else. Something important." Then, hastily, for good measure: "Something that might also help the police."

"I'm sure whatever it is would be real helpful to us, but I still can't discuss this with you."

"Look, I'm just as anxious to clear up this case as you are. No—*more*. I have a niece I'm very concerned about here—a sweet, thoughtful girl who had nothing whatsoever to do with any murder. And no matter what it takes, I intend to make sure she doesn't end up getting this thing pinned on her. Do you know why she's having this trouble now? Because she *is* such a good person. She felt so awful about tossing the drink that night that she couldn't let it rest; she had to apologize. Even though, God knows, Raven Eber was certainly asking for it."

"I can appreciate how you're feelin', Ms. Shapiro, I really can," Brady said when I'd wound down. "But we're still in the process of gatherin' evidence; no one's assessin' any blame here."

Yet. My mind supplied the word he hadn't spoken, and my lips were suddenly parched.

"That's beside the point," I told him. "I just don't understand why you can't be a little more cooperative."

"Because this is an official police investigation, and I can't take a chance on anybody gummin' up the works and getting in the way of my doin' my job."

"I wouldn't get in your way, I assure you. And anyhow, considering how long this has been dragging on, I'd have thought you'd be glad of some assistance." It spilled out before I had the presence of mind to bite off my tongue.

Instead of blowing up, though—as he had every right to do—Brady grinned. Which really infuriated me. It was just so . . . so patronizing. And then he inquired in this ultra-patient tone, "Do you remember when you came to see me that last time?"

"Sure I remember."

"Well now, as good as I can recall, when I told you what it was you wanted to know back then, I made it clear that was but a one-shot deal. Does this sound familiar to you?"

"Yes, it does but—"

"I'm afraid I'm just gonna have to keep you honest and hold you to that bargain we made." So saying, he righted his chair and put both palms flat on the desktop—preparatory, I realized, to getting to his feet. I was maybe two seconds away from being tossed out of there—but very politely, of course.

It was definitely time for some sort of drastic measure. And I could think of only one thing. . . .

"You don't understand how difficult this is for me," I said, snuffling. "Ellen wouldn't hurt a soul, not a soul. And I can't bear to even imagine her—" Breaking off, I now squeezed my downcast eyes shut to assist them in their task. It worked quite nicely, too; in an instant they were overflowing. I didn't even attempt to wipe away the tears that were rolling so freely down my cheeks. Casting a quick, surreptitious glance at Brady, I could tell that he was extremely uncomfortable.

I felt genuine pride in how well I was pulling this off. I mean, the way I look at it, you do what you can with whatever it is you've got. Does a man forego using any superior strength he might have when it could assist him in apprehending a killer? Of course not! Or forget that. Did you ever hear of anyone leaving their gun in its holster because it provides them with an unfair advantage?

"Oh, don't do this," Brady was pleading now. "I never could handle that sorta stuff."

"I'm sorry, but I just can't help it," I wailed—but not so shrilly as to offend—while at the same time rummaging around in my handbag for a tissue.

"Listen, I don't know why I should let you finagle me like this—and don't think I'm so dense I haven't figured out that's just what you're doin'—but for some reason I'm gonna give you your way, irregardless. Only this is it. You're not to come sniffin' around here anymore, you understand that?"

I blew my nose as I nodded.

"It was an anonymous phone call. It came in on Thursday afternoon."

"Anonymous!" I scoffed.

"Turned out to be true, though, didn't it? At least, partially. You gotta admit that much."

I did no such thing. "I don't suppose you recognized the voice?"

"'Fraid not. Caller—a woman—managed to pretty much disguise it."

"Well, did this caller of yours say what *she* was doing wandering around the house at that hour?"

"Never had a chance to ask her. She hung up too quick."

"I guess that means there was no time to set up a trace."

"You got that right."

"I suppose you've questioned all the girls about this?"

"Just Ms. Miller and Ms. Eber. They both deny it was them, of course. I haven't talked to the other two yet, but I expect it'll be more of the same."

I expected so, too. "There's one thing that really puzzles me, though," I brought up then. "Why do you think it took so long for whoever it was to report this?"

"Who knows? Took that long for her conscience to kick in, maybe."

"Conscience?" I muttered scornfully. "The way everyone felt about Raven Eber? I doubt that. My niece is the only one of those girls who's even sorry she's dead."

"Maybe that's true. But then again, maybe it isn't."

"You—"

"Listen, I'm sure your niece is a very fine person. The thing of it is, though, even nice people sometimes commit terrible acts." The protest leapt to my lips, but Brady put up his hand. "Now hold on. I'm not sayin' that's the case with Ms. Kravitz. I'm just sayin' I find it happens sometimes."

And then he placed both palms flat on the desktop again. Only now he was out of his seat in almost the same motion. And not even two minutes later, I was shown the door.

Driving home, I asked myself the same question I'd posed to Brady: Why *now*, after all this time? What could have triggered that damned phone call?

I shook my head in bewilderment.

Think! I ordered.

All right. Let's see. . . . Had anything transpired lately regarding the case? The only thing I was aware of was my visit to Jean Brooks on Monday.

Well, could it have had something to do with that?

Not very likely, although . . . Wait a second. Maybe we were getting somewhere, after all. I'd made up that story about someone claiming to have seen *Jean* coming out of Raven's room, and then Jean contacted her sorority sisters about it. Could this have prompted one of them to come forward about Ellen? I supposed it was possible, although after mulling it over for a couple of minutes, I really didn't buy it.

It was maybe five miles later when I reminded myself of something else. Hadn't I also told Jean that I suspected Raven had been murdered? I had. What's more, I knew Jean had mentioned *this* to Ellen, too. And I didn't doubt the girl had passed it on to the others in the group, as well.

And now the haze was clearing.

That's what could have provoked the phone call! No, no. Not *could have*—*did!* I was suddenly certain of it. And furthermore, the call had been made by the killer herself!

Follow my logic.

Just when it looks like this whole Raven business is going to go away, along comes yours truly talking foul play. Which would definitely have made it nervous time for the murderer. And so she—one of those four charming friends of Ellen's— decides to put somebody else in the hot seat. And who better than the person who'd turned up at Raven's door that night?

The caller, of course, hadn't made any mistake. She was well aware that Ellen never went into the dead girl's room. But she could still get plenty of mileage out of my niece's unfortunate timing.

Knowing Ellen (as the perpetrator most certainly did), she wouldn't deny attempting to visit the victim. Uh-uh. She was much too up front for that. Her denial would be reserved for establishing that she hadn't set foot inside that bedroom. *Well fine*, the killer must obviously have been thinking. *Let her do her denying until the cows come home.* The fact is, she'd now be placed at the crime site at about the time Raven met her death. And what's more, she'd never seen fit to mention this interesting bit of trivia to the police.

And that's when I realized the killer was damn lucky Ellen hadn't spotted her, too.

And this, quite naturally, led to my asking myself one thing more:

Why not?

I conjured up that hallway in my head. As far as I could remember, there didn't seem to be any convenient little recesses in which to conceal yourself. Besides, Ellen had been pretty positive no one else was around then. But that didn't wash, of course. The murderer had to have been there *somewhere* to know about Ellen, didn't she?

And then it came to me that there was really only one place Raven's murderer *could* have been: behind the victim's door, waiting anxiously for the sound of Ellen's retreating footsteps.

Funny, isn't it. Once I'd forced myself to acknowledge that I was dealing with murder, I immediately found something to confirm it.

But where, I asked myself then, *do I go from here?*

Chapter 29

It was almost 3:00 when I returned to the city. After dropping off my car at the garage near my apartment, I stopped off for a quick hamburger—I hadn't had anything to eat since breakfast. And thus fortified, I was soon off for D'Agostino's.

Now, I hate food shopping on Saturdays. In fact, there's only one thing I hate worse: a refrigerator with nothing in it. So inspired by these images of my three bare shelves, Spartan freezer, and empty vegetable bin, I took on the crowds and the chaos.

Forty minutes later, I had a cart that was so jam-packed it was even tough to wheel it up to the checkout counter. Besides being in dire need of all kinds of edibles, I'd run out of things like cleaning supplies and laundry detergent and even toilet tissue—I had let myself get down to practically the last square. The eight double plastic bags it required to contain my purchases must have weighed a ton. I swear the delivery kid gave me the fish eye as I was leaving the store.

Once I was back in my living room, I turned on the TV to relax for a little while, catching the tail end of an old Nelson Eddy/Jeanette MacDonald movie. And then—the food order having arrived—I settled down with a big bowl of grapes and the file on Raven Eber. I intended to go straight through my notes extra carefully—from beginning to end. I didn't make all that much headway, though, because the phone rang when I was only at the top of page four.

"Why haven't I heard from you, you tart?" the voice demanded as soon as I lifted the receiver.

"Bruce?" I can't imagine why I asked. I mean, who else would have opened like that?

"Do you know it's been three days now, and not a word? I even waited by the mailbox this morning, hoping the mailman

would deliver a little missive from you. A card or a note—
something! But I don't have to tell you, do I, that he had to
disappoint me. Level with me, Desiree. Do you take pleasure
in keeping your admirers dangling like this?"

"I restrained myself for your sake," I answered, trying to
erase the smile from my voice. "Men have been known—with
only the tiniest bit of encouragement—to fall so hopelessly in
love with me they never recover."

He laughed. "Not bad. You're showing some improvement
at this. But of course, you've still got quite a way to go. Anyhow, get—"

"Besides," I interjected pointedly, "I have no idea of your
address. Or your phone number either, for that matter."

Bruce's response was a low, soft chuckle. And then, unde-
terred, he went on. "As I was saying, get yourself dressed, and
I'll pick you up in an hour and a half. That should give even
you enough time." He didn't wait for a reaction. "And spare us
both any of that 'I'm sorry but I'm busy tonight' crap," he
added, mimicking this conceivable turndown in a very unflat-
tering falsetto. "You're much too contemporary a woman for
something like that."

I checked my watch. Well, he was moving in the right direction, at least. It was only after 6:00 this time. "Make that two
hours," I said. (I couldn't let him have things completely his
way, could I?)

"An hour and a half," he repeated firmly. Right before
hanging up.

I put down the phone, furious with myself.

Sometimes I just don't understand what makes me tick.
Why had I agreed to go out with this man again? I mean, he
really had his nerve, phoning me at the last minute like this—
and for the second time in a row, too. And then to top it off, he
even refuses to let me take an extra half hour to get ready!

And it wasn't as though I didn't have anything to do tonight,
either. I had something extremely important on my agenda:
trying to uncover a killer so I could prevent my niece from
being her stand-in. Which certainly should have taken prece-
dence over making myself available to this inconsiderate, insensitive, and egotistical . . . bozo . . . whenever he deigned to
call. *And after all*, I concluded (totally ignoring that telltale little flutter that I despised myself for feeling), *he isn't even really your type*.

We!l, I supposed I'd better get ready, since like it or not, I did agree to see him. But one thing I knew: After tonight, there would be no more outings with Bruce Simon.

We went to an Italian restaurant in the sixties. And that was another thing! He never even bothered to ask if I liked Italian food. But at any rate, the meal turned out to be pretty great. Ditto the rest of the evening, with Bruce's conversation every bit as witty and stimulating—but impersonal—as it had been before.

After dinner we walked down the block to a little cocktail lounge where they had a piano player who sang Cole Porter and Jerome Kern. Bruce ordered a couple of Brandy Alexanders for us, and by then I was so mellowed out from the music and the wine I'd consumed at dinner and, yes, the company, too, that I barely gave a thought to the fact that I'd have preferred an anisette.

About two hours later, we were in my building, standing just outside my apartment. My key case was clenched in my fist. Bruce held out his hand for it, quickly unlatched the two locks, and pushed open the door. Then turning back to me, he grabbed both my shoulders and kissed me. And not on the forehead, either.

It was quite a kiss, too. Long and hard and passionate. When we broke apart, I was practically reeling.

Bruce smiled his sardonic smile. "A preview," he informed me. And then without another word, he left.

I didn't awaken until just past 10:00, at which point I opened one eye to check the clock and then promptly fell right back to sleep. It was 11:15 before I opened an eye again. But this time, even though I was still extremely resistant to the idea, I dragged myself out of bed.

As soon as I'd had enough coffee to function like a human being, I dialed Ellen.

"I went to see Chief Brady yesterday," I told her.

"What did he say?" she asked warily.

"Only that that story he got about you came via an anonymous phone call."

"Do you mean that somebody called Brady just to implicate me?"

"It seems so."

"Well, it wasn't one of my friends," she retorted sharply. "It must have been someone who worked for Sybil—she had four in help. I'll bet it was that Hannah again."

I was aware of how much Ellen would have liked to believe that. I'd have liked to believe it, too. But unfortunately, that wasn't the way it was. "No, it wasn't Hannah," I told her, hating to have to say the words. "It *had* to be one of your friends."

"You can't be sure," she protested.

"Look, Ellen, who else there that weekend had a motive for murdering Raven?"

"*Murdering* her? But what's that got to do with the phone call? I'm not following you."

And then I explained the theory I'd worked out in the car. "Don't you see? It fits in with all the facts," I pointed out when I was finished.

"Oh, my God," Ellen murmured. After that, she was silent for a moment. And when she spoke again, it was in this small, incredulous voice. "Are you saying that one of my friends wants to see me arrested for murder?"

"That's not what I'm saying at all. What I'm saying is that one of them is willing to sacrifice you in order to divert suspicion from herself."

Another "Oh, my God." Then an instant later, a whispered: "Who?"

It was apparent she was addressing the question more to herself than to me. Nevertheless, I wanted to respond. "I don't know," I told her. "But I have every intention of finding out. And this time around," I said meaningfully, "I'll even manage to come up with the truth."

Chapter 30

It was absolutely imperative that I get down to the serious job of detecting I'd shirked the day before. Of course, this required that I first banish all thoughts of Bruce from my mind. Also that kiss, which was still making me feel weak-kneed and shivery. But I guess I'm stronger than I give myself credit for. Because soon after my conversation with Ellen, I sat down at the kitchen table with my notes, a lined yellow pad, a few ballpoints, and a clear head. And then I started to read.

I reached the part where Brady mentioned those charred bits of paper in Raven's ashtray. And I threw down the page in disgust.

Talk about ignoring the evidence! I hadn't been able to explain that damn piece of paper, so I'd just decided it wasn't important. Imagine. Before this case, I'd never been satisfied until every last loose end was tied up. Yet ever since I began looking into Raven's death, I'd been closing my eyes to one dangling thread after another.

Well, it was time to neaten things up.

I'd go through the rest of the file keeping that burnt paper in mind. If I really concentrated, there was a good chance I'd come across something that would clue me in on what it might have contained. I thought back to my conversation with Brady. Would it have even been possible to make a bigger ass of myself? I'd actually suggested to him that it could have been the remnants of a grocery list in that ashtray! *A grocery list?* Please!

I rolled up my sleeves (figuratively speaking) and went back to work. But when I closed the folder more than two hours later, I still didn't have an inkling as to what that paper was all about. In fact, the only thing I'd gotten out of my labors was a pulsating headache.

I took a twenty-minute break, along with a couple of extra-strength Tylenols, and then I started all over again.

Now I worked at an even slower pace, lingering over practically every word. But without any more success than on my earlier try.

It was close to 7 o'clock when I put down the last page. I didn't know when I'd felt so frustrated. (But of course, all I'd have had to do was think back to practically any investigation I'd ever been involved in.) I was still convinced it *had* to be there: that small, but vital piece of information that would lead me to the killer. In fact, who knew how often I'd come across it since Raven died?—each time failing to absorb its significance. Just as I'd done now.

Enough about the case, I told myself firmly. Quite a bit earlier my stomach had started growling and gurgling like crazy. And I didn't blame it—I hadn't had so much as a crumb for lunch. It was about time I focused on stifling those increasingly loud complaints I was being subjected to.

I managed to narrow the menu down to hot dogs or frozen pizza, but it was really a toss-up from there. And in attempting to reach a decision, I appeared to be on the verge of sprouting a brand-new headache.

The phone call spared me.

"It's Harriet, Dez," my across-the-hall neighbor Harriet Gould informed me. "Have you eaten yet?"

"No. But I was in the process of thinking about it."

Harriet laughed. Then she said in this wry tone, "Listen, I figured I'd be going out to dinner with my little family tonight. But Steve and Scott had tickets to a Yankee game"—Scott being her college-age son of whom she speaks in nauseatingly glowing terms on most occasions. "Only they forgot to mention their plans to me. And I just looked in the fridge to see what I could make for myself, and you know something? I wanted to cry. There's practically nothing there!" Recalling the state of my own refrigerator the day before, I couldn't help nodding empathetically at that. "Anyhow, would you happen to feel like grabbing a bite out?"

I told her that would be great, and she said she'd ring my bell around 8:00, if that was okay. I was about to say 8:30 would be better—you know how poky I am—when she added apologetically, "I'd make it earlier, but I'd better take Baby out before I leave." *She'd better, is right.* Baby, her retarded

Pekinese, boasts, along with his many other attributes, a weak bladder, that—I don't care *what* Harriet says—he makes not the slightest attempt to control. But at any rate, after learning she could even manage to get in a little dog walking by 8:00, I was too embarrassed to request an extension.

We had dinner at a Chinese restaurant on Lexington Avenue, and Harriet suggested a couple of dishes I'd never tried before—dishes that were listed on the menu with these little red stars in front of them. "Don't worry, Dez," she assured me, "they're really not that spicy."

Well, I consider anything capable of setting your insides on fire *that* spicy. Plus I swear that between them, the Orange Beef and General Tso's Chicken managed to remove almost every last vestige of skin from the roof of my mouth.

When I got home, it was a little past 10:00. And after changing into my nightgown, I started the new mystery I'd picked up a couple of weeks ago. But I couldn't seem to get into it. Maybe because I wasn't feeling all that terrific. So within a few minutes I was in the kitchen, putting up the tea kettle. Two cups later I came to the conclusion that tea wasn't the answer to General Tso's Chicken.

Padding into the bathroom, I checked the medicine chest. I so seldom suffer from indigestion (an old friend of mine—Tim Fielding—once accused me of passing it on to everyone else instead) that I wasn't even sure I'd find any help there. It was a nice surprise to discover a roll of Tums hiding behind the iodine bottle. The only trouble was that the expiration date was December 1991.

I took two, anyway. And they were about as effective as the tea had been.

At any rate, after that I figured I'd watch some TV for a while. But struggling through two excruciatingly boring programs was enough, thank you. So I turned off the set and went to bed, far from optimistic, however, about my chances of falling asleep.

Things went more or less as I'd expected, with a lot of tossing and turning and some intermittent pillow punching. I wasn't actually in pain, you understand. I was just damned uncomfortable—and wide awake, to boot. At some time or other, though, I must have dropped off for a couple of minutes, because I remember seeing myself in a forest. And it was getting darker . . .

I was alone and lost. Searching desperately for a clearing, I fought my way through the dense growth. Low-hanging tree branches scratched my face and arms. Brambles cut up my legs and tore at my clothes. And the temperature seemed to drop a little with every step I took. Soon the wind began to howl. And I grew more and more afraid . . .

I think I scared myself awake. I really needed that dream! *A mental metaphor, if ever there was one*, I thought, reaching over to the night table for a tissue to wipe the tears from my cheeks.

The hours dragged on without my shutting my eyes again. It must have been going on 4 A.M. when out of nowhere I recalled a little gem of wisdom from Hercule Poirot—or was it Miss Marple? He (she?) said that to uncover a killer, you had to really get to know the victim. Now, this was for the purpose of establishing motive, and of course, the only thing I *did* have here was motive. Just about everywhere I looked, in fact. What's more, with the amount of input I'd gotten, I considered myself the definitive authority on Raven Eber. Still, it might be worthwhile to list all of the girl's character traits on paper. Who knows? Maybe seeing them together in black and white like that would lead me somewhere I hadn't been before. (I'll tell you, I was so desperate at that point, I might have even been willing to try bungee jumping if there was a chance it could make a difference.)

Practically bounding out of bed, I hurried into the living room and once again removed the necessary items from my desk: file, pad, and pens. After which I settled myself at the kitchen table and began scanning my notes.

. . . *didn't know the pool was empty*, I read. I decided that might be worth jotting down. Even though it had nothing to do with the nature of the victim, the pool itself was a prime factor in her death.

. . . *a showoff*, I read. That, too, went onto the pad.

. . . *compulsive need to rise to every challenge*. Onto the pad.

By the time I'd covered the last page in the folder, I'd pulled out so many little sound bytes my fingers were stiff. But those I've cited here were crucial.

Because while not one of them was exactly a revelation, it was these few facts that proved instrumental in the unmasking of a very resourceful killer.

Chapter 31

I didn't even attempt to study the yellow pad that night. That *night*, did I say? It was well past 5:00 in the morning when I put down the pen. Exhausted and bleary-eyed, I barely made it back to bed. Where I fell instantly asleep.

The alarm clock let me know it was 7:30. Damn! I should have turned it off! But as long as I was awake anyway it didn't pay to incur the wrath of Jackie. (Which, as I've already indicated, was a worthy rival to the wrath of God—pestilences and all.) I'd better call and let her know I wouldn't be in today.

Reaching her at her apartment, I explained that I hadn't gotten much sleep and would just be doing a little work at home later.

Her reaction was predictable: "You're not sick or anything?"

"No, I'm not sick or anything," I answered irritably and then immediately regretted the tone. Believe me, I really do appreciate Jackie's concern—I often find it touching. But even so, I have to admit that just as often, it drives me bananas. As it was doing then. So hoping to cut off the balance of the interrogation—which I knew for a certainty to be pending—I added hastily and, I trusted, pleasantly, "I'll see you tomorrow."

It didn't work. "Hold on a sec. You really *are* feeling okay? That's the truth?"

"The whole truth. Listen, I'm completely bushed. I wouldn't have the energy to lie even if I had anything to lie *about*. So if you'll excuse me, I'm going to conk out now."

"Well, all right, if you're positive . . ." I doubt she was actually convinced, though. I think she even uttered a few more words on the subject as I was putting down the receiver. But I wasn't sure. And I didn't care, anyway.

I awoke after 12:00, well past the time I'd planned on getting up. But I had a quick breakfast and didn't bother dressing, so by one o'clock I was once more at my post at the kitchen table. This time to pore over the jottings I'd made on the pad.

An hour and a half later I was through with my poring—which had yielded absolutely nothing. Zilch. I didn't know what I'd expected to find. I only knew I hadn't found it. I gave some thought to sticking my head in the oven but settled for a little profanity. I even had a few choice words for Hercule. (And that old biddy Miss Marple, too, while I was at it.) And then I decided to run away from home.

Leaving everything on the table, I slapped on my makeup, got into some clothes, and made for Bloomingdale's. Where I put the investigation totally out of my mind in order to enjoy spending more than I could afford on some things I didn't need.

I refused to even go near the yellow pad when I came home.

Five minutes after I arrived at work Tuesday morning, Elliot stopped in my office to inform me that the Moody stakeout was on hold for a while. "Debbie—their daughter—gave birth last night. A boy." Elliot, softhearted soul that he is, was beaming paternally. "And Muriel's on her way to Ohio right now to help out. I'll let you know as soon as she's back in town," he said. "Okay?"

"Okay," I answered. But it wasn't. I'd actually been looking forward to another go-round with Muriel Moody. At least with that investigation, I had some idea of what I was doing—even though I didn't seem to be doing it right. What I'm saying is that it would have been a welcome respite from all of my floundering around on the Raven thing. I hated myself for feeling that way, too. I had an obligation to find out who murdered that girl. And soon.

Immediately following Elliot's exit, out came the yellow pad. I decided I'd try a different approach this time. Why didn't I see if I could tie in anything here—any of Raven's characteristics, I mean—with that charred paper? In other words, I wanted to see if I could find a hint of some kind as to what a person like Raven might have written down that night—and then felt compelled to destroy.

Yes, it was a long shot. But I had no idea what else to do. The paper was the only thing I could recognize as holding out some promise it might be a clue of some sort. And besides, after totally ignoring it for so long, I was now close to obsessing about it.

I began scrutinizing my barely legible scribblings, searching for that elusive connection. I'd just completed the fourth page when I had a flash. Maybe I'd been jumping to conclusions here!

What made me so sure it was Raven who'd written that note? After all, there'd been *two* people in the room that night: the victim and her murderer.

And now I asked myself a question.

What if the note or list or whatever it was had been the work of the killer? And what if it was also the killer who had burned it?

I thought about that for a while. It meant tossing aside all of my previous notions, which I was a little reluctant to do. (It bugs me whenever I become aware of just how off base I can manage to be.) But I definitely had to consider a new tack here. I certainly hadn't gotten anywhere with assigning authorship to the dead girl.

So I flipped back to the first page. And there, practically leaping off the paper, was a fact that this time around, immediately turned a light on in my head. I'm talking about the first notation I mentioned —the one about Raven's having no idea the pool was empty. Remember?

Well, I thought excitedly, *suppose the killer, aware of this, had written her a note daring her to take a dive from the balcony.*

Raven being the kind of person she was, you could figure with almost a hundred percent certainty she'd have risen to the bait. Plus, it would have been imperative for the murderer to destroy that note. What's more, I realized, working myself up to a near-feverish pitch, this would also explain the reason the dead girl's nightclothes had been found near the terrace door. I mean, if she'd been pushed—as her brother believed—why would she have shed her nightgown and peignoir first?

Everything suddenly seemed to click into position. It was so obvious, really, once you took a fresh look at things.

But it was only a minute before I returned to earth. With a thud.

This wonderful little scenario I'd cooked up had one tiny,

almost infinitesimal flaw: Why would you put anything like that on paper in the first place?

I was so thoroughly disgusted at being betrayed by my own very questionable reasoning powers that I shoved the yellow pad as far back on the desk as my arm could extend. Forget the stupid pad. I'd just have to start from scratch again. And I reached for my attaché case and removed the file containing my original notes.

I sat there for a moment berating myself, the unopened folder in front of me. How could I have come up with such a ridiculous theory, anyway? After all, what kind of sense did it make for the killer to dare the victim in writing? Still, I found I couldn't completely disabuse myself of the idea. It just kept hanging around in my head somewhere.

Which is why, later, when I got to those few seemingly innocuous words I'd read countless times before, I suddenly saw them in a different light.

While any of her sorority sisters might have presented the dead girl with that challenge, they told me now, *only one would have written it down.*

Chapter 32

I was close to hyperventilating. *My God!* I wanted to shout. *It's over*!

I felt this incredible sense of relief. I had finally discovered which one of Ellen's old school chums was, in her spare time, a cold-blooded killer. I wouldn't even let myself think about the uphill battle I'd be facing trying to prove what I knew. For now, I was content that I knew it.

I had to tell Ellen!

Fingers trembling, I dialed the first two digits of her Macy's number. Then I quickly replaced the receiver. No. This was not the way to have her learn about her very good friend the murderer. Better to lay that kind of news on her in person. And besides, I was suddenly eager to do just a little more digging before I spoke to her. I wouldn't be surprised if there were other important clues that I'd managed to overlook.

Going back to my original file now, I concentrated on the notes I'd made of my conversation with the perpetrator. Sure enough, it didn't take too long before I learned that there *was* something else. The girl had made a slip! I couldn't believe I hadn't picked up on it at the time. How could I *not*? I wondered, slowly shaking my head in disbelief.

Of course, one explanation was that until a few days ago I'd been hell-bent on proving that this homicide wasn't a homicide at all. But for obvious reasons, I didn't regard this as a particularly satisfying answer.

I reread the critical page again. One thing disturbed me about what I could now appreciate as the killer's damning words. There *could* be an explanation for them. And although I quickly came to the conclusion that this was very unlikely, I'd have to check and make sure, one way or the other. There was a good chance Ellen would be able to clarify things for me, and I'd been about to call her now, anyhow.

Lifting the receiver once again, I reminded myself that the murderer's telltale remark was only insurance evidence. No matter what I learned concerning that remark, I could still be confident I had the right person. The *real* evidence against her, the thing that positively shouted her guilt, being that charred piece of paper.

As soon as I heard Ellen's hello, I asked if she was available to meet me for dinner that night.

"Gee," she told me regretfully, "I promised to grab a bite with this friend of mine at the store—one of the other buyers. She said there was something she wanted my advice on." And then cautiously: "Why, what's up?"

"Nothing that important. There's just this little matter I'd like to talk over with you. Whenever you're free, that is."

But I was practically devastated. I mean at this point I couldn't wait to unload! I'd even selected an appropriate site for this summit meeting of ours. I'd planned to suggest— *strongly* suggest—that we pay a return visit to Irving's Kosher Delicatessen (where Ellen had so reluctantly briefed me on Carol Sue). No, as far as I knew, the fare hadn't improved; it remained America's crummiest deli. And no, I hadn't taken leave of my senses—or at least my sense of taste. I had no illusions that the pastrami was so much as a single notch above putrid, and I was well aware the French fries were even worse. (I couldn't bring myself to even contemplate Irving's strudel.) But the place did have two distinct advantages: (1) It was very convenient to Macy's, and (2) it was invariably close to empty—and understandably so. We could probably sit around forever, if we wanted to. Besides, who knows? The knobelwurst and baked beans might actually turn out to be edible.

Well anyway, it looked like I'd just have to contain myself for another day. And then I had a thought. "Any possibility of your stopping by for coffee after you've finished your dinner?"

"Something's wrong," Ellen said flatly. "Let me call Rita and cancel. I can be—"

"Don't be silly. Nothing's wrong. I wanted to see you about something, but it'll keep. Maybe we can get together tomorrow."

"Does it have anything to do with the murder?"

"Yes and no," I hedged. I didn't dare get any closer to the truth. Believe me, there wasn't even a possibility she'd have let me off the phone without my divulging the killer's identity.

"Listen, I'm sure it's not going to be a long drawn-out meal—we're just going to a coffee shop in the neighborhood here. So I don't see any reason I can't come over after supper."

"Fine," I said. I didn't realize I'd been holding my breath until I let it out.

"I'll see you later then."

"Uh, Ellen? It doesn't matter how *much* later. You know I'm up till all hours."

"All right. But I'll make it as soon as I can."

I couldn't let her go yet. I still needed her input with regard to what I hoped would turn out to be the killer's incriminating words. And it would have required a restraint of which I am constitutionally incapable if I'd been willing to wait until tonight for that, too.

"Hold it a minute," I just about barked. "Before you hang up, I have to ask you a question."

"Shoot. What did you want to know?"

"It's about Raven's lingerie . . ."

Ellen wasn't able to break away as quickly as she'd anticipated, and she didn't show up until close to 11 o'clock—her bedtime when she's at home. If I'd let myself, I would have felt guilty about keeping her up so late.

We were seated at the kitchen table, which contained in addition to my infamous coffee, two generous slices of Sara Lee cheesecake. "I didn't have any dessert at the restaurant; I was counting on something like this," Ellen informed me, helping herself to a heaping forkful. "Mmm. This is *so* good." Two or three minutes later she seemed to remember why she was here. "Oh. What was it you want to talk to me about?" she asked, digging into the Sara Lee again. "And what was that business about Raven's nightgown before?"

I shoved my own cheesecake to the side, untouched. Which was maybe a first in my life. I was so wired that for an instant I could hardly talk. "I know who killed Raven."

"Oh, my God," Ellen murmured, putting down the fork almost in slow motion. "Who?" I could barely hear the word.

Now, I'd made one incorrect assumption after another—as

you're well aware—before solving the mystery of Raven's death. And I couldn't help it; it was thoroughly relishing my success. (Maybe because it had taken me so long to achieve it.) I even managed to convince myself it would be too much of a shock to my poor niece's system if I just blurted out the name of the perpetrator. "Bear with me for a little while, and I'll tell you," I said.

"But—" And then she stopped herself. Ellen had been through this kind of nonsense with me enough times before to realize that no amount of protest would prevent my milking this thing for all it was worth. "All right. Go ahead," she told me resignedly.

"Well," I began, "it was concentrating on those charred bits of paper that put me on the right track at last."

"What charred bits of paper?"

"The ones found in the ashtray in Raven's bedroom. You did know about that, didn't you?"

"Oh yes, of course. That Saturday at Sybil's Chief Brady questioned all of us about it. I almost forgot."

"You're not the only one; I almost did, too. And what's even worse, in the few instances when I did give it any thought, I assumed that what we had there was the remains of a note Raven herself had written. Nothing important, I decided. But then a few days ago, it belatedly occurred to me that I could very well have been overlooking a clue of some kind." I began gathering steam, the words practically tumbling out now. "Well, after that I started trying to figure out its significance. And this morning, all of a sudden it came to me that maybe Raven had nothing to do with that paper. That it was equally likely to have been the killer's handiwork. And then I got this idea. Just suppose she—the killer—had dared Raven to take a dive into that pool from the balcony. Well, Raven not being aware there wasn't any water in the pool, what do you think she'd have done?"

"She's have taken the dare," Ellen answered quietly.

"Exactly! But of course, then I had to admit it wasn't too logical to think that kind of thing would have been written down. I mean, why not just *say*, 'Raven, I dare you to dive into that pool.' Or 'I'll bet you can't still dive from here like you used to.' Or whatever."

Ellen made a face. "You're ri—"

I was too revved up now to listen. "But later when I was

reading over my file again, it struck me that it actually would have been logical for *one person* to put the challenge in writing."

Sitting back now, I waited for a reaction.

Ellen did her chomping-on-the-lower lip thing for a minute or so. Then locking her eyes on mine, she demanded, sharply, "Well, tell me. Who was it, for heaven's sake?"

"The girl who couldn't talk."

"What do you mean 'couldn't talk'?"

"Because she had laryngitis."

"Oh, my God. Winnie."

Chapter 33

"Was I the one who told you about the laryngitis?" Ellen asked after a short silence interspersed with a few more oh my Gods.

I shook my head. "Sybil mentioned it. She said Winnie was in such bad shape that Friday night she couldn't even talk."

"It was Winnie, then, who sent Raven the invitation in the first place. Am I right?"

"Had to be, I'd say. In light of what transpired later."

"So her intention was to get Raven there just so she could murder her?" With the posing of that question, Ellen's large dark brown eyes seemed to almost double in size.

"Let me put it this way. Why else would she go to the trouble of inviting her?"

Ellen nodded acceptingly. And then a moment later she said, "If that's the case, though, there are a couple of things I don't understand."

"Like what?"

"Like how Winnie could possibly have known the pool would be empty that weekend."

"She couldn't. My guess is she had another little treat planned for her favorite sister-in-law. Like maybe a little something surreptitiously slipped into her drink. I really have no idea just what she had in mind. But at any rate this opportunity presented itself with the pool. And it was the perfect way of making the murder look like an accident. All Winnie had to do was get Raven alone, present her with that dare, and let the girl's basic nature take it from there."

"So she waited for her to come upstairs after the cocktail party," Ellen mused. "And then she sneaked down the hall to give her the note."

"That's right. And pretty soon Raven was diving headfirst into solid concrete."

Ellen shuddered. To tell you the truth, we both did. "I suppose Raven was already d-dead when I came to her room?"

"I'm sure of it."

"Oh." You could almost see her turning things over in her
mind now. "But why didn't Winnie just rip up the note and
flush it down the toilet?"

"I think we have you to thank for that. My guess is you
turned up right after Raven went off the balcony. Before Winnie had time for any flushing. I mean, how could she be sure
that when there was no response to your knock, you wouldn't
decide to just poke your head in the door?

"That's why it was so absolutely imperative to get rid of the
note—and fast. I doubt she would have wanted to take the
chance of keeping it on her; I wouldn't have, in her shoes. It's
the one material piece of evidence against her, you realize. But
anyway, as it happens, she was in luck—or maybe not, as it
turns out now. Because there on the table, probably right in
front of her, is a box of matches. It's her chance to dispose of
that damning piece of paper on the spot. And that's what she
does. *Now* if you should peek into the room, well, she's
clean."

"But how could she have explained away the fact she was
even *there*? Considering how much Raven and Winnie despised each other, that is."

"Oh, it would have been easy enough to concoct something." But Ellen looked doubtful. "Here, let me give you an
example. She could claim she thought it over and for Dick's
sake decided they should try and make peace. And she could
further claim that she figured she'd better see Raven that night,
before she changed her mind and backed out. Okay so far?"

"I'm with you. Go on."

"Well, then she could say that when she knocked on the
door and there was no response, she couldn't understand it—
she was sure everyone had already come upstairs. So she
thought she'd have a quick look inside just to see if everything
was all right. And there, lying in a jumble over by the terrace
were Raven's nightclothes. *Good Lord!* she could rasp as soon
as you made your entrance, *you don't suppose she dived off
the balcony, do you?* Or some gestures to that effect.

"Of course," I added, "given Winnie's resourcefulness,
she'd probably have been able to come up with a better story
than that. She could even say that Raven had asked to see *her*.

But the point is, without that piece of paper, there would be nothing to dispute whatever cockamamie crap she chose to hand out.

"And," I concluded, "even if the remnants of the note were still smoldering in the ashtray when you walked into the room, do you think that under the circumstances there's even one chance in a million you'd have noticed something like that?"

"No, I don't suppose I would have." Almost at once a thought seemed to strike her. "But seeing that I *didn't* go into the room, why not flush the ashes after I walked away?"

"In all probability because she was so frantic to get out of there. Also, maybe from her point of view, there was nothing in a few ashes to really tie her to Raven's death. As long as the note itself was gone, I mean."

Ellen sat there quietly with her thoughts for a brief time. Then she looked at me sadly. "You know, it's hard for me to accept that Winnie was the one," she told me softly, this bitter truth apparently becoming real to her at last.

"Which of your friends *could* you accept as a killer?" I put to her.

"You've got something there," she conceded, smiling wanly. But only an instant later, she frowned. "The thing is, though, Winnie's from a very religious background."

I couldn't decide whether she was attempting to convince me that I was wrong or to get herself to believe that I was right. Although I suspected it was the latter. "That didn't stop her from having an abortion, did it?" I responded tartly.

"Maybe not. But then afterwards she felt just awful about it. I don't think it was something she ever got over, either. And anyhow, it's really not the same thing."

"No, of course it isn't. But—"

"Oh!" Ellen exclaimed then, sparing me the task of attempting to draw some sort of parallel. "You haven't told me why you asked if Raven always wore ballerina-length nightgowns."

"I was coming to that. Okay, to fill you in, Winnie was trying to get me to accept that Raven's death was an accident, and she was telling me that Raven must have decided to rehearse her dive for the next day. And then she went on to say how she could just imagine her slipping off her peach ballerina nightgown before taking the plunge. Something of that sort. I think this was supposed to make the whole thing seem more real to me—painting a picture like that. Or could be she was just nervous; people tend to run off at the mouth when they're nervous. At any rate, Winnie explained that she knew what Raven had been wearing because she saw her things on the floor the next morning." I took a deep breath. Now almost beside myself with excitement, I demanded, "But you see, don't you? That wouldn't account for Winnie's knowing it was a *ballet-length* nightgown."

At this, I expected to see some sign of comprehension on Ellen's face. But she was looking at me uncertainly. "Well, like Winnie said, it *was* right there on the floor," she ventured timidly.

"That would explain her knowing the *color*. But how could she possibly judge the length of the gown from just seeing it dumped there like that? You'd really have to see it *on* someone to be able to tell that."

"I guess you're right," Ellen responded reluctantly. "But wait a minute. What if that's all Raven wore nowadays? Ballet gowns, I mean."

"Do you think Winnie would be privy to that kind of knowledge? Don't be silly! I doubt they ever spent one night under the same roof together since college. And if, by chance, Raven did sleep at her sister-in-law's once or twice, it would hardly make Winnie an authority on her nightgowns."

"That's true." But this, too, seemed to be offered with reluctance.

"Besides," I pressed, "most probably Raven would have worn a robe. So Winnie wouldn't have even gotten a look at her in her gown. And incidentally, as for the particular little number she took to Sybil's, Dick mentioned that it was brand-new. Raven went out and bought herself that nightgown and peignoir outfit just for the occasion."

"Well, it looks like that's it, then," Ellen murmured as she abstractedly lifted her cup for a first sip of now-cold coffee. She was so lost in thought she didn't even wince. And when she stopped sipping, it was only long enough to present her next question.

"Do you think this can actually be considered murder? Legally, I'm talking about. What I mean is, Winnie didn't actually *do* anything to Raven—nothing physical, anyway."

"I wondered about that, too. So I asked Pat about it, and—"

"Pat who?"

"Pat Sullivan. You know, of Gilbert and Sullivan."

I purposely threw in the firm for the sake of some levity—however brief—and Ellen giggled on cue. In spite of all the years I've been renting space from Pat and Elliot, she still has that same reaction whenever she hears the name. "I'm sorry, Aunt Dez," she said once the giggle was out of her system. "You were saying?"

"Pat informs me that since the intent of her action was to cause Raven's death, Winnie could be charged with second-degree murder. Which means that if she's convicted, she could be put away for a long, long time. Maybe permanently. The penalty for second degree is twenty-five years to life."

The response was a somber "Oh."

"What's the matter?"

"Nothing. Not really."

"Do you consider it too stiff a punishment?"

"It's not that. Not exactly, anyway. It's just that Winnie was in such a horrible position with the way Dick felt about his sister and everything. I don't know. She may have just been in such a state of despair that . . . oh, I don't know." Ellen was looking totally miserable.

"Think about Raven for a second. Okay, she was a bitch. An A-number one, four-star bitch, in fact. But did that give Winnie the right to cut her life short like that?"

"No, of course it didn't. I feel awful about Raven. I really do. It's just—"

"She was even willing to frame you, for God's sake," I reminded her.

Ellen's comeback spoke volumes for the boundless charity of her nature. "She must have been at her wit's end," she said. And then: "You don't actually know Winnie, Aunt Dez. She's basically a really good person. And she's always been a very good friend, too."

I choked back the sarcastic retort. (But I imagine you can pretty much guess what it was.) "Well, don't feel too sorry for her," I substituted. "That sentence presupposes there's even enough evidence to indict her in the first place. And as of now, I have no idea how I'm going to be able to prove a thing." Then to myself I added—mostly in an attempt to bolster my confidence—*But I'll find a way.*

And with this, I reached for that untouched slice of Sara Lee.

Chapter 34

Ellen slept on my sofa Tuesday night; it was much too late for her to start traipsing all the way downtown to Chelsea. The next morning I was just setting the table when she walked into the kitchen, looking really awful. Being at my most tactful before coffee, I put it to her this way: "You look really awful."

"I didn't sleep too well. I kept thinking about—about everything."

"I know how upsetting this is for you," I said gently. "I wish it didn't have to be like this."

"I know you do, Aunt Dez." She was standing in the middle of the floor only a couple of feet away from me, staring off into space somewhere. After a minute or two, though, she met my gaze. "You were fantastic—to figure this thing out. I don't believe anyone else could have done it. I honestly don't."

I think I may have beamed. And the especially nice thing about Ellen's compliments is that whether they're deserved or not, she truly means them. But anyway, I was about to make the kind of faint protestation I felt was expected of me when she murmured, "I want you to understand something. It's not that I feel Winnie should get away with what she's done—you do realize that, don't you? It's just that this whole thing makes me very sad."

Her eyes seemed to be growing misty now, so I said brusquely, "Listen, you'd better shape up this minute or I won't let you fix breakfast for us."

She was able to produce a halfhearted grin before taking out the frying pan and getting down to business.

I wasn't in any big hurry to leave for the office that day, dawdling over a second cup of coffee after Ellen went to work.

When I showed up, it was late enough to provoke a malevolent glare from Jackie—but not so late as to inspire a lecture.

Sitting down at my desk, I mentally reviewed what I'd so recently regarded as my coup. Now one day removed from the initial glow of success, I faced the truth. While the facts I'd uncovered were enough to convince *me* that Winnie had murdered her sister-in-law, coming up with sufficient proof to convince a jury was going to be tough.

And I was even more anxious about my chances with Brady. That was really the critical part—persuading Brady of Winnie's guilt. You see, while I felt very strongly that she should be made to pay for her crime, right now I had to regard that as a bonus. My overriding concern was presenting the police chief with the kind of evidence that would let Ellen off the hook.

I hung in until close to 6 o'clock, trying to devise some way of making a really solid case against Winnie. But I drew a blank. I just couldn't figure out how I could possibly nail her—short of getting her to confess, that is.

So in the end, that's what I decided to do.

I contacted Winnie at her office on Thursday morning. "I was wondering if we could get together for a few minutes. Something's just turned up with regard to Raven's death. Nothing really important"—after all, why put her on her guard?—"but I thought you might be able to clarify a couple of things for me."

"Well, I could try," she said lightly enough. "I'm going to be in Manhattan on Saturday—beauty parlor again. Why don't we meet at 'our place' "—a little titter accompanied this suggestion—"around a quarter of four. Okay with you?"

"It's fine."

After a very long rest-of-Thursday and an interminable Friday, I strode purposefully into Lonnie's Coffee Bar at 3:45 on Saturday afternoon, right on time for our appointment. My jaw was set determinedly, my shoulders squared—and my heart threatening to burst through my ribcage.

There were only three or four other people in the place. So it wasn't too hard to spot Winnie, who was already seated in a booth toward the back—the same one we'd occupied before, in fact. A beige mug was clutched in her hand. And an empty

plate sat at her elbow, the scant two or three crumbs remaining
a giveaway it had recently been occupied by something chocolate. Probably a brownie.

"Let me get you some coffee," she offered, starting to rise.

That made me feel about a hundred and two. If she'd added
"ma'am," I'd have slit my throat. I put a restraining hand on
her arm. "Thanks, but I'll go pick up a cup myself. Be with
you in a minute."

When I returned, she didn't see me at first. She was much
too preoccupied with glaring down into her coffee mug. I
noted the furrows in her brow and the deep ridges above the
bridge of her nose. *I must have her damned scared* was the
happy thought that flashed through my mind. But then I immediately recalled that those lines were permanently etched on
her face.

She looked up as I slid into the booth and smiled pleasantly.

I smiled back. At least I hoped I did. There's a good possibility, though, that I might have produced a grimace. The fact
Winnie was a killer was one thing. I mean, while I have this
natural animosity for people who see fit to take other people's
lives, well, considering what the victim had put her through,
it's likely I'd have eked out some compassion for this girl. *If*
she hadn't attempted to finger Ellen for the deed.

"How have you been?" she asked.

"Good," I responded, still smiling (or maybe grimacing).
Following this, I politely inquired as to the state of her own
health and that of her husband. And then before this hypocrite
could get around to feigning an interest in Ellen's well-
being—which was almost certainly next on the agenda—I decided it was time for a swallow of hot coffee. After which I
proceeded to cough. "W-wat-er!" I cried out in a choked
voice.

Winnie immediately ran to get me a glass. At that point, I
opened my handbag and turned on my tape recorder. When
she came back, I was all set.

I took a few sips of the water, responded to her ostensible
concerns, and then kicked off with my old standby. "Look,
Winnie," I said, "someone—someone who hated to get you in
trouble—has just come forward and told me she saw you leaving Raven's room that Friday night. But I figured I should wait
and hear what you had to say before reporting it to the police."

"Whoever it was must have made a mistake," Winnie informed me calmly, almost ingenuously. "I went straight to bed after I came upstairs."

Of course, I'd expected as much. But I did have to start someplace, didn't I?

"That's what I thought at first," I responded. "But this person was positive it was you she saw."

Winnie shook her head, her getting-limper-by-the-minute lemon-colored curls joining vehemently in the denial. I was not distressed to note that Tino—I recalled the name of her hairdresser—still wasn't doing right by her. "It wasn't me," she maintained. And then she added, "Besides, as far as I know, the police consider Raven's death an accident. So I wouldn't make any difference, anyway."

At this, she looked so pleased with herself that I longed to punch her silly moon face. But I settled for clenching my fists under the table. Then I let out a long sigh, and in a voice tinged with regret I said, "Don't you think it's time we leveled with each other, Winnie? I've strongly suspected for some time now that you killed your sister-in-law. And it appears that's finally been confirmed."

"Are you crazy?" she shot back, her tone shrill now. "Or is it your so-called witness who's nuts? I didn't kill Raven because she wasn't murdered. And nobody saw me leaving her room because I wasn't there. I really don't know what you're after here, but I don't think I'll wait around to find out." And picking up the handbag alongside her, she started to rise.

"I know about the note," I said then.

She sat back down. "What note?" she asked in a tone that revealed absolutely nothing.

"The note that dared Raven to dive into a pool she didn't know was being repaired."

"I wish I had some idea what you're talking about." The words, however, were belied by Winnie's appearance. Her complexion was now a deep, dark red, and for a fraction of a second she looked at me with fear in her eyes.

"It had to be you," I told her evenly. "You were the one with the laryngitis, the one who had to write out the words because you couldn't say them."

"And where is this note?" she challenged.

"You set a match to it, if you recall. But I have proof it existed."

"Maybe. Although I have my doubts. But one thing I do

know: I had nothing to do with any note." And once again, Winnie shifted in her seat as if to leave.

"And then there's the nightgown," I said quickly.

The shifting stopped abruptly. "What nightgown?" I had the impression she was genuinely perplexed now, and I decided it was quite possible the girl never even realized she'd slipped up there.

She leaned forward almost eagerly as I went through the business about her knowing the length of her sister-in-law's nightgown.

"I don't remember saying it was a ballet gown," was the response. "And if I did, it was an assumption, or maybe that's just the way I pictured her. Raven often wore ballet gowns when we were at school. Ask Ellen. Of course, come to think of it, she probably wore baby dolls just as often. Anyway, it appears I was right, doesn't it?"

I wanted to throw myself down on the rust-colored quarry tiles and kick my legs and pound my fists on the ground. Not a very mature thought, I have to admit. But this girl was making a monkey out of me. Or maybe she was just giving me the opportunity to make one out of myself.

You see, I hadn't honestly expected to get anywhere with that eyewitness story. You never can tell, of course, but the truth is I'd tried variations on that baloney in at least a dozen instances and in all sorts of cases, and if it had actually worked today, well, it would have been the first time. And I hadn't counted on much from the note, either. I mean, the girl would have had to be certifiable to just come out and admit to authorship. But *this* seemed to offer a real possibility that she'd trip herself up. And I'd kind of been pinning my hopes on it.

Ideally, she would have said, "I knew it was a ballet gown, because I saw that same nightgown on her before." Which, of course, she couldn't have. But I'd have settled for as little as a brazen, "It's your word against mine." Maybe that would have at least raised a question in Brady's mind. Only Winnie refused to give me even that much.

I suppose I should have called it quits then. But in my mind's eye I could see that little tape recorder whirring on in my bag, so I plodded ahead. "What kind of person are you?" I said. "How could you do this to Dick?—the man you claim to be so crazy about. Whatever Raven was, he cared very deeply for her." And then I proclaimed dramatically, "When you killed her, you killed a part of him, too!"

"That's just why you can be sure I *didn't* kill her. Dick means everything to me. I'd never have done anything to deprive him of his only sister." She was something like the voice of reason here, while I was sounding more and more like Cheetah. Plus she seemed so sincere and she was looking at me so unflinchingly with those soft, warm eyes of hers that I panicked. *My God! Could I have been this wrong?*

And then she stood up. "I have to take off—we're having company over for drinks at seven. Listen, Desiree, I hope you believe me. Anyhow though, give my love to Ellen."

But as she turned to go, I caught this smile on her face. I've tried to describe that smile many times. *Triumphant* is the best I've been able to do.

But at any rate, it erased whatever doubt I had.

Chapter 35

After Winnie left, I had another cup of coffee—I don't know why—and then I headed home. The answering machine was blinking at me when I got in. *Bruce!* I thought. I was excited in spite of my still-raw wounds. Excited, even, in spite of my willing myself not to be.

I checked my watch. 5:30. He was definitely improving.

But when I pressed Playback, it was Ellen. I can't say I wasn't disappointed, but her message did make me chuckle.

"I'm anxious to know how you made out with Winnie. Please call. I have today off, so you can reach me at home—I'll be here till about quarter of seven. Then I'm meeting Mike. We're having dinner at this new Italian place on Sixteenth Street that Ginger who lives in my building—you remember Ginger—says we positively must try. And then we'll probably take in a movie. There are a couple of good ones around now. Unless Mike's too tired, of course. In that case, we'll just . . ." The tape ran out before Ellen did.

I dialed her number right away.

"Oh, good!" she exclaimed when she heard my voice. "I was hoping, you'd get back to me before I went out. What happened?"

I filled her in on my afternoon, and she listened attentively, her only comment being one measly "Oh, my God"—but at which point I can't remember. And then when I was through, she said hesitantly, "Umm, you're still so sure it was Winnie?"

"If you had seen her face when she was leaving that coffee bar, you wouldn't be asking me that."

"Well, what's next? What are you going to do?"

I hunched my shoulders, then realized this might not be the best way to communicate. "I haven't even had a chance to think about that yet," I verbalized.

"Don't worry. You'll come up with something," my fan club's only member stated firmly. "I know you will."

It was about ten minutes after my conversation with Ellen that the phone rang a second time.

Bruce! I thought again, excited again.

But it turned out to be the second call that wasn't the one I'd been hoping for. Which heaped a little added gloom on my already far-from-happy psyche.

"I was wondering if you felt like grabbing a bite out later," said my neighbor Barbara.

I declined the invitation for both our sakes. "Thanks, but I think I'd better pass; I seem to be coming down with a cold," I alibied.

Supper that evening was soup and a sandwich. And after that, I sprawled out on the sofa and put on the TV. Tonight, I was not going to give another thought to the murder—my brain was practically screaming out for some vacation time. I also had no intention of wasting a single second on Bruce Simon. Not even to wonder why he hadn't called. But when the phone rang at a little past seven, my adrenaline—much to my annoyance—went haywire once more.

Only it wasn't Bruce now, either. It was Pat Martucci. "I had to let you know; Burton asked me to move in with him this morning!" she informed me gleefully.

"That's wonderful! I'm so happy for you!" I responded. I swear I was glad to hear her news. I only hoped my enthusiasm was breaking through my despondence.

I guess it made it, though, because then she said, "I knew you would be."

We chatted for a few minutes longer, and I was waiting to see if she'd mention Bruce at all. When she didn't, I knew that meant she wasn't aware I'd seen him since his move to New York. (Pat doesn't expend any unnecessary effort on discretion.) I was thinking that maybe I should say something about it myself—although there really wasn't much *to* say—when it suddenly became a moot point. "I have to hang up," she told me. "Burton just walked in with a pizza."

My vacation from murder was short-lived, ending as soon as I got up the next morning. There was really no escaping it—I had to find a way to do *something* about Winnie. But for that entire miserable day, I wasn't able to come up with even a glimmer of an idea as to what that something might be.

It was on Monday that Dick Eber called.

"Why did you meet with Winnie Saturday?" he asked.

I think I may have gasped—that really threw me. "She *told* you?"

"No. I was in her office today—I went to pick her up for lunch. And I saw it on her calendar."

"Didn't you ask *her* what it was about?"

"She was pretty vague. Winnie tries her best to protect me."

"Well, uh—"

"Listen, if I came into the city later, do you think you could give me a few minutes? Please. I could be there by six."

I didn't know how to refuse. "All right," I agreed. But very reluctantly. The truth was, I'd rather have eaten a can of worms—*live* worms—than say what I would have to say to this poor guy tonight.

The bell rang at 5:58.

I opened the door of my apartment to a very white, very nervous-looking Dick Eber. "Thanks for letting me come over," he said, shaking my hand.

We sat in the living room. And after he turned down my offer to fix him something to eat and likewise refused the proffered coffee, tea, Coke, wine, and liquor, I steeled myself for inflicting further damage on the man.

"You found out something about how Raven died. I know that," Dick stated flatly. "What was it?" With the question, he seemed to become even paler.

"I'm really sorry I have to tell you this. But well, I recently discovered some facts that, well, that convinced me you were right all along. Your sister's death wasn't an accident."

For a moment he didn't speak. And then he asked in this tremulous voice, "Do you know who killed her?"

"Uh, yes, I, uh—I do. And I'm really sorry. Believe me, telling you this is one of the hardest—"

"You're not going to say it was Winnie!"

"Look," I responded softly, "I'm sure this must be the realization of your greatest fear. But the—"

"You're wrong! Winnie had nothing to do with Raven's death. I'm positive of it. And you're also wrong about my ever being afraid of anything like that. I've always known better."

And then after a minute or two, he put to me tentatively, "What kind of proof do you—do you think you have?"

And so I proceeded to apprise him of the note and the nightgown.

"You call that proof?" Dick demanded when he'd heard me out. "My sister could have been the one who wrote that note— to remind herself of something."

"And then burned it afterwards?" I disputed gently.

"Well, who knows?" he retorted, flustered. "Maybe it was something she didn't care to have anyone else see."

I wanted to leave it at that. But the words came out anyway. "And the nightgown?"

"It's possible Raven decided not to take the new one away with her. Maybe she took the same gown she wore at our house last winter—she stayed over one night, you know—and naturally, Winnie would have recognized it."

"Winnie would have told me that on Saturday. Besides, you don't really believe Raven would have brought another gown. Not after buying one specifically for that weekend."

"You bet I believe it! Raven changed her mind, that's all. She used to do that a lot. Hey, don't *you* ever change your mind?" His tone had grown belligerent, but I could hardly take offense. The pain was so clearly etched on his face that it hurt to look at him.

For once, I just kept quiet. And then, much more calmly, Dick tried to win me over to his side. "Listen, Winnie and I have done a lot of arguing about how Raven died. As sure as I am that it was murder—that's how sure she is that it was an accident. Or maybe it's only that she thinks an accident would be easier for me to live with. But anyhow, never once in all this time has it so much as crossed my mind that Winnie had anything to do with what happened to my sister. And do you want to know why?"

I obliged him. "Why?"

"Because of the feelings Winnie and I have for each other. She would never hurt me like that."

"I'm so sorry," I murmured yet again. And I was. Sorry his sister had been murdered. Sorry his wife was her murderer. And sorriest of all that I'd been the one to lay everything out for him.

"You don't have to be. Not about Winnie. There's just no way she could have killed Raven," Dick insisted.

I didn't have the strength—or the heart—to argue the point.

I was seeing him out about five minutes later, and he was already across the doorsill when he stopped and turned to me.

"If I thought Winnie was responsible," he said, his voice gruff with choked-back tears, "I wouldn't have anything left." And then very, very softly: "Nothing at all."

Chapter 36

I spent Tuesday practically incommunicado. I tell you, I was Greta Garbo with a hennaed head. From the second I got into work until I left for home, I kept a rock-bottom profile. The door to my cubbyhole stayed closed. I ate lunch alone at my desk. I even had Jackie hold all my calls. (Which, business being so thriving lately, totaled exactly one—from somebody wanting to sell me a subscription to the *Daily News*.)

I needed to think. And so I did.

First, I thought about Dick Eber—and immediately my eyes started to sting. The way I saw it, he was his wife's real victim. The one you could really care about, anyway. What a toll this thing had taken on the man! I couldn't devote any more than three or four minutes' worth of sniffles to him, though, because that would have meant running downstairs to the store for another box of Kleenex.

So I soon moved on to brooding about Winnie. And about Ellen. There was every likelihood Winnie was going to get away with murder. But even worse, of course, was the possibility Ellen could end up being the fall guy.

And then I realized something.

While it looked like there was nothing I could do about that damned Winnie, Ellen was another story. Maybe I could still accomplish something there. If I went to Brady with what I'd discovered, it might just be enough to at least cast some doubt on Ellen's guilt. Not that I was all that hopeful, really. But it was the one hope I had.

I figured I'd better call and pave the way for myself first, though. Brady certainly hadn't pulled any punches about the welcome I'd receive if I showed up there again.

At a little before 3:00, I nervously dialed the Clear Cove station house.

"Mertz," a masculine voice informed me.

"Is Chief Brady in?" I asked.

"Nope."

"Uh, is he gone for the day?"

"I'm not sure."

"So he could be coming back later, then?"

"Yeah, maybe." Nobody could accuse this guy of running off at the mouth!

"Well, thanks," I told him grudgingly.

"Yep. Glad to help."

I tried my luck again just after 4:00. This time, a woman answered the phone, and when I asked for Chief Brady, she put me right through. She didn't even request my name first—undoubtedly a big plus, under the circumstances.

The chief wasn't very pleased to find me at the other end of the line. Which is describing his reaction in the most glowing terms possible. For a couple of seconds there, I was even afraid he might decide to hang up on me. (While this, I knew, wouldn't have been at all in character, I could see where our last meeting might have been sufficiently off-putting to inspire that sort of response.)

But when I told him I wanted to see him, his tone was only mildly reproachful. "I thought we had ourselves an agreement," he said.

"Yes, I know. But this time, *I* have information for *you*."

"Is that right." It wasn't a question.

"Honestly, it's the truth."

"And just what kind of information are we talkin' about here?" he asked skeptically.

"I know who killed Raven Eber!"

"Is that so." He didn't sound the least bit impressed.

"But I have proof! Look, let me stop in and talk to you. I'll just take a few minutes of your time. You—"

"Come by tomorrow mornin'. Say, around ten."

"I'll be there. And thanks. Thanks a lot."

But by then I was expressing my gratitude to a dead phone.

For what was left of the afternoon and all of Tuesday evening, I was a total wreck. In fact, the anticipation of that appointment in Clear Cove had me so on edge I didn't even think about Bruce. Well, not more than two or three times, anyway. Five, tops.

*   *   *

It was 10:00 on the nose when I walked into Brady's office—suffering from a constricted chest and buckling knees, I might add. He jumped to his feet. He even smiled. Not a big smile or a very sincere-looking one. But still, it was more than I expected.

Once we were both seated, though, he didn't waste time on pleasantries. "Well now, what is it you've got for me?" he asked immediately.

I imparted the same information I had already given out three times in the last few days. Brady's face was impassive straight through the recitation.

I concluded with, "So you see how everything ties together, don't you?"

He nodded. Not so much in answer to my question as in appreciation of what he'd just learned. Or at any rate, that's how I took it. His words, however, were noncommittal. "Maybe so," he said.

"Uh, I was thinking you might still be able to check the ashtray for fingerprints just in c—"

"That's an excellent suggestion, Ms. Shapiro. It surely is. And I thank you for wantin' to help. But there's some things that occur to even dumb yokel cops like we've got in our little group here. We managed to think of dustin' for prints all by ourselves—right after the discovery of the body, if you want to know. And to save you the trouble of askin', we didn't exactly come up big there."

"I'm sorry. That was stupid," I mumbled, a sudden rush of warmth alerting me to the fact that I was just as red-faced as I deserved to be. "It's only that I'm so excited about this new evidence."

"Well now, I can see where you might be. And incidentally, what you've been tellin' me makes a lotta sense. It answers one question, anyway, that's been hangin' me up all along."

"What's that?"

"I've been speculatin' on why if it wasn't an accident, if she didn't just decide to dive into the pool on her own, the victim would get out of her nightclothes. So this scenario of yours would certainly take care of that, wouldn't it? But even so, I've still got kind of a little problem with your evidence."

I looked at him questioningly.

"I just don't know what it is I can do about it."

"I thought—"

"If I was to bring it to Manfredi—he's our DA—he'd throw me out on my keister."

"Look, I'm aware this isn't the kind of proof that would lead to a conviction or anything. That's not why I came."

"Well then, why don't you tell me why you did come."

"I was hoping that what I found out would get you to change your thinking about Ellen. About her maybe being the one responsible for Raven's death."

Brady put both elbows on the desk then, his fists propping up his chin. "You can stop worryin' about your niece," he said kindly. "There's no reason to concern yourself with that anymore."

You convinced him! I thought. And suddenly, for the first time since I walked into this place breathing came easy to me. If it had been anatomically convenient, I'd probably have begun patting myself on the back just then. With the explanation that followed, however, the self-congratulations came to an end.

"As a matter of fact," the police chief continued, his tone confidential now, "the case was put in our inactive file right after you were here last. Not because I didn't think that young woman was murdered—in spite of a coupla holes here and there, I was certain of that almost from the beginnin'. But I just couldn't see a way in hell we were gonna be able to prove it. And this new information of yours notwithstandin', I still don't."

Well, so what if I hadn't made the difference? At least Ellen was safe. The reason, after all, didn't matter. "So then there's nothing to worry about—with Ellen, I mean?" I had to hear it again.

Brady grinned at me. It was a Cheshire cat kind of grin. "Can I level with you?"

I tensed up. That question always scares me. "Sure."

"You know, I got this kind of . . . call it 'intuition.' Always have had. And the thing of it is, try as hard as I might, I just couldn't see Ms. Kravitz as bein' capable of killin' anyone."

"You mean—"

"What I'm sayin' to you is, I never did consider her very much of a suspect."

When I returned from Clear Cove, I went straight home. I was too filled with emotion to go in to the office. Even if there'd been anything to go in for.

I could hardly wait to talk to Ellen. But she was out to lunch when I phoned, and she didn't call back until close to 3:30. At which point, I was like a crazy person.

My response to her "Aunt Dez?" could have permanently damaged my vocal chords.

"You're not a suspect!" I screeched.

"Thank God," she whispered. And after it had a little more time to sink in: "But how come?"

I related my conversation with Brady.

She giggled almost manically at the part where he admitted he'd never had her pegged as a really serious candidate for murderer. Her reaction being, I have no doubt, a much-needed release from the strain she'd been under for so long. Pretty quickly, however, she turned serious. "I don't know how to thank you—for everything," she murmured, sounding like she might be considering punctuating this with some tears.

I didn't want to take the chance I was right. "Listen," I put in hastily, "just before I left the station, Brady said he might try his luck and take a crack at Winnie himself. He told me not to get my hopes up, though, that it was a long shot he'd get anywhere with her."

"He certainly won't be able to do anything right away. I was talking to Sybil before. She said Winnie and Dick left for the Bahamas this morning. They went for two weeks."

I remembered then that the first time we met, Winnie had mentioned how anxious she was to get Dick to take a vacation. Well, it looked as if she'd finally gotten through to him. "That's okay," I responded. "I guess it'll just have to wait."

Now, knowing Winnie, I was hardly under the illusion Brady would be able to make any headway there. Still, I felt a little let down.

"I haven't told any of them, of course," Ellen said then.

"Told who about what?" I mean, talk about non sequiturs!

"Told the others about Winnie being . . . well, the one."

"And Winnie? Have you heard from her lately?"

"Not in quite a while."

"I would have been pretty surprised if you had. But listen, speaking of Dick before reminded me. He came to see me Monday night."

"Were you expecting him? How is he holding up?" And then right on the heels of that: "The poor guy. You know, every time I think about him, I could cry."

Oh, hell! But it was too late to back off now. "He's still hurting badly," I answered, bypassing question number one for the moment. "Maybe more than ever after our talk." And I recapped our meeting for her.

"So he didn't believe you, huh?"

"He really couldn't let himself, don't you see? With Raven gone, who else does he have but Winnie? If he accepted the fact she was his sister's killer, he wouldn't have anybody at all."

There was a brief pause before Ellen pronounced, "Then I'm glad you weren't able to convince him."

I considered that for a few seconds. "You know something?" I said. "I suppose I am, too."

Chapter 37

I can't say I hadn't toyed with the idea of picking up the phone myself. After all, this *was* the nineties, wasn't it? and I *was* a with-it, liberated kind of woman, wasn't I?

The more I thought about it, though, the less inclined I felt to get in touch with him. If he wanted to see me, he'd do the getting in touch. And if he wasn't interested enough, well then, I wasn't, either.

But the real, absolute truth was that I was just plain chicken. What if for some reason or other I ended up being sorry that I called?

And then on Wednesday night, just before 8 o'clock, the phone rang—and there he was. The same old bantering, ball-busting Bruce.

"Why haven't I heard from you?" he teased. "You've got to stop this hard-to-get business."

Almost reflexively, I fell into our game-playing mode. "I've been away. An African safari."

"No fooling? I always said you were a fascinating woman. Where in Africa were you?"

"I'm afraid I can't give you any specifics." I lowered my voice. "The government sent me."

"Ohh. Well, if that's how it is . . . But listen, enough of this nonsense. Let's talk about something much more interesting: dinner."

The man was really too much! It takes him practically for-ever to call, and when he finally does, he hasn't even got the decency to lie and tell me he's been desperately ill or some-thing. Plus he waits until it's almost bedtime (you can see I'm not above a little exaggeration to make my case), and then he expects me to drop everything and go out with him. "I'm afraid I have plans for tonight," I snapped. There, I said it!

And I should have said it the last time, too. And the time before that.

"Hold on a second," Bruce protested. "Who mentioned tonight? I was talking about Saturday."

"Oh." I was too taken aback to manage anything more. But a silly-looking grin—I just know it was silly-looking—was spreading across my face.

"Well?"

"Saturday's good."

"Glad to hear it. I assume I've given you enough notice so you can get your shopping done."

"Shopping?" I echoed.

"You know, for our dinner." A well-placed pause. "I just assumed you'd want the opportunity to reciprocate."

Now the power of speech abandoned me completely.

"If you think I'm being too pushy, though . . ."

I had no idea how to handle this. I mean, can you believe the chutzpah of this guy? Still, he *had* taken me out for two very nice meals (three, if you counted our initial blind date). And I do love to cook. So it wouldn't exactly kill me to make him dinner. "As a matter of fact, I do. Think you're being too pushy, that is. But you can come anyway."

"What a gracious invitation! I accept. And I'm really looking forward to it. I understand you're a gourmet cook."

"Pat?"

"Correct. She slipped that into a phone conversation I had with her the other day. I got the feeling, somehow, that she was trying to get me to ask you out. She didn't seem to have a clue that we've been seeing each other."

Now, I wouldn't exactly call a couple of dates "seeing each other." But I let it pass. "I didn't want to make her jealous," I said dryly.

Bruce laughed. "Then it's good thing I didn't enlighten her. Well, I'll see you Saturday at seven."

"Seven-thirty," I corrected. Just to be contrary, really. And before he could counter that: "It's my dinner, remember?"

We hung up about a minute later. And almost at once this old saying sprang to mind—I'm sure you've heard it: "Be careful what you wish for—you may get it."

The fact is, I'd never before had such mixed feelings about anyone. And it seemed I just kept right on getting more and more confused. Do you know, I hadn't said a word to Ellen about having gone out with Bruce? Not since filling her in on our blind date all those months ago. And I couldn't even put my finger on why.

It was almost as if Bruce Simon had become my own guilty little secret.

I went into the office on Thursday wondering how I was going to occupy my time there all day. I could, of course, tackle my one unstraightened desk drawer. Or even start working on my files. Or I could just sit around and do nothing. I opted for the nothing.

I was in the process of staring at my fingertips when Elliot bustled into my office. "Oh, I'm so glad you're in," he said a little breathlessly. "Muriel's back."

Thank God!

"I only this minute hung up from Herm," he went on. "Tonight, she's supposed to be playing bingo. She told Herm she'd be leaving the house around seven-thirty. So, are you available?"

You bet I was! "Yes, sure."

I felt suddenly revitalized. And it wasn't just because I was happy about having a job to do, either. What really had me pumped up was that, for me, this was a kind of consolation prize. I mean, while you could hardly place Muriel and Winnie in the same category, still, I now had a crack at zinging it to at least one miserable, conniving bitch.

At 7:06, I was at my post on the Upper West Side, parked in the same spot I'd occupied on my last Muriel stakeout. As before, I sat crouched in my seat, hands on the steering wheel, key in the ignition, and eyes riveted to the Moody front door—with an occasional nervous glance across the street at the home of my sexagenarian nemesis.

Muriel's sudden appearance on the stoop took me by surprise—it was only 7:15 then. *Anxious to make up for all of those missed performances, no doubt*, I meowed to myself.

She was looking very elegant this evening in a pale blue silk dress with a matching jacket, her striking silver hair immaculately coifed. I had ample time to study the woman, too—it took close to ten minutes for her to flag down a vacant cab. But I soon found myself wishing she had hailed any cab but.

I mean, this guy drove like a madman. I don't think he took

a single corner on all four wheels. Which meant I couldn't, either. At one point I may have grazed a parked car. I'm not really positive—I didn't dare slow down. I *know* I came within a breath of crashing headlong into a bus. And I undoubtedly put the fear of God into one of those obnoxious delivery boys who persist in riding their bikes on the wrong side of the street. Forced to yield to my Chevy (which I can report was at least traveling in the right direction), he went crashing into the curb. I could hear him screaming obscenities at me for half a block.

By the time the taxi came to a merciful stop, I was shaking from the top of my head straight down to the toes of the butter-soft Ferragamo pumps I'd picked up on sale a few months back. For a minute or two, I didn't even have the presence of mind to look and see where I was. And then I glanced at the street sign. We were on East Seventy-third Street, and Muriel was just getting out of the cab. A moment later, she walked into a large, canopied building.

Double-parking, I quickly followed her inside. But she was already out of sight by the time I entered the lobby.

"May I help you?" the short, paunchy, singularly unfriendly doorman inquired.

"I just drove my cousin here—she came in not more than two minutes ago—and she left something in my car." How was I supposed to work up a decent lie with this guy scowling at me like that? Nevertheless, I proceeded gamely. "Uh, her . . . house keys. She won't be able to get into her apartment later without them." And when he didn't respond: "Silver hair? Blue dress?"

"I know who you mean," the man informed me, ice in his voice.

"She didn't mention who she was coming to see; she just asked if I could give her a lift."

"Exactly what is it you would like me to do?" Mr. Frostbite demanded impatiently. *Christ, this guy was intimidating!* Or maybe he only seemed that way to us wimps.

"Well," I suggested timidly, "I thought you could buzz the apartment—the one she's visiting—to let her know I have her keys."

The way I had it figured, when the doorman rang up, I'd try to stand close enough to get a peek at the apartment number. But if that didn't pan out, there was also a good possibility he'd mention the tenant's name. You know, "Mr. Smith, I have someone down here with your guest's house keys." (And of course, once I found out what I needed to know, I'd be out of there like a shot.)

He seemed to be purposely taking his time in responding, and awaiting his ruling, I began to fidget, shifting my weight first to one leg and then the other. And now a small white poodle charged through the open door. In tow was a thin middle-aged woman, puffing loudly. The doorman touched his hand to his cap. "Good evening, Mrs. Felton," he said in greeting, his tone at least ten times as civil as the one he'd apparently reserved for me. "Nice night for a walk, isn't it?"

"(*puff*) Evening, (*puff*) Frank. Fine night," Mrs. Felton was able to get out as the poodle pulled her determinedly along.

By the time Frank favored me with his attention again, I was digging my keys out of my handbag to use as a prop. I dangled them in front of him.

The look he bestowed on me then—which fell somewhere between skepticism and out-and-out disbelief—made me aware that there must be something wrong with this picture.

"Oh," I mumbled, doping it out, "I just shoved them in here automatically." Patting my bag, I supplied a tepid little smile. "Habit, I guess."

"Why don't you leave those with me," he said curtly, holding out his hand. "I'll see she gets them."

"I wouldn't feel right doing that. Uh, couldn't you maybe, umm, just tell her friend about them while I wait?" I ventured courageously. "Believe me, it's not that I don't trust you; I do. But you could get busy or something, and well, I'd just feel better if I knew for certain she'd been notified that they were here."

The doorman smiled. And it was an extremely nasty smile. "If that's the case, I can't help you. I have too much to do to bother with that now."

I persevered. "I'd really appreciate it if you could make the time," I told him, hastily removing a bill from my wallet.

He barely glanced at the ten dollars in my open palm before declaring haughtily, "I don't want your money. Or your fishy story." After which he *really* leveled me. "You're not even that good a liar," he said. And then he turned his back on me in an infuriating gesture of dismissal.

Walking over to my car, I was seething with anger. Imagine. Critiquing my performance like that! I mean, considering that

I had to improvise right there on the spot, it was just extremely unfair. And what kind of a supercilious snot won't even accept a little bribe? The thought flashed through my mind that if the bribe hadn't been quite so little, he might not have been so high-handed. But I quickly dismissed the notion. Uh-uh. He was too much of a snot to succumb to a twenty, either.

And then my rantings against Frank were suddenly aborted. The instant, in fact, that I spied the souvenir some nice policeman had so thoughtfully left for me under the windshield wiper.

Well, the way things were going, it figured, didn't it?

At this point, it wouldn't have taken much to convince me to call it quits for the night. But receiving no encouragement at all, I embarked on a quest for a parking space. Given my present mood, however, I didn't have a whole lot of optimism it would prove to be worth the effort.

Anyhow, I finally found a garage five blocks down and a block over. And as soon as I unloaded the Chevy, I signaled a passing cab. I had the driver drop me at the apartment house right next to the one at which I'd just been so royally received.

Standing in the shadow of the building, I reached inside my handbag and fumbled around for the small camera I'd packed in there earlier. I told myself that there was always a chance Muriel's host would escort her downstairs, presenting me with the opportunity of capturing them on film together. (I wouldn't allow even a thought to the possibility the pair had cut out while I was driving around trying to find somewhere to deposit the car.)

I laid hands on my little Minolta at last, and removing it from the handbag, I propped myself against the wall. Now I would wait.

At 10:12—about fifteen minutes after I had concluded that I wouldn't be able to remain on my feet for another second— Muriel emerged from the adjacent building. In the company of Frank.

The doorman promptly whistled down a taxi for her. I stayed put until he was back inside, and then I hailed a cab of my own and went to pick up my car.

Half an hour later, I was home—and so overwhelmingly frustrated that I positively ached to have myself a good, long cry. But I was too exhausted to manage it.

Chapter 38

From the instant I woke up on Friday, I was so preoccupied with Muriel Moody's outsmarting me again, albeit unwittingly, that there wasn't even any space left over for thoughts of Bruce—or tomorrow's dinner.

But at least I finally had a lead.

I'd return to East Seventy-third Street this morning. Another doorman would be on duty now, and there was always the chance I could learn something from him. In any event, I had no doubt he'd be more agreeable to deal with than my buddy Frank. But then that was pretty much a given, wasn't it?

At around 10 o'clock, I phoned Jackie to let her know I wouldn't be in until the early afternoon, and then soon afterward, I caught a cab to Seventy-third.

The nameplate pinned on the chest of today's doorman said John. And John was as tall as Frank was short, as thin as Frank was heavy, and—what counted—as congenial as Frank was not.

"Good morning," he said, welcoming me with a smile.

"Good morning. I wonder if you could help me."

"I'll do my best."

"I'm trying to locate an old friend. We used to live next door to each other, but then she moved, and we lost contact. I haven't seen her in, well, it must be over five years. I'm particularly anxious to get in touch with her now, because a few months ago when I myself was moving, I came across a brooch of hers under the sofa. I couldn't believe it. We thought she'd misplaced it, and we had both searched everywhere for it. She really treasured that brooch—a family heirloom, I think it was. Anyway, I didn't have the vaguest notion of how to even begin looking for her—I'd heard she relocated, you see, and was living somewhere in the Midwest. All I knew—" I cut myself short at this point. I was turning this thing into a miniseries, for God's sakes! "At any rate," I went on, getting to the crux of my tale, "I was driving past here last night, when I spotted someone coming into this building who looked very much like my friend—in fact, I'm sure it was Muriel. I double-parked and jumped out of the car. But by the time I made it into the lobby, she was gone. I described her to the doorman who was on duty then—Frank, his name was—but, well, he wasn't very accommodating." I sighed extravagantly. "It was so disappointing. I only missed her by seconds."

John's expression was sympathetic, but I thought I'd seen a knowing little flicker cross his face at my criticism of his coworker.

"There was some woman standing here, though," I continued, "when I was talking to Frank, that is. And she said she knew who I meant. She told me my friend had just taken the elevator upstairs and that she wasn't a tenant, but she *was* a frequent visitor. I asked who it was that Muriel came to see, but unfortunately, this woman didn't have any idea. She suggested I check with you." And then I put in quickly, "She mentioned how nice your were. She mentioned it twice." (Well, that sort of thing usually turns *me* into Silly Putty.)

"I'll try to help," John responded, obviously pleased. "We got lotsa people living in this building, and they get lotsa company. But if it's someone who's around that often, I suppose I should know her. Tell me what your friend looks like, why don't you."

"I can do better than that." Opening my handbag, I took out two snapshots—the best likenesses I had of Muriel Moody.

The doorman spent all of about three seconds examining them, and then he handed the pictures back to me with a grin. "Sure. I recognize that lady. She comes in here pretty regular—to see Mr. White, up on ten. Ten-H. He's at work now, but I don't think he'd mind if you was to give him a call this evening—sometime after seven, you'd better make it. Morgan White—that's his full name. He's a real fine gentleman."

"Thank you. Thank you so much. I'll do that. Uh, by the way would there be a Mrs. White?" It was, after all, possible that the guy's wife traveled and that he and Muriel got together at his place when the Mrs. was out of town.

"Oh, no, Mr. White's an old bachelor. Far's I know, he never tied the knot."

I was glad to hear that. Naturally, I would have had to do what I had to do, regardless. Still, it was a relief to learn that there wasn't a second innocent party who'd be hurt because of these over-aged players' overactive libidos.

But John had put a different interpretation on my question. "Mr. White *does* have a housekeeper, though—she's in by around twelve usually. So if you don't feel like waiting for tonight, you could stop off a little later if you want; she might be able to help you."

"Great. That would be even better. I can't tell you how much I appreciate this." I pressed a bill—a twenty—into his hand.

"It's very kind of you, miss," he said, pocketing the money. (Now, that's my kind of doorman!)

I told him I'd be back soon, while simultaneously glancing at my watch. It was already after eleven.

As I headed for the coffee bar on the next block, I wondered why I was taking the time to talk to the housekeeper. At this juncture, I should just let Elliot know I had the name of Muriel's lover and then wait and see how the client wanted to proceed from there. I mean, Moody might be satisfied to merely confront his wife with the identity of her playmate. On the other hand, he could require tangible proof she was actually engaging in adultery. (While I don't *do* those kind of pictures, I have this once-in-a-while associate I call on in circumstances like that who's a very talented photographer. Also a very trustworthy and sleazy human being.) What I'm saying is, there didn't seem to be much of a reason for me to question the woman. And especially not then.

Very quickly, however, I managed to justify the decision to pay her a visit. I did it the way I usually do when I'm about to go ahead with something that doesn't make an awful lot of sense: I told myself that, after all, you just never know.

"She went upstairs about five minutes ago," John informed me when I returned to the building. "I mentioned you wanted to ask her something. I didn't say what—I figured it might be better if you took care of that yourself."

"And?"

"She said no at first. She was sorta scared it could get her in trouble. But I said she didn't have to worry; you were on the level"—I cringed at that—"a real nice lady, I told her you was. 'This isn't a scam or nothing' is what I said to her. Anyhow, I let her know it was important and that it would only take a few minutes, and she finally said okay."

"I appreciate that. Thank you."

"You can go right up. Her name's Maria— Ten-H," he reminded me. He was picking up the intercom as I walked off, probably to alert Maria to the fact I was on my way.

When I got to the apartment, there was a chain drawn across the barely open door, and a dark-complexioned woman was peering out at me with wary eyes. She was about my height and seemed to be almost as wide.

"Maria?"

The woman nodded.

"My name is Mrs. Grant," I began, "and I have this old friend who, I understand, visits Mr. White quite often. There's a good chance you might have met her. Are you here evenings, too?"

"Only maybe once every two, three months when Mr. White he has a dinner party." She spoke in faintly accented English, and her voice, to my surprise—considering the fact that she seemed to be guarding the apartment like a pit bull—was soft and pleasant.

"I have some pictures of my friend with me." I groped around in my handbag. "Here they are." Producing the snapshots, I thrust them through the eight inches or so of open door. "Do you recognize her? Her name is Muriel Moody."

"What is it you want to ask me about Missus Moody?" she said, ignoring the photos in my outstretched hand.

I dropped the pictures back in my bag. "Then you know her?"

"*Sí.* I know her."

"Does she come here many evenings?"

"I can't say about 'many.' Like I tell you, I don't work for Mr. White many evenings. Why are you asking me these things?"

"Well, you see, I just came across something valuable that belongs to her—something she lost—and I'm trying to get in touch with her so I can return it."

"I don't have Missus Moody's telephone number. For this,

you will have to ask Mr. White." So saying, she closed the door another few inches.

"All right, I'll do that. And thanks very much for taking the time to talk to me." I slipped a twenty-dollar bill through what was now a very narrow opening.

"No, no!" she responded emphatically with a wave of her hand.

Withdrawing the money, I thanked her once more and began to walk away.

I was about ten feet down the corridor when I heard a faint "Missus Grant?"

It was a second or two before I realized that was me. (When you lie, it really helps to have a good memory.) I turned to see Maria standing out in the hall and retraced my steps.

"I hope you tell me the truth and you not here to make any trouble for her. She's a nice woman. And Mr. White—he's very close to her."

You can say that again! "Oh? You know this for a fact?"

"Well, sure. She's the only sister he got."

Chapter 39

"He's her brother! Her damn brother!" I informed Elliot excitedly, marching into his office about a half hour later.

The face looking up at me was expressionless. And then slowly, understanding crept into the kindly brown eyes. "You're kidding! You mean it's *Morgan* Muriel's been meeting?"

"You *know* the man?"

"I've met him a couple of times at the Moodys'." Grinning impishly now, Elliot shook his head. "Well, whaddaya know. Morgan."

"Why would she sneak around to meet her own brother?"

"Because last year he and Herm had a falling-out—something about a business deal—and Herm forbade Muriel to have anything more to do with him."

"*Forbade* her?"

Elliot spread his arms. "Yeah. I agree. But I'm Herman's friend and his attorney—not his conscience." Then getting up from behind his desk, he clapped a hand on my shoulder. "Nice work, Dez, thanks. See? I told you you'd get the job done."

"At least I was able to give you some good news. I imagine your client will be pleased to learn that his wife wasn't cheating on him after all."

Elliot stood there for a moment, rubbing his chin. "I hope so," he said pensively. "But to a man like Herman—well, adultery might have even been preferable."

I didn't bother going into my cubbyhole. Right after that report to Elliot, I started my weekend.

On the way to the apartment, I made an all-important stop at my neighborhood D'Agostino's to pick up the necessities for

Saturday's dinner. And then as soon as I got home, I fixed some lunch for myself. After which I sat at the kitchen table with a second cup of coffee for an extra fifteen minutes, just so I could spend some quality time cursing Charmaine.

I certainly couldn't depend on that once-every-millennium cleaning woman of mine to show tomorrow. Not with her track record. In fact, there were times I wondered if she even existed. (Maybe she was only the product of a mind that's allergic to dusting and vacuuming and scrubbing toilet bowls.) At any rate, when I ran out of epithets, I gritted my teeth and gathered together half a dozen different cleansers, three kinds of brushes, assorted rags and sponges, and the rest of the requisite paraphernalia. And then I got busy.

It took me close to three hours to whip the place into some sort of reasonable shape—just reasonable enough so that Bruce wouldn't think I was a total slob. Not that I really cared what he thought, I reminded myself. Anyway, I didn't attempt anything major, so there'd still be plenty for Charmaine to do in case she did put in an appearance. Which was really optimism carried to the nth degree.

That evening I prepared the hors d'oeuvres and dessert for tomorrow's meal. And let me say—with no pretense of modesty whatever—that it was going to be quite a meal.

To accompany our drinks, I was serving a shrimp mousse. Also, mushroom croustades, which, if you're not familiar with them, are these tiny breadcases filled with a delicious mushroom mixture. After that, we'd have onion soup. And for an entrée, chicken breasts sautéed with sherry and oranges and almonds. There'd be a side dish of rice and, naturally, a great big salad. And we'd finish off with chocolate mousse flavored with Grand Marnier.

Bruce definitely didn't deserve a dinner like that was what I decided. But, fortunately for him, when it was too late to change the menu.

He was on my doorsill fifteen minutes earlier than expected—at 7:15. Of course, considering that he'd originally wanted to make it 7:00, I suppose I got off lucky. (But wouldn't you know he'd be sure to at least split the time difference with me?) Anyhow, since I had just finished dressing by then, I wasn't too put out by his early arrival—or the message I was reasonably certain it was supposed to be sending me.

He brought a nice bottle of chardonnay. That is, I assume it was a nice bottle—not being exactly a wine connoisseur. It didn't come with a twist-off cap, at any rate. And it tasted just fine.

We were seated across from one another in the living room, and Bruce had already had half a glass of the chardonnay, consumed any number of croustades, and scarfed down three crackers piled high with shrimp mousse. And that's when he said, "You look very nice, by the way."

Now, I hadn't exactly expected him to keel over in a dead faint at the sight of me, but I was a little disappointed that the compliment came so late and carried so little conviction. Especially since I was really very pleased with the way I turned out that night. In fact, if I can believe my mirror, I was bordering on fetching. Most of the credit for that going to the two-piece cotton dress I was wearing, which is this very pale shade of pink that manages to do wonders for my coloring.

I must say, though, that later on when it came to the dinner, Bruce was a lot more generous with his praise. "Pat certainly wasn't kidding when she told me you could cook," he enthused at one point. And not long after that: "You know, Dez, I might consider letting you make another meal for me someday. How's tomorrow night?"

The black look I gave him was meant only half in jest.

"Just fooling around," he informed me, laughing. "Next week'll do."

Over dinner, there was lot of verbal sparring. And I can't complain that I didn't enjoy it. Or Bruce's company. But by the time we were finishing our dessert, I suddenly felt like I was OD-ing on clever repartee. "Are you aware, Bruce," I said then, "that you've never really told me anything about yourself?"

"I have no idea what you're talking about," he stated pleasantly. "I've told you what I do for a living and where I work. I've told you I'm divorced. You know I'm originally from Chicago. You even know I've got a cousin named Burton Wizniak who's cohabiting with a woman named Pat Martucci." He grinned. "So? What else is there?"

"I'm serious."

"Okay. Then ask me whatever it is you want to find out, why don't you."

Damn him! It wasn't supposed to be like this. We should be gaining at least *some* insight into one another's lives and feelings naturally, as we spent more time together. I mean, interrogating people might be part of my job, but this was a *relationship*, for Christ's sake! Well, of some sort, anyway. Still, if I had no other recourse . . .

I started off with "How many years were you married?"

"Six. Actually, almost seven."

"Umm, what happened?" I did ask it with a lot of compassion.

"Nothing that specific. We just stopped caring about each other as much as two married people should, that's all."

"Both of you?"

"More or less."

What is "more or less" supposed to mean? "I guess you parted on friendly terms then," I put to him.

"I don't think I'd call it exactly friendly."

I hated what I was doing. And every time I opened my mouth, I hated it more. I was growing increasingly resentful of Bruce, too. If he'd been at all forthcoming, I reasoned, we wouldn't be going through this. "How long ago was it that you split up?"

"It'll be nine years this November."

"I think you mentioned once that you didn't have any children, right?"

"A hundred percent correct. No kids."

I'd had enough. I asked what would definitely be my last question. "Your wife—did she ever remarry?"

"No, she died instead." He seemed to be scrutinizing my face, as if to judge the impact of the words.

"I'm so . . . I'm so sorry," I told him, unnerved. Well, that's what I got for being such a busybody. "I shouldn't have pried."

"Suicide," he said, ignoring the apology. "She slit her wrists a week after the divorce became final."

At that moment, I got the very strange impression he was confiding this just to make me squirm. To punish me for putting the screws to him like that. When I opened my mouth to say something, though, he cut me off good-naturedly. "Listen, I hope you're not going to tell me you're sorry again. I

like you a helluva lot better when you're giving me a hard
time." I noted that his voice was raspy now, the way mine gets
sometimes when I'm trying to fight back tears. And an instant
later, his lips curved in a faint, poignant smile.

And I melted.

Reaching across the table, I covered his hand with my own.
And before I knew it, he was beside my chair, pulling me gently to my feet. And then he kissed me. Kissed me until my legs
began to give away.

After that, well, one thing just seemed to lead to another. . . .

Chapter 40

Why? I asked myself.

Was it the pity he invoked in you last night?

Or the sparks that have been there all along?

Or were you just plain horny?

If I'd been pinned down for an answer, I'd have had to say that it was most likely all three.

The truth is, I had never before gone to bed with anyone unless there was some sort of commitment—on both sides. Even if the commitment was only to friendship. Here, though, I wasn't sure I even *liked* the man. And as for Bruce's feelings, well, while I couldn't be certain of them the outward signs hardly inspired confidence.

I mean, he hadn't so much as elected to spend the night. Not that this really surprised me. Actually, what did surprise me was his bothering with an explanation.

"I had to bring a lot of work home from the office this weekend," he's said (probably lying like a trouper). And he'd even embellished on this: "A new client. I figure I'll have to get up by five if I'm going to be ready for a nine a.m. meeting Monday."

Now, I have to admit something. I wasn't comfortable enough with Bruce to be particularly anxious to have him stay over. But still—and okay, it's perverse—I wanted very much for him to want to.

Anyway, all day Sunday, I listened for the phone—while at the same time insisting to myself he wouldn't be calling. And he didn't. And I was beside myself.

I just couldn't seem to help it.

Forget that I had misgivings about this new turn in our relationship. And yes, I was unhappy about the way he appeared to be handling it. And of course, as you well know, I'd had reservations about the man from the minute I met him. Still, just the thought of seeing him again, and I tingled. And then cursed my untrustworthy body for betraying me like that.

By Monday morning, I was so antsy I decided to give myself a treat day. Before I left the house, though, I had to find out how things had worked out for Muriel Moody. So when I phoned the office to let Jackie know my plans, I asked to speak to Elliot. He was in court and wasn't expected back. Well, I supposed that all I could do was hope for the best.

Immediately after the call, I was off to the beauty parlor. I spent a couple of hours having my hair and nails done, and by then it was time for lunch. I decided on this Italian restaurant in the East Sixties. I'd eaten there a couple of times before, and the food's really terrific. And what a coincidence the place happens to be so close to Bloomingdale's!

At any rate, not long after what turned out to be a pretty expensive meal, I was busy gifting myself with a pearl-and-gold bracelet (it was on sale) and a gorgeous Oscar de la Renta scarf (it wasn't). And then for some reason I still haven't been able to fathom, I ended up springing for a Waterford jam jar—which I have yet to find an occasion to use.

On the upside, though, at least my extravagance gave me something besides my love life to moan about.

At 9:30 Tuesday morning, I was in Elliot's office.

"How did you make out with Herman?"

He shook his head sadly.

"What happened?"

"He threw her out of the house; that's what happened."

"Oh, no!"

"I'm sick over it. Muriel doesn't deserve this. She's always been a damn good wife to Herman and a wonderful mother to Debbie."

I can't imagine what Elliot must have been thinking *I* was thinking, but apparently he found it necessary to justify himself then—just as he'd done when initially presenting me with the case. "Look, I have to admit I've never exactly been Muriel's champion. Probably, I got the idea she wasn't too fond of me, so very childishly, I made up my mind not to be too fond of her, either. But still, I did my best to prevent something like this." And now he explained once again how he'd tried from the beginning to convince Herman to consider a marriage counselor or, at the very least, to talk things over with Muriel. And all the while, that round, pleasant face of his kept getting pinker and pinker as he grew increasingly more agitated.

"You did everything you could," I told him soothingly. But I can't say for a fact that he even heard me.

"Dammit! He's acting like a stubborn old fool!" And picking up a pencil from his desk, he paused just long enough to snap it in half—which I suppose was mild-mannered Elliot's version of a temper tantrum. "If Muriel had been caught cheating on him, that might have been one thing," he mumbled, speaking mostly to himself. "Although even then . . . This way, though, well, the woman's entitled to stay in touch with her own brother, for heaven's sake." And now he gave me his full attention. "I tell you, Dez, I wish I'd never gotten involved with this rotten business."

Ditto! But to Elliot I said, "Listen to me. There is absolutely no reason to put this on yourself. Herman's your client, and you carried out his instructions. If you hadn't, I promise you, he'd only have found someone else to handle things."

Elliot nodded. But the words didn't really seem to cheer him up any. Or me, either, for that matter.

That night, I was in a truly masochistic mode.

I could hardly wait to usurp the blame for Muriel Moody's troubles and transfer it from Elliot's shoulders to my own. I determined that if I hadn't discovered she'd been secretly meeting with her brother, poor Muriel would still be cozily ensconced in her West Side brownstone. In my eagerness to assume responsibility, I conveniently blocked out all thoughts of her stupid, macho, ego-driven husband—who, it is conceivable, might in some way have contributed to her unfortunate circumstances.

And then when I'd sufficiently milked this situation, I switched over to Bruce. Naturally. Who still hadn't called. Also, naturally. Which is what had no doubt triggered all of this self-abuse to begin with.

How could I have let myself get physically involved with this person?

And now I promptly—and with much malice—ticked off all his faults in my head, including a few there'd been no indication he even possessed. (Like stinginess. And acquisitiveness. And emotional instability.)

And right after this, for the first time since learning of her existence, I got around to considering Bruce's dead wife. And all of a sudden, it occurred to me that my sympathy might have been misdirected.

I mean, by what sort of twisted reasoning did I pity *him* because *she'd* committed suicide? She was the one no longer breathing. And after all, they were already divorced at the time of her death. More important, yet, I had no way of knowing just how much Bruce himself had contributed to that desperate act of hers. And what was it he'd told me about their *both* having fallen out of love? Well, if that was true, why should she decide to take her own life so soon after the divorce? The person to feel sorry for, I decided, was *Mrs.* Bruce.

Nevertheless, when the phone rang at 10:30, I jumped off the sofa—and knocked a vase off the coffee table in my rush to pick up.

It was a wrong number.

On Wednesday morning, I let myself off the hook. By the time I got to the office, I accepted that I was not to blame for wars or famines or swarms of locusts. Or even minor, more personal disasters like Muriel Moody's. And who's to say she wasn't better off without that miserable husband of hers, anyway?

I even gave myself absolution for being so weak as to become interested in a Bruce Simon.

All in all, I was feeling almost chipper that day.

And then just before 4:00, Jackie buzzed me. "Your niece is here. I sent her on back," she told me.

Ellen? I couldn't remember the last time she'd dropped in on me at work out of the blue like this. Come to think of it, in fact, it had never happened before. It was kind of a nice surprise.

But the instant she came into the room, I stiffened. She had no color at all. And there was an expression on her face that frightened the hell out of me. Was it shock? Fear? Horror? I couldn't decipher it.

I only knew that something was terribly wrong.

Chapter 41

"What's the matter, Ellen? What's wrong?" It had taken a moment before I was even able to dredge up the courage to ask.

Ellen was standing on the other side of my desk, opposite me, fumbling around in her purse. "I'll show you."

"Sit down, why don't you?"

She didn't move an inch, rejecting the suggestion with a quick toss of her head. And now she extracted a thin folded-up newspaper from her handbag and walked around the desk to position herself next to my chair. Opening the paper she set it down in front of me, carefully smoothing it out. It was turned to page four.

"What's this?"

"A Long Island newspaper. The *Fairmont Weekly Clarion*." Her voice was curiously flat and a little tic had suddenly made its debut in her right cheek. "Sybil called me this morning. I couldn't understand why she was so insistent on meeting me for lunch today. It was to bring me the paper." She pointed at an article at the bottom of the page. "Go ahead, read it." And then although it was easily about eighty degrees in my cubicle that day, she shivered.

And I read:

Local Pair Perish in Paradise

Wire Report

PARADISE ISLAND, THE BAHAMAS—
Richard Eber, 37, and his wife, Winifred Eber, 29, of Stonehaven, New York, drowned Saturday while vacationing at the Sea Palace resort here.

Authorities report that the couple remained on the beach after a brief tropical rainstorm that hit the island at just past 11:00 A.M. sent other hotel guests scurrying for cover. According to Alice Colletti, another guest at the hotel and apparently the only witness to the tragedy, the pair then went into the water at Mr. Eber's insistence.

"I was sitting right next to them when it started to come down," said Colletti, of Springfield, Illinois. "She—the wife—was grabbing up their things. But then I heard her husband convincing her to go in for one more dip."

Colletti, who just minutes after leaving the beach returned to search for her sunglasses, told investigators she noticed the couple in the ocean when she came back. "They weren't really swimming that far out," Colletti said, "and they didn't seem to be in any trouble or anything. A minute or two later, though, I looked over that way again, and they were gone. Both of them."

The Ebers' bodies were recovered early Saturday evening.

Stunned, I lifted my head from the article. At first my thoughts refused to go any further than *poor Dick!* But then I was struck by the awful irony of it all. *Raven died because there wasn't any water,* I mused, *and Dick and Winnie because there was too much.* I turned and looked up at Ellen, my eyes stinging.

"Did you finish it?" she asked, her voice tremulous now. And when I nodded: "Well? Tell me, what do you—" But she broke off. It took a few deep breaths before she managed to start again. "What do you think?"

I realized almost at once what she was asking, but I was so unstrung I didn't seem able to absorb this terrible thing that had happened—not fully, that is. And I was in no condition to offer any kind of response, anyway. Not until I laid hands on some Kleenex and blew my nose half a dozen times. And after all that, the best I could finally come up with was "I don't know." Following which I returned the question. "What do *you* think?"

It seemed to take a very long time for Ellen to reply. And when she did, she was speaking so softly that if I hadn't been looking straight at her, I doubt I'd have been able to make out the words.

"I think," she said, swallowing hard, "that Dick must have believed you, after all."

Here's a preview of the next wonderful mystery featuring Desiree Shapiro, *Murder Can Spook Your Cat.*

"You know, Desiree," Luella said out of nowhere, shaking her head wonderingly, "it's hard to believe you're a private eye."

Well, this is the sort of reaction I'm accustomed to, and most times I can manage to ignore it. But just then, I stiffened. Luella was appraising me thoughtfully, and I knew exactly what it was she saw: someone toting around maybe twice the mileage of those sexy blond make-believe PI creatures on TV. Plus cheeks—and not the ones on the face, either—that extended almost all the way across the damn sofa cushion. And legs that were too damn short to reach the damn floor.

"You don't fit my mental picture of a PI at all," she said.

"Maybe not, but it's what I am." I hoped that didn't sound as defensive as I was afraid it did.

Luella responded with a flash of dimples. "I know. But it still throws me. The thing is, you're not the type. You're so . . . so *feminine.*"

Now, I can't really say if she meant that or not, but I was perfectly willing to go on the premise that she did. *I could really learn to love this woman,* I thought then.

And today, just over five years later, Kevin has come to inform me that she's dead.

After that night I never set eyes on Luella Pressman again.

But I did run in to Kevin one day about two and a half years ago—in the spring, it was—on Fifth Avenue. Right in front of Saks.

He was striding purposefully down the street, heading in my direction, when I spotted him half a block away. I waited for him to catch up to me, and he stopped long enough to hug me briefly and then tell me he couldn't stop. "I'm late for a client meeting," he hastily explained. "I'm supposed to be semi-retired, only I seem to be busier than ever these days." He said it ruefully; nevertheless, I suspected he was pleased. "Look, I'll phone you soon, and we'll have lunch. Okay?" He was already moving on.

"Okay. Great!" I called out after him.

But that time he didn't keep his word.

And today my old friend was sitting in my living room, his eyes moist and red-rimmed, his mouth set in a thin, tight line, and his hands in constant motion, fidgeting almost nonstop with the fabric of his chinos. He looked at least ten years older than he had not even three years before.

"I apologize for not calling first; I should have," he had said when he rang my doorbell a few minutes earlier, at just before noon. "But I decided to take the chance you'd be home."

And now, after two or three gulps of air, he was apologizing again. "I'm sorry to intrude on your Sunday. I probably should have waited until tomorrow and come to your office to talk to you. But I . . . well, I couldn't get myself to do that."

The second alarm in my head went off at the word "office," the initial alert having sounded the instant I saw his face. "What is it, Kevin? What's wrong?"

"Luella's dead." It came out in a hoarse whisper.

"Your wife?" I responded stupidly. I like to think that was because I was so stunned.

"Ex-wife."

"*Ex*-wife?" I parroted, stunned again.

"Luella and I were divorced a couple of years ago. Not very long after you and I bumped in to each other on Fifth Avenue. Do you remember that?"

"Sure I do," I told him, after trying without success to swallow the lump that had formed in my throat.

"But I never stopped caring about her," Kevin said. "We remained very good friends. Maybe even better friends than when we lived together." And reaching frantically into his pants pocket for some tissues now, he produced a fistful and dabbed at his eyes.

"I'm so terribly sorry," I murmured while he was ministering to himself.

He mumbled a choked thank you before blowing his nose. It took a few moments before he was sufficiently composed to speak again, and then he said in a quiet, even tone, "You know, Desiree? Half the time I can't even believe she's gone."

"She'd been ill?"

"No. Luella was in perfect health."

"Then—"

"She was murdered."

"My God! Who did it? Do you know?"

"That's what I'm hoping you can find out. You will help, won't you?"

"Of course I will. I'll do anything I can. When was she . . . when was she killed?"

"Yesterday."

The next question was obvious. And I was afraid to ask it. I mean, I had these strobe images of poor Luella's terrible fate. I saw her covered in blood, lying on the cold hard pavement with her throat slit as two young punks fled down the street with her handbag. In the next instant I envisioned her sprawled on the bed in this flimsy white nightgown, her lovely face purple, a thick silk drapery cord wound tight around her neck. Only a few feet away a black-hooded man was tearing through her dresser drawers, scattering her dainty personal possessions everywhere. I even squeezed in a picture of her squashed body on the subway tracks, a deranged street person (naturally, I made this perpetrator a male, too) looking down from the platform, laughing maniacally.

For a second I shut my eyes to blot out the horrifying tableaux I'd foisted on myself, and then moistening my lips, I forced myself to say the words: "How did it happen?"

"I'm afraid you'll have to wait for the answer to that one," Kevin responded sheepishly. "We both will."

I let out the breath I'd been holding. "I don't understand."

"Hortense—she's the housekeeper who comes in four days a week—well, she found Luella on the floor of her office yesterday afternoon, just before one o'clock."

"She was already dead?"

"Yes. Or anyway, she was by the time the paramedics arrived. And the police have no idea how she died. They're conducting an autopsy."

"Then what makes you think it was murder?"

"I told you. Luella was in excellent health."

"Those things happen, though, Kevin. You hear about it all

the time. One day a person is fine, and the next . . ." I left it to him to fill in the rest.

He was shaking his head.

"Maybe they'll find that it was a sudden heart attack," I suggested optimistically. "Or a stroke," I added brightly. Not that either alternative would be cause for a celebration, but from where I sit, they beat having to live with a loved one's murder.

"No," Kevin pronounced firmly.

"But how can you be that positive? You don't even have a suspect in mind."

"That's not precisely right. The truth is, I don't *know* who killed her, not specifically, that is. But I would bet everything I own in this world that one of Luella's stepdaughters had a hand in this. Or maybe even all three of them." And taking a few more tissues from the seemingly limitless supply in his pants pocket, he swiped at his eyes again.

"Luella had three stepdaughters?" I asked, surprised at that for some reason.

"From her first three marriages."

"Her *first three*—"

"That's right." Kevin broke in before I'd even had ample opportunity to express my astonishment. "And the girls all continued living with her after their respective fathers died— or in one case, after her father walked out. At any rate, Luella saw to their material needs, but I'm afraid she didn't give them that much attention. Her writing was incredibly time consuming. It really took an awful lot out of her."

Oh, come now! We aren't talking any War and Peace *kind of epics here. We're talking Aunt Whosis drags those twins of hers to the wherever, for heaven's sake!*

It was as if Kevin had crept into my head. "I realize that *Aunt Lulu and the Twins at the Circus* and *Aunt Lulu and the Twins at the Ice Cream Parlor* don't sound like great literature," he told me, his tone amused and defensive at once. "And they're not, of course. But Luella's books were highly entertaining—much more inventive than most children's stories. And she was a perfectionist; she put herself under an awful lot of pressure. It does seems to have paid off, though. It's an extremely popular series, you know."

And now his voice grew confidential. "But besides the Aunt Lulu books, she was also working in a different genre—somewhat covertly. Had been for more than ten years, off and on.

It's a historical novel set in fifteenth-century Spain—the time of the Inquisition. Naturally, something like that requires a great deal of research. And of course, being Luella, she was never satisfied with anything she'd written—I used to tell her she was noodling the thing to death. Anyway, progress was terribly slow—what with the noodling and the research and her Aunt Lulu commitments. Actually, I don't believe she ever even got to page 200."

And now Kevin sighed. "But the point it's taking me forever to make is that because of the demands of her career, I'm afraid the girls sometimes got short shrift."

Aunt Lulu didn't have time for her children, I mused. I mean, the irony of it!

"Yes, I know," Kevin said, exactly as if he were poking around in my head again. "But you can appreciate, can't you? that under those circumstances it was even more to her credit that she kept the kids with her. And it isn't as if they were ever neglected," he asserted. "Connie's great with kids, and she served as sort of a surrogate mother to them."

"They're all adults now, I assume."

"Yes, and out on their own. But they stay—stayed—in very close touch with Luella. She insisted on that."

"Why, if she wasn't that fond of them?"

"Oh, but she *was*—in her own way. Especially once they were older. It was kind of a funny thing about Luella. She was really very family minded." My eyebrows must have shot straight up to my hairline at that one. "It's true," Kevin maintained. "The girls all spoke to her on the phone several times a week, and they came over to dinner often. Listen, it was practically on penalty of death or—worse yet—disinheritance that they miss spending a holiday or birthday with her." And chuckling a little: "Particularly when the birthday was hers." And then he added with the slightest, saddest smile, "Hey, I never said Luella wasn't eccentric, did I? That's one of the reasons I lo—I felt the way I did about her. But what I'm trying to make clear is that while she and her stepdaughters got along just fine at this point in time, the fact remains that she'd kept herself pretty distant from them while they were growing up. And that can certainly hurt."

"She wasn't abusive to them in any way, was she?"

"Oh, no! Nothing like that. Just detached." And now Kevin sat there silently, plucking away at his pants leg, and I got the definite impression he was weighing something in his mind. Finally, he said reluctantly: "Uh, well, she did lose her temper once in a while, and so she'd do a bit of screaming. Sometimes. She used to tell me how bad she felt even now about not having had more patience, more time for them when they were younger. It wasn't her fault, though," he added quickly. "Luella was just a terribly nervous person, and she _was_ busy with her work. But anyway, that could hardly be characterized as abuse."

He seemed to be looking at me for confirmation, so I obliged. "No, of course not."

"Actually, the girls always claimed to be very grateful to her for raising them." He locked her eyes with mine at this point. "But I wouldn't be surprised, Desiree, if one of them had some secret resentment toward her that had been festering for years."

"And you think this resentment just boiled over?"

"No, no. But obviously, whoever did this had no great affection for her."

"You mentioned something about disinheritance before. Was Luella a wealthy woman?"

"I was just getting to that. Luella was worth millions. Although for a while I had no idea of that. I was aware she did pretty well with her books—she wrote close to sixty of them. But writing isn't as lucrative as you might imagine. I only found out about the _real_ money once we were married."

"The _real_ money?" I seemed to be echoing half the things Kevin said to me.

"That's right. Luella's mother came from a fairly well-to-do family. Not exactly _rich_ rich, but extremely comfortable. Anyhow, she died when Luella and Connie were young, and their father—who was the executor of the estate—made some pretty shrewd investments with the inheritance she left. He passed away about twenty-five years ago, but before he did, he managed to assure his daughters would be set for life." The next words were spoken slowly, with emphasis. "And their heirs, as well."

"So you think Luella was killed for her money?"

"I'm convinced of it. And I also think that Connie's afraid I could be right. She's always been so close to the girls, though, that she's reluctant to admit it, even to herself. But when we talked yesterday and I told her about my suspicions, she said that it might not be a bad idea to have you look in to things. To put my mind at ease is how she phrased it. But I have a feeling she wanted to settle things in her own mind, too. At any rate, I promised her I'd get in touch with you immediately." A fleeting grin now. "Actually, I had already decided to ask for your help. The moment I heard about Luella."

For a brief time after this, neither of us said anything. I was still attempting to absorb the fact of Luella's murder—if it *was* murder, that is—while Kevin was occupied with pressing a fresh couple of tissues into service.

"There's something I don't understand, though," I said to him when I broke the silence. "Why now? Why not kill her years ago? Or years later, for that matter. Unless . . . Was there anything that might have precipitated things?"

"Exactly." And with this, some of Kevin's tension seemed to evaporate—for a couple of minutes, anyway—and he sat back in his chair for the first time. "Luella had begun dating someone about three or four months ago," he explained. "Bud Massi, the man's name is. And it seems Massi's starting up this new company—some kind of educational software thing—and Luella planned to invest in it. I don't know just how much she agreed to lend him, but it was a substantial amount, from what I understand. And what made things even hairier—from the girls' point of view, at any rate—is that there was a good chance he might have become husband number five. And who knows how much money she would have sunk into his company if they'd married? Or how sound a business venture the thing was? Look, she could even have changed her will in his favor."

I wondered then how Luella's taking up with a new man had affected Kevin himself. Just as I wondered what had led to their divorce. But this was hardly the time to try to find out, common decency told me. And I was too fond of Kevin to ignore common decency's dictates.

"Incidentally, Luella and I had dinner just last Sunday and we talked about her relationship with Bud," Kevin added. "She insisted it wasn't serious between them. Only I wouldn't have made book on that. Not from the look on her face whenever she mentioned his name."

"And her stepdaughters might not have believed her, either," I mused, directing that mostly to myself. And then to

Kevin: "I suppose you know for a fact they were her beneficiaries."

"Oh, yes. Luella herself told me. And not that long ago, either. The girls get all of it, except for some personal stuff she left to Connie—jewelry, things of that nature. Connie didn't need the money. She was even more well fixed than Luella was. Over the years she'd bought and sold quite a lot of property, making a pretty sizable profit on her investments."

And now he leaned toward me, and there was a new urgency in his voice. "I want you to understand, Desiree, that I've always liked those girls, all three of them. And that's God's truth. But I feel in my gut—no, I'm *certain*—that one of them, at least, is responsible for Luella's death." He pressed his case. "Do you really think it's a coincidence that so soon after entering a relationship that could adversely affect her stepdaughters' financial prospects, a healthy woman—one without a single serious physical ailment—suddenly becomes a corpse?"

Well, of all the things I don't believe a PI should put any stock in, coincidence is the thing I don't believe most. If you follow me.

"You may very well have something there, Kevin. Let's see what the autopsy report—"

"But according to the police, that could take *weeks*. And didn't you once tell me that the more time that elapses, the colder the trail gets?"

I couldn't argue with that. Of course, it would have been helpful to know there'd even been a murder before I started hunting for a murderer.

Still, I'd gone down this road before, and everything had eventually fallen into place. I was about to agree to begin at once, but Kevin seemed to take my acquiescence for granted.

"I think it might be a good idea for you to pay a *shiva* call—tomorrow, if you can make it—so you can meet those girls." And now, a little uncertainly: "Uh, you do know what *shiva* is, don't you?"